# SWITCHING SIDES

## Marilyn Bos

*A WENDY WINKWORTH MYSTERY*

**Sharing a ride with two street kids brings disaster!**

Produced by Flat Sole Studio
398 Goodrich Avenue, St. Paul, MN 55102
*www.flatsolestudio.com*



*Library of Congress Cataloging-in-Publication Data*
Names: Bos, Marilyn Janice, author.
Title: Switching sides / by Marilyn Bos.
Description: Minneapolis : Flat Sole Studio, [2016] | 2014 | Series:
    A Wendy Winkworth mystery | Description based on print
    version record and CIP data provided by publisher; resource
    not viewed.
Identifiers: LCCN 2015050427 (print) | LCCN 2015045792 (ebook)
    | ISBN 9781938237201 (ebook) | ISBN 9781938237195
    (softcover)
Subjects: LCSH: Women private investigators--Fiction. | GSAFD:
    Mystery fiction.
Classification: LCC PS3602.O825 (print) | LCC PS3602.O825 S94
    2016 (ebook) | DDC 813/.6--dc23
LC record available at http://lccn.loc.gov/2015050427

**Credits**
Cover Art by Nancy Allan
Book Production by Flat Sole Studio

**Acknowledgments**
The author is grateful to the following people who contributed to this
work: Amanda Tourville for developmental editing, Zoe Barta for her
suggestions, Jim Scheller for line editing, Nancy Allan for cover art,
and Mary Logue for the final critique.



Printed in the United States of America.

# Switching Sides

A Wendy Winkworth Mystery

WINKS BOOKS
Minneapolis

**1**

I'm Private Investigator Wendy Winkworth, the dickless dick.

Late one night in September 1955, I got stopped on the highway by a state cop who said I was driving tipsy. I didn't think I needed to be arrested, but I failed to get to "H" in reciting the alphabet so he may have been right.

In Cassville, Illinois, a fiftyish matron escorted me to a jail cell. She was dressed in a puffy-sleeved blouse, billowy skirt with frilly pockets and purple heels. After unlocking a cell door, she gestured me in.

"I give up," I slurred. "Who'd you go as? To the Halloween party, I mean. Were you Shirley Temple?"

Her lips pursed. "Settle down. There's your bunk. There's the washcloth."

I shut up. No way could my liquored tongue keep up with Shirley's extreme sobriety.

The hall light dimly illuminated a cell that contained two sets of bunk beds, each lower occupied by a supine form. I climbed wearily to my appointed berth. "This is no good ship Pollilop," I muttered to the inmate directly below.

"Damn right," that gal mumbled. The cell door clanged shut.

In the morning, cradling my pounding head against the thumps and bumps sounding from below, I leaned over the side. I forced an eye open. My two roomies were wrassling on the floor. One, a large girl, had the other down and was beating on her. That smaller gal shielded her face while trying to stuff a cookie into her mouth.

Was this hell?

'Shirley' appeared at the front of our cage. "Lisa, get off her!" she ordered. "I'm making coffee. You'll get some if you behave. Prossie too."

"Gimme aspirin," I groaned from upstairs.

The smaller inmate, Prossie, consumed a last bite of cookie as the girl straddling her screamed, "That cookie was mine!" Must have been a good cookie to cause that much trouble. The bigger girl, Lisa, sprang to her feet and threw herself onto a bunk. Drawing her knees into a fetal position, she shook with sobbing. Dressed in a sweater and skirt set that looked expensive, she couldn't have been older than seventeen. I noticed that the sweater was torn and missing buttons.

Prossie, in a skimpy shift dress, looked like a hard-bitten collector of bedroom miles. Prossie: birth name or occupation?

I rubbed my forehead. What a hangover.

I surveyed my bleak surroundings. A toilet, a sink, a fringed hand towel and washrag draped over a rack. I glanced down at myself. I was still in my traveling outfit of barn-red denims, flannel shirt, grayish socks, and tennis shoes. My shoelaces and belt were missing along with the shoulder bag. Confiscated, I figured. Wished I remembered more.

I lowered myself gingerly off the bunk and down the ladder. "First time in jail?" I asked the lump that was Lisa. She sniffed, didn't look up, didn't reply.

"Lah di da, thinks she's hot shit 'til she ends up in here," Prossie assessed.

I had become a PI because I liked excitement. But I didn't want to go to jail for it. Last night, I'd strayed from my course. While incarcerated, I'd stay mum about my profession. Not the setting to declare myself on the side of truth and justice.

In a career of triumphs, along with a few defeats, I'd sunk to a new low, charged with knocking a roadside mailbox kerflooey, assaulting the arresting officer, and basically driving drunk. I didn't recall any of those deeds, just the cop reading them off in night court.

Four whiskey sours and the companionship of two truckers in a roadhouse are what stick in my mind. The truckers had bought my last two drinks. I needed companionship as much as they did, but when their talk grew suggestive, I excused myself to use the ladies' room and give them time to cool off. But one trucker slammed in after me. I yelled for help but no one came. Luckily I was able to trip the drunken fool into a stall. He stumbled and his head smacked the toilet. He was out, and so was I, pushing the screen from an open window, diving into my '49 Pontiac Chieftain and speeding away from there.

Anyhow, the fine was 500 bucks. Since I had only $20.86, I accepted the alternative— three days in the hoosegow.

How had I ended up practically broke? Sad story upcoming. Two days earlier, in up-state Illinois, I'd posted $5000 bail for my brother Norris, who had been indicted for burglary. Norris had a long history of teetering toward illicit activity and occasionally toppling over. As kids, we had collaborated in that respect. Nowadays though, I represent the law.

Immediately after Norris' release from jail, he jumped bail, leaving me a virtual pauper. I assumed in due course he'd send a note of apology. "Nothing matters more than polite manners," our mother had counseled us before taking off to live with the shopkeeper down the road.

Charlotte, as her nameplate said, (not Shirley, although I'd been close) delivered our breakfasts on individual trays, two aspirins included with mine. The meal tasted home-cooked: cinnamon roll, two eggs over easy, crisp bacon, and bracing coffee in a china teacup. I gorged while maintaining the disagreeable expression required of a con.

"Nasty slop, ain't it?" Prossie said and grinned at me.

"Terrible," I said, licking my lips. "By the way, I'm Wendy."

Lisa didn't touch her food, just glowered at it.

"I'm Prossie. Nice to—" Abruptly the woman turned away and addressed the kid. "Hey, Lisa, I'll be polite and ask this time. If you're through with your meal, can I have it?"

"No. It's mine." Lisa squished her spoon around in her eggs and took a small bite.

"Free food, nobody turns that down," Prossie griped.

Charlotte returned with a scrub bucket and mop and proceeded down the hall, banging and swishing, spreading suds over the cement floor. She began to sing "As Time Goes By."

"'You must remember this, a kiss is just a kiss,'" she warbled pleasantly. As she passed through a door at the far end, her voice gained intensity.

When she came to, "Hearts full of passion, jealousy and hate," she belted out those words as though the mop stick were a microphone. "'Woman needs man,'" she screeched, "and SHE must have her mate!"

I was pretty sure of the actual lyric: 'Woman needs man, and HE must have his mate.' I'd certainly check that out later. Like heck. Once out of here, I'd forget this scene like a bad dream.

After a distant door slammed, the song abruptly ended.

"Charlotte sure sounds serious about somebody," I said.

"Charlotte got dumped," Prossie filled me in. "Hasn't forgave the bastard." Prossie must be around here a lot to pick up all the gossip.

"Jeez, I'm starved," she exclaimed through a bite of cinnamon roll. "Had a long night. All the guys say they're in love with me. Yeah right."

From her bunk, the sullen teen spoke. "You don't know anything, either one of you."

"Yeah?" Prossie shoved the last bit of roll into her mouth. "Tell us what we're missing."

"Forget it." Lisa lowered her head.

The kid stabbed at her bacon. "I'm here because I found the love of my life," she said after a moment.

"Oh, jeez," I said.

"My boyfriend and I took some stuff from a store. I thought we'd be put in the same cell, you know, like Bonnie and Clyde."

Prossie snorted.

"They think they own Rolf," Lisa sneered, lost in her own little world. "They think he'll do anything they say."

"Who's Rolf? Who's they?" I asked. "What do they want him to do?"

The girl took a mournful breath. "They are my parents, the Plinkos, and Rolf is their star violin student. He's also the love of my life."

"Plinko," Prossie whooped, draining the rest of her coffee. "Them's the damn music teachers in town! We're sharing sweat with a celebrity!"

"Big deal," Lisa said glumly. "They're not as great as they think they are."

"It is a big deal," Prossie said. "They're famous. They teach young fiddlers how to have big-time careers so they can make lotsa money."

"They train young violinists to be concert artists." Lisa put it properly.

"Where you from anyhow, Wendy, that you don't know about the Plinkos?" Prossie was exasperated. "They're all we got in this berg."

"Across the big river. Iowa."

"Mmm. Rube country."

I didn't challenge. When in Rome…

"Rolf is the best violinist in their program," Lisa declared. "Some day he'll be famous around the world."

Prossie yawped, "Lisa Plinko-plunk went Rolfing."

"So, Lisa, what did you steal?" I asked, ignoring Prossie.

"A bed lamp. We did it for fun."

Prossie guffawed.

Lisa spoke seriously to me. "You hook the bed lamp over a headboard on a bed. We don't have the headboard yet."

"Or the lamp either." Prossie said. "But you got the bed? You don't look old enough to be living out."

I summed up. "Your parents don't like that you and Rolf are together so you're making plans to leave town with him." I set my empty tray on the floor.

"They hate that we're together. Probably his parents will too when they find out."

"If they're rich like you," Prossie said, "they'll bail him out of here."

"They don't know about us. They're missionaries in South Africa, busy converting the natives. They're from Germany. Last name's Nitschke. Rolf has the cutest accent."

"Hard to resist that," I said. I had no fondness for Germans. It was too soon to forgive and forget. During the war, I'd read the list of American dead each week. And I'd seen photos of the concentration camps.

But I felt a pang of pity for the chubby girl and commiserated, "Sounds like you're having a tough time. My first love was tough for me, too." Dang it, only two hours stuck with these people and I'd begun to care about them.

"What was your dad like?" Lisa asked me out of the blue.

"Like yours, in that he was famous," I said. "Best burglar in the area."

"Way to go!" Prossie approved.

"Oh, gosh," Lisa said and then rallied: "Was he nice?"

"Very. I loved him." I surprised myself by tearing up, maybe because of the present environment. Maybe.

"I didn't know my old man," Prossie contributed.

Lisa ignored her. "When I was a kid, I adored my daddy. I thought he knew everything. He's from Rumania. Played a lot of violin concerts there, with bombs going off all around him."

"But you don't think much of him now," I prodded.

"I hate him. Rolf's the only person he thinks about now. I don't matter."

"Your folks will buy you out of this," Prossie assured her. "You'll be home in no time."

"They better. Wish they'd hurry. They're probably trying to teach me a lesson." Tears trickled down her cheeks. "They'll blame this on me. I know they will. They'll say I talked him into it."

"Tough shit," Prossie said. "They still have to take you back. Big news in town if they don't. Gotta keep fooling people about how wonderful they are."

"Rolf and I will go live in Holland." Lisa wiped her eyes with her sleeve. "He loves the violin but he hates the music school."

Mid-morning, the clack of footsteps approached the cell. Lisa leapt to the bars. Led by Charlotte, a well-dressed, middle-aged couple appeared at the front of our cell. The man was tall and big-chested, with longish gray hair, large black eyes and a prominent nose. The lady was round-shouldered and plump. She had a pretty, if rather doughy, face. Her eyes were a very light blue-gray.

"Finally!" Lisa gripped the bars. "Get me out of here!" The woman recoiled as though struck. The matron pursed her lips and retreated down the hall. This wasn't looking good.

Lisa's dad addressed his daughter in a foreign accent. "You have embarrassed us once more."

"Rolf's in jail too." The woman spoke with an unmistakable twang: deep south origins, I reckoned, cornball accent, like mine or so I've been told. This well-dressed woman was a hill person a few times removed.

"I want to come home," Lisa pled. "Mommy, I'm scared."

"Rolf has a wonderful future that you're ruining," the woman said, ignoring her daughter's plea. "They don't even allow his violin in here."

"No stage show? Unbelievable," I wisecracked from the sideline.

The parents' eyes scanned me like they just realized I was present. Deciding I was nothing of consequence, they returned to the girl.

"Your mother and I want you to be good girl, at home, in school and in church. In Rumania, you would have been—" Dad withheld the punishment, but his voice was dangerously deep, leading me to understand that the guy was furious at his kid. He passed long fingers through his lustrous hair. When next he spoke, he was a calm and controlled daddy. "Simply we do not understand why you choose this very wrong path."

"Your father and I have decided that you stay here overnight," the mommy said, voice cracking slightly. "You need to learn that you can't get away with this sort of thing."

"No, no, get me out! Please!" Lisa sounded absolutely panicked.

The father clutched the mother's arm and marched her off, their footsteps retreating down the hall. She tried to look back until he grabbed her elbow and propelled her forward.

"Wait, please! Is Rolf getting out?" Lisa screamed after them.

"Yes-s," Daddy replied with a hiss, stopping at the end of the hall but not turning around. "He must practice his violin for the contest. But you are to remain here." The couple rounded a corner and were gone.

"I hate you! I hate you!" Lisa's venomous cry echoed down the empty hall. Frantically waving her clenched hands, she burst into wild, bereft sobs. I brought the dainty hand towel to her.

Prossie stepped to the bars. "You people got money, cars, pearls. Wait till the town hears you won't bail out your own kid," she yelled at the couple who were likely in the parking lot by then.

I patted Lisa's shoulder. "Sorry. Guess you're stuck with us."

"Couple a jerks," Prossie analyzed.

Lisa collapsed to the floor and wept raggedly.

I almost felt sorrier for her than I did myself. This girl was absolutely terrified of being left in here. She had counted on her parents to arrive and deliver her from the underworld.

"Hey, it's gonna be okay," I consoled, rubbing her shoulder. "Only one more night. It'll go by quickly."

"No, no, no, it won't," she wailed, nearly hysterical. "You don't know —a policeman tried to—" She shook her head violently.

"Tried to what? Come on, tell us," I urged.

"Oh, oh," Prossie growled. "I think I know already."

Lisa took deep breaths until she was calm enough to speak. "A cop got me down, got my skirt up and was pawing me. Said he'd kill me if I told. But then Charlotte pounded on the door and called and called until he had to let her in. But before he did, he said he'd come for me in the night if I told. He'd do me right in my own bedroom— that's what he said. He meant it too." Her body trembled and the tears started again.

"It's Harris. That fuckin' Sergeant Como Harris," Prossie said. "He did me last time I was in, and didn't pay for it neither." Prossie paced the small cell in agitation. "Wendy, the jail and the police station are connected. That asshole comes by, pulls you out and hauls you over without seeing the light of day. But jeez, she's just a kid. I never heard of him doing a kid before." She paused, examined me. "You're pretty, Wendy, kind of. So you better watch out too."

I absorbed that backhanded compliment before asking Lisa for the sergeant's description.

An explosion of words: "He's a creep. A slimy, greasy, oily-faced pig. He's got a big mustache and a fat mole that he pressed right up to my face." The girl pointed to her face and shook her head to get rid of the awful sensation.

Prossie confirmed, "That's Harris to a tee."

She sat down on the other side of Lisa and patted the girl's arm. "Don't bother reporting it. The town council won't do nothing."

"I know I can't tell." Lisa shook her head. "If I do, he'll kill me. It'd probably be just another embarrassment for my family."

The day progressed. Prossie's pimp paid her fine, she processed out and, I assumed, went back to work. Her departing advice for Lisa: "Keep your chin up."

With the two of us alone, Lisa chattered on about Rolf. I got to feeling I knew the boy. But Lisa's worship of her beloved was probably overblown as seems to be the case for first infatuation.

Finally I interrupted her soliloquy to offer advice: "Sometimes trouble gathers slowly, Lisa, so gradually that you think you can handle it. But it will grind you down and lead to very bad things. Things you never saw coming. Then you realize what you've lost along the way." At that moment in my wounded life I wanted to convince the girl that she was lucky to have what she did. Life could be easy for a kid with parents (both of them) in the home and enough money for a comfortable future.

But she soon had enough of my wisdom. "Why are you in here if you know so much?"

I gave the responsible, adult, answer. "I made a terrible mistake. Went drinking with friends, just having a good ol' time, driving drunk afterward. I usually don't do that kind of thing. But sometimes, you know, like anybody else, I fall short."

She thought about that for almost a second. "I'm going away with Rolf," she announced. "We have friends who will help. We'll stay with them awhile. Until we can get tickets overseas to Holland. Mexico first."

Yeah, that's right next door to Holland, I wanted to say. But, in her defense, it is closer.

**2**

Lisa was released the next morning, in such a rush she didn't say goodbye. I remained the lone female guest of the Cassville jail until the conclusion of my sentence. On that fourth morning, Charlotte led me down the hall and through a door into what looked to be the police squad room. The scrubbed-shiny floor smelled of freshly applied polish, still a bit sticky.

A uniformed cop snoozed on a long bench.

"He alive?" I asked.

"Mostly." Charlotte slammed the door and the man awoke, sat up, and stuck a finger in his collar.

"Mumph," he said.

"Morning, Officer Shulz," Charlotte said primly. She guided me past the booking counter and a couple of desks with scattered papers, into a large office, "POLICE CHIEF" in raised letters on the door, stale smoke hanging thickly in the air. Several plaques lined the wall, their brass plates spit-shined. "BEST OAR CARVED: 1946," said one, below a huge wooden oar. Two others were for "BEST DECOY: 1948 and 1949," with colorful wooden quackers on shelves below their plaques. There was no more recent award.

We moved to a lustrously polished desk on which lay my shoulder bag and a paper sack. I dumped the sack's contents, including my PI license, into the purse.

Fortunately, when not on a case, I keep my Beretta .25 in a pocket under the passenger seat in my car. The pistol hadn't been discovered, or so I assumed. At least it wasn't with those items. I didn't ask. But I did inquire as to the whereabouts of my Pontiac.

"Impound lot, east of town." Charlotte flicked a hanky at a smudged spot on the desk.

Rain was tapping against a row of dirty windows. I had to ask, "This place sparkles, but you don't do windows?"

The matron responded tersely. "Not since he tore down my pull-back curtains. Took away my typing duties too. Reduced me to just another cleaning lady."

"Sad," I said, wishing I hadn't engaged her. I just wanted out of there. After counting my last $20.86, I stuck it the shoulder bag. Charlotte handed over my Timex. It hadn't kept on ticking. I wound it and buckled on the leather strap. I reclaimed my shoestrings and laced them into my tennis shoes. The bag, with its gold turn-lock and spangles of embedded metallic flecks, I draped over my shoulder.

Then Charlotte surprised me by handing over a cashier's check for $100. "Someone's purchased your services." She gave me a long hard look. "Wendy, this is a second chance for you, if you are any kind of a reputable private eye, beings so many of them are nothing more than back-alley thugs."

"Speaking of integrity," I reacted, "why didn't you report Sergeant Como Harris when you discovered him messing with Lisa Plinko?"

Charlotte's lips flopped open. At first the reply came slowly, and with a stutter. "Who- w-who would I have reported it to? Sergeant Harris runs this place. He had sent me out to buy mimeo paper, but the store closed early so I got back sooner than he expected. The office door was locked. I pounded and called until he let me in." Charlotte was talking fast as if she couldn't spit out the words fast enough. "I was surprised to see her with him. He'd had his way with some ladies of the night, I knew that. But the Plinko girl didn't say anything. And she was fully dressed."

"She was terrified," I said. "Her sweater was torn, buttons missing. Considering Harris's reputation I'd have been suspicious."

Charlotte's tone sharpened and she became defensive. "I got her away from him and gave her two sugar cookies. You may not have noticed, being stewed out of your mind, but I stayed in the next cell overnight and the next two nights too, keeping watch over you. If I'd reported him to the higher ups, I'd have lost my job. Everyone loves the great Sergeant Harris and the town lowlife know to steer clear of him. He's cleaned up the fancy houses pretty good."

"The way you're defending him, I have to wonder if he's the lost love who done you wrong," I said wryly.

"Don't be ridiculous," she spat.

She prodded me toward the office door. "Your employers will contact you at the Cassville Manor Hotel. It's the fleabag rattrap two blocks down and one block east. They got you a room there. You better get yourself a coat, though. It's cold and wet outside, unseasonable for late September. Salvation Army's three blocks farther on from the hotel. Twenty dollars should be more than enough to buy a coat."

Although curious as to who my employers were, I didn't ask because, mainly, I wanted out of there with no more talk. Charlotte was right, the weather was bitter. Rain struck the pavement in torrents. As I stepped into the weather, a memory flashed, of making a futile grab for my leather jacket as the state cop dragged me out of my Pontiac. Oh, geez, that was when I'd slugged him.

A block later, I took refuge in a drug store where I bought toothpaste, a soap cake, a Coca-Cola, some licorice twists and, for a dime, an Ellery Queen paperback, a choice between that and a newspaper. I figured the book would last longer and be timeless, comparatively. And I can't do without my licorice.

Arriving at the Cassville Manor Hotel, five floors of seediness, I pushed through the revolving door into steam heat and a pungent smoke smell. For a moment I stood soaking in the warmth. Several heavily dressed old-timers lounged in worn leather chairs, their balding heads stuck in newspapers, threads of smoke spiraling upward from cigars.

I checked in with the desk clerk and took the elevator to a second floor room, paid for by my mysterious client. I tossed my shoulder bag onto the double bed, and exited immediately to an unexpectedly frigid bathroom down the hall where, despite the cold, I spent five minutes reveling in the privacy freedom offered. Back in the room, the bed was double-sheeted and pillowed, a tatty Army Surplus blanket folded at its foot. A bureau, nightstand, wooden chair, and rusty sink completed the ensemble. The tan walls were marred by a yellow undercoat spotting through. So far, nothing uplifting about Cassville. After drawing the window shades, I peeled off my wet clothes, washed them out in the sink and hung them over the towel rack. I hollowed out the pillow's middle with my fist, lay down on the creaky bed and immediately fell asleep. Three days of being incarcerated was exhausting, particularly when down the hall a monster cop lurked. In the early morning I awoke in a cold sweat and put my clothes back on damp. I'd be wrinkled but clean when the client arrived. In bed again, I read the Ellery Queen while finishing off the licorice and the Coke.

At 9:00 a.m., three sharp raps sounded on the door. I dog-eared the paperback on page 205, almost to the end. I pulled the shades, switched on the overhead light and opened the door.

Lisa's parents posed in the door frame. Mr. Plinko wore the same gray cashmere topcoat, a gray homburg perched on his head. Mrs. Plinko was covered in mink fur. She had added a hat with silk flowers on a wired net base. The couple smelled faintly of mismatched perfumes.

He led off. "I am Mr. Miki Plinko. As you recall, I am Lisa's father." His dark, liquid eyes watched me for affirmation. I did recall and so nodded. "I am from Rumania," he continued. "This is my wife, Mrs. Ada Opal Morphew Plinko, whom you have met as Lisa's mother."

The mister took a step inside and glanced around the shabby room. "Three dollars a night for this?" he grumbled to his wife. "Good idea for waste of money."

"We've come to ask you for your help in bringing Lisa home. She's run away again," Ada Opal said.

I pointed her to the chair, and left him to drift toward the windows, where, hands clasped behind his back, he stared out at the cloudy gray day.

Taking a seat on the edge of the bed, I asked, "So this isn't the first time she's run off?"

"Truth to tell, no." Mr. Plinko spoke to the window. "But, thank God, Rolf is home and once more practicing with faith."

"Lisa told me about Rolf and your school for violinists," I said. "He's your best student?"

"Yes," Mrs. Plinko replied. "We're very concerned for him. And his fondness for our daughter. The police matron told us you were a private investigator. She said Lisa had taken a fancy to you."

I asked why my profession had come up.

"I asked the matron if the jail stay had humbled Lisa to accept our authority," she explained. "The matron didn't know, but said that at least our daughter had befriended the detective rather than the—" Her lips tightened. "On the drive home, I asked Lisa about you. She said she liked you. Said you admitted to making a serious mistake and that you weren't an habitual offender of the law. She said she could confide in you, not like with us. That's a low blow she levels frequently. That we just don't understand her." She paused to fuss with her gloved hands. "We want our daughter back home. We hope you will help us and convince her to return." The light blue-gray eyes fluttered, holding back tears. She fanned herself delicately.

"Lisa has deep feelings for Rolf," I said. "How do you plan on dealing with that?"

"Lisa and Rolf may go on accompanied dates—" she started, but it was Mr. Plinko's blunt response that dominated: "I have last words."

I let that sink in as he added, "Rolf Nitschke, sixteen years old, is the outstanding talent. He is the special one we teachers all wait for."

"Are all your students as young as he is?" I asked.

"No. Other four are older. Twenties."

Since the attempted rape of their daughter had not been mentioned, I suspected Lisa hadn't told them. Not the thing to confide to this disconnected family. But these people should know what jail had cost their child. I said, "While she was in jail, a cop tried to rape your daughter."

Ada Opal gasped, her hands flying to her mouth. Miki spun away from the window and sputtered, "She told you that? I doubt it. It is another of her stories. If it happened, she is covering her part in it."

I scowled at the implication, that the girl had lied or even initiated the act.

Ada Opal addressed her husband. "Lisa is a good child. That's a fact." She took a lengthy breath. "As a small child, Lisa would go down on her knees, cling to us, grab our legs, our arms, anything to be noticed. She invented stories to gain our affection. I suppose I wasn't the best mother," she lamented. "Busy all the time."

Mr. Plinko went to his wife and patted her face. "Dahling …" His voice trailed off. Facing me, he recovered strongly. "We spend years to build our music school—Plinko Music Academy—"

She finished his thought. "—school for promising young violinists."

What a pair. A veritable Frick and Frack.

"Only recently do we feel secure to resign our positions at Cassville State University so we may run full-time the school. Daughter must grow up, behave." The man slapped the back of one hand into the palm of the other. "There must be end to this so we may devote ourself to life's work."

"What if Lisa chooses not to return to you?"

He paused before saying, "You bring daughter back of own will, to obey rules of household and finish school. A bonus for you if you accomplish this. Otherwise you tell us of her location and we will arrive to bring her home. If she does not obey, perhaps we send her to private school in another state."

A reformatory for wayward girls was my guess. And what did Lisa's mother want? She had reacted with distress to the overnight jail stay for Lisa, but hadn't contradicted Miki's skepticism about the assault.

"We only mean to impress upon you how much Lisa's return means to us," Ada Opal stated. "And to Rolf's future."

My distaste for these people could hardly be exaggerated. They were putting the future of some musical prodigy before their own daughter. My family circumstances were a bit shaky, but I'd never allow for that. Norris was the only relative whose whereabouts I sometimes knew. My other brother, Jim, had vanished years ago into the enclosing arms of a religious sect.

Was this family worth the trouble? Might Lisa be better off away from them? But need trumped ambivalence. I needed a bankroll and quickly. If the licensing board got wind of the DUI, my PI license might be suspended or even revoked. Best take advantage while I still could. I named the additional amount it would take to purchase my services. It was considerable and would test this skinflint to the limit.

Sure enough, he protested, "We pay retainer already. Now you want more?"

"There will be travel expenses, perhaps other rattrap housing. This is a standard fee."

"Pay her, please, Miki," the woman begged.

He uttered a scornful, "Americans," while digging into his pocket and withdrawing a wad of bills. He separated some and handed them over.

I stuck out my other hand for a handshake. Forcing a smile, he tapped my fingertips.

"We see you are eager beaver to get started. You have bright eyes and bunny tail," he said. She corrected, "Bushy tail," and added, "Mr. Plinko means no offense." I went to her, shook the galaxy of rings on her limp right hand. "I'll locate your daughter, and try to convince her to return home. From the little I know of her, she seems far too naive for life on the streets."

"Exactly." Ada Opal nodded. "She was raised with everything. It's impossible to know how things went so wrong. But may we expect a good ending?" I nodded vaguely. Good ending for whom? Just me, maybe.

I asked if either of them knew where their daughter liked to spend her free time. Ada Opal started to speak but her husband beat her to it. "Of late, we are not let in on her life."

"She goes to high school? Where?"

"Cassville High. Not attended for one week."

"Does she have friends?"

"She does not bring young peoples to the house."

Of course she doesn't. "Does Rolf also attend Cassville High?"

Ada Opal shuddered. "Heavens no. I tutor him personally."

Ah yes, the Special One.

"I will need to interview him," I said, taking a pen and a notebook from my shoulder bag.

"Not allowed," Miki responded sharply. "He must not know we hired detective. It would drive them both away." Miki shook his head for emphasis. "My boy is back in nest now. We believe there is no contact between them, but she will try. We keep close track on him."

"We fear Rolf will vanish into the night." Ada Opal's voice throbbed. "What will his parents think if he just disappears?"

"What will the world think?" Miki said, throwing his hands up. He scrawled their phone number in my offered notebook. "Ask for Mr. Plinko," he instructed. "If a strange voice answers, say you have talented child and search for teacher. Leave number and I will call you."

We agreed if the case wasn't concluded in a week, we'd meet at Delmer's Cafe, on the trunk road ten miles southeast of Cassville. After giving convoluted directions, Miki said, "This must end quickly for the sake of my poor wife. You see how she suffers. I suffer too, but I can endure longer." He raised his wife from the chair. She grimaced, probably fearing he'd snap her bones with Old World solace. After a brusque good-bye, he guided her out the door as though she were blind.

I cashed the $100 check at a Farmers and Merchants Bank two blocks over. Under an empty gray sky, I walked a block more to the Salvation Army store where I bought a loose-fitting black overcoat, a long black dress with a belted waistline, a veiled black hat and scuffed black Oxfords. Lastly, brown workman's gloves—no black ones in stock. Not my typical attire, but an idea was brewing in my mind.

In the first eatery I encountered, I devoured a huge meal. Fortified, wearing the thick coat, with bundles in hand, I walked to the impound lot a mile from town. At the lot I paid the fee and retrieved my Pontiac Chieftain. I was relieved to see my leather jacket still on the passenger seat, and to feel the .25 in the hidden pouch under the seat. My brown suitcase was still in the trunk.

After parking near the hotel, I repaired to my room where I changed into the black dress, combed my hair, clapped on the hat, veil up, and examined the results in the mirror. Not quite perfect. I wiped off the lipstick I'd dabbed on earlier. Now, staring back at me was a drab little religious gal in a too-big coat, her foreign roots across the ocean in Rumania. To complete the transformation, I'd borrow the Gideon Bible from the nightstand.

If I remained Wendy Winkworth, a drunk recently released from the local jail, notoriety would precede me, a disadvantage in getting information about Lisa's whereabouts. At the high school, I intended to present myself as a Salvation Army lady; its soldiers served the world over, and it seemed the only organization without stain or blemish. A suspicious individual would have to be downright crass to cast aspersions on the credentials of such a righteous soul.

**3**

I called Miki Plinko and advised him of my plan to present myself as his Rumanian cousin, a lady of unyielding faith. He resisted. "In my position, I cannot allow lies." Eventually, after I refused to back down, he morosely agreed to schedule an appointment for me with the school authorities. "Or my wife will do it. It is more what she does."

At 10:15 the next morning, garbed in unfashionable black, I met with the principal of Cassville High in his sparsely furnished office that contained only a desk, two wooden chairs, and high shelves holding many textbooks. There were no family photos; the only personal touch was a framed PhD on the wall. Three tall windows looked out upon leaves blowing past on the windy, sunny day. Dr. Carl Swaney greeted me with a vague smile, but worry lines quickly returned to the corners of his mouth. Clad in a double-breasted blue suit, he had spritzed himself with a woodsy masculine scent. He was a tall, slender, long-faced man with frazzled, rust-colored hair. Wire-rimmed spectacles completed the careworn academic look. A scrap of toilet paper clinging to his face told me that his skin cut easily under the razor. I successfully resisted the urge to pluck off the fragment.

"I am Miss Plinko of the Salvation Army, on visit from Rumania." With hand extended, I greeted him. It had registered that peoples from Rumania avoided English contractions, coveted plurals, and despised conjunctions. I pressed on. "I am here in Cassville, U.S.A., on duty but, too, visiting relatives—Miki Plinko? Truth to tell, my name is really Plinkofrunz, but Miki shortened his to American, and thus I do too also." Always augment a lie; it increases the believability.

Dr. Swaney's mouth barely opened. "Mrs. Plinko called about you."

"Cousin Miki's dear daughter, Lisa, has …" I lowered my voice as if reluctant to speak of family shame in public, "…left home. How do you say…ran away?"

Dr. Swaney nodded slightly.

"My cousins are eager to return her. I offered to visit with …" I dropped my voice to a near whisper "…school authorities …" the dark inflection indicated I might be dealing with the Gestapo, "…and offer aid to those bless-ed of my kinship." What had I just said? No matter, he caught the gist.

"I doubt I can help because Lisa hasn't been in school lately."

"Yes-s," I hissed. "We are too sadly aware Lisa has left this most excellent education. Did she leave behind friends as well?"

He pushed up on his eyeglasses. "I guess. The Cheeley boys, Charles and Chuck. They're brothers."

"Oh dear," I said, nearly losing my act. "Is not Chuck and Charles the same?"

"Some might think so." Swaney smiled wryly. "Not the Cheeley clan. Lisa was a straight-A student before she became involved with them. Both boys are currently on suspension. With their departure, she lost what friends she had."

"Does Lisa have interests outside of… activity beside the school?" Keeping up the charade was more difficult than I imagined.

"She plays a nice game of hoops. Hoops—basketball, that is." He raised his voice and punctuated, "Basketball - is - an - American game," while pantomiming shooting a basket. When I nodded enthusiastically he returned to the normal tone for English comprehenders. "Lisa is a member of the First Methodist Church team. They play against older ladies who work at the tractor plant. Lisa holds her own. She has muscles like tire irons."

"Heavens forfend." I wrinkled my nose at the foul smell of masculinity housed within a female personage. "Where do the athletesses play this hoops?"

"At the YWCA, downtown."

I had seen the wide, one-story masonry building halfway up a steep hill while on the way to retrieve my car. I asked Dr. Swaney if he had the Cheeleys' home address.

He yanked open a caved-in bottom drawer that apparently had been dealt a savage kick and produced a card. I copied the address in my notebook.

"I doubt you'll find them at home," Swaney said. "They're hard to locate when not in school." He glanced at his watch. "I'm sorry, I have a meeting to attend." He opened the office door to usher me out. "'Good-bye, Miss Plinkofrunz. And good luck if you make contact with the Cheeley boys. You'll need it."

# 4

That afternoon, wearing my usual jeans outfit, I visited the YWCA and saw what I'd come for.

Lisa was at the gym door dressed in tan slacks and an angora sweater, a large brooch at her neck. The expensive ensemble fit her very well. She was watching the action inside. Beyond my sight line a basketball rat-a-tatted, commands were barked, rapid footsteps pounded.

"Judas Priest," I blurted. "If it isn't my old jail house partner." I went to Lisa and we bumped arms.

"How come you're in here?" she said.

"Needed exercise after gettin' out. Do they got a track?"

"Nah, just this court and you gotta sign up before they let you on it."

From the gym, an up-tempo of screechy shoes ended with a referee's whistle.

Lisa and I retreated a few steps into the shoebox lobby. Four chairs, a sofa and a coffee table filled the space.

"The company league's playing now," Lisa said, resting a hand on a chairback. "They'll be outta here in ten minutes." Her voice and demeanor were welcoming. The girl needed a friend. "They know me here," she said. "Nobody will complain if we go in and shoot baskets. I've left home. If my folks show up, they'll try to haul me back, but I'll just run again."

"Tough tiddy," I said, while wondering why the kid would display herself in public, practically begging to be spotted. Still hoping the parents would acknowledge her right to love Rolf? I knew Miki wouldn't relent. Ada Opal I wasn't sure of.

I bounced on my toes to demonstrate how in shape I was.

She assessed. "You're pretty short for basketball."

"I'm quick. They called me 'Spirit' on my last team." I sprinted to a long Formica counter, reached across and snatched a wallet that lay, among other purses, on a low desk just the other side. I dug out three fives and pocketed them. It happened so fast, that pile of pocketbooks in plain sight, serving as it did, a larger purpose. After years of law-abidingness, at least when sober, I'd again become a thief.

Lisa gaped. I stepped toward her, saying simply, "I need money. I'm on the street just like you." Would she buy that and accept me as someone other than the upright soul I'd earlier claimed to be?

When she said, "How about sharing?" that settled that.

"Thought you were rich," I said.

"Not anymore."

I took out a five, crumpled and flipped it to her. I tossed the empty wallet back over the counter. It hit the desk on the other side. Nice aim. I moved toward Lisa. We both reacted when there was a swishing sound and a bone-thin lady ducked through a fold of curtains that hid a rear area. Eyes forward, with nary a peek our direction, she proceeded to the counter and briskly arranged some pencils and pens.

"Desk monitor," Lisa whispered. "She's here all the time."

I nudged the teen toward the gym. "Let's go in there."

On the floor, hefty ladies were grunting and puffing while lunging after a basketball that skittered for its life. I asked Lisa if the desk monitor knew her.

"Dorothy? Yeah, sure. I'm here a lot."

"I think she spotted you and went in back to call your parents. Let's get out of here unless you want to go home and make a deal with the folks so you can see Rolf again." If the kid agreed, that would be the easiest bonus I'd ever earn. I thought she might be ready to give the folks another chance.

But that was not to happen. Lisa stepped toward a coat rack to the right of the gym entrance and slipped into a wool jacket with a fur collar. Through the gym door, trotting along the court's edge, she headed toward the back. I hurried after. Before the door swung to, I glanced back. Dorothy was peering around the frame. I suspected another emergency call upcoming, describing Lisa's companion as a small lady with a bright-eyed, bunny-tailed aura.

We exited through an outside door into the moist air of an alley between a row of low-lying buildings.

Lisa said, "You can bed down with us overnight, if you want."

"Who's us?"

"Friends. You'll like 'em."

I had to accept.

## 5

We hurried from the alley and turned right onto the sidewalk, strolling to the top of the steep hill where I'd left the Pontiac.

After a circuitous drive, Lisa instructed me to turn right onto a derelict block with barren flatland beyond. At 6:55, the evening was descending into fall's early darkness. Eight run-down houses made up the block, four to each side. Lisa pointed out a dilapidated green frame house as our destination: 822 Plum Street.

"Needs some fixing up," I ventured.

"You can drive onto the lawn and go around back. Nobody minds." I lurched the car over the crumbling curb onto the yard's cratered surface, parking near the back porch.

We got out of the car and stood in the brisk air as Lisa filled me in. "My friends found this place. I paid the rent for this month, in cash from my savings. That was before my parents closed the account." She snorted. "My friends gave phony names to the landlord, so there's no sign I'm staying here. Didn't ask our ages or for identification or anything," she laughed. I wasn't surprised. The way the place looked, the landlord would have rented to a three-year-old if he toddled up with the money.

"October rent is coming due," Lisa continued. "If you're staying, you can help out with that."

"You left a warm breakfast for this place?" I asked. "Come on, it's a dump."

"Hey," she said while opening a rickety screen door that might have blown off in a strong breeze. "You're talking like my parents. I'm sick of old people telling me what to do."

"Yeah, so what if I'm eighty-five years old, don't I look younger?" I spoofed.

"I do what I want," she said, not acknowledging my attempt at humor, "and Rolf will go along. We're expecting money to come in soon."

"Really? Rolf is rich too?"

"Shhh. The guys might be sleeping so be quiet." She opened the back door with a key and we entered the darkened kitchen.

Under a naked bulb light, a two burner stove with curved legs had known the Depression. Beside it sat a cast-iron sink with copper faucets. A late '40s Westinghouse refrigerator, one of the first to replace the icebox, stood across from the sink.

In the gloomy living room, we skirted a folding table that was set up near a rocker. I watched my step, barely missing kicking an already toppled wastebasket and avoiding some squashed sacks and empty beer bottles. Lisa's not so high-class pals were nowhere to be seen. Arriving at a tilted davenport, tufting springing from the arms, Lisa directed me to rest my bones (I chose the uphill side) while she went to click a switch that brought to life two low-watt bulbs in a Gothic chandelier, its iron dome furred with dust.

I heard foot clomps and rustling and a teenage boy suddenly appeared at the bottom of a stairway near the front door. Of average height, he was a stocky kid, olive-skinned, with thick jet-black hair and pretty lips. There was an Oriental cast to his limpid brown eyes. A good-looking teen in dirty jeans, a hapeless sweater and worn-out shoes. The kid ran a hand through his hair, much as my absconding brother Norris did. Would I be condemned to see signs of him in every winsome young man?

Going to the boy, Lisa said, "Charles, this is my good friend—" her face clouded, "I forget your name."

"Wendy." I rose to greet him.

"Wendy lifted a wallet at the Y with fifteen bucks in it," Lisa said.

Charles wasn't impressed. "For Christ sake, Lisa, what are you doing bringing her here?" He scowled at her before fixing his gaze on me. "You'll be sorry if you tell anybody about us," he threatened in a low voice.

I was saved from the awkward moment by a second youth scampering down the steps and nudging past the first. This kid looked like the other one, perhaps a year or two younger, also wearing dirty, shapeless clothes. But where Charles' features were well proportioned, this boy's were a bit lop-sided, the left side of his face slightly flattened, as though he'd been dropped at birth.

Lisa introduced us. "Chuck. Wendy."

"Yup," the kid said, grinning. His voice broke slightly, in the throes of changing.

I nodded at him. His hands clasped and unclasped in a way that made me wonder if he had IQ trouble.

Charles strode past me to the rocker, swept comic books to the floor, and, never taking critical eyes off me, planted himself. "Where you from?" he asked in a reedy, expressionless voice.

"Iowa." I sat back down on the sofa across from him. "Met Lisa in jail," I added.

"How long you staying?"

"Not long. Gotta raise money to get back home."

The malformed kid, Chuck, scooted an upholstered chair close to his brother and sank into it. "You know you're dead if you tell on us," he said, sounding almost cordial.

"Shut up, dummy," Charles said to his brother.

"I get the message," I said.

"Wendy's got a car," Lisa said. Charles' eyebrows rose slightly.

Chuck slapped his thigh. "Hey, Wennie, how you make money? Steal stuff? That's what we do."

Charles leaned forward. "Shut up. Just because you look goofy, don't mean you have to act goofy."

Across the room, a plaintive cry rose from a cardboard box that lay next to a heat register. We all came alert. Something was stirring inside, perhaps a mewing cat.

"You got kittens over there?" I asked. "I love kittens." I rose and prepared to take a little ball of fur in my arms. Instead a pudgy baby stared at me from the box, its blanket balled into a corner.

I stepped back in surprise. "Where'd that come from?"

"It's our sister, Betty," Charles said. "She's ten months old." Betty was ugly, fat, with lumpy cheeks, a wide flat nose and big nostrils. She began pulling on the box flaps, trying to sit up. She let out an aggravated wail.

Quickly Charles snatched her up and tucked the blanket around her. She quieted. "Drafty windows," he observed. Baby Betty reached up and patted his neck. Face close to hers, he said, "The folks left her with us." He cooed and Betty reciprocated with baby noises.

I'm a sucker for teenage boys who pick up babies when they cry. Still, I had to ask, "You guys left in charge of a 10-month old baby? Well, okay, if you say so."

Charles spoke to Lisa. "See, this is what happens when you let strangers in." A memory flashed of Norris saying something similar when I brought a cop to his front door. But this menacing teen was no Norris.

Nimbly avoiding objects in her path, Lisa went to the kitchen. She returned with an opened bottle of beer and presented it to me. I sipped.

"I could use some chips," Chuck said. Booting things out of the way, he wandered to the kitchen and returned with a bag of Old Dutch potato chips. After ripping it open with his teeth, he offered me first dibs. I declined politely.

Meanwhile, Charles had spread the baby's blanket on the folding table and laid Betty on it. He cleaned her with a damp washrag and changed her quickly, using dishtowels for diapers.

"I can't believe how good you are at that," I marveled. He was a lot sweeter with his little sister than with his brother.

"Charles is a good mommy," Chuck affirmed through a mouthful of chips. "He took care of me practically from infamy."

I stifled the urge to correct.

Charles picked up the dirty dishtowel-diaper and the baby. He strode to the front door and tossed the former out. He said to Lisa, "Betty's hungry. Hold her while I get something." He passed off the little one and Lisa seemed to know what to do with her.

Outside a car with a rattly engine drove by, the first traffic I'd heard in the neighborhood.

Charles brought Gerber's peaches and a spoon, and a bottle from the kitchen. After retrieving Betty, he went to the rocker and offered the fruit. For a time, we were all fascinated with watching her slurp peaches as little spots of mush gathered on her. After the fruit was gone, she glugged from the bottle.

Along the way, Chuck informed me, "Babies are messy eaters."

The peacefulness was interrupted by the sinuous sounds of a violin coming from upstairs.

"What's that?" I blurted, but immediately knew, so I shut up and we listened to an exquisitely played melody interspersed with dazzling runs, clean and clear as Heifetz, whom I'd heard several times on the radio. Upstairs the player smashed his bow across several strings causing my companions to dip their heads. Chuck mumbled, "He likes to be perfect."

When the heavenly melody started up again, Lisa said, "It's Rolf, my boyfriend I told you about."

"Oh yeah, the expert fiddle player."

Lisa stood and shouted, "Rolf, come down! I want you to meet somebody!"

The playing broke off and a low, frail voice responded. "In a minute. I have to finish the Paganini."

Lisa hurried to the stairway. "No! Come down right now!" It was a command. Silence and then padded footsteps descended.

Rolf was tall, about 5'11", sallow-faced, with long arms, a long neck, and wide hips. His tangled blond hair fell past his ears. He had bright blue eyes and an aquiline profile. He wore old but clean jeans and a loose, striped T-shirt. He looked like an aristocrat fallen on hard times. Spotting me, he lowered his eyes, but that also may have been to avoid the clutter as he made his way to Lisa. He placed an arm around her and she stretched to buss him on the cheek. "Nasty old beard," she commented after rubbing against his utterly smooth cheek.

"I left my razor at home," he said in a guttural accent.

"You're home now," Lisa said.

"I mean that other place."

"Where your goods are stored," Charles said drily from his post. He stood, spread Betty's blanket on the floor by his chair, laid the baby on it. He brought a saucepan and spoon from the kitchen and Betty began a percussion solo.

After Lisa's introductions: "Wendy—Rolf," to which I responded, "Hi," and he barely acknowledged, Chuck spoke up. "Wennie can drive you back. She's got a car."

"No thank you," Rolf said. "I have my bike."

Lisa and the young genius sat down on the low end of the sofa and again embraced. He hummed into her cheek, "Did you have a good basketball time?"

"Great," she said.

"My little dove," he said, nuzzling her hair, bringing her hand to his lips. An old-world romantic, for sure.

"Where'd you learn to play violin like that?" I asked over Betty's clamor. "Are your parents musical?"

"Nein—"

Lisa yawped, "Gawd no! They're missionaries in Africa, converting the natives. They head the Perfect Truth Church. Isn't that something? The Virgin Mary's got everybody believing she's borne the one, the only, Christ child." Her voice had risen to a screech. Everyone was quelled into silence. This kid was a lot like her dad.

The five of us proceeded to share a couple of potato chip bags, after which Chuck said, "Stupid—" Everyone waited for him to complete the thought. Some seconds passed before, "—I'm still hungry" emerged.

"Newcomer furnishes food," Charles said.

"Oh, sure," I said. "I got a little money. What'd you like?" I pulled out my notebook.

Everyone piled on requests except Rolf, who said, "I will eat at the other place. They like for me to do that. I eat a lot of salad and marinated herring."

Lisa deplored, "Oh, I am so terribly tired of salads."

I jotted down: minced ham, hamburger, buns, chips, beer, orange juice, soft drinks, soup, lighter fluid. Gerbers, batteries, Vaseline, baby powder, milk, chocolate bars, donuts, peanut butter, apples. Once they began it was hard to contain their enthusiasm.

"Planning a safari?" I finally interrupted. No response, not a hint of a smile from any of them. So far in Cassville I hadn't had one belly laugh. A couple of snickers aside, these were serious people.

After Chuck ordered two cartons of Camels," I said sternly, "Enough. You're not taking my last cent. And I'm not buying more beer. You're not old enough." I shouldered my bag and started for the back door.

Rolf checked his foreign-looking watch. "I am late. I must go." He disassembled himself from Lisa, got up, and asked if I would drive him.

"Sure," I said, looking forward to having a private talk. He dashed upstairs and soon came down in slip-on loafers, a bulky sweater and a wool cap with earflaps down. He held his violin case.

After he squirmed in Lisa's clutchy farewells, we left by the back way. I noticed a tangle of dirty dishtowels on the ground beside the stoop.

It was dark except for a distant streetlight. The violinist brought a small bike, possibly European, from the side of the house and wrangled it into the back seat of the Pontiac. He got in beside me with his violin.

A door slammed from the house and Charles flung the rear door of the Pontiac open. He eased in and stuck his knees under the bike.

"I'm going along," he announced.

"Afraid I won't come back?" I asked. He gave me a look and shot at me with both trigger fingers, his tongue clicking appropriately.

Once underway, Rolf directed me to ill-lit side roads. "I bike this route," he explained, "so no one spots me."

"How'd you manage to steal away? Lisa says they keep a pretty good eye on you."

He smiled vaguely. "This evening, all of us violin students went in Ned's car to the picture show in town. But at the first corner, I asked to get out. I made my way back to where I'd hidden my bike and my violin. The others won't tell. Everybody thinks Germans are sneaky anyhow."

"Oh, I'm sure not." I hesitated. Actually, yes we do.

"Rolf likes to keep track of his girl since she's gone to live with other men," Charles said.

"Nothing to that, and trouble if there is," Rolf said evenly.

"Trouble with who?" Charles' voice held a dangerous edge.

"I know guns too," the young violinist retaliated. Whoa, who said anything about guns.

Charles advanced the dangerous mood. "I can smash a violin to smithereens any day I want. And I can have Lisa anytime I want. She lives at my digs. But who wants her? She's a pain in the ass, except she's got money."

Rolf's lips moved silently. Cursing perhaps. He turned to the window and stared out. This was a talented boy with a great future. No way was he stupid enough to tangle with a no-account street kid.

As we headed up a long, gradual hill, I ragged on Rolf a little. "Guess it'd be easier for you if Lisa came back home, wouldn't it?"

The level tone: "Up to her."

"Will it be hard to marry and begin your career at the same time?"

The slightest of shrugs.

"Probably don't have much time to think about that when you're working so hard at your music."

"I guess."

I opted for a change of subject. "Do you like working with the Plinkos?"

"I guess."

"You learning a lot?"

"I guess." The kid was giving nothing away. What was behind the hedging? Weren't the teachers as good as advertised?

"Which Plinko do you study with?"

"Both."

"Why both of them?" No answer.

The hill leveled out and we passed block after block of straight streets in silence. We drove past small homes, an apartment building, people out strolling, a couple seated on a bus stop bench, a park with tall trees bending to the wind, picnic tables beneath a shelter, several blocks of stores and an elementary school, its fenced-in playground empty.

At one point, I twisted to speak to Charles in the back seat. "How you doing back there?" He glared back with an intensity that made me uneasy. I somewhat regretted leaving the .25 in its nest under the passenger seat.

As a curved road wound up a short residential hill, the houses and yards became larger and the paved road turned to gravel. A minute later, Rolf instructed me to drive past a sizable two-story Colonial home, the only house on the block, and park behind a gray DeSoto that had four young people milling around it. A dark row of four cabins was to the side of the road. Thick woods crowded up behind the cabins.

Rolf identified the young people as, "My movie-going friends." Remaining in the car, he studied their horseplay as he delivered an assessment.

"Miki is the musician," he said. "He is nice. There is not much new to learn so we enjoy the lesson. It is a meeting of musical minds.

A lesson in name only." He turned toward me, his eyes opening wide. "Could anyone teach me anything? I came to America already complete." He savored his stature before saying, "Ada Opal is different than Miki. She tries to leave her mark by criticizing everything I do. She makes me work hard, but she has no feeling for the music. For her, it is all about the technique. She tries to knock me down and rebuild me in her own way. For her, you cannot play one note that isn't examined and complained about. She criticizes when you play a wrong bowing or even a tiny bit out-of-tune, like it is a mortal sin. She rides her students as if she's a Jascha or a Yehudi. I am polite but in my mind I resist mightily." He took a breath. "I like Miki very much better. He fills in the hour speaking only of the music, not of single notes. But since I know more than both of them I let them go on about it."

Once Rolf let loose, I got more than I asked for.

"Why did you come to the U.S. for more study if you're already so much better than everybody else?"

He made a face. "Because that is the way of it. No matter how good you are, you must work with famous teachers. With their backing, that is the way doors open for you."

Lisa had said as much, that her parents knew how to promote their students. We sat in silence for a time and observed the outdoor scene.

The Plinko home was large, but not as impressive as I expected, considering the teachers' supposed fame. Evidently Plinko satisfaction lay in musical endeavors and not possessions, or maybe the Plinko Music Academy wasn't as lucrative as I'd imagined.

Rolf broke our silence. "Sometimes what Ada Opal says is useful. She means well." He seemed almost embarrassed by his hubris in criticizing the famous instructor.

I gestured toward the row of cabins beyond the house. "Is that where the students live?"

"Yes, but I live with the family." Rolf got out, claimed his bike from a scowling Charles and went to join the others. They greeted him with friendly laughter.

6

Upon our return to the house on Plum Street, Charles was out of the car quickly, flinging open the passenger door and grabbing the food and supplies I'd bought on the trip back. Chuck met him at the bottom of the back steps. The two boys were already devouring slices of salami when I got in the door.

"Save some scraps for Lisa and me," I said.

Chuck held up a slice and said, "This is yesterday's dinner." He seized two more salami slabs. "And this here's today's." I said no more.

In the kitchen Charles helped me unpack. He placed the twelve Gerbers in the cupboard next to some Jell-0 packets and two boxes of instant milk. I laid the bread on the sink counter and stuck the real milk in the refrigerator.

But then Charles flipped my key ring at me. I snagged it in mid-air. Astonished I asked, "How'd you get my keys?"

"You left them on the counter." He bared his teeth in a fake grin.

The baby was first to be fed after the boys' initial glut. Betty consumed ravenously while the rest of us ate and then swilled down Cokes.

After a while Chuck leaned back, swigged, burped, and pontificated, "We lost our family but got us better people."

"Yeah, ones with money and a car," Lisa guffawed.

I inquired how the Cheeley family had been lost.

Charles burped slightly longer than his brother, showing him up a little. "Pa died from cirrhosis a year ago. He was a drunk. You miss him, Chuck? Can you believe it's been a year?"

Chuck opened his mouth for a burp, but couldn't muster anything. "Yeah," he said. "We was fourteen."

Charles corrected, "You fifteen, me sixteen. In March, Ma ran off with her boyfriend. To New Mexico she said. She left Betty to us. Thought she'd be back by now. Those boyfriend things never last long with Ma, but so far she's stayed gone." He ran his fist over his nose and wiped it on his sweater. "After that we went and stayed with William, some of our kin who lives in the holler. Two room shack. Gave us a corner in one. Had to, otherwise we'd a made serious trouble." The food made Charles talkative, almost friendly.

Outside a barking dog abruptly ended the story. Lisa jolted erect. Betty began to wail and Charles laid her in the box. Chuck hurried to the front window and drew the shade on the barking and the darkness. It was the undercurrent of menace I'd grown up with: outcasts forever watching their backs.

Charles emerged from a closet with a sawed-off shotgun. "No problem," he assured. "Probably just a stray dog." He sat down and laid the weapon across his knees. Below, Betty's cries subsided into gurgles. The dog's yapping came less frequently.

"Careful with that weapon around Betty," I cautioned.

"It's okay. She can't reach the trigger." I guessed that was supposed to be funny.

Not into wasting breath, I said, "Lisa invited me to stay overnight. You mind?"

"Not anymore." Charles rubbed his belly. "We'll be on our feet ourselves, soon."

"We got plans," Chuck said excitedly. "We're gonna—"

"Turn the bulb on, stupid," Charles snapped. Chuck closed his mouth and his face clouded over.

I was pretty sure those hushed-up plans were illegal. After a few minutes of alert silence, Charles stood and placed the gun across the chair arms. He reclaimed Betty from her box and, signaling for Chuck to take the gun and follow, he started upstairs with the child. Cradling the weapon like it was his own baby, Chuck followed. It was 10:20, Timex time.

Halfway up, Charles called back, "Night, ladies."

"Don't let the bedbugs bite," Chuck added, giggling.

I hoped he was merely repeating a saying.

Lisa picked up her fur-collared jacket and headed toward the stairs. "I got my own space upstairs. You can sleep on the davenport."

After she'd gone, I curled up there. It smelled like dog. Instead of bedbugs, I'd probably get fleas.

The next morning, the gang was up early. They seemed even more jittery and on edge than the night before. I thought the increased tension might be uncertainty over housing so, graciously, I pulled out my billfold and paid half of October's rent whereupon they became slightly friendlier. Still, it was a seriously silent breakfast of Cokes and donuts. About 8:15, I left the house and drove downtown. In the hotel lobby, I took two messages from my box, both from Ada Opal. Before returning her call, I went to my room, soaped up using the lavatory, combed my hair and dabbed on lipstick. I dressed in a fresh outfit and packed my suitcase with a few clothes for the move to Plum Street. I grabbed a pillow, but left the Salvation Army outfit. My employers were paying for the hotel room so I'd keep it and visit frequently for naps.

I ate a real breakfast at a corner restaurant—half a cantaloupe, three scrambled eggs, bacon and a stack of pancakes. I negotiate better with disagreeable clients after a good meal.

It was raining lightly when I got back to the hotel. Blinking away moisture, I dialed Ada Opal from the phone by the reception desk. She picked up quickly, informing me that they hadn't called the police after receiving the YWCA monitor's sighting of Lisa because, from Dorothy's description, they knew Lisa was with me.

From the background, Miki spoke up. "I have informed Methodist Church and public school to be on outlook."

"Where is Lisa now?" Ada Opal asked.

"With friends. She's not ready to come home yet," I said. "She's still seeing Rolf. Can't you keep that kid at home? It would improve my chances."

Miki squawked, "What? They were together?"

"Yes," I said. "Yesterday early evening. They were together for at least for three hours."

Ada Opal piped up. "Rolf was supposed to be at the movies with the other students."

"He didn't make it."

Miki's voice dropped as he said to his wife, "Why hire the detective? We can use Rolf as bait, follow him, bring her home ourselves."

I needed that bonus. "You drag your daughter home and she'll just run again. The next time she'll hide even better so you never find her. And Rolf will tag along. They'll both be gone." I changed the subject. "Let's talk business. How much is my bonus?"

"One thousand dollars," she said, while, simultaneously, he yammered, "You peoples are always about the money."

Maintaining my poise, I said, "Okay. A thousand dollars. Let's meet to sign an agreement. How does 11:30 this morning sound?"

Ada Opal agreed to the time and confirmed the site we'd agreed upon: Delmer's Cafe, on the trunk road ten miles southeast of Cassville. I'd ask the hotel clerk where to find that trunk road, also what a trunk road was. We rang off after Ada Opal thanked me for my services. Miki added nothing, the phrase obviously not in his vocabulary.

My next task was to visit the library to check newspapers for articles on recent baby snatchings. It gnawed at me that baby Betty did not have the slightly slanted eyes of her supposed brothers. That, along with the Cheeleys saying they expected money to arrive soon, roused my suspicions.

I left the car where it was and retraced my steps down Main Street, walking two-and-a-half blocks to South Avenue where I turned left and went uphill to Adams Street. The library, a brownstone building in a fancy architectural style that included several peaks, took up most of the block.

Seated at a long table with smudged fingerprints on top and a couple wads of gum stuck underneath, I discovered that the *Cassville Courier* (published Mon, Wed, and Sat) offered no reports of kidnappings. Not the last word on the subject. Contacting the authorities brought greater risk to the victims. But it did occur to me that Betty might have a different father than the Chucks', maybe the boyfriend the mother had fled with. If so, that guy must be a homely fellow.

**7**

Under cloudy skies, I returned to the Cheeley domicile where the air was thick with cigarette smoke. The three kids had loosened up a bit from earlier and we sat around and chewed the fat while snacking on donuts, potato chips, Cokes and Gerbers. About 10:45, we added milk and orange juice.

At 10:57, I changed to the barn-red denims and white shirt and added a light linen jacket, leaving my leather jacket on a chair. Outdoors, I turned up my collar against a brisk wind. The rain had stopped, but the sky was overcast with the threat of more precipitation. As I backed the Pontiac off the lawn, I saw the brothers at the window, watching, hungering for access to my car. No way were they getting it.

Ten miles southeast of Cassville, beside a dirt road, Delmer's Cafe was a tiny outpost on a bare stretch of flat land. Two trucks, a pickup, and a blue Plymouth Roadking were parked in the graveled lot. Our appointment was for 11:30, and it was exactly that when I emerged from the Pontiac and the Plinkos did likewise from their Roadking. Inside the café, a middle-aged waitress met us, her blonde hair piled high except for one straggle drooping over an eye. Her nametag, pinned onto a folded hanky, read "Darlene." Where possible, I like to know the names of the people around me. Darlene ushered us to one of three booths, away from four rough characters in overalls seated at the short counter.

Ada Opal only wanted tea. I ordered a chicken salad sandwich, French fries and a side of green beans. It had been days since I'd eaten anything green.

"We are eating? I did not think so," Miki grumped as the waitress eyed him, pencil poised.

"Aren't we here just to talk business?" Ada Opal inquired.

"It's lunchtime and I'm hungry," I said. These cheapskates had met their match. And I knew the man would pay; around here the man always did.

Miki took an exasperated breath. He snapped at the waitress, "Beef commercial dinner and tea."

In several trips, glasses of ice water, tea bags, cups, and a pot of hot water arrived along with the entrees.

Miki jiggled a bag in hot water, before stirring in five sugar cubes. "Lemon?" he asked severely of the waitress. She brought him a sliced lemon, toot sweet. He squeezed both halves in the tea.

"Lisa's caused so much trouble," Ada Opal sighed. "Tell me why I miss her so much."

Miki grunted. He cut off a piece of gravy-sloshed sandwich, chewed, and chased it with a slug of tea. His wife immediately added hot water to his cup. I could see the famous man was used to being fawned over and she was used to fawning.

I answered Ada Opal because he hadn't. "Lisa's your daughter and you love her," I said simply. Part of me wanted to reach across the table and take her hand. She was obviously miserable.

Miki asked how the Salvation Army impersonation had gone.

"Fine, no problem," I assured him.

"Do not dress up again," he warned. "I cannot defend you beyond belief for I have reputation to uphold. We are very well-known in town."

"Small town people are such gossips," Ada Opal added. "Miki slipped the jail matron $10 to keep quiet." Oh boy. Charlotte didn't seem to be the tight-lipped sort.

"Let's get down to the business of upholding your reputation," I said. I tore a lined page from my notebook on which I'd handwritten and signed the following:

"A CONTRACT BETWEEN PARTY OF THE FIRST PART PRIVATE INVESTIGATOR WENDY WINKWORTH AND PARTIES OF THE SECOND PART MIKI AND ADA OPAL PLINKO

All Parties agree to the following:

A fee of one thousand dollars in cash is to be paid to Wendy Winkworth, Private Investigator, when Lisa Plinko returns home of her own accord, and when all three parties, Miki Plinko, Ada Opal Plinko, and Lisa Plinko, agree to the following stipulations:

1. Lisa Plinko must agree to reside at home with her parents.

2. In return, said parents will allow Lisa Plinko and Rolf Nitschke to mingle in the home, in non-sexual friendship, and to attend various events outside the home, with appropriate adult supervision.

3. Until Lisa and Rolf both reach the age of consent, the Parties of the Second Part (the parents Plinko) will continue to support Lisa in the manner to which she is accustomed.

4. Upon Private Investigator Wendy Winkworth's successful return of your daughter to you, both of you will thank PI Winkworth unabashedly, fulsomely and without restraint."

Okay, so that last condition was my little joke.

Miki's cultivated hands positioned the document directly in front of him, while Ada Opal had to twist her neck to see.

When he finished reading, he nudged the paper toward his wife.

He asked if I'd seen Lisa today.

"Yes," I said. "Rolf hasn't shown up, so congratulations."

"Has her attitude seen a change?"

"No, she believes he will visit tonight, so you have to prevent him from doing that."

"All students will again remain indoors." He stabbed at his food.

Ada Opal set down her cup. "Last night Rolf arrived home with the other students about 8:30. He practiced until bedtime at 10:00."

Miki smacked his lips. "He is happy camper when he plays violin. He does not think of her at all."

"Uh-huh," I responded. "Do you check his room during the night to make sure he isn't camping out?"

"Lately I sleep on the sofa in the living room so he can't go by me out the door. Each hour I open his door a sliver and check his bed," she said.

"My wife is almost Dick Tracy," Miki said.

With a vision of a lump of clothing under bed covers representing an escaped inmate, I asked, "Where is Rolf's room? First floor? He could go out the window."

Miki responded. "Yes. On first floor. But not our Rolf. He would not risk hurting his hands. It is big drop to ground."

Yeah, and bicycling six miles to the Cheeleys while hanging onto a violin case isn't risky? I didn't say that but the skeptical look on my face must have, because Ada Opal assured me that "You don't know him like we do."

Miki's pen moved to sign, but then it hovered above the document before he dropped it to the table. He slid his other hand into his suit coat and came out with a pack of Old Golds. He passed one cigarette to his wife and stuck another between his grim lips. They each lit up from gold Ronsons. No one was offering me a smoke these days. Not that I'd have accepted, because I'd definitely quit. For the second time. The last time.

"Just now we need to think," Miki explained.

"Swell," I said. "Take all the time you need, even thirty minutes. If, in thirty minutes, you don't accept these terms, I'm on the road back to Iowa. I've been away too long as it is."

The woman's blue-gray eyes pleaded with Miki's dark ones. She knew the jig was up if Lisa were forcibly returned home; her husband would soon have Lisa enrolled in some remote institution.

Miki snatched up the pen and signed the document. He pushed the paper across to me with such vehemence that his corner crumpled. I slid it Ada Opal's way. She seemed surprised to have a say, but signed her name under his in tiny script. I smoothed the document, folded it, and stuck it in my notebook.

"Darlene, more ice water here," I called, motioning to my glass. "And I'd like a piece of lemon pie."

My water glass was sloppily refilled. The pie was skidded close enough that I could capture it.

After the waitress returned to the counter, Miki said, "Rolf's parents are coming in May. I hope we give them good news."

"They're coming in March, darlin'. Rolf will return to Germany with them," Ada Opal said. "Next fall he'll be back."

I asked what had happened with the shoplifting charge.

"We paid the fine," Ada Oal said. "Now Rolfie has a police record. One can only hope his parents don't find out."

Miki snapped, "I told you I would get that crime erased."

She sputtered, "You can't always buy people off in this country. It doesn't work that way."

"So you say." He jabbed a second cigarette in the ashtray. "Lisa's problem is there is something wrong with her. A craziness inborn."

"If so, she got it from you," she said. Suddenly the two were sniping at each other in such low tones I could hardly hear.

"Miki has relatives back in Rumania," Ada Opal spoke to me. "Sitting in doorways, surrounded by stone walls with peep holes cut in them. They hold guns in their laps and belts of ammunition around their necks, waiting for the next war to begin."

He gave it right back. "And on your side is your crazy mother."

"My mother is a bit ill-tempered," she conceded.

"She is she-devil," he responded.

"Don't you dare talk about my mother that way," she threatened. That stopped him. After pouring hot water over a tea bag, adding sugar and squeezing a drop more out of the lemon, Miki revealed that, "Her mother lives in next town over so I may know her traits."

"Mother hates Miki," Ada Opal said. "She moved up here intending to live with us, but it didn't work out."

"She lives in Watkins now?" I asked.

"Yes-s." Miki slouched back in the booth. Such torment took the starch right out of a man's backbone. When his shoulders hit the seat back, he jolted up and expelled an "oof."

Ada Opal eyed him with concern. "My Miki Mouse, don't get so worked up." She rubbed his arm.

The man must have skipped that comic strip because he took her hand, swept it to his lips and kissed it.

"We're the original odd couple, aren't we," she murmured. "But united in our art. It's what will live on after us."

"This is utmost," he confirmed.

"Uh-huh," I said, trying to move the show along. "Ada Opal, what about your mother? Could she take Lisa for a while?"

"Oh, God no," she responded. "Living just down the road? Rolf would be there all the time."

Miki gave me the names of three different restaurants where, in the future, we could meet. "Out of the way spots where nobody will see us," was how Ada Opal put it. I hoped to be done with the case quickly and never have to enter any of those eateries.

Once Darlene dropped off the bill, the Plinkos stood. He helped her with her coat. I was left to find sleeve openings by myself.

As I drove back to Cassville, my thoughts reverted to the Cheeleys. A cold-hearted scheme formed: I'd engage the boys in a lesser crime, like shoplifting, report them and get them out of the picture long enough for Lisa to weary of the vagabond life. With my counsel, she'd see the wisdom of returning home to three squares, a warm bed, and clean clothes. I'd turn baby Betty over to the authorities where she probably belonged anyhow.

And when the young prodigy's parents crossed the ocean in one of the M months, they'd whisk him away. Trouble over. Bonus earned.

I was feeling quite good about this idea of mine. Too bad others had their own plans.

**8**

It was 1:15 p.m. when I got back to 822 Plum. I parked on the street, sparing the Pontiac the curb. Even though I was still a little nervous around Charles, who wasn't hesitant about grabbing weaponry, and Chuck, who loved cuddling a firearm, I was becoming increasingly confident I could handle any threat from them without resorting to fire power. So once again I left the .25 in the secret pocket of the car.

A humid breeze greeted me as I lugged a bag of groceries up the front steps. Entering through the unlocked door and mindful of the baby, I said softly, "Anybody home?" In the living room, Lisa and Rolf were necking on the dog sofa. Aha, with the parents away, the kids were at play. Baby Betty was fast asleep in her box on the floor near the teens, an empty Gerbers jar tipped beside her with the spoon sticking out. When the couple saw me, they separated, aided by Rolf's gentle push. He murmured a welcome, but Lisa's frown said she didn't care to be interrupted.

In the kitchen, I unloaded the groceries and put them away. Poking my head into the living room, I whispered, "Anybody want an orange pop?"

"Yeah, bring two," Lisa said, sounding only slightly annoyed. I opened an extra for myself, distributed the others, and then went to sit in Chuck's chair.

The back door opened and closed as someone, a Cheeley I assumed, entered the kitchen. Footsteps moved about and then left, the door closing softly. The lovebirds had turned toward the sound and were listening with a kind of expectation.

"That sounded like Charles," I said. "What's he doing?"

"I thought he was coming in here," Lisa said. "He wanted to ask you a favor. I guess he changed his mind."

Out front a car started hard and roared away with a screech of tires. Something about the proximity caused me to grip the chair arms. "That sounded awfully close," I said.

Lisa straightened. "Charles and Chuck might have borrowed your car to go rob the bank."

For an instant, I gaped. Then I swept my shoulder bag off the floor and dug into it. No car keys. I dropped the bag, jumped up, and scoured my pockets. No keys. Damn, had I left them on the counter again? I ran to the picture window in front. No Pontiac. I swung around.

"Which bank, Lisa?" I asked through gritted teeth.

"Farmers and Merchants on Main Street," Lisa said.

Where I'd cashed the Plinko check.

Outrage consumed me. I could hardly speak. "Why didn't you tell me sooner?"

She showed her palms. "We thought Charles was going to ask you for the car. We're all supposed to wait here, not go anywhere."

"Are they armed?"

Rolf answered. "The sawed-off shotgun."

"Goddam it," I shouted. "They'll kill somebody, and use my car to get there." I rushed out the front door. Two blocks up, the Pontiac was turning right, heading toward the main drag. It was traveling slowly, the driver apparently realizing that after hot-rodding away, getting arrested for speeding was no way to start a bank heist. What to do? I already had a record in this berg. I'd surely be arrested for aiding and abetting. I'd be convicted. I'd do prison time. Goodbye youth and so long career.

I took off in a sprint down three alleys before I saw an old pickup parked next to a garage, the driver's door unlocked. Hot-wire.

Gasping, I ran into the open garage, saw a litter of tools and grabbed a screwdriver. I ran to the pickup and pried open the cover under the dashboard. I separated the red wires from the ignition switch and touched them together. After several tries, the motor turned and fired.

I hit the gas and roared out of the alley. I sped the remaining ten blocks trying to remember exactly where that damn bank was. A half-block before, I saw the bank's sign and screeched to the curb. The Cheeleys emerged from the bank, bending low. Bandanas, actually dishtowels, covered their lower faces. When the boys encountered several people on the sidewalk, Chuck raised the sawed-off shotgun and fired into the air. People screamed and dived for cover. Chuck fired again and I could see the glee on his face. To him, this was great fun. Why would Charles give his dim brother control of the weapon? The boys turned right, away from me, and took off down the sidewalk, leather pouches swinging from their belts. The door to Jake's Best Burgers burst open and a cop in blue rushed out with his pistol drawn.

I yanked the pickup into gear and moved into the street. Shots were fired and I saw Chuck slap his shoulder and the shotgun spin out of his grasp. He collapsed sideways against a parked car and slid to the sidewalk where he lay twitching. A step ahead, Charles wheeled, grabbed his brother by the belt and dragged him into the street. Chuck's legs were moving, knees buckling as he tried to gain purchase. Money spilled from both boys' pouches as they struggled to make it across the street.

I gunned the engine and the pickup shot forward. I leaned across the seat and pushed the passenger door open. Slowing down for them, I yelled, "Get in!" Charles lifted and shoved the bloody Chuck in the cab. Then Charles was in, slamming the door, the three of us crammed together on the front seat with Chuck wheezing in pain. I floored it as behind us the popping of small guns continued. Ducking almost below window level, I took the corner on two wheels in a narrow right turn. I saw the delivery truck parked out in the street, but way, way too late. There was a terrible screech of metal against metal as we collided. I was whipped sideways against the door that flew open and I fell out. I hit the pavement hard, my left side scraping against the abrasive surface as I bounced and skidded. Within seconds, a cop was upon me, dragging me into the clear.

Dazed, I looked for the boys, but didn't see them. Apparently they'd managed to flee the coop and the only chicken remaining was me.

The cop tried to stand me up, but when I sagged toward the pavement another uniform stepped in close. "Hands up. Spread your legs," he hollered. Wobbling, I tried to comply, but could do neither so the two of them dragged me to the sidewalk where several gawkers stood transfixed. I mumbled to an older lady, "I thought they needed a lift."

My left sleeve was ripped and my arm was scraped and bleeding. It hurt like hell. When the taller cop twisted my arms behind my back and clamped cuffs on, it hurt worse. My trousers were completely frayed along the outside seam. One tennis shoe had split between the leather and sole. My big toe poked out. While one cop supported me, the other wandered around scooping up money with his left paw and transferring the bills to his right. A bystander ran up to help and the cop appropriated that currency. Startled cries from onlookers sounded from every point on the map. I watched it all dully while trying to regain my senses.

After the shorter cop retrieved the shotgun, the two of them hauled me, my feet barely touching sidewalk, around the corner and two blocks further to the low brick building that I knew housed the police station and jail. During the trip, a cop car, dark blue with white top and doors, kept pace beside us. From the driver's seat a cop with a sizable mustache observed through slitted eyes. The image blurred and I ducked my head and tried not to pass out. A hushed crowd trailed after us; I heard their shuffling footsteps and their murmurs. Why hadn't the cops stuck me in that squad car? Oh. I knew. Because the slow procession was for the taxpayers, to show their dollars put to good use.

In the station, I was hustled to the Chief's office, where two days ago Charlotte had returned my belongings. I hoped she didn't see me now; it would be another black mark for the PI profession. A third cop entered through the back door. The observer with the brush mustache. He was heavy set, with creases under his brown eyes, and a smile you didn't want to return. My addled brain called up Lisa's mention of a mole on her attacker, but this guy's ruddy complexion contained no mole. Neither of the others had moles. My brain was swimming. My entire left side screamed with pain. I fought to concentrate on spinning a story to get out of this mess. I was pretty confident I could do so. After all, I'm the champion of liars.

Mr. Mustache came toward me and jerked my shirt collar. "Who're those guys you're driving for?" he asked. He had minty breath and a sandpaper voice.

"I'm hurt," I gritted my teeth. "Get me a doctor." And give me time to think.

He tapped my face twice. I sagged to show how weak I was, how injured. Think. Think.

"You'll get a doc when I say," he rasped. I noticed he wasn't wearing a nameplate. Odd. The other two bore IDs, Brunanski and Shulz, something like that. This older cop tossed his cap onto the wooden desk. He had dark brush-cut hair. "Good job, boys," he said. "Now go get rid of the population hanging around outside. After that, I want you both out there patrolling for those two bank-robbing bastards." He waved the two cops away. "Don't come back without them." He rocked on his heels and measured me. "I'll interrogate this one myself." Something glittered in his eyes and it chilled me to the bone.

I wanted no part of this interview. I talked fast. "I knew those boys from last summer when they raked my lawn. Today they looked like they needed help, that's all. I didn't realize their complicity in a crime until it was too late—"

Mr. Mustache smacked me hard across the face. The blow sent me reeling against the tall officer, Brunanski.

That guy pushed me away like I was poison and I stumbled against the desk. My face stung from the slap. I regained my balance and said strongly, "I need a doctor and a lawyer."

Shulz tossed the key to the cuffs onto the desk. "Behave yourself now, Sarge," he said. This mustached sergeant had to be Lisa's attacker, but where was the goddam mole?

Brunanski strutted out a back door and Shulz followed, but before going out he cast a vacant glance upon me. He knew what was going to happen and didn't mind a bit. I carry that cop's imbecilic gaze as a reminder of my seething contempt, in my worse moments, toward cops. I began yammering again. "Look, Sergeant, I'm a private investigator. My ID's in my purse." Surely he'd leave a representative of the law alone. Oh, shit. I'd left the purse at the house. I continued, "I'm a friend of the Miki Plinkos, you can call them up, they'll verify my credentials; they're the music teachers in town." He laughed outright. I should have realized the name Plinko hadn't stopped him before. Hands cuffed behind me, I swayed as swarms of dizziness circled like sweat bees. I lowered my head.

The sergeant's thick hands pushed down on my shoulders. His face came up close to mine. "You be a nice girl," he whispered, "and I'll be nice to you." When he turned his head, I saw a fat mole under his left ear lobe. He pushed me steadily down onto my knees and then, with a final shove, onto the floor. I fought and yelled all the way. Where was that damn matron?

Looming over me, Sergeant Como Harris growled, "This is your lucky fuck day."

I bent my knees to my stomach and yelled some more. He kicked me in the kidneys. I screamed with the terrible pain. Vomit trickled out my mouth. "Pig," I tried to say, but the word caught in a bubble of saliva. Harris grabbed my waistband, heaved me to my feet and held me sort of upright by the shirt collar. He struck me across the mouth, getting residue on his hand. He wiped it on my shirt.

He slammed me into the desk. "You gonna get you a lesson." I lunged for him, butting my head into his chest. Out of my mind with rage and fear, I'd lost the battle for sanity. He came for me with murder in his eyes. He punched me in the ribs. I stumbled backwards and my legs gave way and I crumpled to the floor on my back, my cuffed hands trapped under me.

Then he was on me, pulling at my trousers, his weight crunching me, the cuffs digging into my back.

There was a far-off bang of a door against a wall, and I twisted to see the Cheeleys, bandanna clad, crashing in. Harris started to turn but Charles was on him so fast the cop couldn't get his gun from its holster. Charles got to the weapon first and brought it down on the back of Harris' skull with a fearsome crack. Blood spurted. Harris lurched and rolled off of me. Charles straddled him and pounded his head against the tile floor.

Although I'd have liked nothing better than to see the life ebbing out of the bastard, we didn't have time for it. "Get the cuffs off me," I spat, blood and spittle dripping off my chin. "Keys on desk."

With one hand, Chuck pulled me to my feet and helped get Charles off of Harris. After removing the cuffs, Charles stuck Harris' .38 in the back of his pants. I rubbed my hands trying to get sensation back.

Chuck located their sawed-off and leaned it by the door. He was very pale. Bending over, he clutched his arm and moaned. Oh yeah, he'd been shot. Charles took a revolver from a holster hanging on a hook and offered it to me. I tried to grasp it but no use, my hands had no feeling.

"You keep it for me," I said. He stuck it in his belt. "Hurry," I urged, "the other cops are hunting for you." I limped to the desk and scrubbed its surface with my sleeve. I wasn't sure if I had touched anything on the desk, but I wanted to be safe, leave no traces. As I worked, my fingers began tingling back to life. Slipping what was left of my jacket sleeve over my hand, I opened file cabinet drawers and located my DUI arrest papers. I pulled those out, along with some other sheets that my fingers weren't agile enough to separate. I crammed the whole mess into my pants pockets.

The boys worked fast, jerking open desk drawers, flinging aside pencils, pens, paperclips, rubber bands. They stuffed cigars into their pockets. Charles produced a box of ammunition. Using his good arm, Chuck brought out a second box. "I need a sack for these," he said, looking around.

"Use the wastebasket," Charles advised.

"No, no," I said. Touching my jaw, I feared it was broken. "We can't carry a waste- basket down the street. Fill your pockets. We need all the fire power we can get." Where I was at that moment, another siege of Leningrad seemed likely.

We stuffed all the ammunition we could into our clothes and into the bank pouches. Weaving toward the door, I begged, "Let's go, let's go."

Charles dropped the empty cartridge boxes into the wastebasket. Chuck reached across his body with his good arm, pulled out a lighter and set the boxes on fire; seemed sort of ceremonial. Charles swept Harris' cap off the desk, plunked it on his own head and gave it a jaunty tilt forward. "Always wondered how one of these felt," he crowed. I took it and plopped it backwards on my own head. "Feels good," I said. I tossed it toward the fiery wastebasket.

Flames continued to rise from the container as we had a last look at Harris thinned out against the floor. I studied the man for the slightest rise and fall of the chest, but saw none. The boys stuck their dishtowels under their jackets.

"Watch for cops," I said as Charles, supporting me around the waist, hustled me out the back door into an alley where three police cars were parked, one with keys in the ignition. I crawled into the driver's seat and started the engine. Chuck crawled into the back seat. Out the partly open window, I urged, "Come on, come on," as Charles, wielding the sawed-off, smashed the windshield of the second car. He went to the third car and slashed a tire with his pocketknife. Observing, Chuck giggled. Finally Charles laid the shotgun beside his wounded brother and climbed in next to me. Bleary-eyed, I negotiated the alley. We saw no one. Charles guided me onto side streets, down alleys, past sagging fences, and small stripped gardens. I drove carefully, stopping at all stop signs.

Suddenly the town siren blasted and blared continuously thereafter. In euphoria's grip, Charles joked, "Must be an air raid somewhere."

I watched in the rear view as Chuck thrust his good arm out like a one-winged bomber and made machine gun noises. I had to laugh. We had achieved a miraculous victory and were high on adrenaline. But I knew that shortly the full force of the law would be upon us.

When we were well away, Charles said, "Bastard almost got ya." He ducked down below the window and stayed low.

"Why'd you come back?"

"For the shotgun. It's ours." He chewed on his lower lip. In the back seat, Chuck groaned.

"There's an old granary outside of town," said Charles. "Hasn't been used in years. Nobody goes in it, except Chuck to play hideout. We'll leave the car there." I was grateful he had a plan. Charles always seemed to be thinking one step ahead.

Reaching the town's outskirts, he directed me onto the highway. Far away I thought I heard a train whistle through the blare of the omnipresent siren. Not long after, in the far distance, I saw a freight train pass by.

"Bet you'd like to see us hop a freight, get outta your life," Charles said. "If only the trains stopped here." All the while, Chuck, in the back seat, kept groaning. I commiserated. The rush of adrenaline was subsiding and pain was hammering at my ribs. My beaten face hurt and I could feel my body stiffening up.

Charles directed me to drive down a long gravel road that led to the doors of a decrepit wooden building set out in the open. He jumped out. Chuck tried to exit, but instead collapsed against the door in frustrated sobs.

"Stay with her," Charles ordered. Chuck lifted his leg back in the car and big brother closed him in carefully.

Boards and strips of metal covered the granary's narrow windows. A faded sign above the double doors faintly announced its original purpose. As Charles strained to slide the doors open, one skidded off a hinge. It remained out of plumb but he worked around it. Finally there was sufficient space for me to maneuver the car into the dark interior. I wiped the steering wheel of my prints before inching my way out of the car. The long-abandoned building smelled of moldy grain.

Charles got Chuck out of the car and propped him against it. He took his dishtowel and wiped down the rest of the vehicle. My body hurt terribly, a headache pounded, my jaw felt ballooned and one eye was almost swollen shut. Didn't know where I'd come by that last injury, maybe in the crash. Charles scrubbed vigorously to remove Chuck's blood from the back seat, which only drove the stains deeper into the material.

Along the inside walls of the granary, I saw small piles, of tools, lamps, toy soldiers, and even some framed paintings, all separated as though catalogued.

Chuck was beside me. "Gotta get my stash," he said. He wove toward the piles. "They'll bring a price. Be our safety net."

Swinging his brother around, Charles said, "Sheesh, forget it. We can come back later. Now we gotta go home and lie down." He guided the unresisting Chuck from the building.

On the way out I noticed an empty whiskey bottle protruding from trash near the door. Did Chuck drink or had a bum stopped over? I suspected the last. If so, how long would it be before the cop car was discovered?

Chuck and I clung to each other as Charles struggled to close the granary doors. Particularly difficult was lifting the broken hinge until it aligned with the others.

But finally he managed it and afterward we piled pasture brush in front of the entrance; Charles did most of that too. In pain and useless, Chuck swore through tears and sank to the ground.

"This is the last place they'll look," Charles assured us. "Nobody's found Chuck's stuff yet."

"Or wanted to," I said. "Be tough getting him home."

Charles stuck the sawed-off under his jacket. "We're prit' near Plum Street right now," he said.

"Really." I looked around, surprised. "I'm entirely lost."

The three of us proceeded haltingly along a fence line at the rear of the granary, stepping through dry weeds, moving within brambles, honeysuckle and sumac. We kept well away from the highway where an occasional car cruised by. Walking between Chuck and me, Charles aided both of us. The leather pouches flopped against the boys' sides, the bullets jingled as we proceeded. The ammo's weight added to our slow pace. In about twenty minutes, we reached the town boundary, marked by a sign: "Cassville 17,326 NICE FOLKS." I assumed Sergeant Harris and his men weren't part of that count. Shortly we moved from dirt onto a cracked cement sidewalk.

Chuck peered around Charles to inform me, "I took a bullet, ya know."

I clucked in empathy. "You're quite a man."

I checked my Timex. 3:58. The day was overcast and gray with the smell of rain in the air. After another ten minutes, I recognized the old neighborhood.

I hoped they hadn't killed Harris. I wanted to do that myself.

**9**

Charles helped me up the front steps of 822 with Chuck stumbling along behind. There was no one in the living room except Betty in her box, but a soft rustling sounded and Lisa peeked from behind the closet door. At the bloody, beaten sight of us, she buttoned her blouse and came forward hesitantly. His belt loose, Rolf followed.

"What happened?" Lisa asked shakily. "The sirens went off and we hid."

"It didn't go well," I said.

Charles slipped off Chuck's jacket and helped him onto the davenport. He stretched his brother's legs out full length. The pouch slid off when he unbuckled the boy's belt.

The shotgun fell from under Charles' jacket and left a bloody streak down the side of the davenport. Betty woke up whining.

"Bop me," Charles said to Chuck and the wounded kid complied with a weak heel-of-hand bump. Chuck's complexion was pale and sweaty. He was probably going into shock if he hadn't been there already.

Rolf broke out of his trance, sprinted up the steps and in a moment bounded back down with violin case in hand. He scooted out the front door without a word. Obviously he wanted no part of this. I hobbled after him and caught him wheeling his little bicycle into the street.

As he swung a long leg over the bars, I said, "Rolf, you can't tell. Just pedal like mad for home and play your violin like nothing happened. Okay?" I yanked his arm for emphasis.

"That is my bow arm," he said, yanking it back. "I will not say anything."

He took off on the bike with the violin case hugged against his side. Turning, I saw Lisa at the front door watching his defection. Her expression said: your belt's not fastened and already you're running out?

In the living room, Charles spotted a half-empty Nehi by the couch and tilted it to his brother's lips. Chuck drank greedily. I lifted the boy's greasy head and placed the hotel pillow behind it. I ordered Lisa to collect her things. "We're leaving," I said. My decision; after all, I was the adult here. Outside the siren kept up its terrible howl with multiple lesser sirens joining in. Every tornado siren in the vicinity must have been activated. At my feet, Betty howled along.

"You have bandages?" I asked Charles. He hurried to the kitchen and returned with some dishtowels and an ice cube tray. He also fumbled with a Mason jar of what smelled like white lightnin'. Chuck guzzled a good inch of the drink before he settled back with a slight moan. He seemed to be nodding off. If he falls asleep, he might not wake up, I realized. Painstakingly I pulled down his torn, bloody jacket sleeve so I could get a look at the wound. A ragged gaping hole. I asked Charles to find my purse, and when he brought it to me, I rummaged around until I found tweezers. With delicate precision I separated shredded cloth from the injury, each slight tug producing a wince from the boy. "Okay, it's okay," I whispered repeatedly. Charles poured the white lightnin' corn alcohol into the wound. Chuck screamed once and passed out.

The bullet had skimmed through the meaty deltoid muscle in Chuck's skinny upper arm, tearing open a chunk of flesh and muscle. From what I could see, the shot had exited. I didn't spot any bone fragments, but I wasn't about to dig for them either. Charles stanched the blood flow with ice cubes and a towel.

"We need a doctor," I said.

Charles didn't answer. He tore a dishtowel into strips and shoved them in my hands. He hurried to the bathroom and returned with adhesive tape. Chuck's breath came in soft whimpers as we worked silently to wrap the wound.

"Charles," I spoke with urgency. "Chuck won't make it unless we find a doctor." Gripping his brother's hand, Charles remained mute.

From her box, Betty's shriek cut through the sirens.

"Lisa, feed the baby," I ordered. The girl stood glassy-eyed watching us.

"Now!" Charles barked.

"Gerber's in the kitchen. Go!" I reinforced. Lisa came out of her trance and scampered to the kitchen.

She came back with food and spoon, and concentrated on feeding Betty, although it wasn't absolute concentration, because at one point while the tot slurped, Lisa whined, "Where's Rolf when I need him?"

Chuck's radio was beside his chair and Charles flicked it on and turned it up very loud to be heard over the sirens. It was always set to the local station, and now we heard a special bulletin that, after hearing of the crime, a citizen had called in to report a police car going east toward the highway. Since the call had been made right before the sirens started, the announcer assumed it was the fleeing robbers.

How long before that granary was searched and the felons apprehended less than two miles away?

Leaving Chuck to his brother, I decided to tend to myself. On my way to the bathroom, I noticed the shotgun, dried blood on the stock and the short barrel. I picked it up, took it to the bathroom and rinsed the blood off under the tub faucet. I had no particular emotion doing this. It was only after viewing myself in the mirror, lip cut and bleeding, eye swollen half-closed, jaw puffy and purpling, that I experienced a moment of extreme panic and vulnerability. I was as fragile as tissue paper. We all were. I washed the blood off my face and neck, wondering if Harris' blood was mingling with mine.

The piercing siren cut off abruptly, leaving lesser alarms to mingle like quarrelsome children. I went to the radio and turned it down. I scooped the bullets out of my pockets and laid them in Chuck's chair.

Charles said, "What'll we do?" He didn't have a next move.

"Where's my car?" I asked.

"In the library lot." A block and a half from the bank.

I expelled breath. "You're not supposed to park the getaway car in the next county."

"Downtown's got one hour parking and Chuck was scared. I had to talk him into it. It took time," he said, as sheepishly as I'd seen him, so far. "Look, the bank was a pushover," he went on. "The guard's probably still trying to draw his gun. It was those damn cops eating next door that spoiled it." He'd recovered his bravado.

We could discuss faulty reasoning later. Or not. But for now, a kid was dying. "You got my keys?" I asked. I was exhausted, had to force myself to keep moving.

Charles raised Chuck's rear slightly, dug into a back trouser pocket and wriggled out the keys. I shouldn't have been surprised that he left the idiot in charge of the keys.

"You've gotta go get that car," I commanded Lisa.

She recoiled. "What? No! I can't drive. My parents never had time to teach me."

"Excellent whining," I said. I snatched the keys from Charles. "Fine, I'll go get MY car." I realized I couldn't be seen in daylight, but waiting for dark might be too late. If I could only reach the hotel where the Salvation Army clothes waited. My body was a mass of pain. Deep regret weakened my knees. How the hell had I gotten into this mess? Why had I gone to the rescue? It was the Pontiac. If Chuck was captured with my keys, the police would try every car in the area to find the right fit.

Rage consumed me, the unfairness of it all. "You stole my car!" I yelled. "Robbed a bank. Who the fuck you think you are?" Charles studied me for a moment before turning back to his unconscious brother.

I clenched my fists and ground my teeth. "You have other clothes here?" I asked Lisa testily. "I can't go out looking like this."

She nodded quickly and motioned toward the stairs.

"Let's go then. Hurry up."

Charles took the baby, and I followed Lisa up the steep steps to the attic. My lungs ached by the time we reached the top. Lisa's bedroom was furnished with a partially de-silvered floor mirror, a battered dresser, and a stained mattress with a crumpled blanket at its foot. The attic had been turned into two semi-private areas by several tattered sheets strung along a rope.

As I peeled off my ruined clothes, Lisa pulled a long blue-flowered cotton dress out of a suitcase. She gaped at the bruises and scrapes on my arm and torso. "Geez," she said in awe, "you're all beat up." I took the billowy dress she offered and stepped into it. Lisa was larger than me and the dress hung on my frame. I gathered it at the waist so that the garment was drawn up tightly. Lisa used safety pins to secure the dress in place. A belt on the tightest hole would help keep the look together.

"My jacket—" Lisa pointed to the doorknob where the fur-collared wrap hung. I donned it and turned the collar up to cover some of my ballooning lip.

Lisa stood back, clasped her hands. "Perfect. In junior high my girlfriends and I used to do this all the time. It was more fun." For that moment she looked like a bubbly child. She doused my wrists with some Orange Spice cologne. "I have a wig you can use," she said. "I'll need it back though. It's going to disguise me when we elope."

"That's thinking ahead," I encouraged, breathing in the pungent fragrance. "Let's see it."

After she placed the curly golden wig on my noggin and it tilted forward, I said, "No, no, it's way too big."

But she insisted we could make do and glued the wig to the crown of my skull with a substance dripped from a bottle. I painted pink lipstick over my swollen lips, powdered heavily, and rouged up with a peach tint. I smeared on dark eye shadow to try to hide my puffed eye. I looked like a clown. But that was better than looking like me.

All of Lisa's shoes were three sizes too big, so I was stuck with my battered tennies. Black Oxfords awaited me at the hotel if I made it that far. Clutching the railing I trailed Lisa down the steps, the wig staying put although tilting a bit rakishly.

At the bottom of the stairway, Charles gripped the newel post. He cracked a half smile at my transformation.

"I'll be back," I said to them. "Have your stuff packed and ready to go."

Lisa walked me to the door. "A city bus comes every half hour," she said. "It stops on the corner a block down. You'll see the sign. It'll take you downtown." Slinging my bag over my shoulder, I set out. I had thought about claiming the revolver that Charles previously offered, but after killing a cop you don't carry his weapon.

After adjusting the wig, I set off in the direction of town, trying to walk without limping, glancing behind frequently for the bus. Fortunately there was no one at the stop and the bus came within minutes. Depositing the dime fare, I kept my head down, my face in the fur collar. All the way downtown, the four other passengers discussed the bank robbery.

"It's a big surprise," one man said.

"I thought this town was safe," huffed an older woman. "What's going on anyhow?"Eleven minutes later, I disembarked and in two minutes I was entering the hotel through a rear door. I hadn't spotted the police anywhere. Did those three crooked cops constitute the entire force? I thought not. Somewhere there had to be a police chief in charge of those mutts. I hobbled up the narrow back stairs to the second floor, took out my key ring and unlocked the door. In front of the mirror, I wiped off the pink lipstick, but left on the dark eye shadow. I'd wear the black hat with the veil down to cover my bruises. I pressed the hat down hard against the springy wig until the wig yielded. I drew the veil over my face.

Soon, garbed in black, including the Oxfords and the overcoat, I stuffed Lisa's flower-print dress into my shoulder bag. If I made it through the day, I'd need to change out of the Salvation Army outfit. I left her fur-collared jacket in the room.

The tennies with big toe out would give me away, so, upon exiting the hotel, I lost them in a trash can. On the sidewalk in the comfortable Oxfords, I moved slowly, erectly, full of dignity and duty, while trying not to hobble. In my left hand I held the hotel's Gideon Bible.

Many folks were out to view the crime scene. A conspicuous displaying of the Bible caused them to shy away; they didn't want to be talked to about God.

It was cloudy and windy; the temperature had fallen some. On the street, traffic crawled by, to see what it could of the remains of dire afternoon events. Across the street a half block up, an Illinois state patrol car was parked between other vehicles. Nearby two officers conversed in front of a shoe store. I cleared my mind of crossing to that side and continued walking in the proper manner, chin uplifted, consumed by thoughts of a better life in the world to come.

At this distance I couldn't be sure, but it seemed one of the state cops was eyeing me, criminality, beauty, oddity, or faith occupying his attention.

Directly ahead a familiar figure stepped from a parked Nash and climbed the curb, a book under his arm. I picked up my pace and tried to walk normally.

"Whoo-hoo, Dr. Swaney," I called to the high school principal. The slender man swiveled and stared. I fluttered my hand. He smiled and pushed up on his wire-rimmed specs to check his certainty as to who approached.

"Miss Plinkofrunz?" he questioned, puzzled by the drawn veil and the new bombshell blonde hairstyle.

"It is Plinko only, in this land," I corrected. My words, from bruised lips, were slurred.

"Lovely day, is it not?" I queried. "Have you heard anything of my niece, Lisa?"

"What? No. I haven't heard anything," he said distractedly. "Say, have you heard about what happened here today?"

I tried to check out the troopers through the flecked netting of the veil. "Why no. What has happen-ed?"

"Bank robbery. They think it was the Cheeley brothers. Remember I spoke of them. The getaway driver was female. She beat a police sergeant within an inch of his life."

I breathed a sigh of relief that the bastard wasn't dead.

Swaney continued. "The officers who found him said he was unconscious and covered with blood. 'That little girl was really mean,' they told reporters."

"Heaven forfend." I clasped the Good Book to my bosom.

"Speculation is that she's a Cheeley too. One of their many sisters," Swaney went on. Lucky for me Swaney was quite the gossip. He held his book forward. "I was about to get some coffee and read my book. Would you join me, Miss Plinko? There's a café just up the block."

"Oh, Mr. Swaney." I fluttered a hand to my chest. "I would love to, but am going to the library on emergency Bible mission." I twitched the Gideon.

His face fell. "Perhaps another time."

"Yes, with certainly," I gushed. "Absolutely I would enjoy to."

He brightened. "I'll walk you to the library. Wouldn't mind going there myself." He glanced at his watch. "It closes soon."

"We'd better get a leg on," I said, hooking my arm through his.

Left blinker on, the patrol car swung into traffic. Gaining speed, it cruised off in the opposite direction. Swaney walked me the two blocks, chatting all the way. He held the heavy door to the library and guided me into the lobby.

Inside he took my hand. "You are hiding an extremely pretty face," he said, gazing at my veiled visage.

"We are modest in my land," I said, removing my hand from his and tipping my netted head lower. The bright lights of the library weren't doing me any favors.

"The lady with who I stay presented me home permanent. She gave me new color."

"Very pretty," he murmured, lips close to the wig. "But, your complexion—it is—why, what has happened to your face?" His voice was full of concern.

I stepped back as he extended an arm toward my veil. "Hah!" I said, gently batting his hand away. "I react badly to home permanents and spray cans. You should see me after I spray the fields back home."

"Goodness, allergies," he said, appalled. "Do you have lotion for it?'

"It will go away. God will make it so."

He nodded. "I'm deeply religious also. I sing bass in the church choir." He cleared his throat impressively.

"Very good. Thank you now. I hope I will see you again, Mr. Swaney." I moved toward what I hoped was the religious section.

"It's Carl," he said doffing his hat and taking steps to follow.

"Ta-ta, dear sir," I said to emphasize my goodbye. I disappeared behind tall shelving. When I peered between the rows, Swaney was rooted, staring my direction. I had to get out of there before he decided to help me find whatever religious text I was seeking. I hustled to the rear of the large building trying to find a back door. Jackpot! I headed into the parking lot where, hopefully, the Pontiac waited.

In the car, I retrieved the .25 and tucked it in my shoulder bag. I shot glances to all sides before leaving the lot. No sign of Swaney or the cops. On the trip "home," I reflected that it had been rather pleasant to speak with a normal, respectable, member of Cassvillian society. At least I hoped he wasn't hiding as much as I was.

## 10

About two miles from Plum Street, I stopped at a gas station. The station attendant was respectful before my humble, veiled, personage. While the car was being gassed up, I went into the store, bought aspirin and swallowed three. My lower back was throbbing where I'd been kicked.

From an outdoor phone booth, I made a call. Ada Opal answered. "Hello, what is it please?"

I spoke rapidly. "Your daughter will return home very soon, eager to discuss conditions that all three of you must agree to. Ada Opal, make her feel at home. Indulge her a bit. Don't blow it. It may be your only chance. If all is agreeable, you owe me one thousand dollars. We'll meet in three days, on Thursday, for breakfast, at 9:00 a.m. Hopefully, this can end very soon." In three days my injuries would be less apparent, if only I wasn't in custody or dead by then. I consulted Miki's map. "We'll meet at the Wayside Inn on the far side of Watkins. If everything works out, and it will if you keep Miki muzzled—if it all works out, you will pay me $1000 cash and I will thank you for your business and be on my way. Is that clear? 9:00 a.m., Thursday. Wayside Inn. Will you be driving the Plymouth?"

"Yes," she said. "It's my car. We'll see you there."

I paid for the gas, then headed for the rest room where I changed into the flower print dress and covered its floppy unevenness with the overcoat. I returned to the Pontiac, tossed the S.A. clothes in the back seat, set the netted hat on the passenger seat, and gunned the car onto the road.

Arriving at the house on Plum Street, I parked close to the back door. I stuck the key ring in my dress pocket. I'd keep track of those suckers this time. I folded the overcoat and laid it in the trunk. From my suitcase, I took a pair of trousers and a shirt. If I encountered trouble, I didn't want to be in a dress.

Charles, with Betty on his hip, placed some of the brothers' belongings in the car's trunk. Obviously we were moving on.

"How's Chuck? He still with us?" I asked.

"Sleeping," he answered tersely. "He'll be alright."

"What's the plan?" Charles sounded like he already had one.

"We're going to the holler," he said over his shoulder. "The witch'll stitch Chuck up good."

I blinked. "A witch? Really? In a holler? Maybe we can afford a veterinarian. What does the bank loot come to?"

"$155.82. And Lily will do the job just fine, for free. She's got magic on her side."

I'd have preferred a vet.

Lisa came from the house lugging a gunnysack.

"You go home, hide out for a while," I instructed. "Don't say anything. You're in big trouble, too. You could go to prison for life for aiding and abetting."

She set down the sack and thought that over.

"After this thing dies down," I added, "you can join us in a safe place. Right now, it's too dangerous for you. For Rolf too."

Charles pushed Betty into Lisa's arms. Heading back to the house, he added, "We don't want you getting killed. So go home."

"Rolf will be at home," she mused. "Will I ever ream him out."

Placing a finger to my lips, I said, "Do it away from your folks. Mum's the word."

"Oh, I know," she said, tears springing. She took my hand and rubbed it. "Wendy, I'm so upset about what happened to you. It's like it was happening to me all over again."

"I was lucky," I said. "The Cheeleys saved my hide."

"They're heroes," she said. "A lot different from Rolf."

On his way to the car with another bundle, Charles said, "While you're home, collect supplies for us. Baby food, lighter fluid, weapons. Money. Hide it so you can bring it to us any second."

"Just like the French Resistance," I said.

"Oh, this is so awful," Lisa lamented.

"It'll pass, but it will be very dangerous for awhile, so lie low," I said. "Cooperate with your parents. Be good. Come on, I'll help collect your clothes."

"Oh, I have everything packed." She shifted Betty to a hip.

"I have to hang onto the wig for a while," I said, "so I need to borrow the glue."

She gestured to the gunnysack by her side. "In there."

I opened it, fumbled around and extracted the bottle from the depths. "We'll drop you away from the house, at a gas station or some place that has a phone. You can call your parents to pick you up."

Part one of my plan: getting Lisa home. Check. Part two: keeping her at home for the requisite amount of time. Not so easy.

Bustling out of the house, Charles gave Lisa a small squeeze. "You know what'll happen to you if you breathe a word of this," he said. He stared at her for a long second.

"I know," she said in a small voice.

"Yeah, keep quiet about it," I reinforced.

A very pale Chuck appeared in the doorway, stood for a moment, then sagged against the door frame. A hunting jacket was draped around his shoulders and he wore a sling fashioned from dishtowels. Plenty of clotheslines around Cassville must be dishtowel short. Charles helped Chuck down the steps and folded him into the back seat of the Pontiac.

Lisa got in beside Chuck after handing Betty off to me. She slid down low, having gotten the point of not being seen near a criminal hangout. I handed back the squirming mass of baby flesh.

"What did you do with my old torn-up clothes?" I asked.

"I guess they're still upstairs."

I rolled my eyes. Amateurs.

On the way to the attic, I remembered to pick up my leather jacket from beside Chuck's chair. Once upstairs, I saw the ruined trousers, linen jacket and white shirt where I'd let them fall. I wadded them into a stray paper sack. I changed to fresh trousers and shirt and slipped on my leather jacket.

I managed to get the blonde wig off my head, although it felt like half of my own hair came with it.

After cramming my lacerated clothing and the wig into the trunk of the car, I ran back to the house and quick-stepped through all the rooms in case we'd left anything. The bullets were gone from Chuck's chair. I grabbed the hotel pillow off the davenport.

As I returned to the car, Charles appeared from around the side of the house carrying a pail filled with dirty dishtowel-diapers. The stench preceded him.

I made a face. "You are not putting that in my trunk."

"It'll be okay." He jammed the pail in next to the wig and some boxes. He slammed the trunk lid down on the stink and went around to the driver's door.

My beloved Pontiac, besmirched and sullied. I didn't feel well enough to engage in a shoving match over an odor.

"Gimme the keys, I'll drive," Charles gruffed.

"Hell you will," I said. "From now on, I'm the only driver of this car. Got that?"

"You're in no condition—" he started but didn't finish. He stalked around to the passenger side just as an old couple approached from the house next door.

"You folks hear the sirens?" the man quavered.

"Yep," Charles said. "We're just going to check it out."

"You'll tell us what's going on," the woman said, "won't you?"

Charles waved dismissively. "You bet." He climbed into the car and we were off.

We dropped Lisa with her gunnysack, and my bloody clothes to lose in a trash can, at a gas station a mile away. On the road once more, we hit the highway.

## 11

I gripped the wheel, intent on staying alert. Despite the throbbing pain in my left arm and side, I was having a hard time staying awake. The car was too quiet, but radio music interspersed with dire bulletins seemed like too much.

I asked Charles how they'd gotten away after the crash.

"Hid in the chicken coop back of a bar. After a while we doubled back to the police station to get our gun back. We hid behind a big piece of plywood in the alley. When the two cops came out without our gun we figured it was inside. We heard you yelling and that was that."

"Thank you." I couldn't say that enough.

About twelve miles northeast of town, Charles directed me onto a winding dirt road that descended deep into a hollow. At the bottom, we parked in front of a beat-up shack on a bare patch of ground where three chickens pecked at the dirt. The sky was coming on dusk.

Charles jumped out to greet a wiry, narrow-faced man in his early twenties who stood beside a massive tree stump. The fellow had long scraggly brown hair and weathered skin stretched tight. But what claimed my attention besides the pistol he was pointing at us was his left eye—something terribly wrong with it. It bulged and skipped around unfocused. He wore dirty dungarees, a bit short, and a faded red wool shirt. He lowered the pistol and extended a fist to exchange bops with Charles. I got out of the driver's side and stretched my stiff muscles and yawned.

The man focused on me. "That your car?" He had a scratchy voice.

"Yup."

He stepped past me, tapped on the rear window, and said, "Hello in there—hi, hi." When he began to coo, I realized he was addressing the baby, not Chuck.

Charles introduced us. "William, this is Wenda." The prattler gave me a cursory nod and went back to making clucking noises at the baby. The Cheeleys had mentioned a relative, William. Apparently this was the guy.

Charles asked, "Where's Lily? She die?"

"Naw. Her house burnt down. About three weeks ago."

Charles glanced toward a site some distance from the main shack, where the earth was strewn with ashes, charred boards and pieces of scorched tin sheeting.

William pointed up a rise to a tiny shed at the top, hay strewn around its base. "She's staying up there now."

Charles faced William. "Chuck got shot."

"I seen he looked sick," was the laconic reply. "Well, Lily's always home."

After Charles helped the wounded boy out of the car and onto his feet, William leaned across the seat and lifted Betty in his arms. He cradled her like she was his own. I'd say one thing about the Cheeley clan: they were devoted to the small fry.

With Chuck sagging between us, Charles and I threaded our way up the rise past small trees and bushes. My left side ached during the climb and that arm burned with road rash.

Chuck's breathing was ragged and his body trembled with the effort of trying to walk. When we were almost to the shed, the door opened and a tiny old lady popped out. Despite the dropping temperature, she wore only a shapeless housedress and floppy red anklets. Her face was leathery and deeply ridged, her fierce, penetrating eyes a deep-set sky blue. I noticed her veined hands, bruised, but the claw-like fingers were clean and the nails pristine. Chuck said, grimacing, "I got shot."

"Get him in here," she responded in a crackly voice.

Charles slipped off Chuck's jacket and we laid him out on a floor covered with surgically clean linoleum. Once down, he began a terrible mucky coughing.

Between spasms, he begged, "Gimme reefer, Lily." She squeezed in beside us, and, ignoring his plea, worked off the bandage. She reached toward a cardboard box on a shelf made of cinder blocks and plywood and withdrew a folded piece of white muslin that clinked a little with what was inside. Setting that on the linoleum, she delved into her housedress pocket and produced a handful of marijuana leaves and cigarette papers. She rolled a joint, licked it, and stuck it between the boy's lips. Charles took the silver lighter from Chuck's jacket pocket and lit the weed. Chuck inhaled deeply. Charles laid the lighter on Chuck's chest where it slid off and fell onto the linoleum during a hacking fit. I retrieved the lighter that was embossed with a pin-up girl's gracefully posed, nylon clad legs, and stuck it in my pocket.

I studied the cramped scene: a pan brewing on a wood stove and herbs bundled in ribbons hanging from wires attached to nails in the steeply sloped ceiling. Mason jars lining the back wall contained dark liquids and lumpy substances. Owl's claws, bat's wings? A thick cloying smell filled the air.

Chuck continued moaning. Charles chucked his chin and soothed, "Rest easy, easy." Chuck's eyes closed, his mouth relaxed.

My head was swimming in witchy images and suffocating smells. I was feeling weird.

"Get out. No room for you here," Lily said, shattering my dizzying reverie. Charles and I retreated into the crisp open air. Charles made his way down the hill where he conferred with William, who rocked baby Betty in his arms.

I remained by the shed door to watch the doctoring. Lily opened Chuck's splatted muscle, which had stopped bleeding. She poured a substance from a Mason jar onto the wound. I identified by smell the same white lightnin' we had used earlier. Lilly dribbled more of the liquid down Chuck's throat after removing the joint. She popped it back in his mouth after he swallowed.

Lily began humming. The eerie sound was like a saw being bowed. She snapped thread off a spool. Lips barely parting, from within the hum she informed me, "Healer string." She pulled Chuck's torn skin together and began stitching up the wound. I expected Chuck to scream in pain but he just moaned and grimaced each time the needle pierced his skin. The ragged stitching took the shape of a lightning bolt. Something for the kid to show off later on. I prayed he'd have the chance.

Lily unwrapped one of the bundled plants. "Wound herb," she said as part of the humming. She stood creakily, put a good portion of herb in a mortar and crushed it with a pestle. She took a tiny bottle from a shelf and dripped an oily mixture into the crushed herb to create a paste. She didn't name the oily stuff. I wanted to ask, but since she seemed to be in a sort of ceremonious trance, I thought it best not to interrupt.

She spread the paste on the wound and wrapped it tightly with a clean cloth pulled from her pocket.

I studied Chuck. His eyes were closed, chest rising and falling shallowly; the end of the marijuana cigarette hung off his bottom lip. Lily removed it and motioned to me for the lighter. She relit the cigarette, dragged deeply, and stubbed it out on the ground outside.

She handed me a bag of spiny dry leaves. "Nettles. Heat hot water, make a tea and make him drink it." She reached into the shadows and handed over a jar of darkish liquid. "Here's some ready made. Don't you drink it. Leave it for the boy. He'll need it." She scowled at me like I was a nettles addict.

"I understand."

Lily retreated inside. Sitting next to Chuck, she slipped a leather cord with a charm on it around his neck. More abracadabra. She wiped his sweat-shined face with another clean cloth taken from the bottomless housedress pocket. "Sleep, sleep, sleep," she crooned. Chuck snuggled his face into her thigh and his breathing came more easily. She struggled to rise on spindly legs. I entered the shack and touched her elbow, intending to help her up but she swatted my hand away.

She started down the hill with me following. On the way she pointed out a plant that, in the darkening evening, looked like your average weed. "There's plenty a this greenery around. It's plantain. Pick the leaves, bruise them, lay them over the sore. It sucks out infection." She said again, louder, "Plantain," to make sure I got it.

"Check," I said. I stooped and picked a cluster of the plants for use as prescribed.

Abruptly she turned and trudged back up to her shed. Left hip throbbing, I went the other direction, to the bottom of the hill where William and Charles were debating our prospects for temporary housing.

"You can't stay," said William, hawking at length and finally spitting. "Whenever you guys are involved," he said, voice phlegmy, "the cops come here first." He shook his head. "They take me in, make things as hard as they can for us. We ain't getting nailed for something you done."

"One night is all I'm asking for," Charles begged. "For Chuck. For Betty, too. We'll hide in the woods. The cops won't stay long. They're freaked out about this place." William gave him a baleful glare.

"Sorry. I know that happened years ago and it's only a story anyhow," Charles amended. What was that about? Another mystery that, right then, I hadn't the wit to explore.

"You get out of here and take this gal and Chuck with you," William said. "Leave the baby. I knew we shouldn't a left her with you in the first place." Wait, was William Betty's father?

"Is June over the pneumonia?" Charles asked.

"Healthy enough to hold a rifle." William pointed. My eyes followed to see a gun barrel poking out of the shack's rough-hewn window.

"June!" Charles addressed the rifle. "How's that pneumonia thing comin' along?" From the shack, a coughing fit that jostled the gun barrel.

Charles sighed. "I guess our sister wants us gone too. Now she's a Bertalow, she don't love us no more."

"Weren't my idea to get married," William Bertalow groused. So. William was a brother-in-law.

"We can keep Betty longer if June's not over it yet," Charles said.

"You crazy? With you on the run?"

The light through the trees was turning grayer. "Let's get Chuck and go," I urged Charles. The woman's willy-nilly gun was making me nervous. "This is no place to hide if it's the first place the cops look. William, if the law comes for you, it might be because of June. Talk is that a Cheeley sister is a suspect. Better get out of here yourselves."

William's good eye lit on me as he swore under his breath. "Charles, what've you done to us?"

"Wenda's giving you a bunch of crap," Charles said. "They're looking for Wenda, somebody small and skinny, not for a fat tub like June."

William scratched his cheek. "Yeah, they are different shapes." He trotted toward the shack with Betty in his arms.

After a moment watching them go, Charles and I started up the incline to fetch Chuck. Approaching Lily, I asked her if she was treating June for the pneumonia.

"June don't believe so the cures don't work with her," she responded tartly.

Convenient. Oh well, best not pass up the chance to consult with a pseudo-medic. "Could you take a look at my injuries?" I asked. "Maybe a poultice or two would help me heal."

Lily grasped my tender chin, twisted it, and felt the bones in a cursory fashion. I slipped off my jacket and she peered at my badly scraped arm. "You're okay," she said. "You're just like June." Guess that meant a non-believer in her mumbo-jumbo. She was right.

The evening was growing chillier as Charles and I aided the groggy Chuck, arm in the dishtowel sling again, down the hill and into the Pontiac. Charles hauled Betty's supplies from the car, including the soiled diapers, thankfully, and deposited them by a stump.

As I moved to get behind the wheel, everything spun. I lowered my head, and leaned against the car. The crash and the beating I'd sustained were catching up. I braced my hands against the door frame. "Geez, I'm tired," I griped to Charles, who was regarding me warily. "Why don't you drive?" I handed over the keys.

"I ain't crashed into a delivery truck in weeks," he said, grinning.

He drove us up and out of the hollow. Upon meeting the highway, he stopped as though pondering which way to turn.

Chuck spoke weakly from the back seat. "Did we save the bullet?"

"Wasn't none in you," said Charles.

"Damn. Now nobody'll believe me." I told the wounded boy about the jagged lightening-bolt scar he'd have and he brightened a little, saying, "Hey, is Mom's old trailer still out there? That'd be a place to go."

"Just what I'm thinking," Charles said.

He put the car in gear and swung right onto the highway, putting more distance between us and Cassville. Buzzing along at a steady fifty, we encountered little traffic.

So we were heading for a trailer. I was familiar with trailer living. Back home in Iowa I lived in a Winnebago and ran my PI business out of it. That life seemed a long way off.

After a while, I asked Charles, "Why'd you tell me Betty was your sister?"

He glanced at me. "I never tell outsiders the truth. There's power in secrets. It's the only power we got." I did a quick think about my own life and realized there was a lot of truth in that. Maybe I was underestimating my young accomplice.

"Is Lily related to William?" I asked after a while.

"Aunt."

"Ah. What happened to William's eye?"

"That asshole cop beat him up."

"You mean Harris?"

"Yeah."

"How'd it happen?"

"Harris caught William walking around drunk in the middle of the night. Hit him in the face with his goddam club. William was fourteen. No one believed a holler kid over Harris. Harris said that William got hit by a car, hit-and-run, and Harris, big hero, pulled him to safety. Harris likes to beat up people who can't fight back. You found that out."

"How'd he get that kind of muscle?" I asked.

"Meaner and smarter than the other cops. And he keeps the bad guys down. The so-called decent folks let it all go on."

"When you had him down, did you pop him one on William's behalf?"

"Wasn't thinking about it. Good idea though." He looked over and grinned. I smiled back; it was easy to like this kid, particularly after he saved your life.

"What's the story about William's place that has the cops freaked out?"

He didn't answer. Perhaps, like any male, he had reached the fill-line of talk for the day. We travelled on in silence.

A mile after passing through the five-block main drag of Watkins, we turned left onto a county road. Soon we cruised past the Wayside Inn. My fuzzy brain knew that in three days I had a date with the Plinkos at that very eatery. That was my last thought for a while.

# 12

Sometime later, a series of jolts woke me up. "Where are we?" I stared out the rain-smeared window and saw for myself—on an ill-lit dirt road, bouncing up to some double gates. Beside them, through driving rain, I made out a bullet-holed sign on a crooked pole. It read: CLOSED NO DUMPING!! LARGE FINE.

Charles got out and put all his muscle into dragging the iron gates through thick mud. After he got them open, he jumped back in the car and drove the Pontiac through. He jumped out again to close the gates. All this was accompanied by Chuck's delirious moaning.

Except for our headlights, the night was pitch black. Charles maneuvered slowly along a narrow, trash-strewn road as rain pelted the car and the windshield wipers swished. On both sides, odd shapes appeared and vanished as our lights moved past.

A quarter-mile or so into what I assumed was a dump, a dark silhouette rose on the right, set back from the road. Chuck roused himself to squeal, "Home, right there!" Charles turned the car until the headlights pinned a large trailer in their beams. Its hulky frame listed slightly to one side like a marooned boat.

Across the road, a burned-out car lurked, hood up. Beyond that an impression of many junkers, a purgatory of wrecked cars. The trailer might be viewed as indistinguishable from the other castaway vehicles. At least, I hoped so.

Charles shut down the wipers and the engine. "Gimme my keys," I said. Leaving the headlights on, he passed the key ring to me reluctantly.

"Cut the lights," I said. "Might be somebody in there."

"By now he knows we're here and we got the fire power. Besides we need the light."

I handed over the penlight I always carried. "This'll do."

He flicked on the penlight and shut off the headlights.

He snapped his fingers at Chuck in the back seat and the kid gave him the shotgun.

"You stay here and watch the car while we check things out," he said to his brother.

I slipped my bag over a shoulder and felt the security of the .25.

With the rain beating down on us and our tiny light illuminating the path, we squished through wet leaves and trash toward the trailer. Close up, I saw it was missing a wheel.

Up three steps and Charles turned the doorknob. The metal door stuck on its warped frame, then opened hard. He sidled through, the shotgun in the crook of an arm. I followed and met grit underfoot. The three-wheeled beast swayed a little to our footfalls. Charles panned our light around. Gouged walls, cracked linoleum, shiny paneling, a potbelly stove. "We're alone," he announced. The penlight identified a couch that I collapsed on, using my purse as pillow. With the .25 an unyielding lump against my head, I said, "Gimme a minute to rest." I was stiff, sore, wet, and cold. I didn't care what kind of rat trap we'd landed ourselves in.

The trailer's interior smelled damp and moldy. Even so, it was dry. Charles slammed outdoors. Repeated trips brought in supplies, two sleeping bags and Chuck. Charles got him settled in one of the bags.

Charles dug into the supplies for his flashlight. Finding it, he inspected corners and floor moldings.

"—rat droppings, spider webs—" he muttered. I shot up straight, my body screaming. He knocked down a thick web with the flashlight.

"Somebody's got to stand watch," I said, wiping my eyes. "You maybe killed that cop." My back ached.

"We wore masks. You didn't. You're the one in trouble."

I staggered to my feet. "Hell, I'll go out and watch."

"Hey, take it easy," he said. "I'm the healthy one. I'll hide in the car and take care of anybody who shows up."

I sank down on the couch. I tried to stay awake, but the rhythm of rain rattling against the metal roof took over my brain and I lapsed into a deep sleep. I had no idea if Charles stood guard and would never question him about it if I survived the night.

# 13

I was awakened by a raucous murder of crows. Faint light falling through the windows showed the boys, one snoring lightly, in their sleeping bags. I was cold and damp. I sat up and slowly stretched. Oh, that hurt. I dug in my shoulder bag for a compact mirror. The swelling on my eye and jaw had gone down, but the bruising was getting worse. I also had a groove in my cheek from lying against the gun in the shoulder bag. I flexed my jaw, forced a yawn. I was headachy and stiff, with a terribly tender body, but the dominant feeling was gratitude that, so far, I had dodged a bullet. I dug in the shoulder bag for a comb and tugged it through my tangled hair, trying to keep my sore arms close to my body.

I gingerly slipped the bag over my shoulder and cat-footed to a grimy window. The rain had stopped. A rosy arc heralded the rising sun. Everything seemed peaceful except for the crows. The black-and-white Pontiac, filthy with mud, sat at the ready. I needed to hide that car.

I was the only suspect absolutely identifiable. Charles, bandana in place, had come upon Harris so fast that the cop probably hadn't gotten a good look. Chuck had remained near the door until Charles had Harris down and out. Even if Harris believed it was the Cheeleys, could he prove it? If he was in any shape to prove anything.

I opened the trailer door and stepped outside. Water dripped off the roof onto my head. Ducking, I scurried down the steps and sank into oozy ground. Across the road, a community of junked cars greeted the day.

I stepped back a few paces to view the trailer. It was about thirty-five feet long, twelve feet high, and eight feet wide. Three small windows in front, their frames twisted, the glass cracked into spider web patterns. Plentiful tendrils of sodden vine lopped over the side of the roof; some curled over a window. A tin chimney spout stuck out of the back of the trailer. For the potbelly stove.

Avoiding bits of broken glass, splintered wood, pieces of metal, and other, undefinable, trash, I trudged behind my new home. There were no windows back there and I squatted to pee.

Business accomplished, I noticed a defunct electrical outlet on the lower right side of the trailer. Wind rustled the few leaves left on trees. The stirring of a thorny bush signaled a small animal scuttling by.

Slogging down the road past broken crates, a battered door, a bike frame, a piece of luggage, I came upon a pond with a cluster of watercress floating on top. I resisted the urge to drink. Boil it first, but there'd be no fires today; the smoke might be seen.

Before heading back inside, I retrieved my black overcoat from the car trunk. Charles was sitting up and scratching when I pushed open the resistant trailer door. He acknowledged me with a grunt.

"Uh-huh," I answered, eyeing the slashed wood cabinets and tatty café-style curtains. A round table top was upside-down on the floor, its center post sticking straight up. A matching couch sat across from the one I'd claimed.

I set the overcoat aside, sat down on my couch and removed my soggy shoes and socks. It felt good to stretch my toes. Chuck woke up with a snort and a mewl of pain.

Charles slid out of his sleeping bag and rustled through the supplies. He opened three cans of baked beans and distributed them. Silently, we spooned the contents into our mouths. Each of us drank a Nehi and I swallowed two aspirins.

Suddenly Chuck was tearing at his bandages. Charles grabbed his hand. "What're you doing? Stop it!"

"I wanna see my wound," Chuck whined.

"No! Shut up!"

The injured kid dissolved into tears.

I let him cry for a minute, then said, "Chuck, listen, I got a great idea." He snuffled and tried to pay attention. "You can have a peek at your wound if you drink Lily's tea first."

"That awful stuff?" he whined. "I can't drink no more of it."

"You have to," I said, "because Lily's a witch and she says you have to drink it."

Chuck took two quick swallows before gagging. "Ew, tastes like water soaking in an old log."

"'Cause that's what it is," said Charles. Chuck chased the potion with healthy swigs of white lightnin'. Medicinal necessity.

Fortified, the boy peeled back the bandage to reveal an angry gash, the stitches barely holding the ragged sides together. He turned gray at the sight.

I found Lily's sack of plantain leaves and, after laying one on the wound, I re-wrapped the arm. The boys watched wordlessly.

"Now I'm going down the road, take a dip in the pond with the soap cake. No one else is invited," I said. I grabbed my overcoat and one of the pails that Charles had brought along.

A short time later when I returned half-frozen from sloshing icy pond water over me, I left the soap and pail in the middle of the floor as a hint. Soon Charles said to Chuck, "Now we're gonna have to wash off." He picked up the necessary accessories and led Chuck, uncomplaining, outside and down the steps. I watched from the door. Seeing all the junked cars in daylight, Chuck slapped his thigh and exclaimed, "It's the car center of the world!" A moment of glee before he bent over, writhing in pain.

Charles pulled at his brother and off they went at a dragging pace. Twenty-five minutes later when they returned, Charles banged down the pail and said in a mocking falsetto, "I feel refreshed. You feel refreshed, Chuck?"

But the injured boy had collapsed miserably onto his sleeping bag and was dead to the world in almost no time.

We were wearing the same clothes, but smelling a bit sweeter. My extra trousers and shirts plus the blue-figured dress and the black Salvation Army garb lay in the Pontiac trunk. Better air those garments out after they had resided next to the diaper stench. And I'd bring in the hotel pillow.

I pondered dropping by the Cassville Hotel for the rest of my belongings, but, no, Wendy, don't be stupid. You have to stay away from that town. Be cool. With Lisa presumably at home, in two days I'd meet with the Plinkos, collect my well-deserved earnings and flee this coop. The Chucks would survive; that sort always does. In a former world, without parents, Norris, Jim and I had.

Charles turned the radio on low. The local station was basically country music. After twenty minutes of twang, a special bulletin came on, repeating old news about the missing cop car sighted heading east. Then, breaking news: this morning a driver had passed three hitchhikers, two women and a limping man, thumbing their way west in the opposite direction, toward Wahoo City. The driver reported that right after he passed he had seen in the rear-view a farm truck slowing to pick up the hikers.

Charles hooted, "Could be us, if they think we're two gals and a guy instead of two guys and a gal."

"Who's the extra gal?" Chuck asked woozily.

"Don't look at me," I said. The band of three was fortuitous but it wouldn't be long before the cops figured out they had nothing to do with the robbery-assault.

A half-hour later, another announcement: the female suspect was believed to be a "Wendy," last name uncertain, something like "Winkley."

"Jumping Jehosaphat, we're harboring a criminal." Charles grinned wryly.

Having stolen my drunk driving arrest record, I had hoped no one would make the connection. Neither the two officers nor the sergeant had bothered to get my name. This had to be Charlotte's doing, tying the two circumstances together. The matron got my first name right, missed a syllable on the last. Of course she had also told the authorities that I was a PI. I had verified that fact with Harris, if he was still alive and remembered. Not hard to check out the PI claim; the U.S. hadn't that many female PIs with the first name of "Wendy." Miki Plinko had registered the room at the hotel under my real name. The cops would have that room covered. And if my profession made the airwaves, it would take a hell of a whopper to justify it to the Cheeley boys. The gloomy prognosis: one way or the other, I'd be nailed.

About 3:00 p.m., the three-chord serenade was again interrupted for a special report: schoolmates of the male suspects, the Cheeley brothers, believed they had lit out for California weeks ago. Cheeleys always dropped out of school and left town when they got to be a certain age—anywhere between twelve and twenty-two—the late bloomer being Jerry Cheeley who disappeared in the middle of the eighth grade picnic.

"Tradition may save you yet," I told the boys.

The newscaster insinuated that the police were floundering, unable to act without their fallen leader, Sergeant Harris, who was conscious but remained hospitalized in serious condition. It made no sense to me that Harris was their leader. Didn't there have to be a Chief of Police on duty?

Later in the afternoon Charles used the Pontiac's jack to elevate the trailer corner that was minus a wheel. He and I stacked broken cinder blocks under the corner and pretty much got it set right. When we returned inside, Chuck asked if there had been an earthquake.

After a cold baked bean dinner and a small ration of Coca Cola, we cleared trash from behind a junked Chevy and I drove the Pontiac into that space. We piled branches, leaves, and trash on it. I hated the camouflage for scratching the smooth finish of my treasured vehicle, but in the end its soiled presence blended pretty well within the car center of the world.

**14**

The second morning of trailer living, I awoke to Chuck's howls. "It itches! It itches so bad." He was on his haunches, pounding his forehead.

From a prone position, Charles reached to pat his brother's shoulder. "That means it's healing. Let's change your bandage and have a look."

He unwrapped the cloth and gingerly removed it. We had treated the wound twice yesterday, cleaning out the pus, washing it with soap and water, dousing on white lightnin'. After applying plantain leaves, I had wrapped it in fresh towel strips.

I bent down by Chuck. "Wound looks a little better," I said. And it did. The flesh looked less red and angry.

Charles agreed, "Yup. Getting better without a doubt." Chuck quieted as we treated and dressed the wound again, after which I gave the patient the jar of white lightnin'. He lay back and guzzled like a baby with a bottle.

Charles wanted to see if he could get the stove to work. I advised against it because we'd be sending smoke signals to the cops. He went ahead anyhow, piling small sticks in the potbelly and lighting them, making sure the smoke was properly vented.

"We'll only light a fire at night," he advised. "It's just too cold at night for Chuck."

I had to agree. "You'd be a good one to be stranded with on a desert island. Along with nettle tea."

The two of us traded sentry duty for a few hours but no posse came hunting.

Again that day, we ate cold meals and sipped Cokes. Chuck pulled Red Hots, spicy little candies, from a jacket pocket. He blew lint off and dropped the candy on his baked beans.

Later that second day, after treating Chuck's wound again, Charles said, "Wenda, we're running low on supplies. We need food, medicine, bandages. You have to go to Watkins."

"We need beer, too," Chuck said.

"Yup," I agreed, seizing the perfect excuse to go meet the Plinkos. "I'll drive to Watkins tomorrow, pick up necessary stuff. Be risking my life, of course, but it's for Chuck's sake." They eyed me gratefully.

Morning number three: Thursday. Bright light flowed through the three small windows, illuminating many merry dust motes. I slipped on my black Oxfords, left the trailer and went behind the Pontiac to change into Lisa's blue-figured dress. Back on my couch, I lipsticked up and powdered my face to tone down the bruises. I plopped the wig on my head and glued it down. No longer would I be that pants-wearing Amazon who'd beaten up poor Sergeant Harris.

On one elbow, Chuck spoke from his sleeping bag. "You look like a movie star."

Charles, sitting opposite me on the other couch, warned, "If you're caught it's your funeral. Don't squeal on us or worse luck for you." He grinned wolfishly.

"'Course not." I made a face right back. My mood was giddy with the expectation that soon I would escape this scene.

Twenty minutes later, three miles north of Watkins, I drove past the bright red Wayside Inn sign, intending to scout the place first. A station wagon, a coupe, and a green, jacked-up Ford were parked in front of the entrance to the small brick restaurant. A dark-colored sedan was parked to one side. The Plinkos' Plymouth Roadking was not there, but I was early. I cruised past the building, aware that cops like to employ black sedans as undercover vehicles. A bit uneasy, I drove to Watkins, stopped at a filling station and dialed the Plinkos. No answer. That probably meant they were on their way.

Nonetheless, doubt lingered. I retraced my route. Seeing the Wayside Inn sign up ahead, I pulled onto a side road and cut the engine. I left the car and trotted down an alley toward the rear of the restaurant. At a smudged window by its back door, I stood on tiptoe and poked my head over the sill. Up front by the picture window, a tall man in a gray suit had parted the drapes and was studying the parking lot. I ducked and hustled back to the Pontiac. Turning onto the highway, I drove slowly past the Inn. The same black car was there; the Plymouth Roadking wasn't. I drove back to Watkins. No one followed. If seen, I knew that my top half didn't resemble the suspect's.

In a booth outside Mason's Drug Emporium, I called the Plinkos again. Miki answered, an edginess to his voice. "Allo."

"This is Wendy."

"Yes-s," he hissed. "How are you, Miss Winkworth?"

"I'm here, you're not," I stated.

A pause before he said, "Lisa came home, but soon she was taken to police station. She is questioned about her jail companion. You, Miss Winkworth."

Ada Opal spoke. "We did not give the police your name, only that we believed one of the inmates had made friends with our daughter."

"Who was that big guy in the suit you sent to arrest me at the restaurant?"

"Oh, we would never do that," she exclaimed.

"I know what a cop looks like."

She sighed, long and deep. "I believe it was one of the Cassville officers."

Recognition came. Brunanski from the rear looked just as oafish.

Ada Opal was pleading, "Please, you have to turn yourself in. They will release Lisa then. It seems they are using her as a hostage to get to you. Please, I beg you, she is only a child."

I spoke firmly. "I sent Lisa home and you owe me a thousand dollars."

"Yes, yes, we will pay you but not when our daughter is not home," said Miki. "Police keep her because of you."

Ada Opal wheedled, "You can see our point. I'm sure you had nothing to do with that awful robbery and assault of the officer, but you have to explain that to the police. After all, you are a reputable investigator. Aren't you?"

I used to be. "Did you mention my name to the cops?"

"No, no. They think your name is something like Winkly. We didn't argue with them."

"We do not trust police," Miki said faintly.

"They are determined to get to the bottom of this," she said. "I mean one of them was almost killed. You must understand that we can't afford to be seen with you or associated with you. After you've been vindicated, we will pay you. We surely will. Please," she begged. "Lisa is frightened to death."

"You didn't seem so worried when you left her overnight in that cell. Now she's there again and, if Sergeant Harris is up and around, she's got reason to be scared. You know he assaulted her the last time she was in."

Ada Opal gasped. "I never thought that was really true."

"Sergeant Harris is of no harm; he is still in hospital," Miki broke in. "Pictured in paper with head wrapped in bandages."

"Then Lisa got lucky, didn't she?" I slammed down the receiver.

From inside the store, the pudgy clerk was staring at me for looking hot and bothered, I presumed. I finger-combed my iron curls slowly in an effort to calm down. Standing there at the entrance to that dingy store, I experienced a moment of extreme clarity. I wasn't going anywhere. How could I even think of leaving the area while under suspicion of aiding and abetting the assault of a police officer? How to clear myself?

Thankfully Harris wasn't dead. Even if he never regained the ability to remember the event, the other two cops would identify me. I recalled the squatty one's knowing stare, very aware of what was in store for me.

All that passed through my mind as I opened the dirty, speckled door and stepped inside the store. I smiled shyly at the clerk. "Oh boy," I said, "I was trying to remember what I came in here for. That ever happen to you? Busy day catching up to me."

"Wondered if you was having a spell," he said. I strolled around the store, picking up lotion for my badly scraped arm, gauze, tape, Merthiolate and batteries.

By the cash register there was a cigar box filled with little tin hearts. While my purchases were being totaled, I fingered them idly. I recalled being jealous of a girl in my grade school who had worn a wooden heart on a necklace of pretty beads.

Noting my interest, the clerk said, "We can carve your name into one of those hearts with a buzz machine. Only eighty cents. It cuts a hollow in the tin pretty blame good." Sizing me up, he asked, "Now what's your name?"

I smiled back shyly. "No thank you."

Carrying two sacks, I walked around the corner to where I'd parked. At a grocery, I bought food, cigarettes, Coca Cola. No longer intent on enforcing the ban on beer for the under-aged, I bought a wooden crate of twelve bottles in the liquor store two shops down. When all was paid for, I had a couple hundred bucks left.

I drove dejectedly back to the trailer where I was never supposed to set foot again. Charles helped haul in the sacks and the crate. I received no thank you from either boy. They expected no less from their gal Friday. I unstuck the wig gingerly so the glue didn't tear at my skin, and stored it on a cupboard shelf next to canned corn.

I went behind the Pontiac and changed into trousers and shirt. When I came back indoors, Charles had two beers opened. I grabbed one and stalked to my couch. Charles opened another for Chuck. We swilled. Chuck emptied his bottle quickly and lay back and dozed off.

I donned my leather jacket and posed on the couch like a brooding Buddha.

After a while, Charles set down his second beer, finished off a chocolate bar and went outside. He gathered kindling, distributed it in the stove and lit it. "A warm meal will lift our spirits," he said. Although it was still broad daylight, I didn't care enough to object.

I deserved remuneration; I had earned it through good honest work. That is, I had started by working honestly before fate intervened and I'd had to rescue my car and the crooks that came with it. I was certain they'd have been caught and implicated me, but now I was in a lot worse trouble than having my car stolen by bank robbers.

Wendy, Wenda, Wennie, Miss Plinko, whatever you're known as, how do you clear all your names, particularly since you're guilty? If only there were another suspect. Carl Swaney, the school principal, had mentioned a multitude of Cheeley sisters. Maybe one of them was short and petite like me.

Across the room on the trailer's littered floor hunkered the Cheeley gang. Charles, knees up, leaned against the spare couch and ate hot baked beans while flicking through a boxing and wrestling magazine. Next to him, Chuck cradled the revolver we'd taken from the cops that fateful day. Charles allowed him to play with it as long as it stayed unloaded.

I hated to interrupt such a peaceful domestic moment but it had to be done. "I heard in the grocery store that he's recovering in the hospital."

No need to ask who. Chuck sighted down the revolver's barrel and said, "Wisht I coulda blowed his head off."

"Anyhow we're not killers yet," Charles said.

"Don't give up hope," I said before changing topics. "What do you hear from your other sisters, I mean other than June?"

Charles rubbed his eyes, burped, and set down his empty can. "Rita went out west, looking to be in the movies. She's real good-looking. Lanna was around until about two weeks ago. Haven't seen her since. Probably lit out to join Rita. Always was her plan. She spells her name 'L-a-n-n-a', two 'n's' in the middle. She started out 'Lana,' like anybody else, but in grade school, she changed it to make it bigger and better. Actually she spelled it wrong the first day in kindygarten and was too stubborn to admit it."

"Is Lanna small like me or fat like June?"

"Like you."

"Yeah?"

"What are you thinking? Nail her for this? Good luck. Or if you're thinking there are kin around who'll hide us out, you're wrong. They can scarce do for themselves. You saw that with William and June. We don't forget each other though. We show up when we feel like it or when it's time, and it ain't time."

"I want a ducktail at a real barber shop so I can go out on the streets like Wennie does with her wig on," Chuck broke in dreamily. With no response from either of us, he added, "Well, why not?"

"Because, stupe… " Charles shot back, "… we ain't going out until you get that sling off. Let Wenda and her wig take the chances."

"What if Wennie rats us out?" Chuck whined.

"She knows better than to rat me out." Charles brushed his shirttail so it drew up a little. He let it fall quickly, but not before I saw Harris' .38. The threat came automatically. Those boys brought out firearms at the slightest provocation. Lucky for me, they treasured their shotgun so much they challenged a police force for it. Never let down your guard around these guys, I warned myself. They're predators, surviving within their family group until now, when they're forced to trust an outsider. Never totally, though. Sly, watchful Charles, always on guard, I felt he missed nothing.

Charles pulled a bent cigarette from a crumpled pack. Chuck scuttled over and produced a flame from his fancy lady-legs silver lighter. After exhaling through his nostrils, Charles said, "Wenda's wanted too, you know. If she turns herself in, Harris will want to interview her personally."

End of argument, in my mind also.

It was late afternoon and still daylight when I returned to Watkins. In the blue-flowered dress, and my head firmly topped with the honey wig, I told the boys I was going for emergency female supplies.

Chuck's wish for a ducktail brought to mind a plan to disguise my two accomplices. But before I acted upon that, and with the thought that one more phone call might resolve matters, I stopped at a hardware store and used the pay phone to dial the Plinkos. Miki answered.

"What's the situation?" I asked with no preliminaries.

"How are you, Miss Winkworth?" he preliminaried.

"Fine. What's the situation there?"

"Lisa is home resting. She was housed over the nights in that prison. This is terrible ordeal for my child." His voice became rougher. "You are the cause, you who put her through this."

"Nothing to do with me. You put another kid over your own daughter and treated her like an outcast, and now you're paying for it. How's poor injured Sergeant Harris?"

Not the least chastened, he said, "The newspaper says he is at home in bed, with nurse attending to him. A photograph shows his head still very bandaged."

"Poor fella. Same suspects as before?"

"Cheeley boys and other lady Cheeleys they consider also. Also you. Sergeant Harris is not speaking. At least in public."

"The truth will out. Meanwhile, I'd like my pay. Immediately. With no police around this time. Right now."

"We never believe it was you beating up that policeman. Only the police insisted on hearing such from you. You must go in and clear up things with them." Miki spoke in a deceptively soothing tone.

"When I have a moment." My voice tightened. "We have an agreement. I've done my job. Lisa is safe at home and you need to pay me." He tried to interrupt but I spoke over him. "Is there no honor where you come from? This is a simple transaction. No reason for the cops or anyone else to know about our private business. Don't make me come out to your place and raise a ruckus, Miki." Of course, I never intended to show my face in Cassville again, but was aware that the Plinkos would want to avoid a scene that threatened their status and respectability, as if Lisa hadn't done enough already.

Miki hesitated before saying, "I will consult with wife and get back to you. I take her wishes into account in everything." Baloney. The man was buying time. "Call me tomorrow," he said. "And in future do not comment about honor in my country." The smart click of the receiver was meant as a slap in the face. I didn't flinch.

## 15

I drove two blocks to Mason's Drug Emporium and parked in a space around the corner.

"Back again," the clerk said when I entered. "Ever change that dress?"

I smiled prettily. Soon I stood by the cash register with three brown bottles of 3% peroxide, a spray bottle, a razor, blades, and additional toiletries. I was about to transform the boys, and myself, into decent folk.

The cigar box with the tin hearts was still on the counter. No run on those yet. A large customer in an expensive suit, vest, and fedora, was claiming the clerk's attention ahead of me. I waited, mind drifting, awkwardly holding my purchases, there being no room on a counter cluttered with last second opportunities—picture postcards, boxes of chocolates, gum, rubber bands, cellulose tape.

I perked up when the customer said, "Rumor is, the law is finally gonna burn those holler bums out."

"Yeah?" the clerk responded.

"Last I heard. You know there's a whole village living down there, squatting on government land that the workingman's paying for. Living free and easy on our dime while they go around robbing banks and half killing policemen."

Ringing up the fat man's purchases, the clerk said, "It's a darn shame."

The customer's voice lowered. "You know they never found that little girl." Jowls jiggling, he nodded wisely.

"Tiny Tina Haverford. Went in the holler, never came out," the clerk said.

I interrupted. "Golly, I remember that. In the holler. How long ago was that anyhow?"

Astonished at the nerve of a little lady interrupting man-talk, the fat guy muttered, "About twenty years ago," and gave me his back.

"My goodness," I deplored, "I was only a kid but I remember."

"The police are fed up with them Cheeleys," said the fat man to the clerk. "You know how Sergeant Harris is gonna be if he pulls through."

"Them Cheeleys have had it," the clerk agreed. "They sure picked the wrong man to pound on."

"Remember when Harris gave it good to one of them?" the customer chuckled. "Punched out his eye." The truth of that encounter hadn't evaded this man. He glanced at the load of supplies in my arms. "Why don't you let this beautiful young thing pay her bill and be on her way?" He patted my cheek with fleshy moist fingers. It was like a fish's oily tail flapping against me. I blocked a shiver.

After paying, I moved along the creaky wood floor and lingered at the vitamins, hoping to hear more. No such luck. They were aware of me now and spoke in hushed tones. The discussion ended when the large man wheeled toward the door, almost knocking down a cache of toenail clippers. The clerk called after him, "Lord knows you should know, you're the alderman."

I returned to the counter and picked up a tin heart. "I believe I'll take one of these. Can you cut 'Lanna' into it, spelled with two 'n's' in the middle?" That was accomplished lickety-split.

On the street, thankful I'd parked around the corner so the clerk couldn't identify Miss Lanna's car, I got behind the wheel and dumped my sacks next to me. A fire in the holler, you say. And there'd already been a fire that destroyed Lily's former home. Opening my switchblade, I cut off part of the sash to the blue print dress. I lit a match and fanned a flame over the fragment, burning into it two small holes, pinching out the match when the fringe became seared. I held another match to the rim of the tin heart until the edges were scorched and warped. I was creating clues that hopefully would lead the cops on a holler search for poor Lanna's incinerated remains.

Next I drove to a meat market where I purchased two chicken wings. In the car, I scraped off the meat and skin with my switchblade and then scorched the bones.

I drove to the holler. At the bottom, with chickens clucking and pecking around me, I pounded on the Bertalow shack, calling, "William! June! You gotta get out of here and take Betty with you!" No response. No gun barrel poking out the window. No hacking cough from within.

I hurried up the rise to Lily's shed. The door was open, her witch essentials there; she was not. I scooted down the hill and again posed in front of the Bertalow shack. I shouted, "The cops might try to burn you out! You gotta go and take Lily with you!" Silence. Swirling wind stirred the brush.

I made the rounds of the expanse, repeating the warning in front of tangles of thistles, aiming my voice at shrubs and trees in case the clan was hiding. I came upon a pristine stream, the water so clear that at the bottom tiny stones sparkled in the sun. The lost child, Tina Haverford, had disappeared in this holler. She might have wandered right up to this stream. Reached in farther and farther for a pretty stone and lost her balance. If, back then, a holler person had found the drowned body, what would have been his inclination? Notify the police and fall under suspicion? Or bury her post-haste.

I went to the site of Lily's former, already burned-out home, and made a pile of ashes with my foot. I placed the mangled tin heart and the scorched blue-flowered cloth within the ashes. I spread the chicken wings so, to me, they looked like hand bones, and covered the whole display with more ashes. I tamped the whole pile down. I laid burned tarpaper and some hefty stones on top.

In case anyone could hear me, I bellowed, "Leave this stuff alone. Whatever happens, it's for your benefit. Chuck is recovering. He says, 'Thank you, Lily, I'll remember you forever!'"

An hour later, I parked in the dump behind the junked Chevy. After changing into trousers and shirt, I entered the trailer and told the boys of my plan to make us all over. They could see the smarts of it. If I had disguised myself with that new hairdo, why couldn't they do the same?

I gave the boys haircuts and peroxided the hell out of what was left. Their black hair turned a coppery orange color. My own hair ended up a dirty yellow, not the silvery platinum blonde I'd hoped for. Even after cutting my hair into a chin-length bob I still looked awfully much like me, so I didn't kill off the honey-blonde wig. All this was done by flashlight and candlelight so we wouldn't know the true extent of our transformation until the next day.

But the boys were already ecstatic at their flashlight-lit results. Charles believed he looked hot, "like James Dean." Chuck could see himself surfing in the ocean out west. How they arrived at those conclusions, I wasn't sure.

Now my companions were a step closer to mixing with impolite society, but Chuck, in the sling, shouldn't be seen in public until he was less visibly injured. I supposed Charles could abandon his brother at this point if he had the inclination and the guts, but I didn't think he would. Chuck was the one person in the world who respected and needed him.

After the thrill of transformation wore off, Chuck extracted paper bags, a deck of cards, a pen and scissors from a gunny sack they hadn't yet got around to unpacking. He set them side-by-side on the floor. Around those piles he placed stubby candles and lit them with his lady-legs silver lighter. Painstakingly he put the playing cards in order. Where there were gaps he cut the brown bags into card size and with the pen drew goofy replacement cards, including one of a silly loony joker. He quit when he had a full deck, real and fake. All this was done with infinite patience, the tip of his tongue protruding as he created his art.

Charles extracted a cribbage board from the gunnysack and the boys settled on the floor to play. I had thought cribbage the province of old people. I held off commenting that it was easy to know which cards were fake. Whatever kept them occupied.

The three of us sat amid Cokes, cigarette packs and cardboard ashtrays. The smell of candle tallow mixed pleasantly with the potbelly's smell of burning wood. It was downright cozy.

The cigarette pack was offered. I took a smoke right along with the boys. I would be nicotine free when I got back to real life. If ever.

Chuck pulled out his lighter.

"I'm getting this," he warned me, as though I might challenge him for the right to light my smoke.

"Gorgeous lighter," I commented.

"Gift from Dad," he said. "Only thing he ever gave us and he gave it to me," Chuck bragged.

"Big deal," Charles said.

With dramatic flair, Chuck produced a click, and flame sprang to my tobacco. With my first drag, the old sensation of release flooded back. I deserve this, I justified, casting aside two years of abstinence.

Since Chuck was essentially one-armed, he'd start out holding the playing cards on the sling side, then transfer them to the uninjured side. Occasionally he'd guzzle from the jar of white lightnin'. The guy was obviously feeling better.

After they were deep into the game, I spoke up. "I heard a rumor in town that the cops might burn out the holler people."

Charles sprang to his feet, swinging his arms. "Why didn't you tell us sooner? Gimme your car keys, I gotta go warn them."

I got up beside him. "Relax," I said. "I went to the holler today. Didn't see anybody, but I know they were there hiding. I yelled out about the threat of fire. I know they heard, they were there, I know it." Charles gave me a stony look and held out a hand for the keys.

I placed my hands on my hips. "Lily's potions were still in her house so they hadn't gone off anywhere. So don't you go off half-cocked and do something dumb."

Charles looked me over, took my measure. A short step and a punch and I'd be down. I slipped my bag over a shoulder to be nearer the .25.

"It's a stand-off," Chuck yukked and slapped his thigh with his good hand.

"Flyin' fuck," Charles breathed. His shoulders slumped a little. Voice breaking, he said, "Sergeant Hair-ass better not try anything on William. He'll hurt Betty too."

"Hair-ass," Chuck echoed. "Hey, Wennie, what'd you yell out at the holler? Say again what you yelled."

I repeated for the slow learner. "I said get out because the cops might come and burn the holler down."

"Got it," Chuck said and struck his thigh again.

Slowly Charles cooled off and, after a minute or so, resumed his seat and crossed his legs Indian style.

For a while the brothers played silently, cramming the matchsticks they used as pegs into the cribbage board as though the holes were too small. The crisis seemed over, but I knew it yet festered. I re-joined them on the floor and left the bag over my shoulder.

In the middle of the third game, Charles thumped the floor. "Harris beat William up and blinded him, goddammit. If that bastard comes into the holler, William'll take revenge. He'll kill him."

"Harris is in no shape to do anything now." Again I sought to calm him down. "Maybe the fire thing is just big talk. The guy who was telling it wasn't a cop, just a town official."

"Yeah, well, he better be just blowing off steam." Charles turned over a real card, picked up his pseudo-peg and jammed it home so hard the matchstick snapped.

At bedtime he saw me sticking my key ring in the shoulder bag and curling up around it, my black overcoat covering me. I hardly slept that night, expecting him to make a sneaky move to grab those keys. Nothing happened except both of them did a lot of restless turning in their sleeping bags.

In the morning over scrambled eggs Charles said, "If you're not going to give me the keys, get me a bicycle so I can go warn June and William."

"We should have kept that cop car. We could go get it now," Chuck said.

No response to that. Two of us were still reasonably sane. Had the car been discovered yet? Nothing on the radio confirmed that.

Chuck took an exploratory bite of egg. "I can't eat these, they're burned," he whined. "Cook some more." He waved his fork at Charles.

"Shut up!" Charles yelled. Rage mottled his face. If that kid wasn't at the end of his tether, he was close.

Chuck grabbed the aspirin bottle beside him and swallowed a handful. He washed them down with white lightnin'. "My arm hurts real bad," he whined. "It's pounding right off my body."

"It's healing," I said extra soothingly. I turned back to Charles. "I can't afford a bike."

"Fuck you," he snarled, "get us one anyhow." He had become ash-white with anger.

"If you think I'm gonna steal a bike when I'm already wanted for robbery and assault, you got another think coming," I said more firmly.

Brandishing the fry pan, Charles sprang up. "Gimme those keys."

"No," I barked. "And, hey, that's the new fry pan I just bought. Be careful of it."

"Jesus, I've had it," he roared. "Begging a woman for money and a car. And being nursemaid to a dumb sonuvabitch forever."

He hurled the fry pan across the room; it crashed against the wall. Scrambled egg flew. "Gimme those fucking car keys." He reached behind his back, flipped up his shirttail. His hand returned without the .38, but he had made clear the stakes.

"Fuck you, calm down," I said. I slipped my bag over my shoulder.

If Charles reached for the gun again, I'd have to respond. The last two days he seemed agitated beyond reason. Cooped up and ready to blow. I stepped toward the door.

"Going to get us a bike?" he gritted.

"I'm leaving," I said.

He took a step toward me but there was a tentativeness in his approach. "You're just a broad keeps a toy pistol in a sparkly purse. You even know how to load it?"

"Test me," I said evenly.

"Who you think you're playing with?"

"You wouldn't like it if I told you." I backed toward the door and gripped the knob and yanked. The door creaked open with its customary resistance.

"Better hurry," he said. "I can see the piss running down your leg."

Out I went, slamming the door. I quickstepped to the Pontiac and swept foliage off it. Pebbles flew as I sped out of the dump. Nobody shot at me in my retreat.

For half an hour, I cruised up and down the highway, about ten miles each way. I composed myself to the hum of the tires against the asphalt. I considered what it would mean to run out with no bonus, in effect to surrender. I stopped at an Essex station, bought gas, chocolate bars, doughnuts, potato chips, cigarettes, and picked up a complimentary book of matches. I lit up in the car. Smoked all the way back to the trailer.

When I reached "home," my watch read 11:30. Charles was outdoors collecting brush for the stove. He didn't look up. I parked behind the Chevy, stalked past him without speaking and went into the trailer. Chuck wasn't there. I leaned out the door. "Where's your brother?"

Charles paused holding twigs. "Walked out to the highway to catch a ride to Watkins." His tone was cool and controlled.

Irritation rose in spite of myself. "My God, with that bad arm, he'll be identified and reported. What a jackass. He might just as well walk right into the police station."

"Don't call him names." Charles returned to his task.

I stalked by him to my car, yanked the door open and called over the top of the Chevy, "Chuck is going to get us all caught. I'm leaving." I had laid only one tree branch on top of the Pontiac's hood and I tossed that off. I couldn't spend my life clearing off a vehicle every time I lammed out.

Charles strutted across the road. "I think it's better we split up. I do better with just the family around, anyhow." The nerve of this kid; one minute out of his mind with rage, the next supremely rational. I was the sensible one, which means I should have arrived at that conclusion first.

I climbed into the Pontiac and revved the engine. "You called it. From now on, you're on your own." Charles stepped backward into a patch of thorns as I reversed out and sped away.

## 16

Free of the dump, I drove southwest and found an old tractor road where I concealed the car within a stand of firs. I ate a lot of the treats I'd bought for my fellow felons. Tall corn filled an adjacent field. A half-hour later, the peace of the countryside was broken when a farmer came through on his tractor.

I stayed there the rest of the day and all night, taking short exploratory walks and dozing fitfully. In the morning I found a gas station with good coffee that helped clear my mind. After all the boys and I had been through together, I felt as though I was part of an outnumbered band of misfit warriors. That made it hard to run for the hills now. To surrender. Especially not knowing what would become of Chuck.

I drove back to the dump entrance and parked inside the gates. Trotting beside the curving road toward the trailer, I darted looks over each shoulder and listened for sounds of police presence. Rounding the last bend, I saw a flash of Charles' face through the trailer window.

I scanned the area. From behind the trailer, the nose of an old Ford automobile stuck out.

As I've said, cops normally arrive in late-model sedans, not decrepit old beaters. I scuttled behind the trailer and examined the green 1930s model Ford. A few rags and sticks were piled on its hood.

I entered the trailer where both boys were seated on the floor, eating cereal and bananas. Chuck's cereal was mushy with milk, the nearly empty white lightin' jar by his side. I was relieved to see him.

"Saw you coming," Charles said, not lifting his head.

"You bring doughnuts?" Chuck asked.

"I ate 'em," I said.

Charles pushed the cereal box toward me. It toppled over. "There's some left," he said. "You want it?"

I got a bowl, filled it, and went to my couch to eat.

"Where's your car?" Charles asked.

"Left it at the gate."

"Didn't think you'd be back."

"Looks like you got a car of your own."

"Yep." Chuck beamed at me, his mouth full of bananas.

"So now another car is stolen," I said. "Keep this up, the locals will have to walk everywhere. The authorities thought you boys were in California, now they know better. They'll start hunting for you all over again."

"Got the wheels in Watkins, not Cassville," Chuck said defensively. "Nobody saw me."

"Well, somebody drove you to Watkins, didn't they?"

"Yeah, but only to let me out. They was going on to Carolina."

"Anybody see you take the car?"

"Don't think so. I looked around." While hunting for a bike, he went on to say, he had come upon a car with the keys in the starter, a sign that it was meant to be. Was Chuck a kind of idiot savant, whose special talent was extreme luck?

"Guess you guys can manage for yourselves," I said. "Don't need me hanging around. Makes me free as a bird."

Chuck yukked, "Ma used to say that. Didn't mean nothing."

"Yes it did," Charles said darkly. He reached for a Coke, flipped the cap.

I settled on my couch. I was home safe, with the same old companions and familiar smells around me. I vacillated between desperately wanting out and being reluctant to leave these two boys to fate. I should have been worried about my own skin, but they had saved my life.

Later that afternoon, they painted the old Ford gray with stubby brushes and paint that Chuck found in the dump. When they finished, a few spots of green filtered through the gray overcoat. They wrested 1953 plates off a junked Olds, and Chuck artfully changed the "3" to an "8." After Charles scornfully pointed out that it wasn't 1958 yet, they smudged the "8" with a mixture of gray paint and mud.

Now the Cheeleys had mobility.

## 17

Any plan the Cheeleys had to defend their loved ones was doomed because that night the holler went up in flames. After supper, Chuck ran in yelling for us to come look; the clouds in the sky were all gray and smoky. We rushed to the radio. In about ten minutes a special bulletin interrupted. Dunn's Hollow was on fire, shacks in flames, squatters rousted. An onlooker with a set of binoculars reported seeing a human-like figure on a hillside, trapped in one of several blazes. In the distortion caused by intense heat the figure vanished within the flames.

According to the report, Sergeant Como Harris and his men had been met by a mighty conflagration when they arrived at the site to make an arrest. The officers surmised that the fire had been set by residents as a diversion to allow violent criminals to escape. My throat tightened at the news that Harris was up and at 'em.

The boys listened in shocked silence. Harris was capable of anything. And I'd heard the alderman voicing approval of such a barbaric plan. When the bulletin ran once more, Charles went to the wall and beat on it with his fists.

Squatting, Chuck took a cigarette from the pack on the floor. He tapped it repeatedly against his thumb, trance-like, before finally lighting up. Even then, his hand kept jumping until the silver lighter spun away to the floor. Going after it, he landed on his bad arm and let out a yelp. He asked, in a pitiful voice, "Think Betty's all right?"

Charles turned toward him. "William'll get the family out…" he said. "…but if them cops killed Betty… " He shut the radio off. We sat in silence, in fury and sorrow.

After a while, Chuck asked, "Should I load my revolver? Drive our new car over for a look?"

"No! No!" Charles and I roared almost in unison.

"Tell you what," I said, trying for a level voice, "I'll drive to Watkins and catch the scuttlebutt on the streets. Maybe I'll hear talk about the stolen Ford too. You-all stay put. I'll be right back."

Climbing into the Pontiac, I felt an overwhelming sense that if I wanted to make it to my thirty-first birthday I should flee northern Illinois quickly. Sergeant Harris was on the rampage, and I was high up on his list. The thought consumed me so completely that I had to draw several deep breaths to even drive.

But as I wheeled the car on the road, anger swelled as I thought of the figure in the fire. Likely it was Lily: an old woman who just wanted to help people. The hunger for revenge grew. I'd cooled off on desiring to be the agent of Harris' death. But I'd sure like to slap the handcuffs on him and hand him over to those who could legally provide retribution. I tried to push that thought aside now that escape seemed the most rational thing to do.

I blew out breath. One more try at the Plinkos. Then maybe I'd have the money for a dignified withdrawal.

In Watkins, I called the Plinkos from an outdoor phone booth. A familiar young voice answered, low, with a Teutonic inflection. "Plinko residence. Yah?" Violin strings plucked.

"Wrong number," I growled and hung up. After five minutes, I tried again. Rolf picked up faster this time, blurting, "Lisa? Is that you?" I replaced the receiver. Ten minutes dragged by. Once more I fed in coins and rotated the dial. This time Miki answered.

I began, "Miki Plinko—" before he interrupted with, "Miss Winkworth, where are you? Lisa has vanished. Do you know to where she is?"

I let my head hit the phone booth glass. "No idea. How long has she been gone?" Damn. Her disappearance and the words "Cheeley mobility" attracted like magnets.

"From yesterday…" He sounded short of breath. "…when we bade her goodbye at 8:15 morning until this day,1:40 afternoon, when we arrived back home from out of town."

"Did she take anything with her?"

"Food and toiletries. Also $17 cash money a student left on top of upright piano." In the background, Ada Opal chimed in. "My red wig is missing." Oh, oh, another peruke bound for the border.

Miki explained the circumstances. "We locked all of her belongings in a spare room from the moment she came home four days ago. But we were granted opportunity to conduct master class at Chicago Musical College and we could not say no. We told our Lisa that we trusted her to do right, so she will be good and feel good for doing good and make us proud, and good." He paused to let the pile-up of 'goods' fade. "We left two clothes outfits for her. She paid back trust by taking those dresses and running off."

"Did you ask Rolf where she might have gone?"

"Oh, he does not know anything. He is very much worrying. He will play Town Hall recital on February 21 at 3:00 afternoon and until this happens he practices like mad dog. Now he stands by phone and plays through his concert music like wooden doll."

There was a scuffle and Ada Opal's voice came on the line. "Please help us. We're sorry for any misunderstanding. We're eager to make it right with you. We can meet in public or any place you say."

Brought up short by the offer, I said, "Why are you so willing to be seen with me now? You were scared to death before."

"Because the papers say you have an alibi and are no longer a suspect and that the police are concentrating on the Cheeley girls and their brothers."

I made tiny circles in my peroxide-coarse hair. Since I had no alibi, this had to be a cop trick to draw me into the open. "We'll continue meeting in private," I said. "My start-up fee is $200. Also pay me $1000 of the $2000 that you owe already."

"We'll pay your fees," Ada Opal declared. In the background Miki huffed in protest.

"Rolf can't afford this distraction," she said to her husband. And to me: "He eats his meals by the phone. Our fear is that Lisa will persuade him to join her."

"How did it go with Lisa while she was home?" I asked.

"We wrote a contract and she signed it. Obviously it meant nothing to her."

"Okay, put Miki back on."

In mid-speech, he came on: "—for meeting tomorrow at Eats Dining Room on Cherry Street in Wahoo City. 3:00 afternoon. When patrons have cleared." I agreed to the meeting. I recalled seeing Wahoo City on the map, to the west of Cassville. One caution though: to reach the place meant another trip through my least favorite town.

"Did you tell the cops I posed as a Plinko cousin while investigating Lisa's first disappearance?" I asked.

"Ahhhh, I swear not, did we not, dahling?"

"Honestly, we had forgotten all about it," exclaimed the dahling.

The two seemed frantic over the disappearance of their daughter, but they might be equally fearful that their bushy-tailed PI would abandon them. Consequently they might be lying through their teeth. As Lisa's pal, I was their only link to her whereabouts.

"One more thing," I said. "There was a major fire in Dunn's Hollow tonight. Have you heard if anyone died in it?"

Ada Opal replied in a tentative tone. "There was some kind of blaze; we saw a rosy hue from our house. The local paper comes out in two days. I'll hold one for you." She paused. "Does this have anything to do with Lisa?" she asked nervously.

"No," I assured her. "I just like to know what's going on. Back to business. You understand that in renewing my employment, you agree to me possibly appearing again as Miss Plinko in order to gather information about your daughter's whereabouts."

"Brilliant," said one.

"Absolutely," cried the other. I pictured their heads bumping together.

"No funny business when we meet tomorrow," I warned. "If I sense any kind of police presence, any kind at all, you'll never hear from me again and Rolf may well end up playing in a mariachi band in Mexico."

Before vacating the phone booth, I dialed high school principal Carl Swaney. He seemed very pleased to hear from Miss Plinko. The number of people adoring me was on the rise.

I garbled on in Miss Plinko's dulcet tones: "Assigned mission to buy used clothing for poor peoples in Palatine City and elsewhere. Could you spare time to aid, please? So much clothes and I have two arms only."

"I'd be delighted," declared Dr. Swaney, smitten by my misrepresentation. I needed a respected figure to help me with my errands tomorrow, one of which was selecting clothes for the Cheeley boys. Before ringing off, Swaney and I set 10:00 a.m. tomorrow for carrying out our good works.

"Perhaps afterward," he said, "we might have that long delayed cup of coffee."

I giggled. "Would like. See you in jiffy."

I aimed the receiver at its holder but not before Swaney said, "'Jiffy' means quickly. Until ten tomorrow will be an exceedingly long wait for me."

"Yes indeed," I replied. "Must go. See you. Bye-bye." I placed the receiver gently in its cradle.

# 18

It was dark the next morning when the Cheeley brothers made their maiden voyage in the stolen Ford. I had slept soundly during their departure and they left no note. At dawn, I went to wash myself in the pond. When I came back, I plopped into a broken-back chair in Chuck's furniture sector to await my companions' return. Just as at the granary, Chuck was categorizing the dump's holdings. So far the furniture sector contained only the chair, two deformed table lamps, and one bedpost. Just to its left, small appliances held three misshapen pans and a battered toaster. Tools were to the left of the appliances. I took all of this in, including the ever-present smell of decay, and an occasional pelting by bits of wind-borne litter.

In about an hour, I heard the distant sound of a motor, and soon the Ford chugged around the last bend and pulled up in front of the trailer. The passenger door opened and Chuck scrambled out. Lisa was next, emerging from the back seat. She looked fresh and classy in gray wool slacks and belted green jacket with a mouton wool collar. Charles stepped from the driver's side and posed with the shotgun.

Fairly skipping to the girl, I cried joyfully, "Glad you're back." And it was true because now I knew where she was. How had the boys known where to collect her? Had Chuck called her while he was in Watkins?

I pecked Lisa on the cheek. "I missed you. Hard being the only girl here."

"Missed you too," she said, putting her arm around my shoulder.

I asked Charles how they'd known where she was.

"We checked for the signal. We decided that if we got separated, she'd go to Plum Street and put a string around the mail box to say she was inside."

"What if the house had been rented out?"

"Paid for through October, remember? You paid October."

"Oh. Yeah."

The installation of Lisa Plinko took awhile. After directing her to the couch opposite mine, I helped unpack her two fancy outfits and we hung their hangers on nails protruding from the wall.

Lisa hauled in a wool coat and a blanket with a pattern of scurrying puppies. From a shopping bag, she withdrew myriad make-up items, three bottles of Bayer aspirin, five cans of soup, a loaf of brown bread, a bunch of Archie comics that she gifted to Chuck, and a container of Old Spice cologne that was a present for Charles.

Next appeared Ada Opal's red-haired wig. "I'm not loaning this out," Lisa warned, after glimpsing the deterioration of the honey-blonde wig.

She donated $13 to the communal pot. Charles took charge of it. Presumably she kept $4 for her trouble.

About noon, the honey-blonde wig and I left the dump with the stated intention of shopping for treats for Lisa, who, when she thought it over, was not as ecstatic as she'd first been about living in such dire digs. Soon after settling in, she had broken into great weepy sobs and begged for us to return to Plum Street.

Driving onto the access road and into the glen of firs where I'd recently parked over night, I got Miss Plinko's clothes from the trunk and morphed into the Salvation Army lady. Once the wig was securely anchored, I stowed my Wendy clothes in the trunk.

In Cassville, I parked in the library lot. At a dignified pace, I proceeded to the bus depot down the block where I plunked a quarter in a locker slot and withdrew the two keys. The locker would be mine for five days. That should be enough time for my latest plan to pay off. I hooked the keys onto my key ring.

As Miss Plinko, I shopped at the Salvation Army, buying two pairs of slacks, two long-sleeved blouses, a flannel shirt, a somewhat frayed black cardigan, a blue denim kerchief, some grayish tennis shoes, and two pairs of socks, all for myself. Lastly I purchased an ornate plaster cross. I stashed those things in the Pontiac and waited outside until an old Nash drew up across the street with Carl Swaney at the wheel. In greeting, I waved the Gideon bible.

The principal was clad in a rust-colored wool suit and matching vest. His hair matched his suit; he looked like he was oxidizing.

"I think it's grand that you carry the Good Book with you," Swaney said as he approached.

"Often I must enter dark places where souls are flustering."

"Floundering?" he guessed.

"Yes, clearly. But accompanied by such a man as you, I do not need the Good Book so much. I'll just bestow it in the car." I opened the Pontiac's door and, never letting Swaney out of my fond eyesight, gave Mr. Gideon a behind-the-back flip onto the front seat.

Swaney grinned, getting a kick out of my devotion to him and the backward toss too. Of the Pontiac, he commented, "There's a lot of power under that hood."

"It is lended to me by the arch—" no, no, not a Catholic diocese "— sector." Verbal mishaps were closing in. I had to do some boning up on my native land and faith, and soon. "It is away more car than I need," I finished.

He took my arm and guided me toward the store. "With a car like that," he joshed, "you can escape from the dark places mighty fast."

Miss Plinko was too serious to respond to that witticism. "I must need men's clothing, medium sizes, for the poverty-struck youngsters of the Palatine sector," I said as we headed down a dusty aisle. "Oh, is not this lovely," I cried, holding up a man's ruffley pink shirt.

"No, no," Swaney said. "Not pink, not for a tough boy. Here's a shirt for a big strong penniless kid." He grabbed a tailored shirt with a back pleat, large enough for a grizzly on all fours. With much deference, I let him select the rest of the rough-and-ready male duds, including two huge, slightly worn, wool jackets and two pair of scuffed work boots.

At checkout, he inquired after the clerk's son.

"Thank you for asking, Dr. Swaney," she replied. "He's in the library studying hard of course."

Recognizing a spoof, Swaney smiled. "He's not a bookworm, that I know. But he's very good with his hands."

She nodded. "He loves that old Hudson. Always fixing it on his own in the backyard."

"Mrs. Hawkey, this is Miss Plinko, from Rumania. She is here visiting her cousin, Miki Plinko, the noted violin professor. Miss Plinko is a member of the Rumanian Salvation Army."

"Or its equivalent," I said to ward off skepticism. Mrs. Hawkey bundled the purchases in wrapping paper and tied them tightly with twine.

After loading the clothing and boots into the Pontiac's trunk, Swaney brushed off his hands and said, "I believe it's time for that cup of coffee. What do you say?"

"Oh, yes, Dr. Swaney, but before we do, I must an errand to perform. I must go to place named Dunn's Hollow to leave something for old lady who resides there. Her name is Lily." If Sergeant Harris were on the scene, I wanted the protection of a proper citizen, an educator after all. Despite being apprehensive, I was determined to bring my plan to fruition.

At my mention of Lily, Swaney's face fell. He passed a hand over his mouth. "Miss Plinko, I have something to tell you and it is very bad. For news like this," he took my brown-gloved hand, "I shall need to know your first name."

I was stunned. I had no idea what that was. Once more I was failing the thoroughness test. "Hospador," I spouted. Once committed, I could only elaborate. "I call myself 'Hospador' in this country. You see my birth-name is mostly consonants, impossible here to pronounce. I have add some vowels for Americans." As was my wont, I provided an extra touch of authenticity, if I hadn't provided enough already: "In Rumania, the 'H' is silent, not so here." I paused for both of us to ingest this revelatory information.

Where had the first name come from? Later I would recall that Hospador was the last name of the little girl in grade school who'd worn the beaded, heart necklace.

"Hospador Plinko, it flows," Swaney decided. "Hospador, it's about your holler friend, Lily. I am so sorry. There was a fire in Dunn's Hollow last night. She may have perished in the flames." He brought my gloved hand to his chest.

"Oh, I didn't know her well," I said, twisting the hand free and hardening my heart to his ministrations. "Still and yet, I must enter that hollow place for I promised that poor soul …this …" I dug into my handbag and drew out the plaster cross. "Perhaps I give to her relatives," I continued, "for console them."

Swaney considered. "It will be quicker for us to check the mortuary first. It's only about four blocks from here."

"No!" I stamped my foot prettily. "For her I promise to visit her residence."

"All right, okay," he placated. "To the holler we'll go. A waste of gas though. You Rumanians are a stubborn people. Miki is that way. I should have known you'd be, too."

"Ah, you have met already my cousin."

"Yes," he paused. "In regard to Lisa's antics." I imagined Miki's strict ideas of child rearing hadn't gone over well with kindly, milk toast Dr. Swaney.

Swaney offered to drive my Pontiac, and I acceded with the advisory: "It is borrowed car, you must obey traffic signs. Devil-may-care men are not for Miss Plinko." He liked that, just to be suspected of being the reckless type.

He drove very slowly, commenting on the slight rattle in the motor, suggesting a trip to the mechanic's was in order. I nodded. I knew I'd wait for Norris as long as possible. He was my mechanic.

About twelve miles later we descended into the holler. The smell of scorch and ash was overwhelming. A brown Watkins cop car sat at the bottom of the steep incline. After pulling the veil down over my chin, I took a hanky from my purse and covered my nose. "So smoky," I said through muffling layers. We drew up alongside the squad car and Swaney shut off the motor. No sign of the cop.

Blackened stumps still smoldered and dead branches drooped from the largest tree still standing. Yellow-dyed rope was looped around burned and stunted shrubbery. The Bertalow shack was a smoldering scrap heap, the surrounding brush scarred. The fire had incinerated Lily's shed on top of the slope.

An officer in a brown uniform approached with a cop's side-to-side swagger. He was of medium height with a round face, tapered waist and broad shoulders. "No civilians allowed," he said brusquely through the driver's window. He did a double take and spoke more agreeably. "Dr. Swaney, what are you doing here?" He looked very young but tiny crow's feet on the corners of his blue eyes marked him as in his thirties.

Carl Swaney was surprised as well. "Why, Bobby Lagerquist," he expelled, "I heard you were on the Watkins force. How nice to see you." He nodded toward me. "This lady is a Salvation Army worker. She's promised to deliver a gift to Lily, an old lady who lived here. I told her I believe Lily died tragically in the fire, but she insists on keeping her promise."

The cop shook his head. "So far, no bodies. I heard that an old gal was killed, but the Cassville police have combed over this whole area pretty good. Early this morning they were out again searching, didn't find anything."

Instantly I understood that Harris and his minions had carted away Lily's remains.

Displaying the cross, I said firmly, "I will leave my present for Lily. When she returns for her belongings there it will be."

"Nobody's coming back here. Ever," the cop said. He stood back and hooked his thumbs through his belt. "Miss, there's nothing here any more."

"Still, I must fulfill promise." I hopped out of the Pontiac and, bearing the cross forward, began marching toward the site of Lily's first home.

Behind me, Swaney explained that, "The Rumanians are a stubborn people, Bobby. We'll be here all day if you don't let her leave the dang thing."

The cop said, "They call me 'Bob' now, Doctor …uh …Carl. I've been Watkins Police Chief since August."

"Oh for heaven's sake!" Swaney gushed. "Congratulations. My goodness, I didn't know. Very impressive." I glanced back to see the pair shaking hands. The police chief looked like a Bobby, as callow and innocent as any Bobby ever was.

"Look, Miss," Chief Bobby called after me, "you can leave your present, but make it quick. I'm keeping civilians away." Voice lowering, he spoke to Dr. Swaney, "There was a parade of them when I got here, searching for souvenirs. Seemed to think devilry went on here or so they said."

I reached the spot where a previous fire had flattened Lily's first home. Kneeling where I believed I'd buried the tin heart, I inspected the surface for identifying small rocks and pieces of roof tin. The murmuring voices of the officer and the teacher followed me as I scraped busily at the ashes and dirt.

Swaney was suddenly beside me. "A hole I dig to place the cross in," I explained. A bit of tin heart appeared. "Why, what is this?" I exclaimed. I dug frantically, uncovered the object and held it aloft. With all the energetic sifting, a scrap of blue cloth had also become visible. "Look, something else!" I cried.

Swaney squatted beside me, his sepia eyes fixed on the cloth that I was dangling. I drew a breath and puffed at the ground to blow away dirt and reveal a bit of chicken wing coated with dust. "Heaven forfend," I gasped, "it is bone." Hastily I scooped away more detritus and exposed the rest of the wing. "It is hand bone!" I identified. At my side, Chief Bobby peered down.

"That can't be a hand," he said. "I think it's a chicken bone."

"No, sir, it is hand. In Rumania I see many dead hands. This is one. Where is body? Has policeman carried it away?" Nearly frantic, I rose and brushed myself off. Chief Bobby's very blue eyes met mine.

"And see, on the heart is a name." I trembled forward the tin heart. "See! It says, 'Lanna.' Lanna must lie beneath. Do you know if missing a Lanna? No body to be found—" I scoffed, "—it is like home in Rumania. People get killed. Nobody cares! Police are corrupt. Everybody is corrupt."

"Young lady, you'll find that the American policeman is very honest," Chief Bobby chided. He backed away when I tried to shove the tin heart into his hand. My glove adamantly pursued its target until he was forced to accept the trinket. He held it up to the sunlight. "It's 'Lenna,' I think," he said.

I snatched the heart back and brought it up close to my netting. "Without a doubt, 'Lanna!' Two a's and two n's." I let the tin drop, and, crouching, I clawed anew in the dirt.

"A hand reaches up from the grave," I proclaimed. "For sure underneath is rest of body!"

Chief Bobby gripped my arm and pulled me up. "Miss, stop that. You're messing with a crime scene."

Swaney picked up the heart. "I knew a Lanna," he mused. "Lanna Cheeley was a student in my school a couple of years ago. I believe she's no longer around." He squinted at the ornament. "It might be 'Lama.'"

I wanted to punch him. "That is animal, not person." Damn that inferior buzz machine. It had done a lousy job of cutting. The scorching and re-heating hadn't helped either.

Chief Bobby spoke with authority. "Put that cross back in your glittery purse. I don't allow anybody to add items to a possible crime scene."

He claimed the tin heart from Swaney and set it on the ground beside the cloth and the wing. "Watch that she doesn't disturb these," he ordered Swaney. The teacher stiffened with guard duty. Bobby strode to the cop car and shortly produced an evidence bag. After donning rubber gloves, he packaged the three clues.

Swaney and I left the young chief as he was lifting a shovel from the squad car's trunk. Back in Cassville, I dropped Swaney by his beat-up Nash. I tutted my regret that there was no time for coffee as the macabre discovery had consumed more of the day than expected. Swaney just seemed thrilled to be part of such an event. He had unwittingly become a co-conspirator in my plan by giving Hospador credibility. It was likely Chief Bobby accepted my role-playing primarily because the respected Dr. Swaney did.

What had become of Lily's body? What would be the declared fate of undead Lanna? If the bank-robbing getaway driver was believed to be Lanna, and she was presumed dead, I was home free. I didn't believe the story of my alibi because I didn't have one.

# 19

In the public library, I prepared for my meeting with the Plinkos by visiting the rest room. Now that Lanna and her blue dress had pretty much been laid to rest, I changed from the black costume to the recently purchased brown trousers. I slipped on the flannel shirt and stepped into the grayish tennies. I unstuck the honey-blonde wig carefully, taking care not to irritate further my forehead scabs. I tied the denim blue kerchief over my dirty yellow hair.

In Wahoo City, at "Eets Family Dining," (est. 1946 by Jacob Eets the sign said) the Plinkos were seated at a corner table. The dining room was busier than I'd have thought for 3:00 in the afternoon.

Ada Opal and Miki were each holding a teacup. Seeing me, he rose, spilling his tea. He scowled at me as she soaked up the puddled tea with several napkins.

"You are late," he grumped. "My wife begins to worry."

I slid into the extra chair. "Better late than never," I said, slapping my notebook on the table.

I saw that Ada Opal's galaxy of rings was missing. Except for the wedding bands both wore their fingers were unadorned. Observing my interest, she said, "We rushed off from teaching so quickly that I forgot to put on my rings. I don't wear them when I teach. You can't wear bulky rings when you play the violin. The left hand shifts rapidly up and down the fingerboard and doesn't want to be hampered."

"Ah," I said, "like a fireman sliding down a pole."

"Well, not quite… " she said. Her eyes widened. "Why, what happened to your face?" The bruising from my beating had yellowed to the point that I thought powder covered it quite nicely. Other signs that remained of the ordeal were a slightly swollen lip and scratch under one eye.

"Thanks for asking," I said. "I was searching for clues on another case and a branch jumped out and struck me." I smacked my palms together. Ada Opal jumped at the sound. "Let's not stall around," I said brusquely. "I want my money, $200 as retainer and $1000 of the $2000 owed from before."

We paused as a busy waitress tossed us menus on a fly-by.

Then Miki said, "I am tired of this. Here is money." He withdrew an envelope from his back pocket and slapped it down on the table. I pulled it in and riffled through the package of large bills before tucking it in my shoulder bag. Now I could leave Illinois with health intact, but I had already decided to stay for the promise of a larger payout.

"$200 is due next week," I said, "and each week thereafter that I'm on the case. At its conclusion you will pay me $1000." I detached one of the bus depot's locker keys. Informing Miki what it opened, I slid it across. "You will place future payments, in cash, in that locker."

Miki grasped the key and said, "This must end quickly, before 'future payments.' Where is daughter now?"

"Boarding with the Cheeley brothers," I said.

"What!" he exploded as Ada Opal gasped, "My goodness."

The adults at the next table glanced over curiously.

I leaned toward Miki. "No more yelling or I'm out of here."

"Calm down," Ada Opal begged, stroking her husband's arm.

Miki waved her away. "The Cheeleys are criminals."

"Maybe so," I said, shrugging. "Miki, Ada Opal, I feel this will be permanent employment, running after and delivering your daughter to you. What plans do you have for keeping her at home this time? I mean what will have changed?"

The man banged his cup down; tea sloshed into the saucer. "She will visit Rumania with me. There she may learn the lessons of proper behavior. I will return alone."

He overrode my dismayed reaction.

"Listen," he hissed. "Rumania is good place for Lisa. She will learn to be obedient child. No more spoilage. As a child with my father we walked village to village to play music and make money. Often we stayed outside over the night with nothing but a loaf of bread and some meat that people gave to us after hearing me play. In the darkness, we heard rats scurrying on edge of woods, waiting for us to sleep so as to eat our crumbs."

Ada Opal demurred. "Darlin', this is not the time to tell your story."

"So we bring Lisa back when Rolf completed his recitals and gone home with his parents," he continued.

"She will be back with us at least by September," Ada Opal said strongly.

"She will return and have full appreciation of life she has here," he augmented.

I asked if Lisa spoke Rumanian.

"She will learn quickly the words for 'yes' and 'please' and 'thank you.'" He glugged his remaining tea. "Perhaps Lisa will grow from silly girl to proper lady and make good match and be good wife there across the ocean."

I didn't know anything about Rumania, but I suspected marriages were a bit more arranged there than in the states. I could see Miki marrying her off to the highest bidder just to be rid of her.

The waitress came to take my order: a cheeseburger, fries, and a milkshake. The Plinkos didn't complain; they were getting used to me. Miki requested more hot water.

"Let me get this straight," I said. "Rolf Nietschke is your project, to mold and make better, but whose project is Lisa?"

Miki clattered down his teacup. "For that time, she will be my Uncle Puju's." He leapt from his chair and made for the restroom.

"Miki is sick over all this," Ada Opal said, flicking a hand toward the rest room sign while his chair yet vibrated. "I've reluctantly given my approval to the Rumanian vacation. I'm aware of the severity of life over there. Miki was hit with a stick when he played badly. Children were raised strictly in those days, no nonsense tolerated. Necessary then, perhaps, but nowadays it's more modern. Less strict. It's what our daughter needs for a short while. She will return when Rolf is safely away."

"I see."

"No, I don't think you do." She became cross and snappy. "Let me tell you a little about my husband. When we first met, I was just a second-rate violin student, working very hard for a concert career that I would never attain given my lack of talent. But Miki recognized what no one else did: that I had an uncanny knack for fixing minor flaws in other people's playing. They came to me, the other students, through the back door, so to speak, for technical advice. My forte was correcting minor errors in vibrato, in shifting, in bow articulation, in acquiring the sheer beauty of sound. Ultimately it's the kind of thing that sets apart one player from another and makes a world of difference to a professional career. Miki saw I had the ability and marveled at it. The sad thing is that I could spot and correct flaws in everyone but myself. That has always been a source of anguish, as well as a complete mystery, to me."

The woman cleared her throat. "We fell in love. Miki is a man of gallantry, although hard-eyed and judgmental when in the musical world. You don't see his brilliance because you're not a musician, and you don't know his past to appreciate what he has surmounted. Right now you see only that he is quite unstrung over Lisa's escapades." She eyed the hall that led to restroom. "Miki and I are bound together in an almost holy endeavor. We are helping a select group of special young people to further great art."

"Aha," I said.

The waitress delivered our orders. I munched on the fries. Ada Opal poured hot water and steeped the tea bag. "Rolf is destined for a fine career that must not be derailed. To waylay such talent is unforgivable, and Lisa, after growing up around all this, should know better than to try. There's something else going on that she would attempt this. Rolf has the selfishness of the artist consumed by his passion. He'll drop my daughter at the first opportunity. I've seen enough of it to know." Her voice dropped. "Shhh. Here he comes."

Miki rejoined us, coldly polite. "Pardon, I think I have picked up bug."

"Sip your tea," she said, refilling his cup and handing it to him. She squeezed a half-lemon for him.

I jumped up. "Excuse me," I said. "I need to use the rest room myself." I needed time and quiet to think this through. In a stall in the ladies' room, I pondered. I went to the mirror, removed the kerchief and ruffled my dirty yellow hair. I sure looked the tough gal. I gathered spittle to reinforce the image, and let loose some toward the toilet. Was I mean or what? I took three sheets of toilet paper and wiped my spit off the toilet seat. I washed my hands and subdued my hair with water and finger. I tied the kerchief back on.

Returning to the Plinkos, I plonked down in my chair and began drumming the table with a finger. I said, "Let's make it easier for you to send Lisa away. Let's let Rolf visit her, and make her more amenable to returning home. I mean you don't want to haul her kicking and screaming onto that Rumanian airplane, do you?"

"Rolf will not visit her," Miki declared.

Heedlessly I continued. "A once a week visit at a neutral location will relax Rolf and it'll ease Lisa into accepting your plans. For sure, it will help Rolf's music, don't you agree?" Miki's face was turning bright red. "Now Miki, before you do another Mount Vesuvius, let me elaborate. The visit will be supervised. There is a woman, an older woman, who boards with the Cheeleys. She's an aunt, Wanda's her name. She teaches the boys manners, etiquette, in addition she does the cleaning, cooking, laundering, and picking up; you know how boys are."

"We have no boys. Only a problem daughter." Miki said.

"Rolf is like a son to us," Ada Opal said. "He has very neat habits. What is Wanda's last name? Is she a Cheeley? I don't like this at all."

I shrugged. "I don't know what her last name is. I just know she's very good with the boys. I've witnessed her love and discipline that's turning them into good little citizens."

Asa Opal peered at me. "Are you this Aunt Wanda, along with pretending to be our Salvation Army cousin?"

My, what a suspicious woman. "Really, Ada Opal, in this life you've got to trust those who try to help you. Otherwise, it's not good for your health." I slapped the table with my palm. "I'll tell you what. I'll bring Wanda out to your house so you can meet her. Wanda is taller and much older than me. She's yellow-haired. She wears thick sunglasses because she has a droopy eye. That eye always seems to be dripping some sort of gunk."

"Inbreeding," Miki spoke up. "I've seen another of that family with something wrong with his eye."

"You will have a lovely evening getting to know Wanda," I assured them. "She'll want a meal of course. That kind is always hungry."

"We do not want those dirty people in our house!" Miki exclaimed.

With a sigh, Ada Opal hoisted the white flag. "All right. Whether or not you're Wanda, I just want my child back."

"Good, that's settled. I believe for a small sum Aunt Wanda will watch over Lisa and Rolf when they're together, to prevent any hanky-panky."

Miki's lower lip trembled. His voice was throttled. "I want Lisa on plane! Now! No more nonsense!"

Ada Opal leaned in and said, "No, darlin', not yet. Lisa must board the plane with hope. I can't bear for my child to hate me."

A short obstinate silence fell before I said, "I think I can talk Aunt Wanda into picking up Rolf on your corner once a week. How about tomorrow? It may take only one visit before Lisa's heart softens, knowing it is your kindness that allows for the trysting. Let's talk specifics. Wanda will drive an older model Ford, mostly gray. What time should she be at your corner? I'll even ask Auntie to keep the cost down to, say, fifty bucks a visit, what with gas, oil, mileage, and tire wear and tear. You can give the money to Rolf to give to Wanda."

"At the least, Rolf's practicing will improve," Ada Opal said weakly.

Miki kicked his chair back for another run to the men's room. In his wake, we sat listening to soft conversations around us. After several minutes, Ada Opal spoke reflectively. "We started Lisa on the violin when she was four. Of course I was her teacher. Miki can't handle the young ones. He's too advanced. By the time Lisa was five her every lesson was excruciating. She hopped around while playing, pressed the bow into the strings for the ugliest possible sound, acted up every way she knew how. One disruptive trick after another. Still I persisted, firmly believing that when she grew older she'd thank me for my insistence that she learn to play the violin. After all, she is the child of two remarkable musicians. And in recitals, when the chips were down, she played brilliantly. Her dad and the violin students were impressed.

"It all came to a head one day when she was six and flat out refused to take her lesson. In desperation, I called for Miki and he came roaring in. He carried her into my studio and set her down. She broke away and flew out the front door with him close behind. She made it to the corner, to the giant oak tree and hid behind it. Every move he made to catch her, she'd sidle around the tree just out of reach. Several of the student violinists were watching and laughing. Miki was furious; he roared back into the house and shouted at me, 'She's not mine!' Ada Opal's voice softened. "But she is his, and mine, forever. That day he slammed upstairs and shut himself in his studio. It's always been push-pull between them. He loves her, I know that, but he just doesn't like her very much." Ada Opal sipped her tea, patted her lips with a napkin.

"She never had another lesson. At the time, I was relieved to be done with the struggle. But now it's my burden to bear that I can't transfer my love of music to my daughter." She took a lace-edged hanky from her purse to blot her eyes.

"No use trying to make the kid into something she's not," I said, actually feeling bad for the woman. "She likes sports. She's very good at them. Must make you happy that she's found something she can do really well."

"Mmm." Not ecstatically pleased, that was for sure. Ada Opal opened her compact and smoothed her face, so when Miki returned, which he did shortly, she was arranged once more.

## 20

In the trailer, Lisa sat on her couch holding a hand mirror and using tweezers to pluck her eyebrows. Charles killed time by tossing empty soup cans at a pail near my couch. Fairly anesthetized, Chuck stood staring at the nearly empty white lightnin' jar. Everyone exchanged grunts of greeting. "Scoot over, I got good news," I told Lisa. She slid over and I sat. Charles stopped tossing.

"I was in Goldfarb's department store today," I said. "I saw your mother at the jewelry counter, looking at a gorgeous string of pearls."

"Not for me, I'm sure."

"How'd you know it was her mother?" Charles asked.

"I saw her parents when they visited Lisa at the jail. Give me a break on the paranoia, will you, and let me finish?"

"Pair-o-no-what!" hooted Chuck, taking a swig. "What's that?"

"Anyway," I said to Lisa, "I inquired as to how your mom was."

"So? What did she say?" Lisa asked.

"The first thing she said was that you had left home again. She looked terrible, all saggy and dark around the eyes. She said she missed you terribly, and that Rolf is almost physically ill from missing you too."

"Half of that's true. Rolf misses me, that's for sure." Lisa had become so absorbed in what I was saying that one of her eyebrows was almost gone.

I took the tweezers from her before delivering the punch line. "Your mother is going to let Rolf visit you here."

Lisa shrieked, "Wow!" then recoiled. "No, wait, you told her where I was? D-d-dad and the police will be right outside."

Suddenly at the window, peeking out, Charles said, "Are you nuts? If you were followed—" He took a step to the right and grabbed the shotgun off a shelf.

"Of course I didn't tell her where you are," I said. "Give me some credit. Now if everybody will pipe down, I'll tell you how it's gonna work." I allowed a moment of silence before saying, "They'll let Rolf visit tomorrow."

"That jerk coming here. He'll tell everybody," Charles growled.

"No he won't," I said. "Not if he wants the visits to continue. I'm meeting him at the house at four o'clock. I'll drive the old Ford; I'm not getting my car involved. I'll take back roads, be in and out. With the new paint job and license plate the car most likely won't be spotted as stolen, let's hope. I'll drive Rolf out here; he'll stay a couple of hours with Lisa, and if Lisa wants to see him again, her mom will allow it."

"What about Dad?" Lisa asked.

"It's all good. She okayed it with him."

"The great Professor Plinko. Ha." Lisa's voice faltered. "No, he'll follow Rolf out here."

"No he won't. And if he does, well," I finished scornfully, "I've eluded more than one cop on my tail, and I can sure out-maneuver a classical violin player."

## 21

The following afternoon, as dirty-yellow-haired, sunglasses-wearing Wanda, I drove Rolf from the Plinko compound to the trailer. To appear taller, I sat on boards from Chuck's wood sector that I'd piled on the driver's seat. Mid-trip, I pulled over and tied a dishtowel over my passenger's eyes so as to hide the last miles. Arriving at our destination, Rolf stripped off the blindfold and saw that he was in a car junkyard.

The door to the trailer popped open. Lisa scampered down the steps and fairly flew to the car. Rolf embraced her with one arm while the other hand held the violin case away.

"You got till 6:30, then I have to get you back," I said. Rolf had known instantly who Aunt Wanda was. Viewing our departure from the picture window, the Plinkos hadn't emerged to request an ID. Their main goal was to get Rolf back to concentrating on his music. Oh, and to get Lisa back home so Rolf could concentrate on his music.

Charles and Chuck, in Salvation Army clothes, followed Lisa down the steps. The new pants were baggy on Chuck, less so on Charles. A distinct improvement, nonetheless. Charles forced a handshake on Rolf, growling, "If you turn us in, you'll never see Lisa again."

"I'm not stupid," Rolf said, eyes averted, as Lisa tugged him toward the trailer steps.

"Come on, fellas," I said, "let's take a walk so they can be alone."

The boys and I walked the road for a while, going farther into the depths of the dump than I had been before. To our right, up a considerable grade, we happened upon a narrow trench that broke away from the road and curved out of sight.

We stopped there long enough for Chuck to relate how, when he and Charles had previously lived here, he had seen glittery objects among the torn roots of a tree that had gone down. The shiny balls turned out to be Christmas tree ornaments. When he brought them home, Charles said get rid of them. "If we'd kept them we could have Christmas now," Chuck concluded.

"We'll be gone by Christmas," Charles said. He provided additional history: "A long time ago, pipes ran through this trench. Probably they carried sewage. They're gone now."

On our return, we paused at the pond to enjoy the remnants of a sunny day that was fast darkening into twilight. It was 6:50 and I had my penlight on by the time we rounded the final bend and saw that the Ford was not in the road. I had stuck the keys above the visor and left the car out front; after all it was only for a couple of hours.

We broke into a run. Maybe Lisa had told Rolf to move the car behind the trailer where space had been cleared, but did that kid even know how to drive? I scurried up the rise for a better look. No Ford. I hurried back down. The boards I'd piled on the driver's seat lay beside the trailer steps. The dishtowel-blindfold Rolf had worn lay on top.

"Damn them if they stole our car," Charles said as he banged into the trailer.

I ran up the steps after him. "Doesn't anyone ask permission to borrow a car?"

Behind us, Chuck wailed, "Where's my car?"

Lisa and Rolf weren't in the trailer. Charles gestured in disbelief. "I'm gonna kill 'em both," he said.

I scanned the room. "Her clothes are still here." I took three steps, flung open a cupboard door. "Yeah, the red wig's here too. They're probably just taking a drive."

Charles was by the shelves. "The shotgun's gone. Damn them, they've gone to get money from the Plinkos and not cut us in on it." He spat on the floor. "Fuck 'em."

"Huh?" I asked.

"There's piles of money in Miki's safe. Lisa saw it when she was a kid. The Plinkos are hiding it so they don't have to pay taxes, something about violin lessons they give in Europe. Lisa said she'd tell on them if they didn't cut her in. Now her and Rolf are gone for good with a lot of money of which we're not gonna see any of it."

I dashed out the door; Charles pounded along behind me. At the bottom of the steps, I scooped up the dishtowel in case I needed to mask my face. I raced to the Pontiac and jumped in, jabbed the key in the ignition and revved the motor. Charles clambered in beside me, gasping, "If they use our gun, we'll be the bad guys."

As I was pulling out, Chuck stumbled into the back seat. I aimed to stop the robbery before it started. Wait, wasn't that my aim last time? Bouncing out of the dump, I added a proviso: If a crime were in progress, or completed, I'd drive right on by. Okay, so I'd slow down and let my associates jump out to reclaim their shotgun. From there on, they'd have to rely on Chuck's idiot savant good luck. No more aiding and abetting felonies for this girl.

Desperate minutes later, after a hairpin turn and up a steep hill, we were in the isolated area of the Plinko encampment. It was quite dark. The Ford was parked in front of a lone streetlight at the far end of the block. Chuck said excitedly, "There's my car."

Two people sat in the Ford's front seat, the taller being the driver. If the robbery hadn't yet happened, maybe we could get out of this situation scot-free. I pulled up across the street on the left side of the road, about ten yards short of the Ford.

To our right, lights glowed in three of the four student cabins. A number of violins sounded discordantly. In the house, a light burned on the first floor, and upstairs another light came on.

Charles leapt out and rushed the driver's side of the Ford. Fearing the end of a promising musical career, I was at his heels. Rolf opened the driver's door. Halfway out, he saw Charles and plunged back into the car. Charles was on him, grabbing the gangly youth's sweatshirt from behind and yanking him into the street. The shotgun came spinning out with Rolf, making me think he had gone for the weapon.

Charles swung Rolf into the opened door. Lisa screamed from the passenger seat, "Fight back! Show him! Fight back!"

Rolf stuck his hands in his armpits. I picked up the shotgun and hurled it into the bushes.

Charles hit Rolf a left to the face and a right to the belly. Rolf fell to his knees. He balanced there momentarily and then pitched forward.

"Bastard," Charles breathed, "taking our car, our girl and our money. As if you two soft asses could get away with it." Looming over Rolf, Charles preened in his triumph over a wuss.

I grabbed his shoulders. "Enough. You nailed him good."

Charles yelled to Chuck still in the Pontiac, "Come on! I know how to get money from Plinko!"

"No, sir!" I said, pushing down on his shoulders.

Above the front door of the house, a light came on.

I ran around to the other side of the Ford. In the passenger seat, Lisa was fixed on the sight of her fallen accomplice. I touched her shoulder through the open window. Startled, she wheeled and nailed my jaw with a flailing hand. "Did you get the money?" I asked, wiggling my jaw, relieved it still had feeling.

She shook her head. "Not yet."

I yelled to Charles, "Help Rolf up and see if he can make it to the house. Hurry! We gotta get out of here." Happily there was no sign of Chuck emerging from the Pontiac. The block had descended into almost complete stillness. All but one of the violins had stopped playing.

Charles hoisted Rolf to his feet. Tottering, the boy looked around in a daze. His nose was a bloody mess.

The front door of the Plinko home opened a crack, closed, then opened again, wider this time and the front steps light came on. Both Plinkos appeared, skulking down the steps and moving down the sloped lawn. They halted just beyond the full reach of the exterior light and barely within the street lamp's dim glow. Each of them carried a rifle.

I urged Rolf, "Put your hands up. Go to the Plinkos, tell them everything is fine. Get them into the house. I'll straighten things out later."

"Lisa, is that you? You come inside. Get away from those hoodlums!" Ada Opal shouted.

"You think you're keeping all that money? Good luck! Everybody knows about it," Lisa screamed.

Ada Opal's rifle blasted. The bullet pinged into the rear of the Ford. The recoil knocked the shooter backward onto the lawn. I dropped to the grass, pulling Lisa out of the car and down on the ground beside me.

Ada Opal wailed, "My God, Miki, it went off."

"*Curule!*" he yelled, no doubt an unhappy Rumanian expression. He had dropped flat on his belly into a rifleman's position.

"Cease fire! Truce!" I called. "You're going to kill someone!"

"Call the police, Miki," Ada Opal yelled.

"You do and I'll call the tax-man!" Lisa challenged.

Hands in the air, I rose slowly with the plea, "It's me, please don't touch the trigger!" I peered over the car's hood for Charles, saw him across the street poking his head above a bush. By the Ford, Rolf crouched, covering his nose with a hand. I didn't see Chuck. Presumably he had stayed in the Pontiac.

Three violin students huddled in front of a cabin. The single violin continued its merry tune.

Leaping to his feet, Miki sprinted for the house.

I shouted, "If you call the police, Rolf will be arrested and your daughter will go to jail too. It will make all the papers!"

Rolf opened the Ford's rear door and, mouth hanging open, nose perhaps broken, he leaned in, claimed his violin and then wobbled to the curb.

Lisa struggled to her feet and said forlornly, "Baby, come and hold me,"

Ignoring her, Rolf trudged up the lawn.

Lisa's voice rose. "Hey, come back here! They have to give us money. Otherwise that's it for them."

Miki paused on the top step of the landing. Ada Opal, weaponless, made her way to a peony bush under the picture window. She called, "Here, Rolfie, here Rolfie," like he was their pet dachshund.

Suddenly Charles was beside Lisa, gripping her shoulders. "Bitch, stealing our car and leaving me out after all I done for you."

"I woulda shared," she mewled. He pushed her away.

"Are you fucking that pansy?" he charged.

"No, no, no, never." Her tone changed from frightened to husky. "Oh, Charles, you're such a brute."

I studied the two. Lisa offering herself was a bad sign, or maybe not if it weaned her from Rolf. After all, this was the second time the guy had walked out on her. Most likely though, the wheedling was an attempt at mercy because she still needed Charles.

Up the lawn and plodding up the steps, Rolf reached Miki. The teacher raised the boy's right hand in victory. Ada Opal ascended the steps and took Rolf's other hand. The Plinkos led him through the door and after all were inside, closed it with a definitive "whump."

The three violin students drifted into one of the cabins, but left the door ajar. The solo violin continued being happy.

Face in hands, Lisa wept.

I grasped her shoulders, shook her a little. "Come on, we gotta go before the whole town shows up," I said. "The students will call the cops even if your parents don't. Come on. There'll be another day."

Not with me around, I fervently hoped.

I led the sobbing girl to the Pontiac. She'd travel with me. I told Chuck, who sat alertly behind the wheel, to join his brother in the Ford. Kids who can't get along ride separately.

Charles found his precious shotgun and examined it for dings. I went to him and took it away gently but firmly. He didn't protest. My pissedness brooked no argument. I laid the gun on the Pontiac's back seat.

The Plinkos were at their picture window, Rolf between them, making sure we were leaving.

We took the back roads to the dump. I drew the Pontiac up to the trailer with the Ford right behind. Charles shot out of the Ford and when Lisa tried to exit the Pontiac he was there to shove her back in. She tumbled onto the seat, her hefty legs sprawling out the door. Again she tried to get out.

"You ain't staying here with us," Charles grunted. He pushed her again, not as hard. She grabbed his arm. "You're so strong, Charles," she said in a very small voice. "Like Clyde, you know, Bonnie and—"

"You go find some other dope to fool," he said harshly.

I couldn't afford to let the girl out of my sight. "She's very sorry, Charles. She fully intended to share," I said.

"I did, I did," she pleaded.

"Let it go till morning. We'll all think better then," I said.

Appearing to gain some sense, Charles backed off to let Lisa out of the car. She stood before us a humiliated child-woman, vulnerable and teary. "I'm sorry, I'm so, so sorry," she said while studying Charles' obdurate expression.

"Fuck you," he said. He stepped into her and, with one hand on her back and the other behind her head he pulled her to him and buried his face in the crook of her neck. "You're safe with me," he whispered.

Her body yielded and they clung to each other.

I could only watch. There's no use trying to interfere with nature having its moment.

# 22

It was 8:36 the next morning before Lisa stirred on her couch. Immediately I said, "How you feeling, babes? Want to talk about what happened?" The previous night she and Charles had broken apart quickly as though repulsed.

She raised her head. "What's to say?" she asked groggily.

"Why'd you take the shotgun along?" I persisted.

Considering, she rubbed her eyes. "Rolf with me and a gun? I knew they'd absolutely die when they saw that."

"What's up between you and Charles?"

"Nothing! He's just so different from Rolf…" Lisa's voice trailed off. "So strong. He comes right at you with what he wants."

"Rolf loves you. You'll break his heart if…"

"Will I? That'd show him, wouldn't it? Besides he likes the creature comforts with my parents better than roughing it with me."

I couldn't allow Lisa and Charles to fall for each other and, what, run off together? I had some serious cash at stake. "Lisa, think of how long you've loved Rolf, all the plans you've made and all the experiences you've gone through together."

She got quiet, then weepy, and called me a rat for reminding her.

Later when I announced my intention to visit the Watkins laundry, the boys contributed some of their duds. Not the new outfits. They could be worn for days before smelling bad enough that the wearers would notice. Lisa threw in some dirty clothes, but didn't ask to go along. That was suspicious, because yesterday she'd begged to accompany Wanda and window-shop the stores during the trip to pick up Rolf. Not allowed, of course. What had changed since then? I dreaded to think.

As I went to the Pontiac, I spotted Charles in Chuck's tool sector, amid the discarded metal objects. He was holding a pry bar.

I walked the road toward him, inquiring, "What you need a pry bar for?"

"Fix up that old Chevy." He motioned toward the fleet of disabled cars. "Put it off too long already."

I called him out. "Hey, you, don't go trying to break into the Plinkos' safe with that thing. You'll bring us all down. And here's another piece of advice: don't fall for Lisa. She's more trouble we don't need."

He spat into some dead leaves before giving me a cocky half-smile. "Feel bad I'm turning you down?"

I ignored that.

He wheeled and faced the road. "Somebody's coming." He drew the .38 special.

We crouched and waited. Minutes passed before a stooped old man shouldering a cloth bag came doddering up the road. His unsteady footfalls crunched against the road's litter.

Charles rose. "It's okay, I know him." He stuck the gun in his waistband and approached the guy. "Hey, Davy," he called. He pumped the man's hand. "How be ya?"

The old wreck grinned toothlessly. "That you, Benny? I gotter get a salamander before noon. Lost mine to the lunch pail."

"Gosh dern," Charles said. "Bad luck for sure." He gave the man a shoulder pat. The fellow shuffled on a few steps, saw the tool sector and headed for it.

I joined Charles and we watched Davy paw through Chuck's tools. "Think he'll rat us out?" I asked.

"Davy's a little… " Charles twirled his finger by his ear. "He did prison time for stealing something way back during the Depression, but he doesn't remember what it was. Now he just wanders around. Got no sense to do otherwise. He'll be on the freight train tonight."

As I headed for Watkins in the Pontiac, I saw Charles stooped beside Davy, helping him sort through the tools. Maybe Chuck would interrupt and want to keep everything.

## 23

At the laundry, I handed over the gang's dirty clothes, to be picked up in two hours. From the pay phone booth, I dialed Cassville High School to find out the latest from Carl Swaney.

"Hospador, thank heaven you called," he said. "The police want to interview me concerning the 'Lanna' matter, after school today at 4:00. You have to be there too. They're wondering why they can't locate you. Municipal Courts building. 4:00 today. Can you attend?"

"Oh," I said, "I do not trust those who wear the badge. You will be there?"

"Certainly. The police have ordered me to attend."

"I do not know where this court building is, so you will meet me at public library, okay? We go to building together." I was not going walk the streets by myself if there was an alternative.

"The library, very good," he said. "We can chat on our way. The courts building is not too far away."

"For sure. Will Mr. Sergeant Harris be there?"

"I believe so. I understand he's recovered and is game to go."

Oh, really. Things just got serious. Mr. Sergeant Harris is fair game and he has got to go.

About a mile outside of Watkins, I drove onto a secluded side road and changed outfits to become Hospador. I felt more comfortable with that netting in front of my face.

I drove back to downtown Watkins, parked and killed time wandering through the five-block shopping area. Pausing at a pawnshop window, I viewed the treasures available inside. A ukulele for $2.00. Kind of scratched, but looked playable. I walked on and ate a leisurely lunch in the next block.

At 3:55 that afternoon Hospador Plinko sat next to Carl Swaney in a room in the Municipal Courts Building, a three-story edifice of flaking limestone with tall narrow windows and a high-pitched roof.

To the side of a long table, brown-clad Watkins Chief Bobby Lagerquist and his deputy, Ken Johnson by nameplate, sat in ladderback chairs. Bobby's hands were resting on the table and I noticed that he wore no wedding ring. The leather armchair behind the desk was unoccupied. Saved for Sergeant Harris or maybe the Cassville Police Chief would finally make an appearance.

Gripping my spangly purse with both hands, I sat primly with my feet in the black Oxfords planted side by side. The hat's veil masked my eyes, nose, and chin. My long black skirt and anklets covered the switchblade strapped to an ankle and my black cardigan fell over the holstered .25. I would not be taken so easily this time.

About twenty well-dressed men, conversing in undertones, sat on various mismatched chairs they had arranged to be near friends. Swaney whispered that they were city council members, businessmen, various VIPs.

"That's the mayor." Swaney pointed out a portly gentleman with thinning gray hair, a goatee, and wire-rimmed glasses, leaning toward an associate in the back row.

The fat alderman and the Mason Drugs clerk were in the front row. Both wore suits, ties, and vests, felt hats in their laps. I averted my gaze; after all we had never met.

I shifted my eyes and saw, in a far back corner, William Bertalow in jailhouse stripes, shackled, slumping forward in a chair. At least he had survived the fire. A short, round blue-clad cop attended him, one of the men who had arrested me and afterward left me alone with the cruel sergeant. The other cop that day, the tall one, was bulling his way through attendees toward his partner. When Bertalow raised his bleary head, I saw purplish splotches below the bad eye and that his upper lip was swollen and discolored. He'd been beaten. Was he a suspect in the Harris assault, or had he simply been taken in for having a track record with the sergeant?

It was then that my stomach sank and my heart started fluttering fast and irregular and I became aware that I was terrified of seeing Harris again. As if summoned by my rush of fear and adrenaline, the door opened and Harris, head bandaged, limped in supported by a cane. The room grew silent. Scanning the crowd, the sergeant made his hesitant way to the leather armchair and, with a grimace, lowered himself into it. He turned toward Chief Bobby and barked, "Let's get this over with. I got a helluva lot to do." He addressed the gathering in a more moderate tone. "Chief Bob here has got it in his head, thanks to some of you—" he eyeballed the alderman and the clerk "—that my men are hiding something about that holler fire." Harris' steely gaze passed over Swaney and landed briefly on me. I lowered my eyes and suppressed a shudder.

"Some of you," he went on, "got your dander up about that fire, even though you wanted the riff-raff out and said as much to me many times. And you know as well as I do that riffraff included the witch who ate up little Tina Haverford twenty years ago." There was a communal gasp. "One less witch if she did burn up," Harris rasped, "although God knows too late for Tina." He bowed his head as if in remembrance of the little girl. When he raised his eyes, I saw they were cold and focused. "But me and my troops didn't burn them out," he said. "They did that to themselves with their reckless habits. One of them is under arrest and with us today. Back there." He flicked his wrist dismissively.

Everyone had already spotted the prisoner, William Bertalow, so there were only slight head movements to acknowledge him.

Among this bunch of lambs, someone had to act the lion, so I said, high-pitched but strong, "A second lady also perished."

Harris swiveled and stared. Bracing his arms, he made a clumsy motion to stand for a better look at me, but hesitated when Chief Bobby jumped up.

Addressing the group, Bobby spoke quickly. "The reason for this meeting is that our fire department got a call about 10:15 the evening of the fire. A witness who was in the holler shooting small game called in to report seeing a Cassville police car and three officers there. According to him, they were setting fires at various locations. This witness said people were burning up in the holler."

Harris turned his chair aggressively toward Bobby. "You get his name?"

Bobby slid his chair back a tad and sat down. "Hung up without saying."

Harris splayed his hands in disbelief.

"Sergeant Harris, our purpose today is to determine the facts of the fire," Bobby went on, not subdued after all. "Because it was set deliberately. The evidence is clear. There were traces of kerosene all over."

"That worthless heinie back there set it, then called it in to blame it on our police force," Harris said. "If people died, we'll charge William Bertalow with their murder. He's been known to keep kerosene."

"No phone in holler," I said pleasantly, my shrillness penetrating.

Harris' small eyes shot onto me once more and remained. A peculiar smile formed on his face. I had been recognized. I dipped my head. It was a standoff. Accuse me of bank robbery and assault and I'll accuse you of attempted rape. In support of my charge, I had met two women who had been molested by Harris. If they dared testify, that is. Gloomy prospect.

Every man present had inched forward to the edge of his chair. The room became as still as a cemetery at midnight. I guessed some of Cassville's elite hadn't minded if the holler people were burned out, but killed in the process? Got to draw the line somewhere.

It was a long measuring moment before Harris broke the paralysis. "I know what's up," he said to me. I let my mouth go slack.

"Who's the dame?" he asked Bobby.

"The lady? Her name is..." Bobby checked his sheaf of notes. " ...Hospador Plinko. She's a Salvation Army lady, Miki Plinko's cousin from Rumania. She found the tin heart in the holler."

"Yeah? From Rumania? Like gimme a home where the vampires roam, isn't that their national anthem? Gal's gotta know all about witches." Harris looked around for laughter, but no one complied.

Carl Swaney slipped a protective arm around my shoulder.

"We carry crosses," I said mildly, "to fend off evil ones." I pulled the plaster cross from my purse and held it forward. "Keep away," I said to Harris. There was a chuckle from one brave soul. Sharing the simple humor, Harris grinned tolerantly. This guy believed he had me where he wanted. Right now he was seeking a way to bring me down. Getting a look at my left arm would be a way; it still bore scabs from the truck crash.

Harris leaned back and allowed the leather chair's sucking sound before saying, "I guess I'm on the hot seat. So if any of you have anything to ask me, now's the time. To my face."

No one took the opportunity. After several seconds, Harris set his elbows on the desk and clasped his hands together. "You know, folks, we have only three police officers battling the bad guys in this town, since our Chief is once more sitting it out at home. Apologies to you, Mayor, but it's you and the councilmen that appoint him time and time over again, so don't blame me for this steep rise in crime."

So there was a Chief of Police, someone above Sergeant Harris, who chose to hide out in desperate times.

The mayor glowered at Harris. At least for the moment, it appeared that the mayor of Cassville detested the town's acting top cop.

Harris blew a raspberry. "This whole thing is ridiculous. We've done a thorough search. There's no body or multiple bodies. William

Bertalow back there is the offender in all this. Everybody knows he's a poacher and a squatter. You see anybody in flames that night, William?"

The slumping man didn't stir. One of the blues backhanded William on the side of the head. "Answer the man," he yipped.

The prisoner roused himself to mutter, "Didn't see nothing."

I said, my small voice projecting in the quiet room, "In my country I see men tortured. They have the look of this man."

Chief Bobby broke in. "Sergeant Harris, citizens have come forth identifying the other possible deceased as Lanna Cheeley, last seen in Mason's Drug Emporium where she bought, and had her name engraved on, the tin heart that Miss Hospador discovered. Mr. Howard Mason, the clerk and owner, remembers her and the blue-patterned dress she wore. Fragments of a similar material were discovered in the holler after the fire. They've been identified by Mr. Mason as the same pattern. Some chicken bones were found there also, at first mistakenly identified as human."

Damn. Well, I knew the chicken bones were a stretch.

Bobby drove ahead. "Alderman J. Halstead Sprinkle saw Miss Lanna Cheeley too, that day in the drug store. He gave us the same description. Now the only photograph we have of Lanna Cheeley is of her with her eighth grade class eight years ago. There she's petite and pretty in a backwoods sort of way."

"Just like in the store," Alderman Sprinkle avowed. "A sweet little thing she was in her blue print."

"I recognize you, Sprinkle," Harris jumped in. "And I know where to find you in case I have questions. That's true of everyone here today except the little Salvation Army lady, who just happened to come across these items in a crime scene that had already been searched."

"Find what you want, leave what you don't want," I reacted sharply.

Harris got up and jabbed the cane toward me. "That woman there, she's hard to locate. Anyone bother to wonder why?"

A thump sounded from the back corner. Heads twisted toward the sound. William Bertalow had slipped, unconscious, to the floor. The two officers lifted him back into his chair. He started to slide off again until one caught and hoisted him up. That mutt pressed him against the chair back and held him there.

"That poor soul needs a doctor," I assessed. An older man in the last row was already on his way to William, now semi-conscious and staring.

"That's Dr. Hoffman," Swaney murmured. The doctor helped Bertalow stand and supported the weaving prisoner out of the room with the two doughnut boys following. After they left, leaving the door ajar, Harris crashed his cane down on the table. "I don't know where Lanna Cheeley is but I damn well know where she isn't—in that holler. Bertalow just said as much."

"That poor man, he said nothing," I piped up. People were attuned to my every utterance so I didn't have to shout.

Eyes blazing, Harris' gaze fixed upon me.

I pressed the cross to my cardiganned bosom. "Oh, see the policeman's maddened look," I cried. "That man has tortured soul."

Harris spat, "We'll never find Lanna Cheeley. You never know where a Cheeley is. That one or any of the rest of 'em. The teachers say as soon as a Cheeley drops out of school they're gone outta here, but with another one always coming along to take their place."

"Cheeleys never stop coming," Swaney agreed. There was murmuring consent throughout the room. I wanted to dig my elbow into his ribs, but refrained.

"Mr. Harris Lawman blames all town problems on Cheeleys, I think," I said.

Amused bleats from a few lambs passed through the room. I was gaining audible support. I sensed that many of these men might like to hammer the first nail into Harris' coffin, but just didn't have the guts. They'd be willing to see somebody else try, though, and maybe they'd even offer support.

Harris said, "I must speak with the lady. She's come to our country with the wrong ideas. Beings she's a foreigner, we can forgive her for not knowing how our law works. We all know that Salvation Army ladies do a lot of good, but they aren't fit to speak to city affairs like you fellas are." A little flattery for his fellow city leaders.

"You report to the police station at 1:30 tomorrow, Miss Hospador," Harris continued, trying for a smile but settling for a grimace. "We'll get you straightened out then."

I opened my mouth, but closed it when Carl Swaney spoke up. "Miss Plinko goes nowhere without me. She is an intelligent young woman, but she is also a foreigner. I will be there in case she misinterprets." I breathed a sigh of relief. I wondered if Swaney had a personal gripe against the sergeant. A cop who maimed a school-age child, as Bertalow had been, would not exactly endear himself to a school administrator.

Harris spoke through tautened lips. "Young lady, can you not interpret what I am saying?" He thrust his jaw at me.

"Is very tense and angry," I said.

"I will be at any interview," Chief Bobby said, careful and courteous. Out of his jurisdiction, Bobby wasn't rocking any boats. "But today, with everyone present, let's make what progress we can. Dr. Swaney, what did you observe in the holler the day after the fire?"

Harris dug into a breast pocket, withdrew three pills and gulped them down without water.

At the door, the two cops were back, whispering to each other. I couldn't hear their conversation, but it looked as if they recognized me too. This was getting more and more dicey.

Meanwhile Swaney was testifying in a flat tone, as if in the witness box. "I observed the discovery of the tin heart and the blue-flowered material those men said came from Lanna Cheeley's dress." He nodded toward Mason and the alderman.

"Were Miss Plinko and Chief Robert Lagerquist in attendance on that occasion?"

"Yes, Bob, you both were there."

Bobby turned to Harris. "Sergeant, there is a charge that an old lady, Lily Bertalow, died in the fire."

From the second row, a voice whispered, "Shame if it's true. I had a rash on my arm that Lily got rid of after the doc gave up on it." Someone responded, "Lily sure knew cures the doctors didn't."

Bobby had the ability to focus. "Sergeant, do you have any idea of Lily Bertalow's current whereabouts?"

"On her way west like the other low-lifes? How do I know?"

Bobby pointed at the tall officer, Brunanski. "You were at the fire. Describe for us what happened."

Brunanski was taken aback and it took him a moment to collect his thoughts. He said haltingly, "I was in charge of spraying out the embers with a fire extinguisher. I never saw no old lady."

"How about you, Officer Shulz. Anything to report?"

By Brunanski's side, the short, round cop rubbed an eye and fingered his lips before saying, "Sarge was up a rise. Maybe that's who they seen, Sergeant stretching out his arms. I didn't see nothing. I stayed by the main shack to rescue people, but there wasn't none to rescue. Them people ran away after their reckless habits set the fire."

Well rehearsed, Officer Shulz.

Harris interposed. "I was pulling burning boards off a shed, trying to save anybody inside. But there wasn't nobody in there, including no old witches."

"Ask him, please," I interjected softly, "does he have burns from burning boards?"

Harris snarled, "Do you have any burns, Hospador? You talk like you were there. Let's examine your arms to see if you have burns." Cane flung aside, he bolted out of his chair and hurtled around the table to whack at my left sleeve. Instantly I knew he was trying to expose my road-rashed arm to prove I was the driver of the getaway car. I grabbed at his arm but he flung me back against the wall and my netted hat flew off.

"Ow, ow, ow, you're hurting me!" I screamed.

"Get him off her!" Swaney yelled.

I heard chairs squalling and many quick thudding footsteps and men crying, "Let loose! Let her go!" perhaps wary of laying hands on a police officer.

Bobby's voice penetrated. "Harris, what the hell you doing?" He gripped Harris' shoulder and pulled him away.

Harris snatched at my wig. I pressed it down with all my might. There was a glue-separating tear and the left edge slid a bit.

"It's a wig! She's a phony," Harris thundered.

Bobby and his deputy dragged Harris halfway across the room and threw him to the floor.

"Does it feel good to beat up a ninety pound female?" Bobby said as he tried to catch his breath.

"It's a wig!" Harris yelled.

Bobby studied me and said, "So what if it is a wig?"

"Oh, I am so embarrassed," I said, recovering my Rumanian accent. I nudged the hairpiece back into its scabby slots and explained in a trembling voice, "I wear wig because when as a young child hot lard from frypan spilled on my head. Top of head is scarred and bald, for hair never returned to grow there."

"Oh, you poor dear," Swaney said, taking my face in his soft hands. I gave a few sobs into his jacket and quieted. I retrieved my hat and set it back on, letting the net dangle. Deep inside me, I was furious.

Near me, Officer Brunanski said to his sidekick, "Don't she look like her though?"

The round one stepped forward and peered closely at me. "Nah," he said, "that other one had hair on top of her head."

Harris gimped around the table to the leather armchair and collapsed in it with an extended groan. He smoothed his shirt cuffs and attempted to dignify himself. "Don't worry about me. I'm fine," he said sarcastically. "Defending this town ain't as easy as it looks."

Bobby addressed his deputy, "Kenny, go get the Plinkos down here to verify this lady's identity." Unfortunately, Bobby could focus.

The deputy left to perform his assignment. The councilmen resumed their seats and talked among themselves. I went to the restroom after asking Swaney to wait for me right outside. In front of the mirror, I worked a sprig of my own dirty-yellow hair back under the wig. I despaired of my chances when Miki Plinko was brought in to identify me. His fear of cops, along with Lisa's recent foray to the Plinko home—why would he even want his daughter back? Should I run for the double-door exit now?

The wig looked frazzled and unfixable after this latest incursion. Its purpose had to end. If good lady Hospador survived the next encounter, she had to depart for her native land, and soon.

# 24

When the Plinkos entered the courtroom with Chief Bobby's deputy, Harris planted his chair sideways and gave me a triumphant gloat.

But I saw only my dear relatives. I rushed over and snatched Ada Opal's hand. "Cousins, so glad you are here."

I cupped Miki's jaw in my other hand and stood on tiptoe as if to plant a kiss on my dear cousin's cheek. "Go along with me, bub," I whispered in his ear.

Both Plinkos reacted with stone faces to my affectionate greeting. Nonetheless, I remained close by as Miki made polite inquiries about the health of most everyone there except the subject of the summons. His familiar manner with the group caused me to doubt whether I would survive this.

Ada Opal gave an initial perfunctory nod to the center of the room. This shrewd woman had of course recognized my voice at their home last night. They both knew I had been with the raiding party, so it followed that I knew about the money hidden from the tax collector. That was my leverage. Without alerting Swaney, Harris, or Bobby, I needed to make the Plinkos aware of the penalty for exposing me.

After Bobby brought the meeting to order with a handclap and "Let's get to it," Miki allowed me a furtive glance. I said, "Ah, Cousin, all the important townspeoples are here to meet me. So nice, not like our country, *n'est-ce pas?*" I felt that the French expression granted me an authentic overseas flavor. "So different from Rumania," I hastened on, "where we will be frightened to have powerful men staring at us as though we had not paid our taxes. Horrible, horrible our homeland's follow-up to such an accusation." I looked Miki in the eye. In response, his lip curled slightly.

"Enough of amenities," Bobby said. "Mr. Plinko, can you identify this lady?"

The grimness of Miki's expression, his harsh mouth and condemning stare, told me the jig was up. I slid my hand under the back of my sweater for the .25.

Facing me, Miki stammered, "You c-c-can't expect …" before Ada Opal grasped his arm and said in her sweet southern drawl, "Dear Cousin Plinko, you are correct. There is none of that cruelty on these shores. Both of us are thankful for that, aren't we, darlin'?" She blinked charmingly at Miki.

Miki's eyes widened and his mouth fell open. He mumbled to the floor, "This is my Rumanian cousin. She hails from Rumania." With his arm caught in Ada Opal's vise-like grip, he leaned to me and, mostly hitting netting, pecked at each of my cheeks.

"That's it then," Bobby said brusquely, glancing at Harris, who was sitting, fists clenched on the chair arms, glowering at me. If looks could kill.

## 25

After Carl Swaney and I were ensconced in a booth at Jake's Best Burgers, he watched me swig strong coffee and said in awe, "You challenged Sergeant Harris. Incredible."

I took a large bite of apple fritter, wiped my fingers on a napkin, and didn't answer until all had gone down the hatch. Then I said, "Rumanians are people of courage." I poured another coffee and drank heartily. "But," I confessed, "at home, so bold I would not dare."

"Is it so terrible there, Hospador? Miki said there were terrible shortages during and after the war."

"Ah, you have spoken about our homeland to my cousin."

"Yes." His voice hardened. "There's something callous and uncaring about Miki. Have you found that? But you wouldn't, you're so sweet. He has a bad relationship with his daughter. That's all I really know about him."

"Yes-s. I am sad when he speaks of Lisa. Miki has been through much difficulties in his life. He is, I suppose, made callous."

"Nothing should harden a heart to that extent," Swaney averred. "Especially against his own daughter." He stuffed a hunk of cinnamon roll into his mouth and chewed. "I've been reading up on your country. Fascinating," he said after swallowing.

I laid down my fritter. "Yes-s, but when I am in your country I do not want to think about mine. In your family are there brothers and sisters?"

"One brother. Older."

"And he is also educator?"

"Not a chance." He flapped a hand dismissively. "He went into banking. He's rich. I'm considered the failure in my family."

"But you have much education," I said.

"They'd rather I make a lot of money. Sometimes so would I. I'm kidding. Sort of." He crumpled his napkin, pushed it away, smiled forlornly, and got back to pinning me down. "Your country is in a very perilous location, isn't it? Surrounded by predators."

I nodded grimly. Why had I not spent one hour researching in the library, instead of just rushing through to reach getaway transportation?

"With the Soviet Union right on your border," he egged on.

"Exactly. We live in Transylvania," I said, rallying. After all, I had seen two Bela Lugosi movies. "As Sergeant Harris said, it is where vampires roam."

"You don't really believe vampires exist, do you? They're just legends, after all."

I responded haughtily. "I survived a vampire raid on our town." I picked at a fingernail. "Maybe just big bats."

He snickered. "What town are you from?"

"Very tiny town," I said. "Impossible to understand name in this American which contains many vowels."

"How is the name 'Hospador' pronounced? I mean, in your country?"

I spat out something that I hoped sounded plausible.

"Oh boy." He shook his head. "This is really strange. I don't quite see—your language has a Latinate base, so how did your town mutate to mainly consonants?"

I would have liked to say "the Mongol Hordes," an answer that had served me well in grade school, but instead I admitted ignorance. "Many facts I do not know about my homeland for I have little education. But with all my soul I would die for Rumania flag." I hummed a tuneless, rather jumpy phrase. "National anthem," I identified.

A spate of questions followed. "Have you siblings? Are your parents living? What does your father do?"

"Alas," I said, "Dadda is dead. Mama expired of the bite. I have five brothers and two sisters. All traveling musicians," I said, recalling Ada Opal's tale of Miki's childhood.

"Music runs in your family," Swaney responded. "Your cousin is a wonderful player. I've heard him in recital, and once visited their home out of concern for Lisa. Miki leaves everything domestic for his wife to take care of: family, finances, anything that might distract him from his work. Excuse me for saying so, but he is an arrogant man."

"Oh my, so sad, but of dear blood to me," I demurred, taken back by the vehemence in Swaney's voice. Still, the man was a devoted educator. Witnessing one of his students treated badly really ticked him off.

He pursed his lips. "Hospador, you said you had little education. I'd like to offer you a few tutoring sessions at no charge in whatever subjects you like."

Tutoring, along with some wooing sessions. This guy wanted some sack time with me. "You offer the etchings too?"

"What?"

"Am told Americans entice the maiden into their bedroom with etchings."

He guffawed. "I bet you don't even know what etchings are."

"Like pastries?" I thought it wise to change subjects. "Have you worked in Cassville for long?" Swaney looked slightly put off by my clever response to his offer.

"The last four years as principal." Smiling, he forgave me. "Before that, ten years in the classroom, teaching geography." Yes, of course, he knew Rumanian topography. I was in over my head. Race you to the library if I make it through this.

"How did you get interested in Salvation Army work?" he asked, relentless in his pursuit of every detail. "I would have guessed your family to be Greek Orthodox."

That was news to me. We had to be Methodist or Baptist or something evangelical, didn't we, for the Salvation Army to enlist me? "My parents are—were—" I stumbled on, "devout Christians to helping all mankind, and including people like that poor young man in handcuffs. Mr. Harris is evil, my bones tell me." I shuddered for effect. "It is of no use to talk to him, but maybe that nice Mr. Bobby could help? What is this William Bertalow charged with? Or was he arrested only to confirm certain policeman stories?"

"Bertalow verified Harris' story that he saw no one die in the fire," Swaney said. "Granted, he was forced into it, but Harris got what he wanted, so perhaps now they'll release him. I'll talk to Chief Bob. You are truly the champion of the down-trodden."

"My job," I said modestly. "But for now I am very tired." My voice broke unintentionally. "Please excuse. I must go and rest so I may serve evening meal to the poor up north." I slid out of the booth. Rising with me, Swaney placed a hand on the small of my back. When he withdrew the hand hastily, I knew he had touched the .25's hardness.

The best I could do was, "Cross back there too. Cross in front, cross in back. I am surrounded by God."

"You're very well fixed," he said nervously. I imagined the thought passing through his mind: from a violent country, this poor thing has to go armed. As he studied me, I saw shock in his expression, and also a bit of a thrill.

## 26

Swaney walked me to the library and I left him there. On the drive to Watkins, after darting quick looks back to check I was not followed by Harris and his goons, I pulled onto a side road and changed to Wendy Winkworth attire. In Watkins, I parked on the main drag and picked up the laundry.

With the fresh clothes bundled neatly in the Pontiac's back seat, I decided to complete my transition into brash, grotesque, croaky-voiced Wanda. Innocent, unimpeachable Hospador had served her purpose.

The evening had turned cloudy. People were sauntering in and out of shops, chattering gaily. There was a line in front of a movie theater.

Watkins stores stayed open until 9:00 on Thursdays, so, in the five-and-dime, I found materials for disguise, among them a beauty mark, also known as a black mole. I also bought a pair of lifts. Placed in my shoes they'd raise me about an inch. Back in the car, I took a maroon felt pen from the sack, and drew a tiny, erratic "w" to the left of my lips. If anyone asked, I'd say that my superstitious parents had named me "Wanda" after taking that birthmark as a sign. Deploying black watercolor and spit, I darkened the area above my lips to suggest the vague beginnings of facial hair. I applied ruddy-hued rouge to my cheeks, then put all containers in the sack and dropped it on the floorboard in back. I kind of liked the ugly me that stared from the rear-view mirror.

Three blocks from the dime store, the Army Surplus Store was a nondescript brick building with a rusted horse trough in front. Behind a carpet hanging from a clothesline in the back of the store, I tried on a blousy tan shirt and a flight jacket, its shoulders broad with padding, and airman trousers that zipped up the front. I attached a fabric pouch to the belt for my penlight, a screwdriver, and other paraphernalia. My holstered .25 remained behind a hip. I buckled on a military wristwatch. Brass rings fit the middle fingers of my right hand. I tried on tinted aviator glasses that were more serious than the round sunglasses Wanda had worn while chauffeuring Rolf. I stepped into air force flight boots. A bit loose, but warm with the wool lining. I'd add the lifts to raise me up.

I slipped on thin black leather gloves that were more flexible than the brown workman's type I'd worn as Hospador. There was no mirror in the store, it was an army surplus store after all, so I used my pocket mirror. Brown, brown, and more brown. Looking good.

I also brought a Navy flashlight to the checkout counter, along with a military rain poncho with hood and drawstring, and a white silk scarf, a fashion accessory I'd always envied because it made the wearer a dashing hero even before he saw air combat.

After paying, and it cost a hunk, I viewed my total reflection in the front window. I looked like a long-legged, fierce armor-plated mammal with a tiny top. On my way out the clerk, a narrow man in a sweat-marked Navy cap, asked me for a date.

## 27

A light rain was falling when I got back to the trailer. The weather had cooled and the sky was gloomy and dark. A faint moon glimmered behind passing clouds. I parked the car in the usual spot behind the broken-down Chevy that Charles intended to fix.

Chuck was sitting on the trailer steps.

Approaching him, I said. "It's getting too wet for you with that arm."

"Charles and Lisa are inside. You can't go in. They're busy."

Oh, great. I dropped the laundry bundle and a pack of Cokes, sidled past the kid and shoved open the door. Lisa and Charles were on her couch, in flagrante delicto. At the sound of the door, Charles twisted around and fell backward to the floor. "What the fuck?" he said, scrambling to cover himself.

Lisa lunged for her puppy-dog blanket.

"What do you think you're doing?" Charles said, kind of falsetto. His prick peeked out between his hands.

"Entering my home," I said. Three candles flickered from the floor-dwelling tabletop and the room reeked of Orange Spice. The lovers had set the mood.

Lisa tried wiggling into her nightgown as quickly as possible but it was tangled and stuck on her head and arms, exposing her. In the doorway, Chuck gaped. "I never seen Lisa naked before."

"Shit," Charles said to his brother, "Didn't you tell her we were busy?" He scrambled to conceal his shapely buns in shapeless briefs.

Some of Lisa's lipstick was on his face. "You got no right, Wenda," he whined.

"Some nerve," Lisa squeaked.

"Nerve?" I said. "You're the one who already has a boyfriend. And you're the one who's going to get p.g."

"So? We want a family."

Charles hitched up his trousers. His hairless chest was glowing with sweat. "News to me," he said. He retrieved his red-checkered jacket from the floor.

"Honey, we'll have the money to start over someplace else," Lisa said. So the plan was still on: steal the family money, start a family, every girl's dream.

Charles shrugged. "I don't know. I'm having a good time right now. Good enough for me."

Chuck had taken out his silver lighter and was flicking it on and off nervously. "Are you going away with Lisa?" he asked.

Hair smoothed, pants buttoned, Charles ran his hands down his legs. "Lisa honey, we're just having fun. We can have all the fun you want, but I don't do the permanent stuff."

The girl's voice broke. "I wouldn't have done it if I didn't love you."

"Like you love Rolf?" Charles snickered. "Chick, you're just hot to trot."

Chuck caressed his top trouser button. "Hey, Lisa, can I be next?"

"Shut up," Charles growled.

Lisa sniveled, fat tears rolling down her cheeks. "Rolf and I never went all the way. I only did with you because I saw the way you took care of Betty and I know you'll make a wonderful father."

"Agh." Charles turned away in disgust.

"Fine." Lisa crossed her arms over her chest. "I'll get that money myself and go live in a hotel in Chicago with all the services. I don't need you. I don't need anybody. I'll be rich and you'll be begging in the streets, you just watch."

Charles adjusted his crotch. The money girl was talking about leaving. "Come on, honey," he wheedled, "I'm sorry. Guess I wasn't thinking. You're real special to me too. I love you, too."

Chuck said, "I'd like a piece of that love myself."

"Shut up!" Charles and Lisa shouted in unison. He extended a hand to her. She knocked it away.

"Liar! I can't stand you. I'm going home." She said to me, "They'll take me back, won't they?"

I nodded. "Sure they will. Absolutely."

"Whew, don't get a woman sore," Charles said. "Come on, honey, let's have a Coke. You bring Coke, Wenda?"

"Outside getting rained on."

He gestured at Chuck. "Go get the Cokes."

"Bring in the bag of clothes too," I said.

Chuck went out, while Charles kept trying: "Honey, don't pout. I'm sorry it ended this way with Wenda breaking in on us. Why don't you apologize, Wenda, so we can all be friends again."

"I'm not in the mood," I said.

Lisa stood stock still as Charles squeezed her fingers and leaned in and nuzzled her cheek. He whispered, "You had a good time, didn't ya, hon? I sure did. You were a real good screw."

Lisa shoved him. She retrieved her blanket off the floor. "Hold this up," she said, handing it to me. "I'm getting dressed."

Chuck slipped back in and closed the door behind him. He took a Coke and dropped off the rest.

Lisa went to the water pail by the stove. I shielded her as she cleaned up.

"You even look good behind a blanket," Charles encouraged. In her undies, she brushed past the shielding blanket and moved toward the wall spikes where she removed gray trousers and a paisley-print blouse. Her fingers shook fussing with the tiny pearl buttons. She stepped into calfskin flats that lay beside the coital couch. Removing the mirror and brush from her snap purse, she raked through her locks, dropped the brush on the couch and smeared on lipstick.

Finally realizing how through with him she was, Charles lost his intensity and posed mutely.

I folded the blanket and laid it on the couch. "You want a ride into town?" I asked. A negative shake made me wonder if she was really going anywhere or just tweaking Charles, hoping for a kinder, gentler, boyfriend. She wrenched her body into her wool coat, tied on a scarf, grasped her purse, and announced, "I'm taking a walk." She stormed out, slamming the door.

In the sudden stillness, Charles said, "She'll be back. She's just upset."

Chuck inquired timidly, "Was it me?"

"Naw. Girls get upset easy." Charles glanced at me as an afterthought.

I went after Lisa to comfort her. Right then, I could think of nothing better to say than how stupid she was to have sex with a loser. I assumed something a little more sympathetic would make it out of my mouth.

She'd disappeared quickly. At the bottom of the steps, rain drenching my sleeves, I called her name. No answer. The road curved; if she'd run in the direction of the gates, she'd have been out of sight quickly. But I turned right, toward the pond where there was less junk and more foliage, although it was becoming skeletal this time of year. Still, it was the garden spot of the dump. A discarded couch sat near the pond. It would be soaked through by now, but still a possibility for the substantially garbed girl. I broke into a trot with wet wind curling noisily around my ears.

Approaching the site, I saw she wasn't there. Hesitating, I looked around. There were so many cubbyholes she could have poured herself into, including any of the dozens of wrecked cars. I pictured her sitting somewhere, arms around her knees, weeping unbearably, rejected by her latest man. After calling several times more, I trudged back to the trailer and hefted the soggy laundry bundle on the way in.

The boys were huddled together in the corner. There was something conspiratorial in the way they averted their eyes to my arrival. Had I been the subject of a discussion—she's a bother, what do we need her for? She's not one of us; we can get along without her.

I pointed to the laundry bag. "You should let this dry out."

Nothing accomplished by hanging around where I wasn't wanted. I left the trailer again, going the opposite direction. A protected kid like Lisa would tire of being out in the frigid slop and return soon enough. Oh, don't sell her short, Lisa's a well-built, tough Susie. On the basketball court she'd won against those rugged Methodists.

I decided to search a little longer, wanting to catch her alone without having to contend with the two Cheeleys. "Lisa, come on back," I yelled. "We have Cokes and sweet rolls waiting for you." Suppressing a shiver of apprehension, I jogged back to the trailer.

The boys had found pastries. "What if Lisa woulda wanted some of that?" I asked.

Mouth full, Charles pointed to a lone sweet roll. "One left."

I strode to my couch and stuck a cigarette in my mouth. Since Chuck was too busy chewing to do the honors, I lit up with a match. In all the turmoil, neither boy had mentioned my change of appearance into tough gal Wanda.

I studied them openly; they returned the attention covertly. They'd probably made up their minds to lose me. I stopped the cigarette on the way to my lips because another thought occurred: that Lisa might be on her way to tell Rolf—what—that Charles had overpowered her and forced her to submit? Hoping to stir ardent fires within the German's breast? The result: a confrontation between a Kraut who knew guns and an explosive delinquent who walked the road each day packing two firearms.

Not saying goodbye, I left the trailer and hurried in the rain to the Pontiac.

# 28

Bumping over trash, headlights jumping, I sped out of the dump. On each side of the road, shapes moved in and out of my beams. None morphed into a large girl needing a ride. The iron gates, slightly ajar, indicated she had passed through. I shoved them wider for the Pontiac. At the highway, I hung a left.

It was 21:30 hours according to my new military watch. When I had the chance, I'd calculate normal people's time.

Eventually the rain stopped, leaving the road slick. I steamed past what little traffic there was. The headlights of oncoming cars glared against the wet asphalt.

Past Watkins, at the junction, I turned left and headed for Cassville. Two miles further, I heard a sharp bang and the right rear side of the Pontiac sank slowly. Damn. Flat tire. I pulled off the road beside a field of soybeans. I didn't know who had left what in the dump road but I had hit it. This isolated spot was lit by a quarter-moon, the only sound the hum of electric wires above.

Nothing to do but get the jack, hoist the rear end, slip on the spare tire, wipe hands on trousers, breathe deeply and stretch to get the kinks out. I was almost ready to go. The rain started up again, not heavy, but a constant drizzle. I heard a car approaching; the uneven chugging of its motor sounded familiar. Not wanting to take any chances in the dead of night, I crouched down by the hood of the car as the old Ford chugged on by, Charles silhouetted at the wheel with Chuck beside him, both boys staring straight ahead. The Ford vanished into the night. Surely my supposed pals had recognized the Pontiac. I shrugged and returned to tightening the lug nuts with a wrench.

On the outskirts of Cassville, I stopped at a closed gas station to fill the spare tire. Although quite old, it was holding up. In the city, I slowed to the speed limit. Nearing the Plinko neighborhood, I slowed further, to a crawl, and scanned the area. Would Lisa really have gotten this far? With luck, yes. Standing beside the road with her thumb out, she'd be picked up with no problem because she didn't look dangerous.

In my bones, I felt Lisa wanted revenge on Charles for his caddish behavior and wanted Rolf to inflict it.

Up a curved drive, past large quiet homes, and I was at the Plinko compound. Lights in the home burned brightly upstairs and down. At the far end of the block, Rolf Nitschke stood under a streetlight, violin case under an arm. Hunched against the rain, he was wearing a substantial jacket and a cap with lowered earflaps.

I drew up beside him. He jerked toward me, then halted. I leaned over and rolled down the passenger window. "Do you need a ride?"

"No, thank you, I'm waiting for someone," he said. I turned off the motor, got out and walked around the side of the car. The steady tapping of rain held a fresh fragrance. Although it was at least 10:00 p.m., violins still sounded from the cabins. Another melodious Plinko evening. I released a breath. I had arrived in time.

"Lousy night," I noted. "Get in. You can wait in the car." He closed distance. His nose bore a gash from last night's battle.

"Lisa will be along, I'm sure," I prompted.

"Ya. She and I have spoken," he said.

Peripherally, I saw the Plinko home's exterior light came on. The front door burst open and Ada Opal stumbled onto the landing. Her one long scream split the air. The terror was stunning, as though lightning had zapped me. Instantly Rolf was striding up the lawn, violin case jiggling by his side. I drew my .25 and ran after. Ada Opal screamed again, a multi-syllabic, "He-l-p."

The violin music stopped, leaving only our pounding steps and Rolf's whistling breaths as I raced past him. Peripherally I saw a male student plodding from the cabins, violin tucked under his chin.

"What's the matter?" I yelled. I held the .25 against my thigh.

Ada Opal descended the steps. To my left, rain sprinkled the oncoming student and he pulled up his T-shirt and stuck the violin under it.

Reaching Ada Opal, I panted, "What's wrong?"

Her eyes held a stunned look, her lips a colorless line. "My husband—I think he's been shot. Someone might still be in there." She broke into ragged sobs.

"Who shot him?"

"I don't know." It was an outraged shriek.

"Where is Miki?"

She pointed upward, toward the sky. Knowing Miki's nature, that probably meant second floor, not higher.

"In his studio," she clarified.

Charging by me, Rolf took the front steps in one leap and plunged into the house.

"Wait!" I commanded. Swinging my pistol in arcs, I raced after him. The well-lit living room appeared normal. I lowered the .25 and tried to bring the weeping woman inside, but she resisted, batting at me and saying, "No, I can't see him like that again."

"You've got to point me the right direction," I insisted. She stepped in cautiously.

The male student, who looked to be in his early twenties, poked his bony neck into the room. The skeletal image of his violin and its strings showed through his sodden T-shirt. The pointy end of his bow stuck out the neck hole. He averted his chin to avoid being poked.

Ada Opal wailed, "My Miki is lying badly hurt in his studio." With that Rolf leapt onto the curving staircase.

"Stop!" I ordered. Rushing forward, I pushed the boy into the banister. His long arm reached down, snapped the violin case open and a short rifle dropped into his hand. The case tumbled past me down the steps and I jumped back to avoid it. Rolf's manic eyes darted as he swung the weapon back and forth. When it came my way, I knocked the barrel sideways, slammed my fist down and sent the weapon to the stairs. A quick skirmish and I was in possession of both the rifle and my .25. I leveled the guns at him. His hands shot high and he backed up two steps.

"Keep backing until you reach the top," I directed, "and then get down on your knees." Part of my attention was diverted to the dim hall on second floor.

Complying, he said, "I was protecting you."

"Do I look like I need help?" I'd finally seen everything, a real violinist packing heat. On first floor, Ada Opal grasped the stair railing for support. "Rolfie, a gun? Why?" she breathed. Receiving no reply, she cried, "Help us, Wendy, please." I wasn't surprised at the name, I'd done my best at disguising, but I still had a lot of "Wendy" in me.

"Where's Miki's studio?" I asked her.

"First door to the right."

"No sudden moves, kid," I snarled at Rolf. He had backed off and was pinning me in a deadeye stare.

The light from that first room cast a narrow beam into the hall. With the rifle under my left arm and holding the .25, I edged sideways along the wall. I feared an assailant waited beyond that slightly opened door. Snatching a porcelain ballerina statuette from a small table, I tossed it into the room.

No sound or movement in response to the tiny crash. I backtracked and switched on the wall light. Hugging the door frame, I entered the room fast. The window was wide open and rain spattered past the blowing curtains. The spacious studio contained metal music stands, a roll-top desk, autographed pictures of violinists on one wall. Most importantly, it contained Miki Plinko sprawled on his back on a Turkish carpet, arms and legs splayed out weirdly in death. Blood trickled from a bullet hole in his forehead. The back of his head had splatted out with blood and brains. Powder burns indicated he had been shot at close range. There was a sprinkling of blood on his white shirt. Blood pooled under his left leg, near an odd-looking 9mm pistol that perhaps had been dropped by the killer. Had Miki also been shot in the leg or was that the killer's blood?

The ballet statuette lay in pieces by a slightly ajar closet door. I kicked the door wide open and looked in. A smoking jacket on a hanger. A gun rack, two spaces filled, a third empty. I stuck my .25 in its holster and wielded the rifle.

Moving toward the hallway, I saw Ada Opal backed up against the wall. I went to her and saved a glare for Rolf and the other student who were standing at the top of the steps. "All of you get in here," I ordered, swinging the rifle toward the murder room. I needed to keep them all in sight.

Ada Opal protested, "No, no, I cannot enter," as Rolf proceeded methodically toward me.

The skinny student brushed past him; he entered the room before the other two. I seized his arm. "No farther," I warned. Both males halted just inside the door. "Don't touch anything. Leave it for the police," I directed. I had assumed that Rolf had been armed to go after Charles, but now it occurred to me that he might actually have done this.

"Where'd you get the gun, Rolf," I asked, "or does it just come with being a Kraut?"

A grim smile. "Born with it."

Ada Opal edged forward. Glimpsing the body, she gasped, turned away and spotted the broken figurine. "Oh, not my Limoges," she wailed, pressing her face into the skinny student's wet T-shirt. With the contact, the violin under his shirt twanged soggily. "Oh, Ned," she wailed.

"Shouldn't we cover him up?" Ned asked me shakily.

"Not yet," I said. "Stand clear now."

I took a pencil from a box on the desk, passed it through the trigger guard and picked up the 9mm pistol. I sniffed. A spent ammunition smell. I returned it to the floor. Hopefully fingerprints would tell the tale.

I walked the room and came upon a small safe secreted behind the roll-top. It was open. A quick check verified it was empty.

I asked the widow what the safe had contained. If Lisa was correct, I already knew.

"Money," she confirmed.

"How much?"

She clutched Ned's hand. "I don't know. Miki kept the books." Really? Miki had told Carl Swaney that his wife was the financial engineer.

I asked her what she had seen and heard earlier that night.

Her response was pressed through chokes and sobs that threatened to erupt into hysteria. "Miki and I were reading in the parlor. At some point, he got up and left, I don't know when, I was absorbed in my book. Then, I don't know how long afterward, I—I heard what I thought was a backfire from Ned's DeSoto so I kept on reading. But then there were bumping noises as though something or someone had fallen upstairs. I thought Miki had tripped, so I went to the stairs and called up, was he all right? There was another sharp bang, clearly from upstairs. I knew it wasn't outside. We have valuable art and instruments and we're always concerned about thieves. That's why Miki keeps guns."

I nodded.

"I didn't want to climb those steps," she continued, "but no one else came to help. Where were you, Rolf? You should have been here." She had addressed the young German querulously and didn't wait for an answer. "Oh, Rolfie, this is so horrible! Why do you have our gun?" She reached toward the champion fiddler but when he recoiled, she turned the opposite way into Ned's arms and he comforted her. In his embrace, she softened and wept.

I asked Rolf if he had heard the shots.

"I was outdoors. You saw me. I heard some pops. Fireworks, I thought." He shrugged.

I kept at Ada Opal. "After that second shot, no one could have come past you down the steps because you were right there. Correct?"

She stood away from Ned and gained some control. "Yes," she said.

"Any other stairway?"

"The other end of the hall. It leads to the kitchen."

The curtain was flapping and mist beaded the windowsill. The wall clock, ticking loudly, said 11:36.

I spoke to Rolf. "What were you doing with the gun?"

He shook his head. "Nothing."

"Aw, come on. The police are going to want to know the same thing."

There was a tiny clatter. Ned's bow had slipped from under his T-shirt and tinked onto the floor. He made no attempt to retrieve it, just kept gaping at his dead mentor.

"You've dropped your bow," Ada Opal said in a matter-of-fact tone. First the demise of her statuette, now a fallen bow. In Ada Opal's universe, works of art broke through shock and demanded a clear head.

I quizzed the three of them: "How do you think a stranger got into the house? Are doors left unlocked?" Lisa had a key and Rolf lived in the house. My sliver of suspicion grew to a large jagged splinter: of the smitten German youth and the girl who hated her dad. "We'll have money to start over," she'd told Charles. When I recalled the Cheeleys flying past me on the road to Cassville, the suspect list grew longer still.

Ned answered my question. "The front door is unlocked until 10:00 p.m. so we can come in and get snacks."

Rushing through, I had noticed the bowl of treats in the living room. Now, consumed with deduction, I let the rifle sag. In that careless instant, Rolf lunged and grabbed it. He swung the stock up and whacked my right arm. Grunting with pain, I stumbled.

"Stay back or I will kill you," he said.

Ada Opal underscored his words with a short shriek.

"Ada Opal, you know I did not do this," Rolf said, "but Wendy is not so sure." He addressed me. "You asked who I waited for. My Lisa. My dove. That Cheeley bastard fucked my dove and I want her back."

Ada Opal's eyes widened. "Lisa? No longer a virgin? Shut up. Please shut up!"

Gun pointed at my belly, Rolf continued level-voiced. "Teacher, my violin, my bow, my rosin rest on my dresser. Look after them until I return. Wendy, drop your small caliber pistol onto the floor carefully. If you shoot me, it will not do much damage, but before I go down I will blow a large hole in you."

With thumb and index finger I slowly brought out the .25 and laid it on the floor.

"The pistol on the floor is Italian," he said. "It's a Tanfoglio. Mr. Miki kept it in that open drawer. This short rifle is also from his collection."

"Rolf," I said, "stay and help your teacher. She is very sad."

"I am sad too," he said. He leapt over Ned's fallen bow, ran from the room, and hurtled down the steps. I retrieved my little toy, also avoided the bow, and raced to the landing. Reaching the first floor, the German whirled toward me. I dove flat. He fired. The shot splintered the railing. He was out the front door before I could get a bead. I rushed after and caught a glimpse of him running toward the woods. Going for his bike, I'd have bet.

I returned to Ada Opal, who was kneeling beside her slain mate. "It's all gone, my dearest," she spoke brokenly to the dead man. Tears flowed down her cheeks and dripped off her chin, uniting with the blood sprinkles on his shirt.

"Get up, Ada Opal," I said gently and helped her rise. "You mustn't spoil the crime scene." Whimpering, she collapsed against me. I disengaged myself, went to the window and looked out. The rain beat down steadily. A large elm tree loomed, its stout branches near enough to the window that an athletic person could catch hold of a branch and, risking a good scraping, slide down the trunk to the ground. Beyond the tree, the side yard appeared empty.

"Where's the phone? You gotta call the police," I said to Ned. With no response forthcoming, I repeated, "Where is the phone?"

"Living room," he gulped.

Not wanting to make the call myself, I said, "Go downstairs and call the police." I nudged his leg with my toe. "Rolf's run off. He's blocks away by now. You're in no danger, so go!"

Ned moved as though in a stupor.

"Pick up your bow and take it with you," I said. "Put it and your violin on the sofa. They'll dry out there. Understand?" Ned took the bow by the wood part and walked stiffly into the hall. We barely heard him tiptoe down the steps.

"Come on, let's go downstairs too," I said to Ada Opal. She let me guide her tottery form down the steps. Near the picture window, Ned was standing by a small table babbling into a phone. "Stay with Ned," I ordered the widow. "Stay right here beside him." I helped her onto the sofa next to Ned's instruments. After he hung up, I said, "Keep her here, Ned, until the cops come."

I wanted out. Hang around to compare notes with the Cassville police? I thought not.

I stepped into the rain and scrutinized the area before ducking around the house to the big elm that fronted Miki's studio window. Flashing my penlight at the base of the trunk, I spotted a plug tobacco tin sunk in mud. Slipped from someone's pocket, I figured, in the slide down the tree. Faded and scratched, it was labelled "Bulwark" and bore a drawing of a sailor looking through a spyglass. I left it there, pelted by rain.

I shot my light up into the dark, thick branches. A crow let me know he desired privacy.

Flicking off the light, stepping into shadows, I got the feeling I'd missed something. It came to me with sickening realization. I hadn't seen my car under the streetlight. I hurried toward the street and verified that the Pontiac was gone. Evidently Rolf had stopped running, doubled back and discovered the key in the ignition where I'd left it. Perhaps Lisa, cradling a wad of cash, had joined him and was currently pressed against him as they sped off to a new life.

Scooting up the rise past the house, I ran through a thick stand of pines to the garage. Its double doors were padlocked. To my left, a slight noise and I looked to see a small, thin female student standing in a cabin door framed by indoor light. I flattened myself against the wall of the garage.

The girl remained there for a few seconds before going inside and closing the door. Two violins in the next cabin were playing a duet. I guessed group opinion had left it to Ned to check out the disruption.

A small window on the cabin side of the garage afforded an opportunity for entry. I crouched under it and waited until the duet played a particularly passionate crescendo before whacking the pistol butt against the glass. The pane shattered and I ran my gloved hands along the jagged edges, brushing off the shards until it seemed okay to hoist myself through.

Dropping to the concrete garage floor, I shielded the penlight and identified the Plymouth Roadking near me and a Cadillac next to it. The Coup De Ville was too noticeable; I hot-wired the Roadking. Headlights off, engine rumbling, I stomped down on the accelerator. Upon contact with the thick doors there was a terrible, grinding, bullying sound before the doors conceded. I crashed the Roadking through, zipped down the driveway and screeched a left turn. I switched on the headlights, only one of which still worked, and headed for the trailer. I figured one or both of the avengers would go after Charles and expect to find him at home.

# 29

Either Rolf was a terrible marksman or he'd only wanted to scare me. If the last, it hadn't worked. A little ways inside the dump, I saw my Pontiac parked in the road. I turned off the headlight, pulled up and left the Plymouth's motor idling. I exited and approached stealthily. No one was inside the Pontiac. I took the keys from the ignition and the Navy flashlight and handcuffs from the glove compartment. A half-eaten licorice twist lay on the passenger seat. I covered my very wet Air Force jacket with the rain poncho, slipped the hood over my head and pulled the drawstring tight at my neck. There were puddles everywhere in the road. I headed for the trailer, progressing slowly over the uneven surface.

It was a starless night. The moon appeared occasionally through the clouds, although it seemed more clouds were coming in. Shortly I passed Chuck's large appliance sector. It held only a stove and a prone icebox, both originally discarded in that spot. I was close enough to see the dim outline of junkers and the dark trailer. I knew its residents were skilled at moving around in the confined space even in pitch black.

On all sides, the wind rustled foliage as, with quick glances left and right, I crept into Chuck's tin can sector. A movement across the road drew my attention. My breath caught. On the far side of the junked cars, a figure, surely Rolf, appeared from the depths of darkness.

I dropped to my knees and squatted with hands flat on the ground. A tin can sharp against my left thumb caused immediate adjustment. The moon came from behind a cloud and held the gangly youth in its glow. Skulking forward, kicking trash aside, he bore the rifle like a storm trooper. All that was missing was a bear's angry chuff.

During each of Rolf's noisy swipes I crawled forward the final yards to the trailer. There I crouched, shivering against the cold metal. Rain seeping through the poncho (thought those things were watertight) made the aviator jacket damp and heavy. I stifled a sneeze. Rolf had stopped just across the road. A lightning flash cast him and the litter around him into sharp relief. Abruptly the rain increased from a patter to a torrent. Thunder cracked. The boy hoisted the rifle above his head and tore across the road. When he reached the trailer steps, I charged. It must have been terrifying, a black creature flying at him, the poncho flapping like bat's wings. He uttered a guttural cry and skidded backward. Feet sliding under him, he fell into the mud. The rifle loosened in his grip and I kicked it away. Dropping to my knees, I bunched his collar in my left fist and aimed the .25 at his belly. I growled into his startled eyes, "On your feet, prisoner." Cowering, he crawled into a standing position.

"Hands behind you," I ordered. He complied and I snapped the cuffs around his icy wrists.

I retrieved his gun and secured its leather strap over my shoulder. "Up those steps, mister. Be quiet about it." I was whispering even though no sound had come from inside the trailer. Maybe the boys weren't back, or maybe they were waiting to blast us to smithereens.

Rolf whispered, "I only want my little dove back."

"Shut up about your damn little dove."

I hopped up the steps past him. Holding the rifle to his chin—he did not flinch, rather he seemed stunned—I pounded on the door. "Cheeleys, I'm back," I yelled. "We got company." Nothing. I turned the knob, shouldered the door open and shoved the boy in ahead of me.

I shone the Navy flash around. The room was empty. I mean it was really empty. In addition to no Cheeleys, there were no sleeping bags and no clothes strewn all over. I checked the cupboards where pots, pans and bowls were rarely stacked. The plastic glasses should have been there too, when they weren't tipped over on the floor. Everything was gone, including the cribbage board and its silly deck of cards. The flashlight the boys kept above the door was gone. Only the smell remained: of the stove's burned wood and stale tobacco smoke, mixed with the scent of tomato soup and Orange Spice cologne.

"They're gone," I said softly. "Took my frypan with them. We made scrambled eggs and even bacon once, in that pan." I throttled the wave of nostalgia. Not good to appear sentimental before a captive. The potbelly's door was wide open and an unburned half of my wig hung out. They had tried to destroy as much of me as they could.

My flashlight caught a glitter in a corner. I followed its beam to see Chuck's silver lighter. The kid had loved that lighter a lot more than I did my frypan. What would he do without it? It was the only thing his pa ever gave him. Keeping an eye on Rolf, I picked up the lighter and stuck it in my trouser pocket.

Lisa's clothes and the red wig were gone. Was she with the Cheeleys, or had the boys stolen them to sell at a second hand shop?

I booted Rolf's ankle. "Did you meet Lisa tonight?"

"I was supposed to, but no. You came along and spoiled it."

"Did you steal the Plinko money? Did Miki get in your way? Where's the money? Did you give it to Lisa? Rolf, you're supposed to be smart but you're acting dumber than a box of rocks." I kicked his ankle a little harder.

His face contorted. "I did not kill Mr. Miki! He was my friend. I could share my thoughts with him *auf Deutsch*."

"You seemed pretty stoic at the scene. Used to dead bodies, are you?"

"I am from Dresden," he said. That shut me up. The city had been saturated with Allied bombs. At the time, he must have been about six years old.

"I came out here to get Lisa back," he said sullenly. "She didn't want to be with Charles, I know that. I had the gun and I was ready to use it." He amended, "I mean not really use it, but scare them with it." He shook his head miserably. "But, too late, they've stolen her away."

I wasn't so sure. "Did Lisa call you about Charles? How did you hear?"

"Charles forced himself upon my little—*taube*. She ran from him and caught a ride and called me from a gas station. We said we would meet at the house, take one of the cars and leave with some money. I waited there, you saw me, but she never came. I borrowed your car and came here thinking—I don't know what—I guess that she'd return for her belongings. And I can see that they're gone."

Had the Cheeleys, driving the road to Cassville, seen Lisa making that phone call? Regaled her with apologies and stories of a grand traveling life, just like her dad's, that could be hers, too? Did the three of them go together to the Plinko home, enter through that unlocked front door, complete their murderous business, and escape out the window? It would take someone fairly tall and strong who could use both arms to reach for, and hang onto, that stout tree branch. Lisa was superbly athletic and it would be no problem for Charles. Or maybe they used the back steps for their get-away. Or only one of them went upstairs. The likely one was Lisa, to beg her father out of some money. But somehow it escalated. No, what was I thinking? Lisa would not have been present at her father's death. Too horrible. But I'd keep it in mind.

The Cheeleys had taken my black overcoat. I almost didn't care. I'd spent most of my "it's mine" emotion on the frypan. The rest of my duds lay on my couch. Too shabby to sell, I guessed. I took off the poncho and wrapped my things in it. I sat down, dug an aspirin out of the army pouch and chewed it down. I needed to lose a dull headache.

No time to sit and ponder. I went to the door and opened it. "We're heading out," I said.

At the car, I had Rolf crouch in the footwell below the passenger seat. I unlocked one of the handcuffs, had him to bring his arms up and slide that cuff through the armrest and re-fasten it around his wrist. I intended to take him to Watkins and hand him over to Chief Bobby. I wasn't getting near those Cassville cops.

After leaning the rifle against the car, I dumped my clothes in the trunk, donned the poncho and tied its drawstrings tight to hold the hood in place. The less of me Chief Bobby saw, the better. In the Municipal Courts Building, I'd discovered that, despite his boyish appearance, he was a pretty keen lawman.

Holstering the .25 behind my hip, and with the rifle over my shoulder, I trotted down the road to the Plymouth Roadking. I had left it idling and the motor didn't sound so good. I drove it off the road into unsectored trash.

In the Pontiac, I drove for a while with Rolf crouched at my side, and no sound except the purr of the motor (it had lost that slight knocking sound) and the spatter of rain and swish of wipers. After we'd passed the Wayside Inn, I said, "I'm turning you in, Rolf. You are the dumbest kid on earth. You've shot up your teacher's house, and maybe killed him to boot."

"No, no, don't say that."

"If I leave you to fend for yourself, you'll just get killed in the man-hunt."

He muttered drearily, "I only wanted my little *taube* back."

"You're in over your head if you don't let me help you. You know that, right?"

He raised his head and stared at me. "Yes, yes, I need help badly."

"Okay. Good. This is what's gonna happen: The cops will question you. You will say you've never seen me before tonight. Get it?" I lifted my foot and kicked his ankle. In doing so, I lightened my hold on the wheel and the car jolted with the abrupt change of speed so that his hands were jerked tight in the cuffs.

"Ow! Ouch! My hands are going numb! No, I did not kill Mr. Miki!"

I slowed and brought the car under control. "Sorry," I said. "Ada Opal may think differently. She saw you with Miki's gun."

"Please, my hands have no feeling."

"Lean into your hands so the tension slackens. The police won't hold you for long, because with luck and money, they'll never be able to prove whether you're guilty or not. And when you're released, if you've kept quiet about knowing me, I'll see that you're reunited with your *taube*, despite Ada Opal's objections. Deal?"

"Ya, yes, it's a deal." He dropped his forehead to his arm.

A deal with this advisory: I'd best keep my belongings in the trunk in case he blathers out some ill-advised truth about me. Because, for all of his worldliness, Rolf was just a frightened kid, and a frightened kid is especially vulnerable when the law sits on him and puts on the pressure.

## 30

In the cramped, one room Watkins police station, Chief Bobby Lagerquist lounged in a captain's chair behind a desk. Both he and the deputy, leaning against the files, came to attention when I entered pushing Rolf ahead of me. A portable radio on a desk blared news of the murder. Beside the radio, a small round clock read 1:20 a.m. I introduced myself as Wanda Woods, a private detective from out east. Every mid-westerner knew the eastern population was weird.

"This is Rolf Nitschke," I said in a low growly voice. I nudged my prisoner forward. "He's a violin student, lives in the home where the murder happened that you're hearing about. He was armed, fired a shot and escaped. I followed him to an abandoned dump where I caught him." Talking way down there was difficult. Must be like a fourteen-year old boy never knowing when the vocal cords would seek their proper register.

Chief Bobby asked Rolf if that was his story too.

The boy growled assent.

Bobby deposited him in a metal chair. He secured the handcuffs to the chair after I provided the key. The brawny deputy, Ken Johnson, sat down next to Rolf.

The radiator gave several clanks as the radio roared on with a not-too-accurate report of the crime. The Plinko house had been shot up, several were dead or injured, heirlooms had been shattered, a Plymouth Roadking stolen, the garage a pile of rubble.

"One dead," I corrected, "Miki Plinko, the music teacher."

Bobby asked for my ID.

"On vacation, don't have it with," I croaked. "Visiting old friends, the Plinkos, walked in after the violence was over. Got to work right away. It's my business, ya see, detecting. Nabbed this here bugger in your bailiwick. If you can hold off a coupla days, the home office will send my papers. For right now, we got a suspect here so gotta be satisfied with that." Hoping to stave off questions, I had spoken rapidly.

"Have we met?" Bobby asked. He studied me, then returned to his desk and sat down.

"Nope," I said. "Don't think so. Unless you were at the private investigator's convention in Vegas last June?"

"Never heard of it. You have your driver's license on you?"

Heart sinking, delaying the inevitable, I fumbled with the pouch on my belt. This was looking like the final curtain of a detecting career until Rolf tilted back his chair and brought the front legs down with a thud. He continued rhythmically smashing the chair legs down again and again. His face was tight, lips thin and colorless, eyes squeezed shut. Simultaneously with each crash landing, he grunted, "Nein!"

The deputy jumped up, pushed the boy's knees down and tried to hold them there and keep the chair on the floor. I raised my voice. "Ya know, I feel like maybe we met before too. You ever feel like you lived in a former lifetime? In another world? A Kismet? Brigadoon? What?"

Bobby spread out in his chair, absorbing the noise and my babble while staring into space. He stuck a Kool in his mouth. Remembering Chuck's lighter, I almost said, "Lemme get that for ya," but decided using that silver lighter to fire up a cop's cigarette would be sacrilege. With the scrape of a match against the side of his desk, Bobby got the nail going. "I've spoken with Chief Norman Cass, over in Cassville," he said, exhaling. "He's taken charge of the case. It's the first homicide in Cassville since he walked off the job five years ago."

"Walked off? Why? Couldn't swim with the sharks?"

Bobby shook his head and spoke darkly. "Only took one shark." He addressed his next comment to the deputy. "Now that Harris is down and maybe out permanently, it's the perfect chance for Granpappy Cass to reclaim his territory."

"Yup," Deputy Johnson affirmed while keeping a grip on Rolf's knees. The boy had quieted and was slumped over. "Looks like Granpappy has rose from the dead," the deputy said.

"No way to talk," Bobby remonstrated. "Granpappy, that's what everybody calls the old boy. He likes being called that. Makes him venerable, although it's not strictly factual because he's got no grandkids. Anyhow, five years ago he went home because he couldn't deal with the pressures of the job. At home, he whittles for a hobby. Little wooden people, calls them the Whittlins. Works of art, without a doubt. I saw them once."

I raised my brows, recalling that, during the Municipal Courts meeting, two of the VIPs wondered where the carver of the prize-winning oar was these days.

Rolf had perked up and was listening. Any official thoughts concerning my driver's license had evaporated.

"How does Granpappy Cass get away with running out and still remaining chief?" I asked.

"The mayor, town counsel too, at least most of them, hoped he'd reconsider and come back," Bobby replied. "Most of them can't stand the man presently in charge, a police sergeant who's a pretty nasty customer. And it doesn't hurt that the mayor is Herman Cass, Chief Granpappy's brother. Cassville was founded by Augustus Cass, Grandpappy and Herman's great grandfather… or great-great… I'm unclear on that. Anyhow, the Casses have been good to Cassville."

"I bet Sergeant Harris isn't happy about Granpappy's rebirth," the deputy said. "Being the head of the municipal board comes with the chief's position and the board's in charge of investigating Harris' role in the holler fire. You hear about the holler fire?"

"Yup, on the radio. Think the investigation will amount to much?"

Bobby caught Johnson's eye with a 'let it go' look and the deputy obediently clammed up. The young chief squared off toward me and said severely, "You get that license to me post-haste. I need to know who I'm dealing with. As for the holler fire, charges will be filed if there's enough believable evidence."

I moved on. "You said the town council appointed Chief Cass. And there's a municipal board too? So as to give every man in town something to do?"

"Can't everyone take up whittlin'," said Bobby with a glimmer of a smile.

I allowed a bit of lip curvature as well. "Maybe our prisoner had nothing to do with Miki's death, but his subsequent actions were suspicious," I said.

"I have done nothing," Rolf spoke up.

"Good, young man," Bobby said. "Hold that thought. You can tell it to the Cassville police." He turned to Deputy Johnson. "We'll transfer the suspect over to Cassville. I won't step on Chief Cass's toes." He rose, clapped his hands. "Let's go, Mr. Nitschke, rise and shine." I gave him the handcuff key. He opened my bracelets and returned them to me. Johnson clamped Watkins cuffs on Rolf.

Bobby went to the desk, opened a drawer, pulled out a belt with holster and pistol and strapped it on. The deputy was already armed.

I yawned, patted my lips. "I'll leave you to it. Gotta be getting along. Pooped. Done all I can for one night." I moved toward the door but Bobby had another idea. "No, come with us. You were at the scene." He took my arm. I shook free.

"Sure grow them tough out east," he muttered.

"We're independent types," I said, while realizing there was no way out of this. Once I had accepted involvement in the murder, it was my destiny to meet Harris again and, shortly, that was to happen. The poncho's hood was laced tight and drooped over my yellow hair in case Harris had glimpsed it while trying to separate Hospador from her wig. I was wearing the air force trousers, the big-shouldered fly-boy jacket, and boots with lifts. I had drawn on the "w," glued on the mole, water-colored the faint mustache. Enough? Not even posing as the angel Gabriel would have been sufficient. All at once I felt tissue paper fragile.

The rain had stopped and the temperature had fallen. Before getting into the squad car, I told Bobby that I had to go to the Pontiac and get special glasses as my eyes suffered from albino night vision. He stayed close to me, the untrusting soul, as I removed the aviator's specs from the glove compartment. Fitting them on, I said, "Ah, that's much better."

"Don't see how you see anything through those," he said.

"You wouldn't, I guess." The world had dimmed dramatically but the glasses would obscure more of my face.

Striding toward the squad car, hoping I didn't bump into the curb, I said cockily, "Let's roll."

## 31

At the Plinko home, Deputy Johnson parked behind two Cassville squad cars, their emergency lights blinking. I wondered if the third car was still retired to the defunct granary. Flashing lights swept over the front yard. Every window in the house and in the cabins shone brightly.

Chief Bobby strolled up the sloped lawn to greet Harris, who came limping from beneath the picture window. Remaining in our squad, Johnson twisted to speak to me, thought better of it and clamped his mouth shut as though fearing what his words might unleash. Beside me in the back seat, Rolf rested his head against the car window and remained silent.

My heart was thudding as Bobby led Harris to us. Bobby opened Rolf's door and hauled out the sullen youth. Harris came up beside Bobby. His head was unbandaged. His police cap, bill pulled low, hid some of a deep gash. He stepped around Bobby and peered into the back seat. "Who we got back here?" he said, "the brave dolly who snagged the bad boy?"

I let his eyes meet my tinted glasses before I stepped out the other side of the car. Facing him over the roof, I gritted, "Wanda Woods from New York, just passin' through." I came around the car and stuck out my gloved hand.

Harris took one look at me and struck his forehead. "Goddam, another one," he said.

"Yeah, I thought I recognized her too," Bobby said. "Miss Woods is here visiting the Plinkos so maybe we saw her around town."

Harris' hand was en route to his holster. I gave the paw a comradely punch after I caught up to it.

The devil sergeant peered at the part of my face that was available. He whispered, "Jesus Christ, it is you."

Bobby stepped between us. "Look, Harris, you gotta stop seeing that girl everywhere you look or you'll make yourself sick."

Harris kept his poisonous eyes on me. "You're new, Lagerquist, so keep quiet." He laid his hand over his holster. "Bet you won't be taking those glasses off any time soon, will you, dolly."

"Albino night blindness," Bobby said.

"Yep, have to catch me in daylight," I said. Harris let his hand fall off the holster but he continued to stare menacingly at me.

"So where's Chief Granpappy?" Bobby asked, looking around.

"In the house," Harris said. "I stood his asshole questions as long as I could." Harris covered a nostril with a finger and blew snot out of the other, just missing my right boot. The guy was barely suppressing his rage, and yet there wasn't much he could do with the Watkins officers around.

He shouted in the direction of the lilac bush, "Shulz, get your butt over here. Got a suspect to transfer to the station." The rotund cop appeared from in back of the bush. Tugging on his zipper, he broke into a trot. Reaching us, he laid a firm hand on Rolf, who slumped against the vehicle. Deputy Johnson removed the boy's cuffs and was hooking them onto his belt when Rolf threw a roundhouse punch in Shulz's direction. It didn't come close. I grabbed the boy around the waist and held him until Shulz got Cassville cuffs on him. He gave Rolf a stout kick in the thigh and the kid cried out in pain.

Bobby stepped between them. "Easy does it, Officer Shulz. Threat's over." Harris' gun was out and pointed at Rolf. On its trip back to the holster, it moved tantalizingly toward me.

Shulz glared at Deputy Johnson. "How about some warning before you uncuff a suspect, huh?" He jerked Rolf by the cuffs toward a Cassville squad car.

"My hands," Rolf screamed.

Bobby inserted himself again. "Let up," he advised. "The kid's a violin player, not a hardened criminal." The cop reluctantly let Rolf go, and the boy sank to his knees and rubbed his left wrist as well as he could. We waited until Shulz had the prisoner ensconced in the back seat of the Cassville squad car.

Then Bobby turned to Harris. "I'm going in the house and find out what I can about the murder. You coming?"

"Who you think you are, Lagerquist?" Harris said. "You don't have any authority here."

"Somebody around here needs to act like they do," Bobby retorted. He started up the incline toward the house.

The tall cop, Brunanski, stood just inside the living room. Ada Opal was sitting on the gray sofa next to an elegant old man who wore wool flannel trousers, a cardigan unbuttoned over a dress shirt and a tie with a flying ducks pattern.

Seeing me, Ada Opal spoke with authority. "This is the lady I'm hiring to find my husband's murderer and retrieve our stolen $2000." That amount seemed low considering the importance Lisa had attached to it. But here was another job offer arriving quickly. I'd be rich if I ever collected. I acknowledged her offer with a nod. "Wanda Woods, nice to meet all of ya."

The widow murmured, perhaps for her own benefit, "Wanda Woods she's known as."

At my side, Harris inhaled hard.

Uncorking his long legs, the elderly gent rose so awkwardly that a little wooden figure popped up in his shirt pocket. The carved head had only half a mouth and nose and a single eye, all on one side.

"Chief Norman Cass," he introduced himself in a watery voice. He drew himself up to full height. We shook. He was tall and rangy, with a big meaty nose and a throat prominent with wattles. "In what capacity will you be working for Mrs. Plinko?" he asked.

"I'm a private investigator from out east." I continued speaking at breakneck speed. "The suspect, Rolf Nitschke, stole my car. I followed him to an abandoned dump, took him into custody. He's out front, waiting to be transported to your police station." I turned my face. "Mrs. Plinko, I had to borrow your Plymouth Roadking to pursue Rolf. I'm positive he'll be released, but he has to calm down first." I didn't imply that Rolf might have been involved in the murder, because suspicion would have fallen on Ada Opal's daughter too, and there was enough pain already in the widow's eyes. I slowed my delivery. "You need to notify Rolf's parents about what happened. They should come immediately and bring along a big hunk of cash in case he's charged."

Ada Opal placed her small hands on her tear-stained face. "What will his parents think? And what of his career?" Her voice hardened. "I'm afraid Rolf and I will have to part musical ways."

Chief Grandpappy clumsily resumed his seat next to her. He queried me, "Did Rolf steal the Plymouth and smash down the garage door?"

I had just said I took the Plymouth but I repeated it, slowly, for the old boy, adding, "I was in pursuit of the suspect." I glanced at Ada Opal and imagined I saw "deduct from salary" on her lips.

The chief asked for the present location of the car.

"In the dump that's north of Watkins about fourteen miles. After I captured Rolf, I got my car back and transported him in it."

Chief Granpappy spoke in the clear voice of command: "Officer Brunanski, you will pick up the Plymouth tomorrow. We have enough to do here tonight." By the door, Brunanski emerged from a dreamlike state to nod vaguely.

Two officers, Johnson from Watkins, and Brunanski from Cassville, remained with the widow as Granpappy Cass, Bobby, Harris, Shulz and I left to transport Rolf to the police station.

Reaching the Cassville squad car, Chief Granpappy spoke in a puzzled manner. "I only see two police cars. Where is our third car?"

Officer Shulz, in the driver's seat, responded gloomily. "We didn't need it while Sarge was in the hospital, but we could sure use it now."

That was no answer, but Chief Granpappy nodded as though he understood perfectly.

## 32

At the jail, I remained in the background as Rolf was handed over to Charlotte, billy club flapping at her hip. Shulz accompanied her as she led the prisoner to a cell. Luckily Charlotte hadn't given me a glance.

In the adjoining police station, Granpappy unlocked the office door while ordering Harris to stay in the lobby and man the counter in case emergency calls came in.

Harris threw back his head, blew a heavy breath and dug into his pocket. He brought forth a large handkerchief containing the tobacco tin that had lain at the base of the elm tree. "Pap," he said, "you musta missed this at the crime scene. I guess your eyes ain't what they used to be." He paused, then continued in a half-pleading tone, "I can't be shut out of this. Remember the Gene Clawwitter case and poor half-dead Mabel? I handled both of them cases. Chief Bobby-boy here and Miss Ballsy ain't got my know-how. And remember Tina Haverford's disappearance? You ran that investigation and nothing came of it because of them damn witches."

Granpappy was clearly shaken by Harris' mention of the Haverford case. His wattles quivered as he fumbled for a reply. "I - I remember how cautious we were, searching that holler in the dead of night." He shook his head. "I'll never forget the ungodly bangs and howls of that everlasting night."

"Ye-a-h." Harris prolonged the word. "Anyhow, you cancelled the search, not me." Harris turned his back on the chief.

"You were long gone when I called it off," Granpappy responded testily.

Whirling around, Harris fairly shouted, "Knew I wouldn't get no backup if something tried to eat me alive."

I stood mutely. It was my pleasure to witness two scaredy-ass policemen squaring off at each other.

Bobby broke in, cool and focused: "Back to the present case…"

But not before Granpappy summed up: "The Tina Haverford case was a labyrinthine case, rife with twists and puzzles and howls in the night. As to the other case you mentioned, Sergeant, your rough tactics forced a confession from Gene Clawwitter and he killed himself before he could be brought to trial. But," he sighed throatily, "you do have experience and so I will include you in the discussion of this crime. This time, though, we will rely on deduction, not brute force."

"Clawwitter was as guilty as the witches," Harris muttered, getting in the last word as Granpappy opened the office door. The chief stood aside and waited for me to enter but Harris barged past me. He swung a metal chair backward, straddled it and crossed his massive forearms on the back. The tobacco tin dangled from one hand.

"We need an evidence box for that," Bobby pointed out.

Harris got up and thwumped the tin onto a metal shelf as Chief Granpappy planted himself in the swiveller by the desk.

I'd been thinking about that tobacco tin, its importance to the case. Half the men I'd met in Cassville had brown stains between their teeth, including Granpappy, Harris, and the Watkins deputy, Johnson. Maybe the particular brand held a clue.

But I couldn't concentrate on that when my attention was diverted by five little wooden figures that posed at the edge of the chief's desk. Whittlins. Expertly carved, the three males and two females were about six inches tall. The elements had weathered two, but the other three looked as if they had been born yesterday. Beside them, framed in gold, was a 4X5 vividly colored photograph of a hot air balloon. Apparently the little folk were attending the balloon races. Chief Granpappy had brought his home life to the workplace. The other investigators hadn't remarked on the wooden clan so I kept my mouth shut too.

"The body will be sent to Peoria for study," Granpappy said. "There were long threads under the fingernails. I did manage to see them." He directed that last comment to Harris.

The old chief motioned for Bobby and me to gather 'round. I pulled up a folding chair. Bobby chose a padded visitor's chair.

Granpappy took two sheets of paper off the stack in a wicker basket and laid them side by side on the desk. "This will get us started," he said. Using a black felt-tip pen, he drew the two stories of the Plinko home on the sheets, labeling them FLOOR 1 and FLOOR 2, with rooms, windows and doors identified. He added the outdoor stoop, and the curving stairs between the floors. As far as I could tell, the scene was accurate. He placed a little whittled man and a little whittled woman in the downstairs room labeled "Parlor."

Suddenly Harris stood beside Bobby at the desk. "That's the Plinkos, right?" he rasped.

Granpappy picked up a second male figure and entered it through Picture Window on Floor 1.

Bobby stopped the chief's hand and said, "G.P., we figure the killer walked in through the front door. The students say that door was kept unlocked into the evening."

"Exactly," Granpappy responded smoothly. "It stayed unlocked so the students could enter for their violin lessons and after hours for access to food." After letting that settle, he zoomed the figure through the door, saying, "The killer proceeded up the Steps… " He tipped the figure back and forth, left foot, right foot, up the curved staircase to Floor 2, then hopped him into the Studio.

"The killer enters Miki's Studio and pries open the safe, using some sort of tool. There were severe gouges in the metal," the old man elucidated.

I was riveted on the scene because I knew who had held a pry bar recently.

"There was no tool found at the scene that could have done that kind of damage," he rumbled on, "so we may deduce he carried it off with him. The killer," he added, in case we weren't keeping up.

"But now we must backtrack." He lifted Ada Opal's figure out of the Parlor and started it up the Steps.

Harris interrupted. "The victim goes upstairs before her, doesn't he, because he's the one who gets murdered."

Granpappy's hand paused, then jumped the lady back to the Parlor. In one fell swoop, he plunked Miki down in the Studio, not bothering with the Steps. Rankled by Harris' correction, he went on, "We don't know if Miki Plinko heard something or why he went upstairs. According to his wife, he left the Parlor at a normal pace. She was reading and saw nothing odd in his departure. Indeed, deep in her book, she was only vaguely aware that he had even left."

Nearing the moment of confrontation, Granpappy's tempo quickened and his voice became more dramatic: "Miki entered the studio and the robber attacked him. They fought. Miki had bruises on face and arms. We believe he was struck with the burglary tool. He managed to open a drawer and draw out the Italian pistol. They grappled for the gun." Granpappy bumped the two little men against each other vigorously. "The killer shot Miki in the leg. Miki fell down bleeding." Granpappy leveled the Miki figure. "The killer loomed over him and fired a second shot into Miki Plinko's head, ending his life."

"There mighta been more than one bad guy in that room," said Harris. "Pap, you might need more sticks."

Granpappy sat back and incorporated that theory without adding figures even though two more were available. "The killer, or killers," he went on, "goes, or go, out the window and down the tree."

Harris leaned closer to the diagram. Instinctively I leaned away from him. He said, "Pap, I don't see no tree there." He reached into his pocket, found a nickel and plunked it down at the designated spot. "There's your tree," he said. "Ada Opal runs upstairs, sees her husband dead as a doornail, runs down and out onto the stoop." Harris had taken over the narrative. "That's where the suspect, Rolf, and this gal here… " Harris jabbed a finger at me, "…and a student, Ned Fairchild, met her."

With a testy glance at Harris, Granpappy tumbled Ada Opal up and then down the Steps and zipped the two remaining players over to the Stoop. Then he was out of Whittlins. Snatching the incomplete figure from his pocket, he said, "We'll use this for the student Ned Fairchild and pretend it's alive."

Harris reached to snatch the unborn doll from Granpappy, but the chief slapped his hand away.

"What the hell," Harris said, a hurt expression crossing his face. He recovered quickly, saying, "Those three follow the victim's wife up the Steps." He paused, gazed at Granpappy. "Lights, camera, action, Pap," he prompted. At the cue, the old chief made shimmying movements of all four pieces, two to a hand. I caught Bobby's eye and he looked away sheepishly, as if embarrassed for the old boy.

"During the climb," Harris said, "Rolf pulls out a rifle and this here gal captures it. Rolf retakes it with no problem. He fires a shot into the stair railing—"

"Blam!" Granpappy inserted. Startled, the other three of us flinched.

"—and escapes," Harris finished somewhat anti-climactically.

Granpappy swept a gnarled hand above the reenactment and declared, "There you have it, the story of the Miki Plinko murder."

"Wonderfully clear, Grandpappy," I blurted, giving the old boy a big bright smile. Harris arched his eyebrows, got up with a clatter and strode from the office. Bobby bit the corner of his twitching lip.

In my defense, it's important for a PI to be on good terms with law enforcement because they have access to information through channels denied me. Still, sometimes my brownnosing sickens me. Not in this case. With this cast of characters, I needed all the help I could get.

After Bobby dropped me off by my car in Watkins, I swung north to check out the trailer. I could think of no other place where Lisa might go. I also needed to get rid of the half-burnt wig before the cops found it. And I could use a bed for the night. Presumably, the cops wouldn't be out to the dump until morning, if Brunanski even remembered. I'd keep an eye out for Harris, though, in case he decided to hunt me down.

I parked the car in its usual spot behind the junked Chevy. At 4:05 a.m., the rain had stopped, leaving the morning damp and chilly. Shivering, I took wool socks from my suitcase. I left my very identifiable shoulder bag in the trunk after sticking makeup and a comb into the fabric pouch on my belt.

In the trailer, I hung my wet clothes and the soaked poncho from spikes. I put on the wool socks over the ones I was wearing. Damn those Cheeleys for stealing my overcoat. In the morning I'd vacate the dump permanently and seek a new residence, because, if the cops were any good at all, they'd soon be swarming over this area.

The charred wig by my side, I rested against the wall with eyes closed. My last thought before drifting off was that this room was dead space with the Cheeleys gone. All its flavor, the liveliness, had fled with them.

About 5:30 a.m., there was a noise at the door. I drew the .25. It was Lisa in the doorway, visible in the vague beginnings of morning light. I sat up and slid the gun back in the holster.

"What are you doing down there?" she asked. She glanced around.

"Trying to sleep."

"Where is everybody?"

"The boys lit out. They took everything."

"When's Charles coming back?"

"They're gone, both of them. They won't be back."

After a moment of comprehension, she said, "Who needs 'em? I'm a mess. My head hurts and I have a bad cut on my neck."

I stood to inspect her. There was a fiery raw lump on the left side of her neck. "How did you do this?" I asked. Battling your old man? She touched the wound, winced, went to her couch and collapsed on it. She began to sniffle.

"Your face is scratched up, too," I said. "What happened?"

"Rolf."

I sat down beside her and wrapped an arm around her shoulder, carefully.

"Rolf did it to me," she said with a grimace.

"Tell me," I urged. I'd delay informing her of her dad's demise while trying to ascertain if she had anything to do with it. I couldn't believe she had fired the shots, but maybe she had been there when someone else had.

She gave her version of the evening's events. After escaping the dump, she'd been picked up by a young couple. They stopped at a gas station and waited while she called Rolf from the outdoor pay phone. The two agreed to meet in front of the Plinko home. Lisa asked the driver to drop her off two blocks from the house because she didn't want to seen by her parents. Walking those two blocks, Lisa saw a figure coming down the elm tree in the glow of the upstairs window. It was a man and he hit the ground running the opposite way from her vantage point.

"It was Rolf!" she blurted. "I had been thinking about him and there he was! Running away to be with me but going the wrong way! I ran after him. I didn't want to call out, didn't want anyone to hear me. He ran around the back of the garage. It was very dark there. I called his name real soft, and all of a sudden he was in front of me and he swung at me with something. It hit me in the neck. Wendy, it really hurts."

"I'm not surprised. It looks pretty nasty."

She touched the wound and shuddered. "When I talked to Rolf from the gas station, he was very jealous about me and Charles and what Charles did to me. But I never thought he'd blame me for it. Rolf gets angry sometimes. He said he'd punish me if I ever did it with Charles and look what he did to my poor face." Lisa pulled back her hair and stretched her neck to show me some scratches on her face.

"Honey, the injury on your neck looks bad, but those marks on your face look like scratches. Did you run through pines tonight? Maybe by the garage?"

"I came through some pine trees," she admitted, "near the garage, but Rolf did this. I know it was him because, when I came to and got up, I saw him standing out by the curb with his violin like nothing had happened. I was afraid to go to him." Lisa's expression and tone changed to haughty. "He could stand there all night for all I cared. I'd go back to Charles, be his girl. Wendy, did you ever have two men fighting over you?"

I passed on that. Not the time to recount sexual episodes or make them up.

"I took the next street over so Rolf wouldn't see me," she went on. "I heard sirens and I just flew down the walk. But pretty soon I got so tired that I lay down behind some bushes and rested for a while."

"Poor baby." Rubbing her shoulder, I became aware that she had come in empty-handed. "I don't see your snap purse. Did you drop it somewhere?"

She glanced around, checking by her feet, and under the couch cushion. She became frantic. "Oh, where is it?" She rushed about the room. "My Gucci," she wailed, "I don't remember. I was unconscious and I don't know where I lost it. In the car going out or coming back? Maybe I left it in the phone booth. Oh, Wendy, my Gucci purse."

"It's Wanda now," I said. "Finish your story. Did you get picked up on the highway coming back?"

"Yeah. The guy who stopped for me said I looked pretty bad. When we got to the dump road, he was looking at me kinda funny and didn't want to let me out in the middle of nowhere. But I didn't like the way he was looking at me, so I just jumped out. My knees and hands got all torn up. I don't think I had my Gucci when I jumped out."

"Let me see your hands," I said. I took each in turn. "They look okay. Nothing some lotion won't fix."

"Was that my mom's Plymouth off the road back there? Don't tell me she's here." She almost sounded glad.

"No. I drove the Plymouth in. Rolf stole my car."

"He's not here, is he?" That was asked apprehensively.

"Don't worry about him. He's down for the night."

She spotted my wet duds hanging on the wall. "Whose stuff is that?"

"Mine."

"Where's mine?"

"The Cheeleys took your clothes. And most of my things, too," I said.

More fruitless glancing around. "I don't get it. What of yours was worth anything?"

I passed on bringing up the frypan.

"Why do you think Rolf was shinnying down that tree?" I asked.

"He wanted to get away from them and come to me."

"Did you two decide to rob your parents and he went ahead on his own? I mean, that tree is right outside your dad's studio, isn't it?"

A nod. "Rolf's always strapped for cash."

"Did he change his mind and hit you so he could keep all the money for himself?"

She covered her face. "Oh, we needed that money. How could he do that?"

Nothing more was to be gained by withholding the bad news. "Lisa, something happened at your house tonight, something terrible."

She made a face. "Yeah, I got clobbered."

"Something far worse than that, I'm afraid. Your father…is not with us any more." I paused. "He's gone to a better place."

"Did he go back to Rumania?"

I dug out a cigarette, handed it to her. She stuck it in her mouth. "This is very hard for me to say," I went on. "Your daddy was shot by an intruder."

Her mouth dropped open and the cigarette hung there. She collapsed back on the couch. Surely this was a surprise.

Outside an owl screeched.

"Lisa, he didn't make it," I said.

"What do you mean?"

"He didn't survive."

"My dad's dead?" she squeaked.

"Yes. Whoever you saw coming down the tree shot him and burglarized the safe."

She recoiled from me. "My dad's dead?" she repeated. I waited a moment for the awful news to sink in.

"No. Wait," she said, staring up, eyes wide. "You're saying I saw the killer?" She shook her head adamantly. "No, I saw Rolf. Rolf would never! Then it wasn't Rolf I saw. He would never hurt my dad!" Covering her eyes, she bent forward. "Oh, no," she wailed. "Rolf liked my dad."

I went to her and put my arms around her. She leaned against me and sobbed into my hair.

Lisa had lost her dad, Rolf, and Charles in a single evening.

"Let's get you home to your mama," I said. On the way out, I retrieved the burnt wig.

## 34

The grounds of the Plinko homestead were bordered in yellow-dyed rope and lit by a rotating searchlight. A cop patrolled the perimeter. Harris. I pulled to the curb, my vehicle no longer a secret. Nearing Cassville, I had pitched the wig out of the window onto barren farmland.

Ned Fairchild and the other violin students were out in front of a cabin. A few gawking townspeople stood by.

"Mornin', officer," I said, strolling toward Harris. "I've brought the daughter home."

"Every time I see you, you get uglier," he said, spitting in the direction of my air force boots. He limped off. Lisa gripped my arm and stayed so close to me that we were bumping against each other as we headed up the lawn to the front door. "Don't leave me alone with him," she whispered shakily.

"Same here," I replied.

In the living room, Chief Bobby greeted us. "You here again? You're a glutton for punishment." I was happy it was Bobby. If I'd had to deal with the two Cassville officers so soon after encountering Harris, I might have lost my cool.

"This the daughter?" Bobby asked, noting my companion.

"Yes. I brought Lisa home. She's injured. Someone, the killer most likely, struck her with a hard object. Perhaps a pry bar."

Viewing the injury, Bobby assured Lisa that he'd send for a doctor. He added a perfunctory, "I'm sorry for your loss."

Ada Opal came through the "Parlor" door, if Granpappy's diagram was correct. Astonished at seeing her daughter, she halted and her expression changed to wariness. The girl pressed against my side so hard I almost tipped.

"Ada Opal, here's Lisa!" I said brightly. The two took the measure of each other like feral cats.

Displaying the compassion I was not born with, but acquired from necessity, I said, "Lisa's come home to grieve with you. She needs her mother. Plus, she's been hurt." I turned Lisa's head a bit to display the wound. Seeing it elicited a maternal gasp. Ada Opal took a halting step toward her daughter as the girl studied her cautiously. Suddenly, exclaiming, they rushed into each other's arms and burst into tears. It was as if touching each other allowed them to truly feel the tragedy and their loss.

"Bobby," I said, "let's go outside. There's something we need to hunt for."

"Harris found a pry bar out by the garage," he said. "Most likely used to force open the safe. And if what you say is true, probably use to clobber the girl. If that's what you're looking for, we've got it already."

"There's something else missing. Lisa's purse," I said.

Bobby posed ramrod straight. "Miss Woods, when will I be seeing your ID?" he asked severely.

"Right now that just seems so secondary to our mission," I said, exasperated at his concentration on trivia. "But I'll call today," I added to appease him.

I moved ahead of him toward the double garage. At 7:10, there was enough natural light that we didn't need flashlights. Bobby caught up, and, as we traversed the lawn in the brisk morning air, I related Lisa's story, ending with, "We're hunting for a Gucci snap purse. I think she might have lost it when she was attacked."

"Sergeant Harris checked the area, only found the pry bar, and I checked a little ways into the woods. Is it possible Lisa killed her dad? Did they get along? You said you knew the Plinkos well."

"Yep, I do. She's a troubled kid, no doubt about it. But her shocked reaction when I told her Miki was dead seemed honest. I can't believe she did it."

He wasn't as sure as I was. "That girl's no weakling. Back there, breaking down like that, it might have been remorse."

"Yep," I conceded. "I know there's reason to suspect her, but as a rule daughters don't kill fathers." I was being firm about that. So far.

"Leaving out Lizzie Borden," he said.

Passing a greenhouse on our right, we reached the damaged garage.

"At first Lisa told me it was Rolf coming down that tree," I said as we walked slowly along the outside of the garage and peered into shadowed areas. "She changed her mind after I told her Miki had probably been murdered by whoever that was."

Bobby nodded. "Mrs. Plinko said that Lisa was consorting with some pretty undesirable characters. A couple of teens, Charles and Chuck, from the Cheeley clan. Rolf knew them too. Sergeant Harris thinks they're the ones who beat him up."

"Mmm."

"Rolf Nitschke. How well do you know him?" he asked.

"Never met him before last night. Has he been questioned yet?"

"Nope." He eyed his watch. "Will be, 40-45 minutes from now. I'll be present to keep an eye on Harris."

"Good."

"You know, Wanda, we may have identified the killers already," Bobby said. "Those two kids, Lisa and Rolf, going after the money. The widow believes it. See her reaction when her kid walked in? She was cautious, even fearful. And Lisa says her purse is lost? That's a pretty convenient way to get rid of the money. Maybe Rolf took it as part of their plan and was in the dump hiding it when you cornered him."

"Then where did she get that wound?"

"Just a theory. She could have done it to herself I suppose. Or he could have done it so she wouldn't be a suspect."

"But the first story she told convicted Rolf."

"She retracted it pretty quickly. Or maybe the killer, Rolf or whoever, acted alone, and was surprised by her following him. He clubbed her down and took the purse."

"Yeah, that's possible." Two inventive minds spinning theories.

I saw a black object jammed into a crevice in the base of the garage. "There it is," I said. "That's Lisa's purse."

Bobby slipped on gloves and carefully pulled out the Gucci. "Damn. Supposedly Harris went over this territory."

"He's good, isn't he? What's in it?"

He clicked it open, allowed me a peek. No money, some personal items. We searched further, found nothing, and returned to the house.

Lisa was collapsed in an armchair, crying quietly, her neck greasy with salve. In the meantime, she had washed her face. Free of blush and black eyeliner, she looked very young and innocent. Ada Opal posed protectively beside her.

Bobby held out the snap purse. "This yours, Miss Plinko?"

"Oh. Yes." Lisa dabbed at her face with a hanky. She reached for the purse.

Bobby held it away. "Name the contents please."

"Make-up, lipstick, comb, tweezers… " she detailed.

"Money?"

She thought. "About three dollars and change."

"Money's gone," Bobby said. "Young lady, you'll have to do without your purse for now. It's evidence."

Lisa thunked a fist down on the chair arm.

Ada Opal stepped forward and addressed me. "I must speak privately with you, Miss Woods, about our financial arrangements and expectations." She turned deferentially toward the young chief. "Is that permitted, Chief Lagerquist?"

Bobby considered before saying, "You should be aware, Mrs. Plinko, that all of us in law enforcement are on the same side. We work together."

"Oh, that's not true," Ada Opal replied testily. "Chief Cass and Sergeant Harris hate each other's guts. That's reason enough to have someone outside of the police working for me." I had to admire the spunk of the recently widowed lady.

"Mrs. Plinko is able to concentrate on shattered works of art, or on business, or on just plain common sense when she absolutely has to," I explained.

Bobby filed that before he said, "I can't stop you from meeting privately. I'm sure Miss Woods will fill me in later."

Lisa started to rise. "Mom, I want to go with you and Wendy."

"Wanda, dear," I said.

"No, baby," her mother said firmly. "This is just to tie up some financial arrangements."

"Besides, Miss, I have some questions for you," Bobby said.

"I don't want to be alone with him," Lisa said. "I'm scared of cops."

"Chief Bobby's a good man," I assured her. "He'll protect you."

Gazing up at Bobby's clear-eyed, determined, confident visage, Lisa nodded a reluctant assent.

Ada Opal steered me into the parlor and closed the door behind us. The cozy room contained music stands, chairs, a writing desk stacked with music, a shelf lined with books, some paintings on the wall. This must serve as her teaching studio.

She removed a violin case from a Queen Anne chair and gestured for me to sit, while she deposited herself in a straight-back chair. Crossing her slim legs, she said, "With our savings gone, Lisa and I have very little to live on. Our students will leave, at least for the rest of the term, and most likely forever. Their families will be appalled by this." Pausing, she mussed her already disheveled hair. "Miki was the driving force around here, not me. I never dreamed… We've lived for our art, a rarified existence, granted, above the storm so to speak. Now we're in the middle of a thug's world. First Lisa associating with those depraved Cheeleys, then drawing Rolf in with her." Hollow-eyed, drained of color, Ada Opal was suffering over the death of her husband. Their personal relationship may have been rocky, at least it seemed so to me, but the musical and monetary success that had come from their collaboration was over. She understood that, painfully.

She said, "Wendy, Wanda, whatever the hell you call yourself, I'm hiring you to find our money. There will be a substantial reward. By the way, your disguises and personas are lousy. Why do you do it?"

"To hold Harris at bay," I responded frankly. "Both Lisa and I have had violent encounters with him."

"I know he assaulted her, the bastard. She told me she's terrified he'll drive up in a police car and take her into custody and that will be the end of her."

"I'll do everything in my power to stop that from happening," I said.

She gave me a sideways look. "You were in jail here and that makes Wendy Winkworth a suspicious figure. I can see that Sergeant Harris hates you. But you have an alibi for the bank robbery, don't you, and couldn't have been present when he was attacked. So why does he hate you so much?"

"He's a hateful man," I said. "And one who isn't fond of women."

She nodded. "The circumstances we find ourselves in mean that I have to trust you to help me, and you have to trust me not to tell anyone who you really are. But I haven't been entirely forthright either."

"How so?" For sure, the IRS complication.

"I know you want to make money, at least as Wendy you did, plaguing us to pay even as Lisa drifted in and out of our lives. Well, now, I'm offering an even larger reward," she enticed.

Calling the next, promised, amount a reward didn't change the fact that it was another legally uncollectable amount. "How much is this new reward and when do I collect the last one?" I asked. "After all, once again I've returned Lisa to your care." Considering the circumstances, that was a low blow, but with previous defaults in mind, I didn't much care. "Ada Opal, how much money was actually in that safe?"

She drew an agonized breath. "It's been a long time since I've had to deal with people like you. But I grew up among them and I'm sure it will all come back." Her eyes pierced mine. "$25,000 was stolen, all in cash. As you heard, I told the police only $2000 was in the safe. From what your fake Hospador said, you know why. If you recover the entire sum, your bonus will be one-tenth of it. $2500."

"You haven't come through with my last bonus yet. Or is that money waiting for me in the bus station locker?"

"No it is not, but I will pay. Believe me. I can sell some of our paintings. It might take a month or so but you'll get all your money."

"A month more in this town? Please. Now that Wendy is gone and Wanda has arrived, you will pay me personally. And tell your daughter not to call me Wendy. It mixes up the cops." If I discovered the $25,000, I'd nab my reward before I brought it to her. She could hardly sue.

She read my mind. "You'll probably be rolling your hands in my money first and no doubt will take your cut at that time, but if you take more or disappear, I'll expose you as Wendy What-the-hell and you'll never work again."

"And I'll report you to the tax collector for hiding $25,000," I shot back. "So let's call it even, except this latest reward is only $500 more that the last one. I'll need $3500, now that a murderer is involved."

She moaned, "You'd see Lisa and me begging on the street before you had any pity." She dug her fingertips into the chair arm.

Trying to catch her off guard, I asked, "Do you believe that Lisa did this?"

"Nobody believes that." Said too quickly.

"You seem to."

"No. Really. I don't."

Blood is thicker than water, they say. I was not one to say that was wrong.

"How about Rolf? Could he have done this?" I asked.

"I fully realize that he may have killed my beloved Miki and taken all our savings."

I gave her a moment before saying, "Okay. Let's get our agreement down in writing." We stood together by the desk. With an ink pen, Ada Opal wrote out two copies of the contract. I insisted my name be Wendy Winkworth, for legal purposes, you see.

Folding my copy and tucking it in my military pouch, I said, "One more thing. Speak to your daughter and make sure she knows that Wanda Woods, family friend, has just arrived in town. Wanda has no previous existence in Cassville. If Sergeant Harris finds out differently, he will destroy me, and then you'll never get your money back."

"I understand perfectly," she said.

She went to a painting of a long-necked woman, a Miro? fake Miro? and with my help, lifted the antique gold frame from the wall. She crammed her copy of the contract in the back of the frame, after which it took the two of us to heft the thing back into position.

## 35

Ada Opal paid me a hundred dollars in tens to tide me over until the big pay-off.

I drove to Watkins where I ate and then called Cassville High School asking to speak to Carl Swaney. When he came on, I spoke wispily. "It is I, Hospador." I raced past his thrill at communicating. "I must go back to Rumania so I call to say good-bye."

Thrilled no more, he blurted, "Leaving? Do you know that your cousin Miki has been murdered?"

"I know that. I am heart-broken, but in Rumania we are used to this."

"I thought I'd see you at the funeral and we could have coffee afterward."

Why was Swaney so hot to see me again? He'd never even made a pass at the Hosp.

His lecture voice emerged: "Dear Hospador, the first thing I noticed about you was your scent. You have a lovely orangey smell, did you know? Odor lodges in the most primitive area of the brain, the part that speaks first, not of beauty or vocal quality, but of aroma."

"Mmm." What a come-on, caused by Charles' Orange Spice cologne.

"Hospador," he urged further, "please come to the funeral, attend the burial. Your cousin was a great man and deserves to be honored by his own blood."

"Hmm." My voice narrowed. "I thought you did not like him very much."

"You mean because he was so hard on his daughter. But he also was a marvelous artist and brilliant teacher."

"Yes, I see. But, unfortunate when Major calls me back to my country, I must answer."

"Where are you? I want to see you off."

"Must go!" I cried, "Major is gesturing. Bye bye, Doctor Carl Swaney."

"I'll miss your righteous spirit." He talked fast as though he knew I was about to slam down the receiver. He was right.

I allowed a few stabilizing breaths before dialing Sid Dobrotka, my former boyfriend, at the Burton City newspaper where he was head sportswriter. Our breakup was what led me to visit my brother in Chicago in the first place, feeling I needed a little brotherly compassion. Instead, I had found an indicted burglar who jumped bail and forfeited my money.

When Sid picked up, I confessed that I badly needed his help to confirm the identity of one Wanda Woods, a private investigator from New York City.

He guessed that might be me. "You have a habit of stretching the truth, even about the smallest things."

"When I see you," I said, "I'll explain fully, but right now if you don't help me, I might be arrested, convicted and imprisoned. Oh, and possibly raped. It's in connection with a murder case I'm working on. Aren't you happy I'm productively employed in my chosen field?"

Sid muttered something incoherent. One of our disputes had been over my refusal to get a "regular" job like the secretarial position that had opened up on the newspaper, offering as it did a steady income until marriage when, as policy, I'd be given the axe.

"I need you to send me an official looking document that declares Wanda Woods to be a Private Investigator licensed by the state of New York. Suitable for framing would be nice. Include in the mailing, ten sheets of expensive blank stationery with the letterhead: 'Woods Detective Bureau, Box 3102, New York City, New York.' Oh, and stick a glowing letter from a former client into a separate envelope. It should thank Miss Woods for saving his life after being wrongly accused. With the true criminal incarcerated," I said, as if reading the letter out loud, "I've been free to pursue my dream as a social worker at the Fillies Home for unwed mothers, or something like that. Sign it, Yours truly, Louie." I ended with, "Do this for everything we meant to each other."

"You think I'm some god-blame fiction writer?"

"The letter can be crude. Just make it sincere."

A lengthy silence, before, "When will you be back home?"

"Sid, believe me, I'd love to be there right now. But as soon as possible." My throat swelled with the memory of my cute Burton City trailer and my tiny yard. And Sid at his sports desk trying to pronounce "statistics."

"When you get back you can take me out to lunch. Because you'll owe me big time."

"It's a deal," I said. "Send all correspondence to Henrietta Youngman, care of the Cassville Manor Hotel." I gave the address. I would not reserve Wanda Woods a room that Harris might visit in the night.

At the hotel, Henrietta Youngman registered for the week and paid in cash, no questions asked.

# 36

I dropped by the Cassville police station early the next morning to find Chief G.P. at his desk. In a herringbone tweed jacket over a white shirt and the flying ducks tie, he was with Bobby and Harris, wearing their standard browns and blues. Granpappy welcomed me in. "Pull up a chair. We're just getting started."

"What the blazes you doing here?" Harris asked.

Bobby rose to usher me past Harris' death gaze. "I asked her to join us," he said smoothly. Harris' baleful look changed to astonishment as I took a seat.

"What do we need this ragged dolly for? Pap, tell me you didn't approve this." Harris was incredulous.

"Wanda's here because she's been in on this from the beginning and she has a proven track record," Bobby said, resuming his seat. "Caught an armed bad guy, didn't she? And she's been a valuable liaison with the Widow Plinko."

For a moment Harris was speechless. Then he sputtered, "Has anyone bothered to check her credentials?"

"Her paperwork is on the way, isn't that right, Miss Woods?" Bobby said.

"Right," I said, crossing my toes that Sid was working quickly.

G.P. checked his Waltham watch. "Come on, boys. Um… team. Let's get a move on." We all looked to Harris who was the only one still standing. Growling, he threw up his hands and thumped into the remaining metal chair.

We were just beginning to review the details of the case (no drawings involved, fortunately) when Charlotte entered pushing a wheeled cart. She wore the same high-heeled purple shoes and the Shirley Temple outfit she'd had on the night she locked me up.

Charlotte's rolling cart contained a coffee pot, four bone-colored cups, a cream pitcher, and a billy club. I ducked my head when she entered, but, not to worry, her attention was fixed on Granpappy.

"Those Whittlins, just like the real thing except aren't they awfully cold to the touch?" she asked coyly. She poured a cup of steaming coffee and held it toward the old chief. When he motioned for her to set it on the desk, she tipped forward in her high heels and lost her balance. Hot coffee spewed onto his white shirt and down his front. He squealed and fell back in his chair.

Holding the empty cup aloft, Charlotte cried out, "Oh, so sorry. Do you want first aid? And I'll certainly wash and iron your shirt for you."

Highly offended, he gasped, "You burned me."

"I am so sorry, but I am offering my services," she said with a bit of tartness.

"No, no, not needed." He tugged at his wet shirt. Bobby helped mop up the coffee, while Harris looked on with a dumb grin.

"Woman needs man and she must have her mate," Charlotte said under her breath as she returned to her cart.

This ace detective deduced that once upon a time there had been something between those two.

Charlotte filled three more cups and silently served the rest of us with no problem. Mission accomplished, she zipped the cart out the door.

"Clumsy broad," Harris said when she was out of earshot. He swilled his brew, and mopped his mustache.

"That looked deliberate. What's wrong with her?" Bobby said.

"Could be menopause," I suggested.

"Did that already," G.P. muttered.

The rest of us took out smokes while mulling over how he knew that. Bobby scratched a match against the desk and lit my Camel.

"The results of Rolf Nitschke's interrogation… " G.P. took a folder from the wicker basket on his desk. Apparently he'd decided to change the sodden shirt later. "According to the German lad, the Cheeley brothers, Charles and Chuck, sixteen and seventeen years of age, knew about the Plinko money. Consequently they are suspects. An unnamed woman whom Rolf describes as 'pretty' lived with the Cheeleys in the very trailer where Rolf was captured by Wanda." G.P. indicated me.

Harris cut in. "Yeah, the Hun told us there was a pretty lady out there. I asked if it was you, Wanda, but he said no, definitely not you, not you at all. He got very excited saying that. Why would that be, Wanda?"

I gave him a blank look. "I haven't a clue, Sergeant."

G.P. continued over Harris' snort. "Rolf states the Cheeley boys rode around in an old gray Ford. Tomorrow morning early, Chief Lagerquist and I will take a tracking pair of bloodhounds out to that abandoned refuse area and give the place a good sniff in case the suspects are still hiding there."

Bobby nodded acquiescence.

"Dogs should give Wanda a sniff before they start out," Harris said. "See if they find her smell out there."

I coughed out a lungful of smoke. "Especially since I was out there doing your job, Harris, by taking Nitschke into custody."

"You got no credentials to put nobody in custody." Harris slammed his chair back and jumped up. "Or even to be sittin' here with us."

"I don't have to take crap from you," I flared.

"Whoo, big talker, didn't act so brave before—" Harris stopped abruptly.

"Before what?" I challenged. He ducked his head and sat down.

"Shut up, Harris," Bobby said off-handedly without bothering to look at the sergeant.

Whether impervious to bickering or just plain missing it, G.P. droned on. "Rolf Nitschke is charged with destruction of property. He's been sentenced to ten days and needs to make restitution. His parents are missionaries posted somewhere in the African bush. They can't be located currently."

The meeting degenerated into a discussion of the best oil for your car, the best deal for your money, favorite beers, and how to make a decent Manhattan. I did not participate.

The rest of the day, in Henrietta's hotel room, I skimmed the local paper and the Chicago Tribune, did two crosswords, read a paperback, and caught up on my sleep.

Before our afternoon meeting the next day, I came upon Charlotte preparing to enter the chief's office with her cart. Face flushed, she seemed hyped and ready to do more damage with hot java. The door to the office was ajar and I heard the three cops chatting inside.

"Hold it, Charlotte," I said. "If you're aiming to create another accident, don't do it. You gotta let go whatever's bothering you."

She licked spittle from her lips. Awareness dawned on her face. "You're Wendy aren't you? That drunk in the tank? Why are you acting like somebody else? You have an alibi for the bank robbery, so what's the problem? Sergeant Harris is spooked by you, so I'm not gonna say anything about it."

"I'm only me," I waffled, "but thanks anyhow. As for you—you're messing with the chief's mind and impeding a murder investigation to boot. If G.P. jilted you, it's a shame but get over it. No use keeping a grudge. It'll just eat you up inside."

Charlotte's face collapsed. "Everything is G.P.'s fault," she whispered. "I don't know why I'm acting like this. I'd never do anything to mess him up. We were a secret; he was a married man. I couldn't stand if it got out now."

I wrested the cart from her and guided it toward the women's rest room. "Follow me if you don't want the whole building to hear." She scampered along beside me on her extremely high heels.

I banged the swinging door open with the cart and bulled my way through. She scooted in after me. It was pretty crowded with the cart in the small space that contained only one stall and lavatory.

"You want the affair kept secret?" I asked. I cracked a couple knuckles to give me time to think. "Then we have to make something up to justify your lapse yesterday. How's this? You were aggravated by the loss of typing privileges when Harris took over and G.P. isn't reinstating them fast enough. How's that? I can try to justify that to the boys."

"How'd you know I was the official typist?" For an instant her eyes flashed with more proof of my identity. She had complained to Wendy about losing her typing duties the day my former self was released from jail.

"Got sources," I replied. "Let's keep on subject."

"It was G.P. who fired me. Didn't want the temptation around." She became wistful. "I really thought that after his wife died, he'd marry me. But I guess he never saw me as the wife of a police chief. I was just his affair girl. It was better when he went home and stayed there. I mean I died inside, but it was better than being ignored every goshdarned day." Charlotte's tone became resolute. "I am a good typist. I do want to type again."

"Okay, you got it." I left the restroom and, as usual, entered the office noisily. Wanda always entered noisily. The men had been absorbed in a discussion of the latest fully loaded Ford truck but, encountering my racket, they quieted.

"G.P., Charlotte wants to be the typist again," I said. "That's the reason she spilled on you yesterday. What do you say?"

"Knew it was deliberate," Harris crowed.

"She was just upset over typing?" Bobby asked incredulously.

"Sergeant Harris is our typist," G.P. mused.

That was the one guy I wanted off the street so I said, "Can't Harris man the booking counter? Charlotte can type afternoons."

"If I'm stuck indoors, I don't give a damn what I do," said Harris.

"All right," G.P. agreed reluctantly. I wondered if Charlotte was right about G.P. being tempted, a bad relationship being better than none.

I left the office to inform Charlotte. She nodded agreement smugly and wheeled her cart with its coffee service through the door to the jailhouse.

I rejoined the homicide team. G.P. reported that only Miki's prints were found on the pry bar that was assumed to have opened the safe and then used to strike Lisa. The killer had obviously worn gloves, and there had been a struggle.

The morning's search with the bloodhounds revealed nothing. "It is a surprisingly organized dump," G.P. noted. "Some experienced officer of the state is doing a fine job."

I congratulated Chuck in my head.

In other news, G.P. said a beat-up gray Ford sedan had been implicated in the burglary of a grocery store yesterday in Winchester, thirty-five miles southwest of Cassville.

"I'll check it out," Harris said. "Sure like to meet those guys again."

Bobby reported the highlights of his interview with Lisa, who had been accompanied by her mother, the two refusing to be separated. "When I asked Lisa to verify her earlier statement that Rolf had come down the tree, Ada Opal butted in and said that her daughter had changed her mind. I explained that when I asked Lisa a question I expected Lisa to answer. Immediately the kid echoed Mommy, saying she'd made a mistake about it being Rolf."

"Ada Opal's protecting her prodigy. That's obvious," I said. "Still, I can't believe it was him. He doesn't seem the type to be sliding down trees." But Charles was. In my deepest self, I'd known that the need for money and the crazy fearlessness of the boys worked toward catastrophe. Was Lisa in cahoots with Charles? That would entail a quick reconciliation after the insulting aftermath of their sexcapade. I'd meant to check if the pry bar in the tool sector was still there.

Although if it was gone, that proved nothing. The old bum, Davy, might have taken it to go with his salamander.

Bobby went on to tell of Lisa living with the Cheeleys for a few days in an abandoned trailer at the dump. "She said they stole her clothes and took off in an old gray Ford. Probably it's the one implicated in the burglary in Winchester. Lisa didn't mention a pretty lady until I specifically asked. Then looks were exchanged between her and Ada Opal before the daughter admitted there was an older lady there sometimes. I wonder why such a simple question provoked such a wary response." Bobby gave me a furtive glance.

"How'd the older lady's pretty looks compare with mine, Bobby?"

"No comparison," he smiled. He scooched his chair toward me. "What brought you back to the trailer after you nabbed Rolf? Why did you think Lisa might go there?"

"Because Rolf told me she might head back there to pack up her things," I replied confidently. How keen Bobby was to catch me in a stumble. The young chief opened his mouth to ask more, then closed it, maybe because he'd not add fuel to a flame that Harris could rekindle.

Following the briefing, I drove to the Plinkos to check on mom and daughter, and, not least, to worm an invitation to a noon meal where I might question the violin students. Noontime dining at the Plinkos was to become a habit for me. That first day four students were present while Rolf remained in jail. In the ensuing days, student numbers were to dwindle as expensive cars arrived to claim them.

Although from wealthy families, the two male fiddle students wore basic floppy T-shirts and faded jeans. The two females dressed in flared skirts, cotton blouses and cardigans. After living with the Cheeleys, I found these young people, smelling of shampoo and soap, to be exceedingly clean.

A good detective might pick up scraps of information during informal meals and I did my best, but in each other's company those students were reticent.

During the time of the murder, all had been playing their violins, each sound identifiable by its singular tone quality and the repertoire played. After lunch, I sought out each musician individually, hoping they'd be more open.

Ned responded only, "You know what I did."

The other, pimply, male recalled that his heart pounded and he became quite frightened when he heard the commotion outside. That was it.

"I looked over at the house and saw a shadow by the window," one young woman contributed. "Maybe I only imagined it."

"I heard a couple bangs," the second woman, bespectacled, with abundant black hair, said, "but I only had ten more minutes to go before my practice time was up. It's a rule of the house that we have to practice four hours a day," she elaborated. "I put in my four hours but that's it; I don't owe the violin any more. So I didn't go to check out the noise because I only had ten more minutes to go, then I'd be finished for the day."

Unbelievable. "You mean if somebody has a heart attack right next door and you only have a minute more to complete your four hours, you won't immediately go to help?"

She flipped her hair. "Guess so," she said.

No one at the Plinko compound had cleaned up the pieces of garage door that lay scattered along the driveway. After dinner that first day, Ned said in a strong Boston accent, "Every day when I go out in the morning and the first thing I see is this mess in the driveway, all I can think of is Miki lying dead on the floor. Why doesn't anybody clean it up?"

"Who did it, anyhow?" the other male student asked.

Ned's eyes lit on me. Since Wanda doesn't do cleanup, I stared him down.

At table, when the students spoke of the late Miki, it was in somber, respectful tones. They talked mostly of inconsequential things, how slowly he'd eaten and how he had trouble lighting his Meerschaum pipe, but sometimes they'd dwell on a piece of advice he'd given or wisdom he'd imposed. "Even with all his stage business, Mr. Plinko heard every note you played," Ned said and the others murmured in agreement. Miki Plinko must have been a very good teacher.

The students and I ate in the dining room around a long table. Lunch was served on ceramic Fiestaware in red, green, and yellow glazed colors. Serving dishes and condiments were placed at each end of the table and passed politely down the line. Ada Opal cooked the noontime meals, but she and Lisa ate by themselves in the kitchen. Ada Opal seemed to want little to do with the students. "It is over," she'd pronounced at her dead husband's side.

Once I joined the pair in the kitchen, its appliances and walls color-coordinated in light blue. I took a seat across from mother and daughter. Midway through a fudge sundae, Ada Opal said, "I can see the students think very little of me."

"You're not helping," I said. "It looks like you don't want anything to do with them."

She sniffed. "There was only one of them worth the trouble and he's in jail."

Looking up from her ice cream dish, Lisa said, "I'm responsible, I know that. I ran away and got Rolf in trouble and I didn't get to say good-bye to Dad. Mommy, where is he now?"

"They took his body away for an autopsy," Ada Opal replied. "He's at a mortuary in Peoria." They sought each other's hand until Lisa pulled away to stuff a healthy portion of fudge-syruped ice cream into her mouth.

"Feeding her sorrow," Ada Opal commented after Lisa left. "It's how she's always coped. She's always had problems with her weight." See, that's what mothers are for: to point out your flaws your whole life, whether they're by your side or gone forever.

Ada Opal's face was withered by grief and drained of color. The strange blue-gray eyes, when they delved into mine, were unsettling. Those penetrating eyes had identified a thousand tiny errors of technique in violin players, and I wondered what flaws they saw in me, besides those she already knew about.

Noonish one day, after the students had stacked their plates in the sink, Ada Opal showed me through the house, two stories, capped by a weather-beaten shingled roof. The living room occupied the entire front, the commanding picture window to the right of the front door and two smaller windows to the left.

Upstairs, across from Miki's large studio, there were two wallpapered bedrooms with a bathroom between. The medicine cabinet held several square bottles of Orange Spice cologne, a jar of Mum deodorant and a bottle of Lanvin Arpege perfume.

"Wow, Miki sure liked his cologne, didn't he?" I said.

"He always used too much."

"Kind of a peacock, wasn't he? Dressed in grand fashion and carried himself like he was the cat's pajamas."

"In this business, you must present a confident front."

"He sure succeeded in that," I agreed.

"Miki had his weaknesses like any man," she declared. "And of course wonderful qualities too. I loved him very much. I counted on him for so many things."

Noting the feminine decor of the larger bedroom, I said, "This is a beautiful room. Did Miki sleep here?"

"Miki preferred his own room, out of concern for me. He snored so loudly. He didn't want lack of sleep to affect my teaching."

In that larger bedroom, jewelry spilled out of an ornate box on a dark oak dresser. It looked expensive. Apparently the killer hadn't gone anywhere but the studio. The precious stones would have made quite a haul and been easy to carry. More support for the murder happening unexpectedly. Panicking, the killer wanted only to flee. That sounded a lot like the impulsive Charles.

In the adjoining, smaller bedroom, a pine bureau stood next to a stand-alone mirror. It held Lisa's items: comb and brush, extensive make-up supplies, a frilly handkerchief. On a rear corner of the bureau, a pair of silver cufflinks, left in memory of Miki, I suspected. A walk-in closet held a sparse collection of teenage girl's clothes. The Cheeleys had made off with some of Lisa's wardrobe and diminished finances apparently didn't allow for replacement. Miki's sleek suits hung at the far end of the closet, two still in dry cleaner's packaging, along with numerous slacks and shirts. A bunch of knit ties were draped through two hangers. Miki had slept in this smaller room while Ada Opal claimed the master bedroom. Seeing how he'd dominated her, that was not what I'd expected.

Next to Miki's studio there was a third, tiny, bedroom. I stepped in. Containing unsheeted twin beds, it was obviously not in use presently. Perhaps Ada Opal's mother had slept there before moving out. It had likely been Lisa's before she left. Now that she was back, she had moved into Miki's more spacious bedroom.

A corner room by the narrow back stairway had an office set-up.

I went down the narrow back steps that twisted into the kitchen and met the basement stairs. Rolf's room was next to the kitchen. I peered in, found it to be unusually neat for a teen-age boy.

I returned to the second floor..

Ada Opal was gone, but in passing Miki's studio, I saw Lisa in his chair, red-eyed, crying quietly as she cradled his violin.

"Hey kid." I entered and stood beside her. There was no place to sit, with only the one chair, and the open violin case taking up the bench. "I hope you're not thinking any of this is your fault."

She turned away to bury her face in a Kleenex tissue. "Sometimes I think everything's my fault," she mumbled. She glared at me before returning to the Kleenex. "You always make me feel even worse, you crumby rat," she said through its folds.

I withdrew as gracefully as I could manage.

During my afternoon visits to the Plinko compound, I never heard the sound of a single violin coming from the cabins. Miki's murder had killed the music too.

## 37

Saturday on my way to the daily briefing, I parked an extra block away to buy the morning paper from a child vendor. Consequently I was a little late getting to the station. Slamming into the office at 9:06 a.m., I saw the team members in their customary spots, holding Cokes, chatting about some male-fueled subject. With a great scraping, I got a metal chair positioned just right and my companions thoroughly quelled into silence before I slouched down into the seat.

"That Coke's yours." Bobby pointed to an opened bottle on the desk.

"Thanks." I took a gulp of Coke before smacking the newspaper on the desk. "You read the *Courier* this morning? Another editorial lambasting law enforcement for its lack of action, and there's three letters to the editor reminding us that Tina Haverford's body was never found and no one was ever prosecuted in the Gene Clawwitter case." I glanced at Harris for that one. He bore up.

"The only homicides here in the last twenty years," I continued, "and neither one got solved. So let's meet tomorrow instead of taking Sunday off, or you can resign yourselves to more ridicule." I would have worked an eight-day week I wanted out of that town so bad.

"We do not work on Sunday," G.P. declared. "Absolutely not. It's the Lord's day of rest. Don't ever call me on Sunday."

"Do you think Miki Plinko's killer is taking the day off?" I responded.

G.P. hesitated. "What do you think, Chief Bob? Should we meet?"

"A short meeting might be okay," Bobby equivocated.

Harris stared contemptuously at Bobby. "Lagerquist ain't even a Cassville officer and still we have to listen to his opinion on everything." He took a swig of Coke and mopped his mustache.

"All right. A short meeting on Sunday, beginning at 9:00 a.m., everybody on time," G.P. said. "Wanda, you were late today. It doesn't matter because little is new, except another stolen car report. Something odd about that though."

"I drove over to the Winchester robbery, consulted with the police. They had no luck finding the bastards," Harris contributed.

The door opened abruptly and Charlotte's cart, loaded with frosted pastries, burst in followed by Charlotte. Apple-cheeked, she looked peaceful and pleased to be doing for us. Nonetheless, I jerked up straight.

"I could not resist the fresh rolls in the bakery window," she warbled. "And I've made egg coffee to go with. I'm deliriously happy; I've started typing again."

"Can't stay away," Bobby muttered, but he looked pleased at the treats.

"What's odd?" I asked G.P., referring to his last words.

Smelling pastry, Harris' nostrils flared and he lunged past me to grab the top éclair. "Don't want coffee," he growled. "Got Coke."

Suddenly G.P. was out of his chair and swooping toward his Whittlins. Normally he moved carefully around them so as not to knock any of them kerflooey. The awkward surge caught everyone's attention, including Charlotte's. Coffee pot in hand, she peered around him as he bent over the wooden pieces, shielding them. I rose, saw that a new figure, a shapely female with purple feet, had joined the others. This recent arrival leaned backwards, her puny arms extended as though belting out a song. I drew a breath. I could almost hear "As Time Goes By."

Charlotte's expression collapsed. "Oh, G.P., the real thing is right here, in front of you, in warm flesh and blood." Arms extended, she offered herself.

G.P. recoiled. "No, please, don't. I can't," he begged, a bit of spittle dribbling from his mouth. "Forgive me."

Charlotte's expression changed to one of utter rejection. She reared back and swung the coffee pot. The lid flew off and brew sloshed over the Whittlins and splattered onto the balloon photo. Steam from the pot curled upward as it hit the floor.

Charlotte snatched up the new Whittlin and shoved it down her bosom. "You want your beloved? You've been down this trail before, so come get her."

Eyeing the location and swallowing hard, G.P. remained rooted. A rush of red spread from his neck to his forehead.

Bobby said, "G.P., you can always make another doll."

"That's cold, Bobby," I said. "There's only one Charlotte."

Bobby crossed the room and picked up the pot and handed it back to Charlotte. She stared at it witlessly. "You must leave now," he said. I got ready to duck. Bobby turned his back on her and stepped to the desk where he examined the now soggy-brown photo. He shook his head and pushed the picture over upside-down. "Hope there's a negative," he said.

Charlotte gave her cart a shove, caught up to it and marched it out. We heard her pitiful wails as she crossed the lobby into the jailhouse.

"Someone should cancel that sweet roll order," Bobby said. He bit his lip to prevent a grin from spreading. "G.P, what in hell did you do to her?"

G.P. fell into his swivel chair. Smoothing his hair with a shaky hand, he spoke brokenly. "While I was married to my late wife, I had a little fling with Charlotte. At the time, she was the cleaning woman in the jail. She looked real appealing, chatting with the prisoners, bringing delicious meals in for them. She was so cute and fanatical about it that I appointed her matron to make it official. I awarded her all the paraphernalia of rank: a badge, a cap and her own personal billy club that I carved for her myself, of mahogany and ivory."

With G.P.'s confession, Bobby passed the back of his hand across his mouth and became grave.

The old man continued in a reflective tone. "My wife Lucille was a professional career woman, a fine photographer. She was never home, always out practicing her trade. Often I made my own dinner. Lucille had bought a camera, a Ricohflex Model VII twin lens reflex, with her own earnings. She always strove to be the very best, to get the perfect shot. Five years ago, on April 26, she was taking pictures at a hot air balloon festival when a terrible gust of wind caught the balloon and it plummeted down right on top of her. She kept snapping until death. She always wanted the perfect shot and she got it. Right there." He pointed to the overturned, coffeed picture lying on the desk.

"She went out big," I brown-nosed solemnly, "for the sake of a perfect shot."

There was a moment of respectful silence, before Harris bellowed, "That Miss Charlotte needs to be taken down a notch."

"You shut up!" G.P. cried. "Don't you say a word against Miss Charlotte." He strained out of his chair and stalked toward Harris. The sarge slid his chair back. Glowering, G.P. circled him, lost momentum and stumbled back to his chair. He said, "Even today when I pass by the cell with the one good mattress I miss my Sha-sha."

"Who's Sha-sha?" queried Bobby.

"It's what I called Charlotte. Close to Zsa-Zsa." G.P.'s voice continued to throb as he continued, "I shouldn't have regrets, I know. I was the one who called it off after giving it a great deal of thought. Because Charlotte is a career woman, fanatic about it. Like Lucille was. I lost one career woman horribly. I'll never take up with a career woman again. I want my meals served at home and my wife always there to receive me." He lowered his head and took a shuddering breath.

Harris said, "Pap, why don't you give all this up and retire home to your carvings."

G.P. expelled a whimper and sank lower in his seat.

"You're an asshole, Harris," Bobby said. He went to G.P. and patted his back.

"Pap, you're not needed here," Harris went on earnestly.

"Maybe you're right. Maybe I can't do the job anymore," G.P. muttered.

"Don't listen to Harris," Bobby said. "He wants your job back."

"Come on, Chief, brace up," I urged. "Let's get back to work." But Harris' heartless statement reflected what, at times, all of us thought, that G.P. was at worst slightly loony, and at best, terribly out of touch.

After Bobby announced break-time, G.P. remained hunched over in his chair. The high color had faded from his cheeks and he looked exhausted by circumstance.

Following the break, he remained quiet and withdrawn, not seeking to lead the group and offering no suggestions.

So Bobby took over, briefing us on the news that G.P. had started to impart. The old gray Ford sedan implicated in the previous robbery was found burned to a crisp in some woods, while a mile away, a 1950 Dodge sedan was reported stolen. The oddity to which G. P. referred, was that the remains of the Ford and the theft of the Dodge were actually closer to Cassville instead of further away.

"I'll check this one out too," Harris said. "Looks like the idiots are lost and making U-turns."

I kept still because it occurred to me that there might be a reason for the boomerang route; that the Cheeleys, if it was them, were returning for Chuck's lighter. Every time I used the thing or even touched it in my pocket it seemed to exert the energy of its owner.

That afternoon at the Plinkos, I saw the Plymouth Roadking was back, parked in the wreckage-strewn driveway. Both passenger side tires were flat, the front fender staved in and that bumper badly tilted. I didn't inspect further.

Within the hour two young Negro men in jeans and T-shirts arrived in a tow truck, hooked up the Plymouth and hauled it away. Soon they were back with a salvage truck and spent twenty minutes in silent labor clearing away the fragments of garage door, placing them in the cargo bed and sweeping up afterwards. When they left, the driveway was spick and span.

Also that day, two more violin students packed up and departed in their parents' fancy cars.

That night I drove to the dump and parked behind a doorless, wheelless Hudson. I hid behind the door in the trailer, the .25 beside me, the silver lighter in my pocket, a hotel blanket covering me. I expected the Cheeleys. I was ready for Harris too, just in case, but no one showed.

Sunday morning G.P. did not show up for the meeting. We three investigators waited for him in the booking area because no one had a key to the office. I called his home, but got no answer. With nothing new in the case, we departed quickly.

I drove out to the Plinkos. Of the students, only Ned Fairchild remained. He met me at the curb, said he'd sold his backfiring DeSoto to a dealership, and offered me a heck of a deal: his bike, including two saddlebags and a squeeze ball horn, for a ride to the bus depot at 11:45.

I took Ned up on the offer and soon four pieces of Samsonite luggage, plus his violin, phonograph, a box of '78 records, and a fan lay at the curb. Pausing by the Pontiac, Ned reflected, "I'll never forget climbing up those stairs, wanting to be anywhere but there, and seeing Mr. Plinko lying so flat and bloody."

"Stone-cold dead," I said.

"Anyway, I want to thank you for being there. I don't know if I'd have made it through otherwise."

"Yep," I said. "Just part of the job."

"I need to tell you something," he went on hesitantly, "that perhaps I should have told the police, but I was so in shock, if I did think of it, I didn't think it was important. I don't know that I even thought of it until a couple days ago. Then I got so I couldn't think of anything else. With you working on the case, I thought you should know."

"Yup. What?" I grow impatient with wafflers.

He perused his lips with two fingers before continuing, "That night, right before Mrs. Plinko ran screaming out of the house, I saw a light come on in their basement. Just for a few seconds. Or maybe as long as a minute, I don't know, I was in my cabin, practicing the Saint-Saens. Nothing else mattered except getting those darn octaves in tune."

"You never told the cops about this?"

"No, and now I'm afraid to, because they'll probably want to keep me here longer for questioning and I've got a reservation in Chicago for the 6:10 sleeper to Boston."

"It'll only take a minute to give the police a statement." I was quite matter of fact although my heart was pounding. What did this mean? Was there an accomplice who exited through the basement? Charles escaping out the upstairs window, and Chuck, with the wounded arm, going down the back steps and out a basement window?

Ned tossed his suitcases onto the back seat of the Pontiac, piling them on each other until one toppled off. He shook his head vehemently. "I'm not staying here one minute longer, I can hardly stand this place." He slammed the rear door, got into the front seat with his violin and closed that door. He sat with chin thrust forward and arms folded.

I got behind the wheel, tore a piece of paper from my notebook and Ned wrote down his Boston address and phone number.

After dropping him at the bus depot, I drove back to the Plinko home. Ada Opal greeted me at the door. Her pale face was heavily powdered; the stacked rouge almost clownish.

I explained the situation as divulged by Ned, concluding with "We have to search the basement before I notify the cops. If they find the money first, we're both out of luck, me with my bonus and you having to explain about the large amount they recovered."

Immediately Ada Opal understood and led me through the blue kitchen and down the steps into the large musty basement. Another set of steps on the opposite side led to what looked like the greenhouse. Odd. Most greenhouses are free standing.

Noticing where my attention lay, Ada Opal said, "Yes, it's a greenhouse. Miki fixed it so I could enter from indoors when the weather was cold. I'm a hot house flower, you know, from the deep south."

The furnace, hot water heater, washing machine and dryer, all top of the line, were in the central basement. There was a coal room next to the basement steps. I stepped in. In a corner, a few lumps of coal remained that had been dumped through a ground level window, now hooked closed.

Next to the coal bin, a former cistern contained a steamer trunk and many different-sized boxes stacked deep on wooden shelves. Peering into the dimness, Ada Opal gasped and stumbled against me. "Wendy," she cried, snatching my arm. "I think our tray is gone. Miki's Rumanian tray." She pointed to a space in front of a large cardboard box. "I put it there about a month ago. It's an antique, from the old country. Miki treasured it. My God, it's gone."

"Maybe somebody moved it," I suggested.

"I'm sure I'd have noticed if Miki had brought it back upstairs. It was big and heavy, about two by two-and-a-half feet, a dinner tray we hardly used. It was taking up a lot of room in the étagère so I moved it down here but left it out in the open so if Miki wanted it, it would be right..." She pointed again at the empty space and surrendered to soft tears. "What would it mean to a murderer to steal a family treasure?" she choked out.

"Money. It's probably valuable. I'll have to let the police in on this. They can check the area pawnshops. And it might identify a killer. Who's been down here lately? Furnace man? Plumber? An experienced burglar would scout the place out." My dad always did.

"No one has been down here for months except my family and me. I work in the greenhouse practically every day. It grants me peace and quiet."

I stepped down into the former cistern and examined the sealed boxes to make sure none had been opened.

"It's something that he'd enter this side room instead of getting the hell out as fast as he could," I said. "As if he knew where the tray was."

I checked the windows as escape route. They were all hooked from the inside. A stray thought intruded: that those windows were too high up for one-armed Chuck.

"Let's have a look in the greenhouse," I said.

I trailed Ada Opal up the steps into the warm damp greenhouse where small pots lined concrete benches with an aisle between. Some of the plants looked healthy, others perhaps were dying, but what did I know? Maybe they sprang to life with the touch of a green thumb. Lily the witch passed fleetingly through my mind. She'd had the touch. It was the first I'd thought of poor, presumed dead Lily in a while.

Ada Opal interrupted my musings. "I know my plants need watering. So much on my mind. Miki did so love the herbs."

We traipsed between the benches to a door that exited into the backyard.

"Might be prints on this," I said, examining the smudged surface of the doorknob.

"Probably my gloves smeared the knob," Ada Opal said despairingly. "I'm in and out often."

"The cops have fingerprint equipment. I've got to call them in."

I called G.P. at his home, but no one answered, so I dialed Bobby at his home. Again, no pick up. I tried the Watkins police station and Bobby answered.

"Every third week I work on Sunday," he informed me. "Otherwise Ken Johnson's the officer on duty."

I filled him in on the basement light and the theft of the tray, also about the likely escape route through the greenhouse.

In response, he griped, "You're the original loner, aren't you, searching that basement without the team along."

"It's Sunday. I didn't want to disturb you."

"Let it go until tomorrow. G.P.'s in charge. He has to lead the search."

"Bobby, the man's terribly discouraged. I mean he didn't even show up this morning. Why don't we go check on him? This revelation may be the perfect calling card to get his pulse pounding again."

He thought for a few seconds. "Well, okay," he said, "but the man's going to hate us for spoiling his Sunday."

"Que sera sera. Let's stop by the office first, see what we're getting into. We can check and see if he's taken his Whittlins home. That'd be a pretty good indication that he's gone home too."

I drove to the police station. Arriving right at 1:00, I waited just inside the squad room. At the counter, Shulz was at the typewriter booking in a couple of fidgety young men as Brunanski stood by. The two collars were blond, fair-skinned, one a little taller and thinner than the other, otherwise a matching pair. Were they Cheeleys? If so, thankfully not mine.

Bobby soon joined me and got the office key from Brunanski.

He allowed me to enter first. The blinds were closed so I switched on the light. Five coffee-stained Whittlins lay on the desk. "The photo's gone," I noted. "I know he won't be back. He took that picture because it's the last thing he has of his late wife. He left the Whittlins because there are a lot more where they came from."

Harris walked in so suddenly that Bobby and I both jumped. "What's up?" the sarge asked.

"We're taking the Whittlins over to G.P.," Bobby improvised. "Maybe he can do something to clean them up."

"Crazy old man, playing with dolls," Harris said.

"Playing? Whddaya mean?" I waved an arm. "Look at that championship oar over there on the wall. G.P. is a master carver of both large and small. These dolls are his masterpiece, his Beethoven's Ninth. If there was a contest to show them off, he'd win in a landslide."

Harris sat down in the swivel chair and began a vigorous swiveling. In response, the chair creaked and squalled. "Old guy didn't have the balls for this job, or for fighting off an old cellulose bitch who practically lives in the cell block. I woulda laid out Miss Charlotte at first twitch. If Pap's quit, I'm in charge. And that means you are gone, Lagerquist, back to the sticks where you belong. But, Wanda old girl, I'd love to swap spit with you."

"Doubt I could even find your pencil-dick."

Harris jerked the chair to a halt and gripped its edges. "You got some hair on you, lady."

"Don't answer," Bobby growled. "He's not worth it."

Harris made a noise in the back of his throat. "Goddam set of hairy balls on that one."

Bobby took my arm.

"Don't handle me," I said. I shook loose and strode to the door. Bobby followed.

"Letting a woman tell you what to do." Harris called from the swiveler. "You're pussy-whipped, Lagerquist."

On his way out, Bobby kicked the door shut.

Forgetting about the Whittlins because we wanted no more contact with Harris, Bobby and I took the Watkins patrol car to G.P.'s house, a white Colonial with red shutters, located in a secluded upper-class neighborhood. Bobby pulled in behind a Lincoln Continental. "Back there, that was ugly, Wanda," he said. "Lawmen are supposed to fight the bad guys, not each other."

The scrap of Wendy remaining said, "Gee whiz, I'm so dang sorry." Under the overcast sky, a single light had been left on above the back door so we went there, rang the bell and called G.P.'s name several times.

After a couple minutes, the door opened a crack and the old chief peeked out.

"We wanted to advise you of the latest," Bobby said. "Knew you wouldn't want to wait to hear what we got."

G.P.'s eyes were bloodshot and dull. "Can't I have a day off once in a while?" he said querulously. He opened the door a little wider, stood aside a bit, and we squeezed past him. The kitchen was cream-colored, the fixtures and appliances unmatched and fairly new. A kettle sat on a lit burner.

Sparse gray hair uncombed, G.P. was in blue jeans with one knee torn, and a stained, partially buttoned shirt, its tail hanging out. He wore ragged plaid slippers.

Bobby explained the situation and that a search was required.

"We'd never go ahead without your leadership," I added with eye-glistening sincerity.

G.P. absorbed the information and asked no questions. He just sighed and said, "I'll be with you directly," and went briskly from the room.

The kettle smelled scorched so Bobby turned off the burner. "I've noticed that you're a pretty good brownnoser," he said.

"You're not half bad yourself," I retorted.

"I learn fast," he said.

In about ten minutes, the old man returned shaved and dressed in an elegant working outfit. Marking the time on his Waltham, he took in a huge lungful of air and let it out with a woosh. "Let us begin," he said at the bottom of the woosh.

On the way to the Plinko home, we stopped at the station for Harris, because G.P. insisted, "The sergeant's been on these cases before and has a keen eye for detail."

Arriving at the Plinkos, Harris was the first one out of the patrol car. He had mounted the steps to the front door when Rolf Nitschke burst out of the house carrying a duffel bag and his violin case. Shrinking around the sergeant, he glanced at Bobby and G.P. further down the walk, but seemed not to see me ahead of them.

Harris stared after him, then pressed the doorbell.

Shortly Ada Opal appeared in the doorway. "Come in please. I know why you're here." She paused to look at me. "Rolf is just back from prison. He's moving to a cabin now that they're all available." Later Ada Opal told me that the boy had taken two adjacent cabins, one for his few belongings, the other for sleeping and practicing. The preacher's kid probably considered two whole rooms to himself was living high on the hog.

Ada Opal described the missing tray: "A pattern of leaves, entwined. They were gold, green, blue, in a background of stripes. Red and black stripes."

We made quick work of the basement search, Bobby asking pertinent questions, G.P. clinging to the railing as he proceeded slowly up the greenhouse steps. Harris dusted for prints on both greenhouse doors, but no luck there. Ada Opal's gloves had most likely destroyed whatever evidence there may have been.

I spent another fruitless night in the trailer and returned to the hotel in mid-morning to find that Wanda's documents had arrived. In addition to Harvard-bonded stationery bearing my detective bureau letterhead and New York state PI documentation copied from my Iowa licensure with which Sid was familiar, he sent an authentic-looking degree from CCNY, granting Wanda Woods a Masters of Law Enforcement. The diploma arrived rolled up and banded in red ribbon like the scroll presented on stage at graduation. Sid also included a missive from a grateful former client that was heart-rending. I hadn't detected such empathy in Sid. Maybe he had a new tenderhearted girlfriend who offered suggestions. Sid was my best friend from the past, as well as my lover and, while viewing the package contents in my hotel room, I let fall a few tears in thankfulness, and also from jealousy that he had gotten over me so soon, if he had.

That noon when I arrived at the Plinkos for lunch, Ada Opal met me at the door and asked if I'd like to move into Rolf's old room. "You're here all the time anyhow and it would save me money on both your hotel rooms. And I'd feel more secure after learning that the killer was in the basement, too. I get the heebie-jeebies thinking of some awful, faceless man creeping through the house and finding me. Or Lisa. And then there's shoot-em-up Rolf living right next door." She laughed harshly. "I wish he didn't have to live here, but he's got no other place to go." She made an ugly sound. "I pray the two of them aren't cooking up something that will knock the legs right out from under me."

"Lisa and Rolf are ignoring each other as far as I can tell," I said. "I think that part of Lisa's life is over."

"God grant it," she said.

Rolf did not value Ada Opal's teaching and had spoken disdainfully of her. Ada Opal confessed that, after returning from jail, he told her plain and simple, "I will not study with you." Circumstances what they were, she wanted Rolf out of her life as soon as possible. I couldn't blame her for that.

I accepted the housing offer after setting some ground rules. I was not her bodyguard. I was working on getting her money back and that meant there might be some late nights. I assured her that if I did get home after hours, I'd be quiet as a mouse.

"Oh, make some noise so I know it's you," she responded. She gave me a front door key and reminded me to always lock up. I didn't think I'd forget. I was already preternaturally aware of Harris and that I was baiting him. Was that smart? Yes, I believed it was keeping him off me, at least in the company of others. Our mutual hatred was so obvious that he'd be the prime suspect if anything happened to me.

Immediately after lunch, I returned to the hotel and checked out of Henrietta's room. I was still hesitant about entering Wendy Winkworth's room that the Plinkos had continued paying for, so I gave up on the pair of slippers and the clothes I'd left there. Maybe the management would box them up and I'd see them next at the Salvation Army. For sure the needy would appreciate Lisa's fur-collared jacket.

I returned to the Plinkos and made myself at home in Rolf's former bedroom. On the first floor, next to the kitchen, it contained a single bed, desk, bureau, and closet. There was a bathroom with two doors, one to Rolf's room and the other to the kitchen. That bolt was locked from inside, preventing entry from the kitchen. The medicine chest contained a depleted tube of toothpaste and a container of

Orange Spice cologne. I spritzed some on myself. I wondered if I should invest in the Orange Spice cologne company.

Now that the other students had left, Ada Opal, Lisa, Rolf and I were the only ones eating the noon meal at the house. An icy civility was maintained between the German boy and Lisa. They sat as far away from each other as possible. Young love burns bright and fizzles fast, I decided, particularly if, upon thinking it over, one objects to the other's infidelity. At any rate, Rolf never approached me for help in easing his way back into Lisa's heart and I certainly wasn't going to volunteer.

Ada Opal no longer prepared evening sandwiches and the treat bowl hadn't returned. Okay by me; I had my licorice twists. After wolfing down lunch, Rolf stole away quickly with confiscated leftovers in his pockets. Soon his beautiful music radiated from the cabins. It seemed that when the boy was not sleeping or eating, he was playing his violin.

"I recognize Rolf's type," Ada Opal said, alone with me after one of the meals. "I've dealt with them all my life. A young man of exceptional talent, totally absorbed in himself. Yes, he'd love Lisa dearly for a while, but before long it would wear thin and he'd drop her. There's only one thing Rolf and his kind bear allegiance to and that's the violin. I can imagine them, all of them, praying to their instruments at bedtime. I never wanted her to marry someone like that."

"Like you did," I said.

"I knew what I was going into and we shared our art fully. Lisa has no music in her. All I want is for her to be happy."

"She's not off to the best start."

Ada Opal laughed mirthlessly. "We thought we could mold her into what neither of us was: a concert violinist. What a travesty. It ended fast."

## 41

I spent a third night in the trailer, hoping the Cheeleys would show up. I was lying in a corner near the door when, about 2:30 a.m., the door squeaked open. .25 in hand, I waited. A flashlight zagged around. I recognized Chuck's chunky silhouette. I sprang to my feet and shoved the .25 in his ribs. "Freeze. Give me the light."

"Wennie?" he croaked.

"Yeah, give me the light." He handed it over. I aimed the beam in his eyes. "Where's Charles?"

Covering his eyes, he said, "You scared the life outta me. Charles is out in the car." He looked away and blinked.

"What vehicle you driving now?"

"I don't know the name. It's new. Come on, Wennie, I can't see." I directed the light to the floor by his feet. He peered around, probably seeing fuzzy black blobs.

"I might of left my silver lighter here," he said.

"Yeah, you did. I saved it for you."

"Gimme it." He held out his hand. When a silver lighter did not cross his palm, he said, "What's the gun for?"

"I don't trust you guys any more. You'll get your lighter back after I make sure Charles is where you say. First I'm gonna pat you down, then you're gonna take me to him. Hands up."

"Huh? I don't get it." But he complied and wasn't armed. His skin was greasy to the touch.

I followed him out the door and down the road in the direction of the entry gates. I handed back his flashlight and stepped off into the ditch. I had my penlight if he got smart and turned off his light.

The tops of trees were a dark blur. The moon was moving in and out of clouds. I heard the faint sound of a motor idling. Around a curve, I saw a dark shape in the road. It was a big car. The headlights came on to light up Chuck. I crouched where I was. A late model Buick Roadmaster, the body two-tone, blue or blue-green, its top light-colored, tan probably. In partial moonlight it was hard to tell. The motor was idling softly and there was someone behind the wheel.

"Get him out of the car," I whispered to Chuck. "Don't say I'm here or you're a dead man."

Chuck approached the car. I heard him say, "Charles, I got something to show you." The dome light came on as Charles opened the door. As always, he emerged quickly.

I climbed out of the ditch. "How you, Chaz," I said, the pistol at my side.

"Huh?" he grunted. Recognizing me, he grinned. "You still here?" His face, etched in weariness, appeared narrower than before, the facial fuzz more pronounced than I remembered.

I thought to myself, "You'll be shaving soon."

His mouth opened slightly and I knew I'd said that out loud.

"I helped you get to this point," I said.

"I helped you live," he said right back.

"Okay, but I helped you first."

Except for the purring motor, the scene grew quiet except for Chuck clicking the flashlight on and off and muttering about wanting his silver lighter back.

"Keep your flashlight on so I know where you're at," I said.

"She's got my lighter," he whined to Charles.

"I heard you the twelfth time," Charles said.

"So what you been doing since you ran out on me? Making some money?" I asked.

"William came into some," Chuck said. Charles eyed him murderously.

"Yeah? Somebody die? Anybody we know?" I asked. "Did William steal that $25,000? Or was it you in the house that night? You have the Rumanian tray in the car?" There was no reply. "Mum's the word, huh? This is a gorgeous car. You buy it with the dough?"

"You kidding?" Charles said. "This car's road trash. What dough, what twenty-five grand?"

Raising the .25, I said, "I'm searching the car." Charles' expression grew fierce.

"Stay still," I warned. "Don't reach behind your back or you're dead." I assumed he had the police special stuck in the hollow of his back.

"What bee you got up your ass?" he said, bringing his hands away from his body. He stepped away from the car door.

"One wrong move, you die right here," I threatened again.

"Thought we were friends," he said.

"Not since the day you left without me." I stepped toward the Buick, jerking the gun back and forth, toward Chuck who stood transfixed, and then to Charles, the dangerous one. I said reproachfully, "I gave you boys food, beer, clothing, and what do I get for it?"

"Boo-hoo," Charles said.

"You rob Miki Plinko without dealing me in, and you're stupid enough to kill him. Was that part of the plan?"

"Miki Plinko's dead?" Charles asked.

"Huh?" Chuck said. "Say again?"

"Miki Plinko was murdered," I said. "Like you didn't know. Charles, turn around very slowly, take your .38 out by the fingertips, very slowly, and drop it in the road." He brought out the gun at a snail's pace and let it drop. "Now step aside," I said. He obeyed reluctantly and fidgeted as I came forward. I picked up the weapon, took the magazine out of the handle, ejected the round from the chamber, and tossed the remains far off the road. It took a lot of control for him to watch that gun go. It was an expensive gun to lose, but no way was I keeping a cop's weapon.

I backed away from him quickly.

"Chuck." I waved the handcuffs I'd taken from my pocket. "Go stand by the front bumper of this beautiful machine. Stick one of these cuffs through that slot behind the left bumper guard." I indicated the small oval opening and then tossed the cuffs at him. "Be quick about it," I said, "or you'll be out one silver lighter." Chuck stepped hesitantly toward the car.

I said to Charles, "Grab that handcuff when he sticks it through the other side of that oval hole. Snap it on your left wrist. Chuck, do the same with the other cuff. Snap it on your left wrist."

Chuck's lower lip pushed out. "She's going to run us over. What we ever done to her?"

"Save her life is all," Charles said, poised on his toes, evaluating the chances of overpowering me.

I waggled the .25. "Nobody's gonna get run over," I said, "but don't tempt me."

Charles glanced at the Buick and shifted his feet until he faced me. "Nobody's getting handcuffed to the car either," he said. "Too dangerous in case the brakes slip. We'll go stand in the middle of the road where you can watch us." Chuck began whimpering.

"You're pitiful," I said, "both of you. Okay. Charles, take your brother's hand and stand over there in the headlights. Move straight and slow or this gun goes off." Death threats were piling up. I hoped I was convincing two out of the three of us. Slowly they complied in sidling moves while studying me.

"That's far enough. Stand close together and face each other," I instructed. When they were properly positioned, I said, "Get down on your knees." They hesitated. "Do it!" The pair sank to their knees. "Yes. Okay. Chuck, place a cuff around Charles' right wrist and snap it on and then snap the other cuff around your right wrist." They looked at me blankly. "Move! Do it," I barked. Chuck snapped a cuff on Charles's left wrist. "No!" I shook my head in futility. "Oh well, okay. Fine."

"You really have my lighter?" Chuck asked.

"Yes. You'll get it back when you snap that other cuff onto your LEFT wrist." I could have used a couple Whittlins to demonstrate.

"No," he whined, "it will hurt my arm." He was holding the injured arm close to his body. He wasn't wearing the sling anymore so the wound had slipped my mind.

"All right," I gave up. "Snap the cuff on your other wrist."

Once they were manacled, I approached the car, keeping them in view. "If you rush me I will drive this car directly over you. If you run off in the dark, I'll drive the car right out of here, and tell the cops you're here. You're wanted for Miki Plinko's murder, and you'll never run fast enough to get away from a posse plus every trooper in the state."

"Plinko's dead?" Charles said again.

I opened the rear door and glanced in the back seat. My black overcoat lay in a heap beside a sack of groceries. I rummaged around, but no large tray. If it had been in their possession, they had likely pawned it. With a couple hefty yanks, I pulled the back seat ajar. Nothing underneath but dirt and some loose change. Watching the pair, I hustled around to the passenger side and examined the footwell. I clicked open the glove compartment to discover the old familiar police revolver on top of an ill-folded Illinois map. I broke open the gun. It was loaded. After spinning the six cartridges out onto the road, I threw it far into the darkness.

The registration document that an owner usually strapped around the steering column was missing. I knew better than to ask where it was.

I shut down the engine, pulled the keys from the ignition, and unlocked the trunk. Inside, a spare tire, a jack, a few cartons of cigarettes and Charles's pet shotgun. Mustn't take that or he'd follow me to the ends of the earth to retrieve it. Lisa's expensive clothing and Ada Opal's red wig were scrunched up in a corner.

I slammed down the lid and strode to the boys. "Empty your pockets."

"Do what she says," Charles said, digging. "It was stupid to come back for a fuckin' lighter."

They turned their pockets inside out and dropped the contents on the road. Between them they had $23.17, a pack of M and M's, three grimy Redhots, and five homemade marijuana cigarettes.

"The night of the Plinko murder, you drove past me like a bat out of hell," I said. "Didn't you recognize the Pontiac? Why didn't you stop? You have killing on your mind?"

Charles passed a hand over the stubble on his cheek. "Why should we stop? Tough gal like you, you know everything. That sure includes how to change a tire. Besides we were in a hurry, going to see William and June."

"Yeah? More like going to rob the Plinkos."

He was adamant. "No. William owed us. For taking care of Betty."

"So where's the pay?"

"You got it."

"Twenty-three dollars? You got to be kidding."

"It was more but we spent it. Paid cash for stuff. Gas and food. Ate sit-down once in a restaurant. New feeling."

I took their measure. With their expertise and gall, when had they ever needed to pay for transportation? Charles was more relaxed now, chatting with a woman who, in a previous life, he had grown to sort of trust. Meanwhile, Chuck squirmed and fretted.

"Okay," I said. "Pick up your stuff."

I decided not to go back for the black coat. It would keep the boys warm. I dug into my pocket and tossed the silver lighter at Chuck. It flew over his head. He reached for it and Charles' cuffed arm came along, jerking him sideways into his brother. They ended up sprawled on the road. Behind them, the lighter had skidded into a mushy pile of leaves. Charles growled, "Idiot, you got me all wet." Chuck stretched for the lighter that lay just beyond his reach.

I flipped the handcuff key to Charles. He unlocked the cuffs and dropped them beside a dead garter snake. He stomped on its head and kicked it aside.

Chuck retrieved his precious lighter. Flicking it on and off, on and off, on and off, he squealed each time the tiny flame erupted. "Daddy gave me this lighter," he goaded, his face close to Charles's.

"Knew you'd never have the money to buy one," Charles said.

"How'd William come by the money he paid you?" I asked.

"Guess he took a job. I don't know and I don't care," Charles said. "We didn't stay to talk."

"Where's William living since the holler burned?"

Charles took a step toward the Buick. "Keeping the headlights on runs the battery down," he advised.

"Stay put," I said. I brought the .25 back into the game.

"Don't know where William's at. We met in the holler because it was convenient," Charles said.

I tossed the Buick's keys to him. There was no evidence the Cheeleys had killed Miki. Not much money on them, no tray. And no chance that I'd turn them over to Harris. My PI job was only to return the stolen money to Ada Opal and collect the reward. Along the way, if I could wreak a little vengeance on the sergeant, I'd do that.

Right then I needed to be alone in the dump. Seeing the mashed-up snake had given me an idea.

The boys were quiet as they waited for me to decide their fate.

"You have a place to go?" I asked.

"Just outta here," Charles said.

"Out west," Chuck blurted. "We're gonna be cowboys." For once, Charles didn't demand silence.

"Okay, take your car and get the hell out. Don't come back," I said. "Every so often the cops come here and infest the place." They trotted past me to the Buick. "One more thing," I called after them. "Was Lily with William and June when you met?"

The boys paused by their respective doors. Chuck shot a glance at Charles and decided to take a chance. "That's for us to know and you to find out."

"Yuk yuk," I said.

In the car, Charles started the engine. As the responsible owner of a such a prestigious vehicle, he backed slowly down the road. He'd probably go in reverse right up to and through the gate where there was space to turn around without threat of scratch. In farewell, he pressed the horn and it emitted many tuneful notes.

"See you later, alligator," I said, mostly to myself. I don't think they heard.

I had memorized the Buick's license number and, by penlight, jotted it in my notebook. I'd check to see if it was stolen. Of course it was.

The moon went under the clouds and the night became even darker and very still. I used my penlight to retrieve the cuffs and key. After I cleaned them off against my thigh, I installed them in my army pouch. I slipped on rubber gloves and picked up the crushed black and yellow snake. It was a couple feet long. Its head was crushed and it smelled dead. I took my switchblade and sliced off a hunk and crammed that in an evidence bag. The rest I returned to the road.

Halloween with its witches and ghosts was about to descend upon Sergeant Como Harris. I was intent on making sure of that.

# 42

The Plinko compound was dark and silent when I returned at 4:45 a.m. In my room, I unbuckled the pouch and dropped it by the bureau after removing the snake-filled evidence bag. Someone, I assumed Ada Opal, had carted away the soiled bedclothes.

Shoeless, I picked up the snake pack and went through the bathroom into the kitchen and down the basement steps. It was spooky down there, all alone, in groaning darkness in the middle of the night. By penlight, I went up the steps into the glassed-in greenhouse. Succulents and herbs stood ready to be plucked. I laid the penlight on a bench and took scissors and pruning shears from the gardening-tool box.

I clipped some sick-looking herbs and stuffed them in the evidence bag to mix with ooze of snake. Farther down the aisle I spied a distinctly withered cactus that also found itself in the bag. I picked up the penlight and tip-toed back to my room, locking the bathroom door behind me.

Two hours later, I drove the empty streets to the Salvation Army store where I parked and waited for it to open. When it did, I was the first through its weary doors. I purchased several girls' blouses and skirts, a mop head with thick rope strands, and a sorry-looking broom. A 12-inch cloth doll, clad in frayed trousers, completed the buying spree. Under cloudy skies, I walked to the dime store where I bought cellophane tape, a black 10x13 sheet of artist's cardboard, some watercolor paints, and a brush.

Across the street a fabric shop supplied me with yards of black cotton material. Then on to the grocer's for three Mason jars and eight licorice twists. Those shops were within three blocks of each other.

I returned home. How quickly I thought of the Plinko residence as "home," a consequence of recent catch-as-catch-can housing. I left some of the purchases in the car trunk, the rest I brought to my room where I created a conical hat out of the black cardboard, holding it together with the same glue for the ages that had produced scalp scabs from Hospador's wig. I tried on the witch's hat and it fit perfectly.

I water-colored the doll's hair black and added a dab of black to each eye. I painted on a villainous-looking mustache. Since this replica turned out better looking than Harris, I dripped red watercolor between the eyes and cheeks.

I carried the items to the car and then sped to the daily briefing, which was blessedly Charlotte-less, and where there was no report of a stolen Buick Roadmaster. Harris strained to be polite and G.P. seemed tired. It was a glum nearly wordless meeting that wound down to a period of total silence before Bobby, clapping once, adjourned us.

On the way out, I greeted Charlotte clacking away at the typewriter, consumed one of the day-old rolls on her desk, and then drove to the Plinkos to find Harris already there, ostensibly to patrol the grounds. Why? To threaten Lisa by his very presence?

The sergeant strolled my way, his limp barely noticeable, a sardonic look on his face. I continued my brisk pace right up to him. He blanched at my ugliness; that was routine.

"Why you putting me down all the time?" I challenged him.

"We met before, ain't we?" A tentative statement of something he had once been sure of. All the opposition from others in law enforcement had diminished that certainty.

I shook my head thoughtfully. "Hell no. I'd remember if we had."

"Let bygones be gone if we did meet before," he said. "That's the way a man looks at it, otherwise nothin'd ever get done."

"You got a point. Definitely," I said. "So, the reports we've been studying the last few days… don't it look like the Cheeley boys are traveling around in circles?"

"I said that earlier. Nobody took me up on it."

"Well, I think you're on to something. Look, I want to say… " I stumbled a little because it was the last thing I ever wanted to say. "… I appreciate you working with me. If we keep working together on this, maybe we can solve this murder. Because, you know, let's face it, Bobby and G.P. are too young or too old to take advantage of our experience…" Off and running, talking fast, Wanda was tough to stop. "…what I mean is maybe us two can nab them Cheeleys boys together. Gain some respect for ourselves. I mean maybe them Cheeleys are heading back here for something. What if they hid that two grand from the robbery in the dump and are coming back to get it? Maybe they lammed out till the heat's off and all the time the money's hid in that trailer? I mean they lived there for a while and, okay, it's been searched, but not by experts like us. I mean there might be a trap door in the floor or a space in the ceiling. And what about all them junkers out there? Maybe it's hid in one of them." I had become nearly breathless with excitement. "Or on the trailer roof. Did they even look up there?"

The sergeant's mouth firmed and his slitted eyes watched as I became increasingly animated.

"You pushing me to go out there with you?" he finally asked.

"Gosh, no. I don't need you. I'll go out tomorrow, with the chief's permission, of course. If you want to tag along—I mean I've always worked alone—but you're welcome to come with. Right now, though, I gotta get inside and eat with the family. Tomorrow at the briefing I'll tell Pap my idea and get his okay. Totally up to you if you want to join me." *The chance to get me alone is up to you, pal. What a victory that would be, finishing me off and having a fine festive time "entertaining" the two boys who clobbered you.*

# 43

After lunch and a nap, I drove to the dump. It was 3:00 p.m. and sprinkling when I got there. I knew Harris' shift didn't end until 5:00. I parked behind the cast-off Chevy and, loaded with bundles, slogged through mud up the slippery trailer steps through the ill-aligned door. I wasn't concerned about tracking in ooze, slime, and dead leaves. With what I planned to do, messier was better.

I dropped the packages on the upside-down tabletop. Wearing soiled rubber gloves, I got the table surface mucky and dropped the Harris doll on it. I stabbed a darning needle through a scrap of paper labeled "Sargjnt Haris," in case anyone didn't recognize himself, and plunged the needle through the doll's front. The cloth split with the tiniest sound.

I crammed the mangled snake, its foul smell clinging to the evidence bag, into a Mason jar and added dirty water to murk it up. I followed the same recipe for the herbs and the cactus. I placed all three capped jars on the table next to the doll.

After ripping the children's clothing at the seams and scorching one blouse with a match, I scattered Lily's wardrobe, or maybe it was the garb her tasty young victims had worn, throughout the trailer. Lisa's couch became Lily's bed, rubbed with a bit of funky snake smell.

Standing at the open door, jacket over my shoulder, gloved hand smudging the knob, I took stock. Yes, Lily the witch was back. She had returned from the dead and thoroughly defiled this place. A deflating thought: this was no more than a clever Halloween prank, a scared kid wanting to get back at somebody. I was leaving a lot to my mark's imagination. Harris had blamed Tina Haverford's disappearance on witches. Let's hope when pressured, he really believed that.

I drove from the dump, turned left toward Watkins and went a short distance, then swung another left onto the old tractor road that ran along the backside of the dump. Trees had overtaken that road, among them tall firs that provided a windbreak for the adjacent farm field. I maneuvered the car under overhanging branches so it faced the highway. I was familiar with the spot; it was where I'd ended up days earlier, to decide whether to return to the Cheeleys.

Out into the chilly afternoon, stepping on matted leaves and pine needles, with evergreens looming over me, I yanked Ned's bike out of the back seat. I grabbed the broom and laid it across the handlebars. Patting the Pontiac's hood, I assured her that I would be back soon.

Not much trash in that area, but thorny brush had spread onto the trail that led past the gigantic fallen tree where Chuck had found the Christmas tree ornaments. At that point, the trail began lowering into the trench. I mounted the bike and rode through sloppiness that made it tough to pedal. I was testing how quickly I could get out of there on that bike. A couple of times the tires lost traction in the mud, but I stayed aboard, swaying until I managed to right myself. Like Ike before Normandy, I was too far along in my plan to wait for better weather.

Legs straining, I rode until I reached a location I'd previously selected. There I dismounted and leaned the bike against the earthen bank. This was a spot where the trench was about four feet deep. Standing in that ditch, breathing hard, I unbuckled the bike's saddlebags and removed the black fabric. After draping it around me, its ends dipping into mud, I secured it with a rope belt. I slathered mud over my face, not realizing that, in the process, I rubbed off the fake mole.

For the witch's hair, I stuck the ropy mop on my head and tied it under my chin with a couple of thick strands. I left the witch's hat in a paper bag so it wouldn't get ruined before I needed it. I grabbed the broom and hoisted myself onto the bank so I could see a portion of the trailer, the road, and some of the surrounding area. I unscrewed the squeeze ball horn from the bike and placed it beside the broom. I slid my hand into my jacket for the .25 to ensure that, if necessary, I could be quick-draw McGraw. Hunkering down, I polished off a licorice twist.

It was 4:50 in the afternoon. Harris would be off work in ten minutes. I was betting on him hightailing it out here with hopes of nailing and wreaking havoc on a couple of delinquents who'd beaten him silly.

About 5:35, I heard a vehicle approaching. Shortly it cut off and there remained only the patter of rain and the relentless wind. About five minutes later, I saw Harris, armed with a rifle, bayonet attached, creeping beside the road toward the trailer. When near enough, he sprang from cover, charged up the trailer steps, and banged the door open. Plunging through, he screamed like a banshee. Total silence followed. About two-and-a-half minutes passed before he burst out the door and, voodoo doll held at arm's length, hurtled over the three steps and hit the ground running. He zigzagged down the road and veered into the large appliance sector. There he lit the doll on fire and hurled it into wet trash. The doll flared briefly before the fire died out. Rifle-ready, he zigzagged across the road and crawled into the front seat of a junked Ford. Sitting low, with his rifle snout pointing through the Ford's window, he staked out.

For the next hour, we hunkered in our respective lairs. I figured Harris would stay immobile until complete darkness. Then I didn't know what he would do and maybe he didn't either. I wasn't going to wait him out.

All around were the sounds of wildlife I'd grown accustomed to while living in the dump. Close by, an animal scrounged and snuffled, in the distance a feral cat yowled. Rain spattered against the metal trailer and wind whipped through the trees. In the midst of persistent rustling, Harris fired off a shot, a spit of light from the Ford window. The man was completely unnerved by a witch hovering. Responding to the shot, a flock of fluttering birds rose from the garbage.

Eventually sunset came and a three-quarter moon rose at my back. Twilight lapsed into almost total darkness, with the moon glowing through the sparsely leafed trees. I gathered some pebbles from the ground. Rising, rearing back, I hurled them at the trailer. Enough clattered against the metal to startle Harris, who jumped from the Ford and, not stirring trash, twig, or leaf, crept swiftly, in absolute silence, toward the trailer.

Crouching, I pressed on the conical hat and picked up the squeeze ball horn. When his foot touched the first step of the trailer I stood straight up, hopefully silhouetted by the moon. I honked the squeeze ball horn twice, swished my black cape, lifted my arms and shook the broom. I screamed, "You killed me!" Instantly he fired off two rounds that hit short. As I leapt into the trench, the hat blew off. I flung the broom into darkness, jumped on the bike and pedaled for my life. Three more shots rang out, zinging over my head.

After a time of frantic pedaling that seemed to go on forever, I rose out of the trench and stayed on the bike to ram through rough foliage. Reaching the Pontiac, I slammed the bike into the back seat. The car protested in getting free of the evergreens but she was a good old girl and when we were well away on the highway, I patted her dashboard and told her so.

Speeding down that black, nearly deserted road, I cackled with witchy laughter. Disguised as Hospador I hadn't fooled Harris, and Wanda wasn't fooling him either. But my portrayal of a witch had been an absolute success.

## 44

Back at the Plinkos, I wheeled the bike to an outdoor faucet and scrubbed it clean with a rag. I hid it several yards back in the woods behind the cabins. In my bathroom, I cleaned the mud off my face. That was when I saw my mole had gone AWOL. I'd have to be without it at the 9:00 a.m. briefing tomorrow because the dime store wouldn't have opened yet.

After a restful night's sleep, I got to the station ten minutes early, at 8:50. Creating Wanda's usual racket upon entering the office, I saw G.P. and Harris in close consultation.

"Morning, Wanda," the chief greeted. "The witch is back." He pointed to his desk where lay a scrap of paper, almost ripped in half, on which "Sargjnt Haris" was scrawled.

"Witch left a curse," Harris said. "She's alive. I'm cleared of murdering her."

As Bobby entered, I took a chair on the other side of G.P.

"Sergeant Harris encountered Lily the witch in the dump," G.P. filled Bobby in. "Sergeant, why didn't you check with me before going out there?"

"Had to be done immediately. Ask Wanda." Harris looked at me expectantly.

The chief swiveled my direction. "Wanda, are you in on this?"

I shook my head. "Not a chance." Harris gave me the stink eye.

G.P. opened his mouth to say more but closed it when Harris spouted, "The witch left a voodoo doll in the trailer with my name printed on that paper there and stabbed a needle into the doll." He caught his breath. "I burned the goddam doll up."

I gawked. "Really? A police sergeant destroying evidence?"

"You look fine to me, Harris," Bobby said coolly. "That mean the spell hasn't hit yet? Did you pull the needle out of the doll before you lit it up?" Bobby winked at me.

"If you didn't the curse might still be in effect," G.P. said seriously. "Isn't that right, Chief Bob?"

Bobby smacked the desk. "Absolutely, G.P."

Harris sprang to his feet. "You weren't there so stop shittin' on me!"

G.P. raised his head to follow the sarge's sudden increase in height. He spoke firmly. "Sergeant Harris, you must go back and get whatever is left of that doll. I don't care what shape it's in. And find the needle too."

"We can send them to Peoria for forensics," I said eagerly.

"A needle! How would I find a goddam needle?" Harris yelled.

"Bring whatever evidence remains," G.P. persisted. "We need to know you're not just making up stories to throw us off the trail of you burning up innocent people. Why did you go out there in the first place?"

Harris' eyes slid to me and then he dipped his head. He knew I wouldn't back him up. He growled, "Routine check." He kicked his chair backwards and jumped up. "Wasn't none of this suspiciousness when I ran the town."

Bobby maintained his calm. "Chief, I'll accompany the sergeant to the scene. As a witness."

Protracted silence followed. You could feel the hostility in the room. Finally Bobby said, "Como, you are implicated in a possible murder. At the very least, gross negligence. We're trying to help you here. If we find proof of your account, we'll go from there."

"Como…" G.P. began. Harris blinked at the second use of his given name. He didn't like being addressed in the familiar like any run-of-the-mill Como.

"For now, we'll post a guard at the dump, in sight of the trailer," G.P. went on. "If there's any witches out there we'll bust them."

"I'll volunteer my deputy to stand watch overnight," Bobby said quickly.

"And I volunteer Brunanski," Harris came right back.

"Both can go," G.P. declared.

Harris righted his chair and sank into it. "I'll go back to the dump tomorrow, find that voodoo doll. But I'm taking Shulz and Brunanski with me, not Lagerquist."

"Como is scared," I whispered behind my hand.

"No!" he shouted. "The witch has taken over the trailer. Her shit is all over in there. That place is evil. I want the backup I choose."

"Lions and tigers and witches, oh my," I said, twirling little circles with a finger near my ear.

Harris made furious motions. "That witch cursed me for being a policeman. You know it's true, don't you, Pap? It's what we faced in the holler with poor little Tina Haverford."

Eyes narrowing, forehead wrinkling even more than usual, G.P. processed. Clumsily preparing to rise, he shoved his swivel chair back. When he failed to attain balance, he sat back down, almost missing the chair because it was still sliding backwards from the shove. He raised himself, fumbled for the chair arms and yanked it under him.

Before changing subjects, he smoothed himself out. "The results are back from forensics on Miki Plinko's corpse." He strained to reach the top paper in the wicker basket without getting up. "The red threads trailing from Miki's fingernails are from a man's wool shirt, probably Woolrich brand. Possibly they came from the shirttail because they had battery acid soaked into them. Speculation is that the killer worked around cars and some battery acid leaked onto the shirttail. For that much of the material to be ripped off, it may mean the cloth was old. Supporting that conclusion, the red strands are faded, indicating a lot of wear." He waved the paper as he gazed around. "Does anyone know of somebody around here that customarily wears old Woolrich shirts?"

"Popular shirt," Bobby murmured. "I own one. Brand new."

I said nothing. A faded red Woolrich shirt like William Bertalow had worn that day in the holler. I leaned back and kept quiet. Prove Bertalow's the culprit before letting the hounds at him. During the Municipal Courts meeting he was in jailhouse stripes, but what had he been wearing when arrested? Harris might recall. I sneaked a look at just another Como and saw his eyes light up. He blurted, "I know… " before clamping his mouth shut. "Forget it," he mumbled. I read his mind because we were thinking the same thing. But Harris wasn't about to allow more derision at his expense. Instead, he'd gather evidence and shove it down our throats—William Bertalow clad in a threadbare Woolrich shirt. I needed to get to William and June before Harris did if I hoped to collect my reward, if the Bertalows even had the Plinko money, that is.

As the meeting broke up, G.P. asked me to remain.

"Sure you don't want me to hang around too?" Bobby asked.

Harris groused, "What does she get to know that we don't?" For that moment, their exclusion made them unlikely bedfellows.

After G.P. closed the door on them, he said to me, "Chief Bob is asking a lot of questions about you. That young man is a bulldog. Once he gets his teeth into something he hangs on, and that might be regrettable for you. Is there something in your background you're not telling us? Something steamy, perhaps?"

Just like a man, assuming that the checkered past of a female must be sexual.

"What doesn't Bobby like about me?" I asked.

"I think he likes too much. Maybe he's looking at you closely for personal reasons, you know, boy-girl." His face flushed.

I felt color rising in my cheeks too. "Bobby's interested in me?"

"He talks about you frequently. You look like a man, Wanda. Doll yourself up. Throw on a little lipstick and fluff up your hair. And put some powder over that mole." He did a double take. "Where'd that mole go?"

"Oh," I said blithely, "every once in a while it rolls off when I scratch it. It always grows right back. I'll cover it up better when it re-appears."

G.P. thought that over, but with no immediate action necessary, his expression cleared and he said, "Perhaps you should try wearing a frilly dress and high heels."

Gee, who was that a description of? "I can't do this job in a dress," I said frankly.

"If you were more of a girl… a woman… maybe Bobby'd be more forgiving of any little white lies you've told. If any," he added. "As for Sergeant Harris, he still insists that you are not who you say you are."

Resorting to my usual flippancy, I said, "I yam what I yam, and I know that Harris is, and always will be, a poor excuse for a police officer."

# 45

At the Plinkos, the Cadillac was gone. Yesterday Ada Opal had mentioned the need to shop for groceries. I went to the kitchen to raid the icebox. Like most folks, I called the refrigerator "ice box" long after that appliance had gone the way of the dodo. As I poured milk into a glass, Lisa came in, snacking on a Milky Way. Without speaking, she sat down at the table. She was wearing an oversize man's white shirt, no doubt her father's. Her hair was uncombed.

Taking a seat across from her, I said, "Guess you and Rolf have broken up."

"Yeah. I don't want anything more to do with him, ever," she said, eyes on her candy bar.

"Otherwise, how are you getting along, Lisa? I mean we haven't talked for a while."

Briefly meeting my glance, she said dully, "I'm okay. I just hang around. Mom likes that." She hesitated. "Does she ever talk to you about Dad? About how he died? Who could have done it?"

"Who does she think?"

"Sometimes… sometimes she looks at me like I might know."

"Oh, I'm sure… "

"She thinks Rolf knows something, too."

"Were you and Rolf involved? Somehow?" I asked softly.

She didn't erupt at the accusation, like I thought she might. "No. But she thinks so and so do you."

"No I don't," I said. I hadn't totally absolved the girl but she was way down the list now that William Bertalow had risen to the top spot.

"Dad's funeral is Saturday." She blew into a handkerchief.

"Yes." Not knowing what else to say, I settled for, "Your dad certainly made a lasting contribution to the arts."

"Yeah. He adored Rolf. The other students too. He spent more time with them than with me. I wish he would have loved me like he loved them. Wish I could have pleased him. Now I never will."

"Oh, Lisa."

"To make it worse, I dropped out of school and ran off. I left him here all alone."

"He had your mother."

"Not really. They were pretty much separated except for the school."

"Couldn't get along?" This was new information.

Lisa wadded up the candy wrapper and tossed it toward the blue wastebasket. It went in. She sat back in her chair. "Because of Dr. Swaney," she said.

This was really new information. "How so?"

"They knew each other but kept it a secret."

"Oh, yeah?" I sensed a scandal. And here I had thought of Swaney as awfully shy with the ladies, the way he'd been with Hospador. Now I tried to picture him and Ada Opal necking in the principal's largely sterile office. It was a stretch.

Lisa slid her chair away from me. "I don't want to talk about it."

"I been around, kiddo, I'll understand," I said, sensing that she really wanted to unburden herself to someone. "If you want to tell me, I can keep a secret."

"It's hard to talk about," she deliberated. Nonetheless, with her eyes riveted on copper pots hanging from a rack, she began. "In high school, I didn't like the girls. They always did silly things and were backbiting like mad. I liked boys; they were interested in sports and things that mattered and didn't waste time gossiping. The tough guys were the best; Charles was one. One night when I couldn't stand being trapped at home one second longer, I told my mother I was going to a birthday party at a girl's house that was within walking distance. I wrapped up a present from something I didn't want any more and she said okay and I walked a couple of blocks to where I met Charles. He was driving an old truck and we drove out to the country and parked and walked into a field. There were fireflies everywhere, hundreds of them. Fireflies are magical, don't you think?"

I indicated I thought so too. "What happened?"

"Charles started to run after them and I chased him. We ran through alfalfa, trying to catch the bugs and hold the blinking lights in our hands. We chased each other chasing the fireflies. Finally we ran out of field and stopped, out of breath. It was dark by that time. We were at the edge of town where there was only flat land and the road.

"It was really black except for a small building that had a neon sign blinking on and off and a lot of cars in the parking lot. I was thirsty. I said, 'Maybe they got Cokes,' but Charles said it was a workingman's bar and we were too young to get served, besides I'd get thrown out anyway.

"I recognized the place from one time when my folks and me had driven by. It was a private club they said should be closed down because it was raunchy. I remember Dad was really down on the place.

"Charles went back for the truck. I wanted to go with him, but he told me to stay put. Said he'd come pick me up."

She sipped water and set the glass down hard. "While I waited, I walked over to the building just out of curiosity. The outside of the building looked seedy—broken bricks and masonry— the neon sign was flashing but all the letters weren't lit up. I went up to the big front window. It had blinds on it that were all bent. I looked through one of the openings.

"It was quite dark inside. You could barely pick out faces because of the smoke and all the people. It looked odd because there were only men in there. I looked for women, but saw only men. Then I saw my dad and he was with Dr. Swaney and they were sitting on the same side in a booth and nobody was on the other side. I couldn't believe it; Dr. Swaney's arm was around Dad. I mean, get away from my dad! But Swaney leaned closer to Dad and Dad took Swaney's hand and it looked like he was kissing the knuckles—one, two, three, four! I about threw up! I mean, why would he do that? The whole scene was gross, with the men slowly parading around. Men don't do that.

"I got away from there fast and Charles picked me up down the road. I didn't tell him anything because what I thought I'd seen wasn't right. Maybe I had it wrong and there was another explanation.

"I got home about midnight. Mom was waiting and really mad. She had called the girl and found out there was no birthday. She wanted to know where I'd been so I said I went out with a friend and we got malts and didn't know it got so late. It was a dumb lie; the malt shops were long closed. She wanted to know what I'd really done. By then I was really mad too, and I said I went with Charles Cheeley and she said that damn no-account and did you have sex with him? That steamed me, that she'd think that and I told her so. She was half-way drunk; she'd been hitting the schnapps pretty hard. I knew if I kept lying she'd hit me. She had before and she really thought I'd had sex with Charles.

"So I told the truth. That I saw Dad who was supposed to be at a selectman's meeting and afterward go out with the good old boys was, instead, sitting in that workingman's bar out on the old gravel road, and he and Dr. Swaney were sitting close together on the same side in a booth, arms around each other and hands touching. I felt sick remembering it, and felt worse for having told; I thought Mom'd say something to help me understand it. You know, explain what I'd seen, but instead she slapped me really hard. On both sides of my face. She yelled at me to never say such a thing again to her or to anyone else." Lisa paused to gulp water. Her face was blotchy with emotion.

"It was after that her and Dad split up. She acted very polite around him, and at first he was nice about it, but later on it was like he didn't really care."

She stood agitatedly and ran more water into her glass and sat back down. "I wish I never knew, never found it out. Had never said anything. It's all my fault why they split up." A tear rolled down her cheek.

"Your mom was probably already suspicious, and horrified when she learned you'd found out, because then she not only had your dad to deal with, but you too. Secret lives can destroy families. It's not your fault." I leaned over and patted her shoulder. "Does Charles know about this?"

Lisa nodded. "I told him when we lived together on Plum Street. He said 'The Lonesome Cowboy,' was a dive for fruits. He said he'd never figured my dad for a fruit, but he must be. I said Dad was no fruit, Dr. Swaney coaxed him into it, and Dad put up with it because he wanted not to fight and just to get out of there. But Charles kept at it. 'So Mr. Moneybags is a fairy,' he said. 'I'd go and collect blackmail money from him," he said, "but I don't want to catch what he's got, don't want it to rub off on me and Chuck. So it's up to you.'"

Lisa put her face in her hands. "I was really sorry I told Charles. I should have kept my mouth shut. But the blackmail idea stuck and when Rolf and I went to get money that time, it was in the back of my mind. I never could have done that to Dad, though, and I never told Rolf; he was so in love with Dad—not like that, though."

"No. Rolf admired your father. Do you think that Charles, despite fear of contamination, might have confronted your dad, or Swaney, about this?"

"I don't know. It bothers me if I should tell the police. It can't hurt Dad now and it might help catch who killed him, even if it's Charles. But telling would ruin people's memories of Dad, so… "

"Well…" I said, as though deliberating the pros and cons. "Keep this to yourself, kiddo. Let me think out all the ramifications first."

Firecracker information. Later, lying in bed, I considered options. Had Ada Opal killed her husband? Was she in cahoots with a lover of her own? Of course, she hadn't stolen the money, but she might deeply object to a lover who had. An adulterous husband, the cheated-upon wife, infidelity being an excellent motive for murder. But Miki was the one who drew students to their academy. His death had destroyed her career, her life, really. Ada Opal seemed more practical, more realistic than to let rage destroy her career. She seemed put together better than that.

And Carl Swaney, a homosexual working with children; what a scandal if that were revealed. Did Swaney have a motive for murder? Not unless Miki threatened to expose their relationship. And that wasn't likely, since Miki's livelihood also depended upon working with the young. But Swaney did have a motive for robbery, a lack of money compared to a brother who evidently had lots of it. That was a sore point within his family.

Investigate Swaney first or go after William Bertalow and keep Ada Opal waiting in the wings? I fell asleep fully clothed, mulling over the possibilities, and didn't awaken until the sun seeped through the window blinds. Once out of bed and cleaned up, I gathered my air force jacket and gloves and stuck the aviator glasses in a pocket.

First I called a switchboard operator and determined that the Bertalows had no number. A young man with a family and some money had to have a car, particularly since William was almost a Cheeley. There were three dealerships in Cassville and one in Watkins.

At the second car lot, I hit pay dirt. A short, balding salesman couldn't take his eyes off my manly get-up. He told me that William Bertalow had stopped by a couple of weeks ago looking for a vehicle and what was my interest? His simpering tone, the fluttering eyelids—some guys don't know how to flirt.

"William is my cousin," I divulged. "He said he was looking for a car and I want to get him a pair of fuzzy dice to hang from the rearview. Oh, and if he bought a car here, you'll have his home address on the bill of sale. I need to know where to drop off my gift."

"A Chevy, yeah, that's what he bought, but it's against the law to show the bill of sale to just anybody off the street." He was circling around me, checking me out, front and rear. I turned my head to keep an eye on him.

After we played "Ring Around the Wanda," and again faced each other, I inquired, "What you lookin' at, hon?" I lowered the aviators and batted my eyelashes.

"Baby," he said throatily, "I can't help feeling we have lots in common."

"Oh, I'm sure we do, hon," I purred, "and as soon as I get that bill of sale, we can go some place cozy and find out. Whaddaya say?" I saw his zipper rise. Like taking candy from a baby, this guy.

He managed to say, "I'll get that bill of sale right now," before hustling stiffly into the office. He returned quickly.

Snatching the document from his sweaty hand, I skimmed: $100 sale price, the license plate number, and landed on William Bertalow's address at the Beddy-Bye Motel. I knew where it was, having passed it on the main road to Watkins, about two miles from the holler. I unzipped my jacket and posed, hands on hips. "Let's make tracks," I said, eyes shifting, scouting escape routes.

An engine-knocking '44 Rambler drove into the lot, piloted by an elderly man. "Oh, shit," the salesman said, "I'm on duty. How about 5:00?"

"You got it. See you then, hon." Letting the paperwork flutter to the ground, I swaggered to the Chief Pontiac.

"How's the day goin' so far?" I heard my would-be lover call to the prospective customer.

It was 2:00 p.m. when I pulled into the cracked parking lot in front of the Beddy-Bye Motel. 'Suites Available,' the sign said. Not many cars in the lot this time of day so it was easy to spot the banged-up Chevy parked in front of Number 8 between a couple of 1940s coupes. I rapped on the door to Number 8 and heard movement within its thin walls. I assumed it was Fat June who opened up. The doughy-faced young woman taking up the entire doorway was holding baby Betty and had a flat nose exactly like Betty's. She was clad in a shapeless light brown dress and slippers with white ankle socks. Her mass of auburn hair was neatly combed.

"Hey, Betty," I cried, "how ya doin'?" I gave the kid a chin tickle with a gloved finger. She let out an aggrieved cry and June yanked her back. I introduced myself as "Wenda, Charles and Chuck's friend." 'Wenda' was recognizable as Charles' name for me and not far from 'Wanda.' "I helped take care of Betty when she was living with them on Plum Street. Guess I don't have the magic touch like Charles does," I grinned. "I was in the neighborhood and thought I'd check on my favorite little girl. Don't she look beautiful though."

Betty screwed up her ugly baby face and whimpered.

"She's hungry," June said.

"Such a sweetie-pie," I cooed. Lifting a hand to re-tickle, I decided against it.

William appeared at June's elbow, eyeing me as though I was a sick dog. "What are you doing here?" His damaged left eye drooped, the pupil jumping.

"You know me. I'm Wenda. Charles and Chuck's friend."

"She's came by to see how Betty's doing," June said.

"Okay, you seen. Now you can leave," William said, his one-eyed gaze cold.

I kept a smile pasted on my face and held my ground.

"Oh, come on, William." June nudged her man back to let me through. "We ain't had no company since we came here. And I could use some company," she ended firmly, as I edged past them and headed to a rocking chair and sank into its spongy cushion.

Jungle print drapery covered the front window, making the room very dim. Near the door, a bed was littered with well-thumbed movie magazines. At the far end of the rectangular space, a two-burner stove, sink, small icebox, and a table with two chairs were crammed together. The Bertalows had splurged on a suite. I figured two closed doors on one wall led to a bathroom and a closet. William went to sit on the metal-frame bed that was covered by a quilt of the same print as the curtains.

June's husband wore brown trousers, and a new-looking red and white striped shirt with a brown wool cardigan over his wide shoulders. The clothes were much nicer than when I'd met him in the holler and his hair looked neat and professionally trimmed. It was the new, moneyed William.

June brought a dish of scrambled eggs to Betty but stopped feeding her when the tot spit out the second bite. "Not hungry after all," she assessed. She laid the baby in a buggy beside me.

"What a lovely baby buggy," I said, running a finger over the buggy's hood. Both parents scrutinized my actions. These were people on the fringe of society, wary of strangers.

"How long you know the Cheeley boys?" William asked.

"Some months now."

June jumped in. "What did you do at the house on Plum? Did Betty have enough toys?"

"Oh, yeah, a ball, a pan and spoon." The list was short. "She was a happy baby, ate well, went through the dishtowels like mad."

June relaxed a little, but William remained taut, lips tight, the working eye unblinking while the other swam around.

"Me and him appreciate what you did," June said. She went to sit beside her husband, clasping his hand and gazing at him.

"It was my pleasure," I said. The room lapsed into silence. "Well, how are you all?" I urged along the conversation. "Your brothers told me so much about you."

"You look different from when you dropped by, when Chuck got shot," he said.

"Yup. It's been hard times." I shook my head.

He got up and dislodged his wife's hand. "I'll be back, hon." He touched his back pocket. Not finding what he sought, he gave the pocket a tap. My sensors went up. The guy had wanted a chaw and was feeling for his tobacco tin.

He went to Betty, tickled her under the chin and murmured, "Be good, Little Spit." At the door he grabbed a jacket off a coat rack. He left and a moment later, a car coughed to a start and took off.

"Well, that explains the nickname," I said fondly to the woman. "William was reaching for his chaw, like my daddy used to do. William calls Betty 'Little Spit,' 'cause he's 'Big Spit,' right? Sweet. Lovely."

"Oh, William don't chew," June said too quickly. "From the day Betty was born, he called her 'Little Spit' and we called her that ever since, I don't have no idea why."

I could see June was troubled by my assumption that William had felt for a tobacco tin. I helped her recover. "Charles is a lot like William, very caring with Chuck."

She fingered a button on her dress. "You seen 'em lately?"

"Yup, they was just setting out. Going west."

"Smart," she said. She didn't ask why they might be traveling. In apology for William's rude exit, she said, "He had to get to work, that's why he left so fast."

"Oh? Where does he work? I just got me a job at the Army Surplus in Watkins." With a nod indicating the fitness of that employment, she said, "He works in a bar, serving dinner and drinks." That news set off sparklers. Here was William Bertalow, proclaimed by the town as a poaching holler bum if not worse. What decent establishment would hire him?

"What tavern is that?" I asked. "I'll recommend it to friends.."

"You won't be recommending this one," she chuckled, "but it's a job. It's called 'The Lonesome Cowboy.' Outside Cassville a little ways. You know it?"

"Oh, yeah, the fruit bar. Poor William. What a guy has to do to bring home the bacon."

"The queers hit on him like mad. There's no reason. He never wears a dickey or nothin'. He is just so good-looking. He's had to punch out one or two of them guys."

"Terrible," I replied, shaking my head. "What do you hear from your Aunt Lily?"

"You know her too?'

"Met her at the holler the time she treated Chuck. I was impressed by how she helped him out."

"Don't hear nothing of her. William's taking care of that." I wasn't sure what that meant. From what Chuck implied the last time I saw the brothers, I thought Lily might be alive.

I delved a little. "William's always looked after Lily, hasn't he?"

"Lily convinced him she was his safety, so he'd feel obligated. Lily says harm done to a witch comes back three-fold. You think kin could get hurt if they don't treat her right? You can see by his eye that he was wronged bad by a lousy cop. You think he's cursed?"

"Don't think one thing has to do with the other but you never know," I opined.

I got up to leave and, surprisingly, June rose to hug me at the door. "Thank you for coming," she sniffed. "I get so lonely here." I patted her mountainous back. After I let my arms fall, she went to the buggy and lifted out her hefty child, settling Betty to her bosom. Betty reached up her pudgy fists and the two went cheek to cheek. June trembled a teary smile. "William says I cry at the drop of a hat."

Wheezing, she returned to the bed with the baby. It creaked under their weight. "Real hard living in the holler," she said. "After I got knocked up and we got married, we lived on berries and squirrels and rabbits that William shot. He tried so hard to keep us going but then I got sick and no doctoring except for that cranky old lady. But it didn't do no good, so we asked Charles to take Betty. Worst of all was the fire." She gazed around and her voice dropped. "I didn't mean that about Lily. All old people get cranky sometimes."

Don't be landing on the witch, June, or she'll get you.

"William hates paying for this here suite," she went on, "but I love the running water and the flush toilet. Someday my husband's gonna buy him a leather eye patch. Like the pirate on the rum bottle."

"Better not wear it to work, though," I chuckled, but she didn't smile. "Most of the day you're alone out here, aren't you, I mean, except for Little Spit," I continued seriously. "Now that William has a job, maybe you-all can get to know other young marrieds."

"No. We'll be leaving soon. We're moving away, to California." She swiped at her eyes with the quilt.

I moved to open the drapes. Cold sunlight flooded the room and gave it a positive glow. "Looks like your fortunes have turned and you're living high on the hog now. This is a beautiful room. Job must pay well."

"He brings home nice money."

"Well," I said, "happy trails to you. You deserve them." I was a little surprised I meant that.

After another hug I left, thinking June was not just a potential source of information but an innocent, it seemed, in her family's messed up situation. I felt sorry for her. Before long, she'd need as much compassion as she could come by.

## 47

If the cops recovered the stolen money, I'd be out the big bucks for sure. I figured my best chance would be to get William out of the way. Then June would be alone, isolated, friendless except for Wanda. I doubted that the money and tray were hidden in their room—pardon me—their suite. William was too smart for that.

The guy hated the police. I was betting June would confess to me before he ever opened up to the cops.

"Hey, Bobby. New shirt?" I said when entering the Watkins police station. "You're looking good."

"Nope, same old rag. I haunt the laundry next door." Behind the desk, the handsome man looked up from the pile of mail on his desk and smiled.

I plunked down in a chair across from him. "Office looks good too. Clean as a whistle."

He turned his chair toward me. Before we could continue our badinage, Deputy Johnson came in from the street.

I nodded a greeting. "Anybody got a cig?" I asked. Bobby handed over his pack of Kools and I selected one. He leaned sideways, scratched a match against the side of his desk and lit me up.

"What can we do for you?" he asked.

"William Bertalow's come into some money." I outlined all I'd learned from Lisa and from my visit to the Bertalows.

"'The Lonesome Cowboy,'" Bobby pondered when I'd finished. "That's a members-only club a couple miles outside Watkins."

"Fudge-packers," Johnson said.

Bobby considered. "I had Dr. Swaney in geography class in high school. He's a fine teacher and a decent man. At least I thought so. Lisa Plinko's a troubled teen; mad at her folks and joining up with a rough crowd to prove it. Sometimes kids like that say spiteful things to get back at their parents. But this is really vicious."

I squinched up my lips. Bobby was alpha-male so that opinion was what you'd expect.

"Doesn't make Swaney a killer though," he added magnanimously.

"How about this—" I said. "Bertalow must have seen Miki and Carl in the saloon and maybe the thought of blackmail entered his mind." I pulled a folded sheet of Wanda Woods' bonded stationery from my pouch and flipped it open. "I've made a few notes." I showed off the letterhead as much as I reasonably could to prove Wanda Woods was the real thing. "William Bertalow may have known about the money," I said. "The link there is the Cheeley boys."

"How'd you come by that assumption?" Bobby tore his eyes away from the paper.

"Lisa Plinko knows the Cheeleys. If she told them about the money in the safe, they could have relayed that to William. William's wife, June, is a Cheeley sister, you know."

"I didn't know," he said, mildly surprised. "Another Cheeley sister in town, huh?"

"Or another possibility: Miki could have told Carl Swaney about the safe. I know first hand that Carl needed money and brooded over his lack of it."

"How'd you come by that information?"

"My informant said that Swaney's family looked down on him because his brother had made a lot of money and he hadn't. Made him feel inferior."

"Your informant. Is she a small Rumanian lady about your size?"

I blinked. Was I really fooling anyone here? "I can't reveal my source," I said haughtily.

"I bet she shows up in town about the time you leave," Bobby smirked.

The list was mounting of folks who saw through my disguises. Why hadn't I been exposed? To protect me from Harris? Maybe they all detested him and wanted to see him go. They just figured they'd let me do the deed.

I could tell by Deputy Johnson's alert expression that he was listening and catching clues. I figured he'd not make a move to unmask me unless Bobby did.

"My deputy and I will head out to 'The Lonesome Cowboy,'" Bobby said. "If Bertalow's not there, we'll question the workers and the owner. If it checks out that he wasn't on the job the night of the murder, we'll head on over to the Beddy-Bye for a little chat. William Bertalow's been a thief all his life, but there's nothing violent on his record. The other suspect is Carl Swaney. I can hardly believe he'd rob and murder Miki Plinko."

"Maybe a crime of passion," I said.

"One pervert mixing with another always spells trouble," Johnson agreed.

"I don't think it was blackmail," Bobby said. "Blackmailers set up appointments, but this killer, or killers, snuck in."

"Right," I said. "What about the tobacco tin that William Bertalow reached for but wasn't there? And maybe he took a job to account for the cash he stole from the Plinkos."

The two lawmen strapped on their pistols. Upon leaving, Bobby tipped his hat.

I watched until the cop car pulled out, then went to the door and turned over the "OPEN" sign and "CLOSED" up law enforcement. I returned to the desk and paged through the stack of already opened mail, which was not fascinating. Afterward I thumbed through the wanted flyers. No one I knew was on them, including Wendy Winkworth. Had my supposed alibi actually checked out?

I sat for a couple of minutes, but surviving dead time has never been a strong point of mine. I filled in the next hour and fifteen minutes by opening unlocked drawers, discovering a New Testament Bible, a book on tying knots, and a massive amount of fishing line with a lure tangled in its midst. Pulling out files of past miscreants, I recognized the Cheeley last name in a few instances, but the first names weren't of any Cheeleys I knew.

I went to the restroom and checked the medicine chest. It contained shaving stuff, deodorant, mouthwash, and a package of rubbers. Checking myself in the mirror, I saw a stray hair poking out of my chin. For authenticity's sake, I left it.

Returning to the desk, I spotted a scrap of paper under the phone. It contained three long distance numbers. I dialed each and hung up after a voice introduced itself. The first was to the Better Business Bureau in New York City, the second to the central headquarters of the NYC police and the third called a Nancy Woods with a heavy Brooklyn accent. Clearly Bobby had done his homework regarding Wanda Woods and her detective agency.

It was almost dark at 6:55 when the police car returned. Bobby burst into the station and seemed surprised to see me as if forgetting he'd left me here alone. "William Bertalow was in 'The Cowboy', but ran out the back when he saw us," he said. "We chased him and darn it, we lost him. Owner says he did not show up for work the night of the Plinko murder. Next day he came in, tail between his legs, pleading a headache and begging not to be fired. Owner kept him on. Hard to find workers for that place."

Bobby was at the gun cabinet, removing two Springfield rifles. "We're heading out to the Beddy-Bye. Want to come along?" Outside, the squad car intermittently roared, Johnson tapping the accelerator, raring to go.

Hurrying to the door, Bobby said, "Bertalow won't come quietly. Ever since Harris ruined his eye he's been resistant to cops, and who can blame him."

I followed him out. He locked the office door and asked again if I wanted to ride along.

"Naw, you can handle it." I watched them leave. There had to be a better way to view the event. Being pals with cops was not to be desired when associating with the Bertalows.

# 48

I parked the Pontiac a half block from the Beddy-Bye Motel and shut down its headlights. The streetlight lit an empty cop car sitting at the entrance of the lot. A few spaces farther on, William's banged-up Chevrolet was parked askew. I took handcuffs from the glove compartment and snapped them around my wrists. I planned to arrive as the best friend the Bertalows had. I'd tell them that I'd just escaped from the same police who were now hounding them.

If the cops did find the money, what would Ada Opal say to a much larger amount, $25,000, being recovered, instead of the paltry $2000 she'd reported missing? Not a problem, I believed that smart lady would cover somehow: "Oh, that much? Oh dear, how would I know? Miki kept track of the finances." If she got away with that explanation, I doubted she'd share the loot with me. That belief was based on past performance.

The door to Number 8 stood wide open. Stepping into the room, I was greeted by the baby's whimpers. In the rocker, clutching Betty, June warned, "There's a cop in the bathroom." Bobby stepped out with pistol drawn.

"They arrested me, June," I said, emotionally distraught, "but I wriggled out of the cop car. Never was a police that could hold me." I gazed around frantically. "Where's William, they get him too?" I stepped closer to a seawall of tears from the female Bertalows.

Bobby breathed, "Jesus," or the like. He jammed the weapon in its holster and grabbed me by the handcuffs.

An out of breath Deputy Johnson rushed in the door. "I lost him," he gasped. His jaw dropped at the sight of me in cuffs.

"Wanda escaped, but we got her back," Bobby offered quickly.

Johnson's mind worked through it, and, becoming grave, he went along.

Bobby addressed me. "If it's any of your business, Bertalow went out the bathroom window. The manager saw him running away."

Johnson said, "If they run, they're guilty of something."

"Why wouldn't he run?" June screeched through her tears. "He was scared. A cop almost bashed his eye right out of his head. Wanda, he's only got a sweater on. He'll die overnight of the cold." She rocked frantically in the chair. "You think my husband's stupid? He'll never come back for Christ sake!" Hearing her mama's shrieks, Betty joined in.

Bobby had to shout to be understood. "Where'd he run to, June? If we have to hunt him down, he'll likely get killed."

"I know you'll shoot him down like a dog," June wailed, "even though he don't carry no gun. How do I know where he went? We didn't have time to talk." She bent her head to Betty and rocked her. The baby increased her racket.

Bobby persisted at the top of his lungs. "Where was your husband the night Miki Plinko was murdered?"

June yelled, "When was that? I don't know. At work."

"Tuesday, October 3rd. William didn't go to work that night. Were you with him at the Plinkos? You take that tray from the basement? Now's the time to confess. You'll get off lighter that way."

"I was here with my baby! William was right here with me!"

Bobby spoke into Johnson's ear. I read his lips. "We'll post a stakeout and take Mrs. Bertalow in for questioning." Bobby leaned toward June. "Pack what you need for your child." He turned back to Johnson. "Help her, Ken."

Johnson looked horrified at the thought of packing up that screaming pair. "Bob, there's loads of stuff needed for a baby transfer," he said. "Bottles, baby food jars, diapers, pacifiers, blankets, bleach. How about I stay right here and guard them?"

The Bertalow's anguish abated as Bobby absorbed all the reluctance in that room. "All right," he said. "June, you can stay in this room, but you aren't to leave it. Understand?" She nodded mutely.

"It's the right thing to do," I said. "She's too fragile to have to go through this." I meant June, not the baby.

"I'll put Wanda back in the squad car," Bobby said. "Don't know how she got loose in the first place."

"A surprise to me," Johnson said with a smirk.

As Bobby escorted me out, I said, "June, I'm just an innocent bystander, you know that. I'll be cleared soon, I'm sure of it. I'll bring back baby food and supplies if they won't."

On the sidewalk, as Johnson dragged a deck chair to the far end of the parking lot, Bobby called after him, "As soon as possible, I'll send a car to replace you." The deputy set the chair between two cars as his surveillance post. As Bobby and I walked to the squad car, I said, "I take it you didn't find any money. Or the tray."

"Nothing," he said. "Well fixed for shitty dishtowels though."

He opened the rear door of the cop car. "Get in. You're acting like you're the key to this whole case."

"I'm confident I can be of help," I said.

"You sure got a lot of gall."

"You say that like it's a bad thing," I said. "June's gotta see you shove me into the squad, like you've had it. My car's parked on the street. You can let me out there."

His strong hands gripped my shoulders. "Why there's a soft little thing under all that leather," he murmured, as he gently pushed me toward the back seat. "Duck your head down. You're going in," he said, breath tickling my ear. He placed one hand on my head, the other on an arm, lifted and placed me gently on the back seat. A shiver of desire ran up my spine. It was almost like being laid.

## 49

The day before Miki's funeral, I stood in front of my bathroom mirror in the Plinko residence and examined my hair. It had grown out to where, last night, I'd set it in tiny pin curls and anchored them with bobby pins and VO5 wave cream. Combed out, finger-fluffed, the result was a gratifyingly cute curly look.

I sprayed on Orange Spice Cologne. The idea was to create a temptress within Wanda's parameters. Hopefully Bobby would then concentrate on the person and not on her non-existent history.

After donning the military outfit, I asked Ada Opal for a more feminine blouse to wear on behalf of a lead I was pursuing.

"I've thought that for quite a while," she said and lent me a white silk blouse, puckered down the front, a huge bow at the neck, and ruffled cuffs. Returning to the bathroom, I pulled the ruffles through the flight jacket's sleeves so they stuck out. I drew on "Rhapsody in Red" lipstick with an artist's precision. Scrutinizing myself in the bulky jacket, soft blouse, and Marilyn Monroe hair, I awarded myself a "very sexy" rating. I stuck four cigarillos in the jacket pocket. I had bought them on the theory that they represented the height of European sophistication, at least Marlene Dietrich thought so.

Since it seemed a sin to cover my come-hither blue eyes with dark glasses, I abandoned the aviator shades.

Now I had only to replace the brown combat boots. Ada Opal wore wides; Lisa's looked like clown shoes on me. I knew where else to look.

Pausing on the stoop, the blouse covered by my zipped-up flight jacket, I breathed in the frosty morning and enjoyed Rolf's violin music flowing from a cabin. I heard his beautiful music throughout the day, every day. It granted a bit of normalcy to Music Academy grounds.

On the way to the morning briefing, I stopped by the jail and found Charlotte and her scrub bucket in its corridor. Two thirtyish inmates inhabited my old cell, seated on bunks and chewing and snapping gum as they looked me over.

"Charlotte," I said, sloshing through suds, "I met a really neat guy and I need a new look. You have some high heels you can lend me? Preferably brown."

"You? Met a man? High heels?" she queried.

I sat down against the wall in an almost dry spot and slipped off a boot. "Take a look. Can you outfit me? My feet are tiny and narrow like yours."

All women will fall in behind the goal of snaring a man, as long as it's not their man, so, after the initial doubt, Charlotte didn't hesitate. She click-clopped to the storage room at the end of the hall and seconds later emerged with a pair of tan calfskin shoes peep-toe shoes with three-inch heels and buckled vamp straps. They were so small, I had to ask, "Did they bind your feet as a child?"

"We can force them on. I think. You should paint your toenails," Charlotte said. "Not purple. That's my color." Surveying my new look, she pondered, "How's Granpappy? Does he talk about me?"

"Mmm, he seems kinda reflective," I answered.

"Good," she exulted, as though that meant he was sorry.

The two inmates had come to the front of their cell. The bleach-blonde said, "It's not so bad in here. Something's always happening when Charlotte's around."

My first steps were tippy, but by the time I reached the station lobby I was walking like royalty, feeling tall right up to the ceiling. I entered the office with the jacket open, the big bow and ruffles in full bloom. Bobby, G.P., and my vacant chair were in their usual spots.

Next to G.P., a broomstick protruded from a trash barrel. The two officers, Shulz and Brunanski, were seated by Harris in an outer arc. Everyone seemed transfixed by my appearance.

G.P. murmured to Bobby, "Cleans up well, doesn't she?" He started to rise. I zipped up the jacket to batten down the sexiness. He sat down.

A large drawing covered most of the desk, indicating a drama about to be presented. Four sheets of paper scotch-taped together were labeled: "DUMP—EASTERN PORTION." I glanced at the edge of the desk and saw a single male Whittlin awaiting the call.

"G.P.," I said rather grouchily, "with all due respect, we don't have time for this."

"It is necessary to show the clues that Sergeant Harris discovered in the latest twists and turns of this labyrinthine case," G.P. proclaimed.

"What if we just cut to the highlights," Bobby suggested.

G.P. appeared undeterred. He snatched up three beautifully carved police cars painted in Cassvillian colors and set them in a line on the Dump Road in the drawing. I swooped forward and flicked the last car out from under his finger. It zinged off the desk and tumbled to the floor.

"We don't have that one any more," I said severely. "And that's exactly what I mean. This whole presentation may not prove accurate."

Face draining of color, G.P. sank down in his chair.

My God, I've killed him, I thought despairingly because I had seen how much the old man loved springing his beloved Whittlins into action.

"But you can show-and-tell us about the witch, G.P.," Bobby spoke encouragingly. My apprentice brownnoser gestured toward the edge of the desk where another Whittlin, unfinished, lay. Little more than a rectangular piece of wood, it was painted black. Wrapped around its top was a piece of black cardboard that came to a point.

"Ah," I cozied up appreciatively. "See, that's exactly what I mean."

"Moment of showdown—coming up," G.P. spouted, any grievance put on hold. He brought forth the black figure with the pointy cardboard top and thwumped it down by the Trench in the diagram. Eyes fixed on Harris, he said, "The Witch rang a bell, waved a broom and cursed the Sergeant. As she vanished, her hat blew off." G.P. lifted the cone-shaped cardboard off the black figure's top, exposing the head that was also pointy. He placed the cardboard on an X in the drawing.

"I have marked an X where each piece of evidence was found," he filled us in joyously. "An individual X each clue—for the hat, the broom, the squeeze ball horn, the iron cauldron where the witch mixed her brews, and the Tarot playing card. Sergeant Harris discovered all this evidence with Deputies Shulz and Brunanski observing." He released a breath. "The actual items are in that trash bin." G.P. gestured toward the bin with its protruding broom.

"Ah," I said. I pulled a cigarillo from my purse and leaned for Bobby to light me up. He did, after pausing to take in my very sensual eyes.

"Fingerprints on any of this stuff?" Bobby, always business, asked.

"Washed away," Harris said.

"Do witches even have prints?" I inquired, tearing myself away from Bobby's cerulean gaze.

"Dead ones don't," Bobby said. He shifted to face Harris. "Now, look, Sergeant, I keep an open mind on witch sightings, but that iron cauldron is just an old soup pot that some cook tossed out. And the piece of black cardboard is just that, a piece of cardboard, not a witch's bonnet. And look at the playing card. It's a hand-drawn joker. It's not the fool on some gypsy card."

Bobby was growing more exasperated. "And since when do witches carry squeeze-ball horns? Don't they usually just cackle out their curses? Como, I grant you that something out there scared you, but you didn't see a witch. You said it was dark, maybe the wind in the trees, or an animal, some sort of figment of an overblown imagination. Go home, rest, cool off. Give yourself time to think."

"I know what I saw and what Lily cackled," Harris said through gritted teeth.

We fell into complete silence waiting for G.P. to say what he thought. He sat for several minutes, rubbing his lips, absorbing that last exchange before he rendered a forceful and decisive verdict: "This is a true, supernatural sighting," he rumbled, "as spirited tiny Tina Haverford away." That was what stuck in the old chief's craw: the disappearance of a vulnerable child that he was unable to solve. Therefore, necessarily, this solution also had to be beyond human ken.

But Bobby's piece-by-piece demolishing of the evidence was worrisome. If not Lily the Witch, then who? Harris was not terminally stupid. Who did the sarge know who was female, small, and held a grudge?

Something clicked in my mind. Maybe it was just heightened awareness of the danger I was in. I rose and examined the drawing. "Ya know," I said slowly, speculatively, "when I was a child I used to play connect the dots. You do that too? Where gradually a tiger would form, or an alligator or a Coke bottle? Well, this wonderful work of art that G.P. has created—it's revealed something so significant—"

Lips quivering, G.P. rose to peer anew at his drawing. "What?" he asked, no longer inordinately pleased with himself.

A shuffle of footsteps and everyone was squeezing in beside me. Harris growled, "Chickenshit."

I took a pencil from my pouch.

"Don't spoil my picture," G.P. warned and spread his hands to cover the threatened area.

"Trust me," I said, prying his big paws apart. "I'll draw lightly." I drew a faint line. It ran fairly straight from the "X" indicating the Broom, down through the "X"es for the Horn and cone-shaped Hat, on through the Playing Card "X", then with a sharp right, it headed for the Iron Cauldron "X".

"See what letter of the alphabet is formed?" I breathed in awe.

"'L,'" said G.P. "It's the letter 'L.'"

"And that stands for…" I coaxed.

There was a moment's silence, everyone thinking hard, a faint smile forming on Bobby's puss, before Shulz exclaimed, "Lab-rin-theen!"

"No!" I cried. "Lily! It stands for Lily!"

After an instant for the revelation to take hold, Harris stumbled past Bobby and made for G.P, knocking over the bin, spilling out the broom and a tinkly squeeze-ball horn. He punched the old chief's shoulder. "God damn, thank you Pap," he exulted. "Proves I didn't kill her."

I squawked my chair around and faced the sarge. "The witch is here, on scene," I said darkly, "deliberately laying clues before us. She's warning us that she is extremely angry with someone. Lily believes that someone in this room has done her a grave wrong. According to witch lore, hurt to a witch comes back three-fold upon the doer." I sighed. "How do you kill a witch, Bobby?"

In support, Bobby laid an arm across my shoulders. "Burn 'em at the stake," he said. "Although, that's been tried already and I guess it didn't work."

## 50

The search for William Bertalow continued. Shulz was sent to check the bus depot, Brunanski went twenty-seven miles north to the train station. Doubtful the wanted man had gotten that far, but better to cover all the bases. Tracks ran about a half-mile from Cassville, but the fugitive would have to scoot across a barren landscape and then board a fast-moving freight.

William as hitchhiker? Doubtful, what with the community on alert through radio, newspaper, and word of mouth. There had been no local report of a stolen car, so presumably he was still on foot unless family helped him out. Were there Cheeley family codes, like a circle of stones left on a log, or sticks in a T-shape at a crossroads? The Cheeley boys and Lisa had a code; she was to wrap a string around the mailbox at the Plum Street house to indicate her presence.

Another possibility: the Cheeleys, on the run, had tuned their radio to a high wattage Chicago station and heard about the manhunt for their brother-in-law, the suspected killer of an internationally known musician. Would they return for their kin? Was he as precious as a shotgun or a silver lighter?

If the loot was in William's possession, as I strongly suspected, I had to find it before the cops did to ensure my bonus.

I believed William was still in the area, if for no other reason than to reunite with June and Little Spit. This fall season had been chilly and rainy. Without a coat, the fugitive would certainly seek shelter, perhaps in an abandoned barn. Or what about the old granary? I pictured his joy at discovering the cop car all gassed up and ready to go. He, the loot, and the car would be out of there the first night.

Despite misgivings that I might find cops guarding the granary, necessitating yet another flight of fancy to account for my presence, at 1:00 a.m. I drove there and used my penlight to find a narrow crack between the boards covering one window. Peering through, I made out the squad car's hulk.

The next morning, after Ada Opal asked if I had anything to wear for Miki's funeral, she presented me with a baggy black pantsuit and a vest with a six-button front. She also offered heels but they were too wide. After Charlotte's killer heels the day before, I was happy to wear my comfortable black Oxfords.

I found a parking spot in the almost full Episcopal Church lot. Young men with bulky cameras patrolled the crowd with flash bulbs firing. Ada Opal broke through a milling group and rushed toward me. She was wearing a fur stole over a beautifully fitting black dress. Pulling up beside me, she implored, "See what's keeping Lisa. The service is starting in a few minutes and she's not here. She couldn't decide on make-up and said she'd take a cab in, but where is she?" Ada Opal twisted a silk handkerchief in both hands. "The press is here. Even the Chicago *Tribune* is covering this thing."

"Of course she's coming," I reassured. "Where else would she be?"

"I can't take much more of this," the widow lamented.

"I'll bring her," I said and returned to my car.

On the drive to the Plinko compound, I realized what an important funeral this was to be, not only attended by people who had known Miki, but others there for the sensation, because an exceptional man had been murdered. There'd be lots of ostentation, an elaborate coffin, pipe organ music that never ended, a multitude of gaudy floral bouquets.

Eight minutes later, I parked in the driveway of the Plinko home. Hurrying along the sidewalk under a gloomy sky, I registered how quiet the campus was. Too quiet. No violin playing coming from the cabins. But surely Rolf was at his mentor's funeral. He might even be supplying the big music.

I climbed the front steps and unlocked the door. The house had an empty feel, as though everything had stopped for the observance of grief. Calling for Lisa, I climbed the curved staircase. She was not in her bedroom. The bed was unmade, the dresser cleared of her stuff; only Miki's cufflinks remained. The closet door was ajar and I opened it all the way. My sense of foreboding diminished when I saw her clothes still there, including a sparse new collection. Beyond that array hung the black tea-length dress Lisa had planned for the funeral. So what was she wearing? The uneasy feeling returned full force.

I pounded back downstairs. "Where are you, kid? Let's go!" Sweets were a favorite way to feed a sad heart. I headed for the kitchen.

Passing through the dining room I saw the note folded on the table. Even before I opened it, I knew it meant disaster. Scrawled in childish script, it said, "Dear Mom, Rolf and I are together. He loves me. We're going to NYC because he's a brilliant violinist and will make lots of money and that's where the money is. I only took my coat and scarf because it's cold. I could only find one of my calfskin gloves so I left it. They were mine but you liked them better than I did anyhow. So good-bye, Mom. Dad won't care if I'm there or not. It'll be all about you, Mom.

Love, Lisa"

And she and Rolf had pretended to be enemies. Suspects were fleeing with dismaying rapidity. I re-folded the note and slipped it in my vest pocket. Before going back to the church, I checked Rolf's two cabins. Both were unlocked and empty of belongings.

Back at the church lot, I had to parallel park in the street. I sat waiting for the service to end. Twenty-three minutes later people began filing from the church, led, accompanied, and followed by cameramen.

In the shadowy lobby, with its dark ceiling beams and stained glass windows of gospel scenes, a line of people waited to express their condolences to the widow. A wizened old lady stood beside Ada Opal, surely her mother. We had never met, but I knew she lived in Watkins and hadn't been to the house since Miki died.

Spotting Carl Swaney about five mourners back, I made a quick reverse to get behind him. Didn't want to take the chance of him exclaiming in public, "Hospador, what has happened to you now?" I hadn't planned on encountering him there, and thought he had some nerve to attend. He probably didn't know that Ada Opal knew.

Catching Ada Opal's eye with a wave, I mouthed, "Lisa's all right." For the benefit of nearby mourners I murmured how it was so sad that Lisa was sick and couldn't attend. I nudged through the line and ducked past Swaney to deliver the note. "She explains in this," I said. Ada Opal opened the message, focused briefly and clapped a hand over her mouth.

"Is it bad?" her mother asked.

"She's sick," the widow answered in a clouded voice. She shoved the note at me. "Put this in my purse. It's on the bench over there."

She pointed at built-in seating that ran along the outside wall. I recognized her purse among others and took the note and did her bidding.

When I turned back, I saw Carl Swaney at the head of the line, extending his hand to the bereaved. Ada Opal recoiled in a very stagy manner. Head bowed, Swaney slunk away. He scooted through the double doors and into the parking lot.

I strolled outside where a cameraman was waiting to fire. I gave him a toothsome grin. He lowered the camera. Swaney was weaving through the mass of cars, heading for the far end of the lot.

I made tracks after him. Facing his beat-up sedan, he delved into a trouser pocket. From behind, I gripped his shoulder. He spun, broke free and faced me close up. "What—" he stammered.

"I'm Wanda Woods," I barked. "Tough in there, wasn't it. Widow didn't cotton to ya, did she? It's that 'Lonesome Cowboy' thing, ain't it? I seen you in there with him." I shook my head. "Poor choice of a place for meetin' up, though. Woulda offered you and Mick my digs if you wanted. Cigarillo?" I tapped one poking from my vest.

Yanking on the door handle, he snarled, "What the hell?" The door was locked. He fished in his pocket and produced a key ring within a mashed hanky.

Sticking my faded "w" up to his dodging face, I said, "I'm stayin' at the Cassville Hotel if you need to talk. Mick told me you was everything to him."

Swaney plunged a key in the lock, scrambled into the car and slammed the door.

"I'm Wanda Woods," I shouted at the closed window. "Cassville Manor Hotel! Tomorrow!"

"Freak," Swaney pronounced through twisted lips.

"We'll remember him together! Tomorrow!" I articulated loudly. A few people were gaping. Swaney's motor sputtered, caught, and roared. Tires screeching, he careened away, bumping over a curb, taking out a dogwood shrub. I stood alone in a brisk wind that loosened my pin curls and flattened them to my skull. Insouciantly, I strolled past the gawkers to my car.

I zipped off to the hotel. Caught between thrill and anxiety, I registered as Wanda Woods, paid cash for two days, and rode the elevator to a third floor room.

About 3:30 p.m., I drove to the Plinko residence and packed toothbrush and paste, deodorant, and Orange Spice cologne. I changed to Wanda's military attire and left Ada Opal's clothes on the bed along with a night explaining I was out on the trail.

The house sat in dead silence. The widow had not returned. She was probably holding court at the reception.

I drove to the police station to check on the latest reports. It was late afternoon; neither Bobby nor G.P. was there. Charlotte was typing at the booking counter. "You the only one on duty today?" I asked.

She pulled the overtime report from the typewriter. "Mutt and Jeff are in the lounge. It's where they loaf when Sergeant Harris isn't around."

"Where is the good sergeant?" I asked.

"Searching the holler. He thinks William Bertalow went back there to hide."

William would know the holler's secrets as well as I knew the dump's, but, having seen how desolate the place was, I didn't think there was a nook sizable enough for me to hide in, never mind a tall, gangly man. Although William might hide the money there. If he had it.

"I'm surprised Harris isn't scared he'll meet the witch out there," I said.

"Oh, he's decided she moved to the dump. He's crazy. Says after he kills her he'll open her up to see if Tina Haverford's inside."

"God," I breathed. "I mean, really. If he brought Lily in alive he could just X-ray her."

Charlotte's lips parted. "Are you kidding or as nuts as he is?"

I was spared self-diagnosing by the phone's ring. I left Charlotte dealing smartly with the call, and strode down the hall past the chief's office to the lounge.

Officers Shulz and Brunanski were in the small dreary room that contained a cracked leather couch, a table holding a plug-in coffee pot and some chipped mugs. The air was thick with smoke and burned coffee odor. The toadies were sprawled in sagging leather chairs scarfing down pastry.

"Well, look who's here," Brunanski said. His feet rested on the table up against an open sack. I sat down on the couch and tucked my feet under me.

"Make yourself to home," Shulz said. He held a gummy sweet roll, brown frosting on his lips and fingers.

I stuck a cigarillo in the corner of my mouth, lit up and added my smoke to the room's. I took the last cigarillo out of my pocket. "Who wants it?" After eying each other, they realized it wouldn't be proper to accept something you didn't know where it had been, so they both shook their heads no.

"Strangest thing," Brunanski said. "Been three women come to town, all separate. Never see one with the other, and they're always this size." He pointed at me.

Indeed? Hospador's bouffant wig and Wanda's lifts made individual heights vary by as much as one-and-a-half inches. That must not have been as obvious as I thought. "They all got the same facial features," Shulz said, "although on some there's moles and such." He didn't mention Hospador's bald spot, apparently he'd gotten past that. "You get the feeling that them three ladies might be related."

He yawned. The jagged yellow teeth with spittle and half-chewed pastry attached were an appalling sight. "You got sisters?" he asked.

"Nope," I said. I cleared my throat as though about to spit. Instead I swallowed because I had some civility left. "I heard some stories about a couple of lowlife cops who gave permission for a scumbag sergeant to rape a prisoner. They knew exactly what was gonna happen and didn't do a friggin' thing to stop it."

Brunanski looked at Shulz and said, "You never told me what he was like till we was in the diner."

"You are one weak trickle of piss," Shulz responded. He addressed me. "We thought you was one of the town bumps, like Prossie who don't care what's on top."

I jolted forward. "You got a nerve calling yourselves cops."

"Was you driving for them bank robbers?" the pudgy one asked.

"Huh? Whore and get-away driver too? Busy life. Fuck you." I kicked my legs out and smoothed out my pants until the creases were restored. It might be possible to wheedle some information out of Brunanski; he seemed closer to a human being than his partner. I turned toward him. "So what's the sarge doing about me being such a bother?"

Brunanski shrugged. "Nothing. He's going after Bertalow. And the Cheeleys for what they did to him. Once them three are caught, or dead, he'll come after you. Nothing we can do about it."

"Sure you can," I said. "You want to be a patrolman all your life? Harris holds you back, makes fun of you. Forget any promotion as long as he's around. He needs putting down and you might be the man to do it."

Brunanski eyed his partner. "I reckon G.P. would be easier to work for. He's a good guy. Came out to my farm once in a blizzard. Helped us birth a calf. The vet never made it through the weather."

"Yup, G.P.'s there for you," Shulz admitted. "Remember when he drove out and took Tommy Burke to the hospital while his dad was away at work?"

"Yeah, with his mom crying out on the front steps. Pitiful sight."

"G.P. even brought the kid get-well balloons afterward—agh— he's too much of a soft touch." Shulz reached into the sack, pulled out an éclair and chomped. "He's old. Won't be around much longer. No telling what'll happen then. Right now I got me a job I want to keep. Anyhow, we're making bets about how long it takes before the sarge puts a stop to you, Wanda. Wanta get in on it?"

I was out the door and down the hall before they gave the odds.

Returning to the hotel about 8:00 p.m., I dialed Ada Opal from the lobby phone. When she answered, I asked if she'd heard from Lisa.

"No. I know she's not coming back," Ada Opal said resignedly.

"Stay by the phone. She may change her mind."

"No she won't." That pronouncement was a death knell.

I told her that I'd be away for a couple days and not to worry. I was pursuing a lead. She gave a monotone reply.

"Are you going to be all right?"

"I'm nervous about being here alone."

"Is there someone you can call?"

"No. Good luck with your lead." The line went dead. The lady had had her fill of sympathy from people she judged to be false or useless, maybe both in my case.

I stayed in the room all day Sunday, snacking on licorice and apples, awaiting a call from Carl Swaney. I tried to remain optimistic about the chances. Of course, I was aware of Harris discovering my whereabouts too.

About 5:20 I was buzzed to the lobby phone. After I picked up and identified myself as Wanda, Carl Swaney plunged right in: "I don't believe you. Miki never mentioned you. I never saw you with him."

"I kept out of his way when he was with you. I loved him enough to do that."

A pause while Swaney digested that. Then: "How much money do you want?"

"I don't want nothing. I'm staying in Room 307. We can talk there. Nobody will see you. It's Sunday, nobody moves on Sunday. Eight o'clock, I'll expect you. We can reminisce about our great love. For me, unfulfilled."

"Oh my God," he groaned. "All right."

At 7:30 p.m., with the switchblade attached to my left calf and the .25 against my hipbone, I drew the shades and went to sit on the straight chair by a window. At 7:58, a timid knock sounded.

I hauled Swaney inside, slammed the door, and shoved him against the wall. "What are you doing?" he protested as I frisked him.

I found a yellow Swiss army knife in his overcoat pocket. "Planning to do me some damage?" I tossed it on the bed. It looked like an antique, the blade probably rusted. His overcoat, on the other hand, looked brand new. Thought this guy was a poor schoolteacher. "You bring the cops?" I asked in as croaky a voice as I could manage.

"No. What do you want? Blackmail? Nobody will believe anything you say."

"You did. Look," I sighed, "we both loved Miki and it's awful lonesome not being able to talk about it to anyone. At the funeral, I saw how much you wanted to talk to the widow. When she turned you away, in front of everyone, I could have wept. She must have known about you and Miki."

He teared up but wasn't taken in. "You want something," he insisted.

"Yeah. To talk about the great man we both loved so dearly. Why don't you get it? I was his lover too. Miki liked it both ways. He was married, wasn't he? Had a child."

He stared at me, sorting his options. "His love of Ada Opal had diminished," he said weakly. "When we met, he pushed her aside. She became nothing to him. You wouldn't have really mattered either. He and I had the loveliest moments." The competitive male animal emerging. "When he severed our relationship," he continued, "he said he was going back to her. I couldn't believe it after he had spoken so badly of her. Or was it you he dumped me for?" He flexed his fingers nervously.

"I dunno," I said. "He was dead before we made contact again. I know I meant somethin' to him. Once I went to his studio, to be with him when wifey was away. Miki liked to play. Oh," I giggled, "did we play."

"I don't believe you. If you're telling the truth, what did his studio looked like?"

"Autographed photos of great violinists on the walls, a desk with his fancy pipe on it, a high-backed leather chair, a bench… "

He took over the tune. "… two Italian music stands, a roll-top desk, English style. The high-backed chair was where the master sat and encouraged his young artists to perform their best… "

I continued less enthusiastically. "… a small black safe with curliques on the door. Sent from Rumania."

Swaney sobered. "It was robbed that night."

"How much was in the safe? He never trusted me enough to say."

Swaney didn't fall for another chance to go one-up. "How should I know?"

"Goodness, what's wrong with my manners?" I cried. "Please sir, sit yourself down." I indicated the lone chair. Eyeing me, he came forward hesitantly. I swaggered to the bed and perched on its edge.

After settling in the chair and taking a moment to think over the situation, he sighed deeply and said. "I always knew I was different. I tried not to be who I was, but I could never dig down deep enough to get rid of the 'bad stuff.'" He shifted in the chair, wiped his eyes, and shook his head dejectedly. "It's just who I am," he said.

The man was suffering and I was trying to lead him into confessing murder. Maybe I was a rat like Lisa said.

Swaney raised his head. Staring at the drawn window shades, he said, "Miki and I met when I attended a concert his students gave at the Episcopal Church. Their music swept me off my feet, so much so that I went backstage to congratulate him. No spark passed between us on that first meeting, at least not on my part. Not like you with the head over heels stuff. But I went home transported by the music. I bought books on Rumania and on Beethoven and Spohr and pored through them so we'd have something to discuss. When I felt ready, I called him and asked to have coffee together, just to chat about music and teaching and all of that. We met at a downtown café and went to his house later. He showed me his Gofriller violin and his Peccate and Lamy bows. When I went to touch the Peccate's horse hair, he said, 'Ah-hah, do not touch, you will leave perspiration.' I apologized profusely, thinking he must view me as an absolute rube. Then he held out the violin and when I reached for that, he said, 'Ah-hah, do not touch the varnish. It is again the perspiration that will harm it.' He had that wonderful foreign way of speaking. But I was kind of irritated the second time he admonished me, so I said, 'Well, what can I touch?'

"'Come to 'The Lonesome Cowboy' and find out," he said with a peculiar kind of smile. I had an idea what kind of place it was, but since he chose it, I dismissed the rumors I'd heard." He cleared his throat. "I was never interested in women in that way, so the club's reputation didn't put me off. I suppose it made me more interested. Several nights later in the club, we sat together and after a while we were both pretty hot. We made love in a stall in the bathroom."

"Oh you lucky devil," I sighed. "How I would have loved to be admitted to that place." I jabbed a finger at him. "Mr. Swaney, that is one swell coat you're wearin'. Gift from Mick?"

He opened the garment to display the silk lining. I crossed to touch the lapel with my fingertips. Apparently the need for solace trumped fear because he allowed the intrusion. "Cashmere," he said. "I bought it after he died. He wore one like it. I'd show up at 'The Cowboy' in my old ratty gabardine and he'd wrap that Cashmere around me and we'd embrace all folded up together. He felt so warm and safe."

"Your coat must have been costly. Your job pay well?"

"It hardly pays, except for the feeling of service. I splurged on it to help recover from his death. Have you done something like that?"

"No, although I do smoke more now. Care for a cigarillo?" I withdrew the last coffin nail from my pouch. He made a face of distaste. There was a razor nick on his cheek. I touched it gently. The act was too personal and he batted at my fingers.

"Your skin doesn't care much for the blade," I observed. Oops, had I used those exact words as Hospador? That thought led me to recall how this guy had defended me when I was the Salvation Army lady. Suddenly I didn't want him to be the killer. I took a breath and tried to study him with cold PI eyes. I knew if this man had committed murder and had the cash, I'd turn him in, claim my bonus, and go home.

Almost shyly, he said, "I can smell Miki on you, your love for him. Somehow it clings to you."

I strutted over to the bed and sat down to think that over. Crossing my ankles, I stuck the last cigarillo in my mouth and sucked on it. Everyone emerging from the Plinko home smelled somewhat orange-y. "I was with him so much that he must be in my very pores," I said dramatically. I lit up and blew smoke. "After Mick died, Ada Opal must have told the cops about me and him, because I was arrested and asked some pretty embarrassing questions. Why do you think she didn't tell on you?"

"Reveal that her husband was a homosexual? The woman would never do that." His voice softened. "In my dreams, we'd live on a desert isle together, he and I and all his beautiful things. A child's fantasies. The way it ended, with rejection and death, was far more realistic."

"Carl honey, we're like two peas in a pod."

"No we're not. Do you have a reputation that's threatened? I don't think so. Not around here anyway." He measured me. "You remind me of someone, Miki's cousin from Rumania. Are you from overseas?"

I ran a hand over my lips. "My parents were. They came over from Hungary."

"It's got to be your common heritage that gave you Hospador's nose and lips," he mused. "Your complexion is a little better than hers, though."

"Thank you, I guess." I let smoke drift and hoped it clouded my features. Why didn't this guy suspect a disguise? Most everyone else did. Because that would destroy Hospador's credibility? He had believed her, and had vouched for her, after all.

"Luckily when the cops pulled me in I had an alibi," I pressed on. "What about you?"

"I was at home that night."

"Carl, you seem so fragile. You got to think ahead. After you had the gall to attend the funeral, Ada Opal may decide to let your secret out. The night that Miki was killed, I'd be glad to say I saw you here in the hotel. Or was someone with you that night?"

"I'm always alone," he said bitterly.

I shrugged. "Well, if you need an alibi… " I let it hang.

He rose, buttoned the beautiful coat. Facing me, he planted his feet and said, "What are you like under that mannish outfit? I always wanted to hug Miki's Rumanian cousin for their closeness in blood and their enticing aroma. I still ache for a final hug from Miki. Or just to bury my face in his collar. Or something—to feel him against me one more time."

I stood and said harshly, "For twenty-five grand, I'll squash you in hugs and be yours forever. "

His mouth dropped open. "I knew it. You know that Miki told me about the money. Damn it. He must have told you too. It was his retirement savings that we intended to live on. Did he promise you the same thing? I can't believe—" As Swaney advanced on me, his frown deepened. "You killed him, didn't you? Two shots, you grab the money; it was in small bills so who'd notice? Then you run back here where your alibi is waiting and you split the proceeds. Tonight you got me to open up about our affair so you can blackmail me and get more money."

I backed up to the bed until my calves hit the iron frame. I wasn't afraid of the guy. His physique was flabby, his resolve weak, at least up until now.

"You killed him," I counterattacked. "You were raging, out of your mind like you are right now. Maybe you intended to die alongside him, two star-crossed lovers, but in the end the money was an awful big temptation, so you decided to live it up all by your lonesome instead."

He rushed at me and struck me in the mouth with a closed fist. I spun away and fell against the bed to the floor. Swaney backed away, appalled that he had struck a woman.

On my knees, I extracted the switchblade from under a trouser leg. I swung the blade in short arcs, swiping at his midriff. "Have a taste of this," I snarled and scrambled to my feet. "Where's the money, Carl? We'll be a team, cover ourselves in Mick's money and wrap ourselves in cashmere."

He ran for the door. Flinging it open, he skedaddled down the hall. I let him live.

At 8:10 the next morning, I was sitting in the Plinko living room when Ada Opal came downstairs.

"Please join me," I said, indicating the sofa. "I have some questions for you. You won't much like them, but they're necessary. Another suspect has turned up."

She hesitated. "But you've identified the thief. It's that riffraff, William Bertalow. Now you need to get my money back." The thief, she said, and not "my husband's killer," showing where her priorities lay. She was a practical woman. Miki's death was in the past; the lady was bent on moving forward.

"Why didn't you tell the police about Carl Swaney's relationship with your husband?" I asked.

Clutching the sofa arm, she sat down hard.

"Lisa told me about 'The Lonesome Cowboy,'" I said.

"And drag Miki's good name through the mud after he's dead, even to bring down that queer?" she spat. "I knew Dr. Swaney from parent-teacher meetings. He had no spine, he was a wimp." She looked at me, deep hurt in her eyes. "Our marriage was fine until he intruded. I was a good wife. Swaney came along at a time when Miki was extremely vulnerable, and took him from me."

"Did your married life change because of Miki's affair with Swaney?"

"Of course it did. Out of the blue, Miki begged me to do terribly improper things. Disgusting things… in the bedroom. I refused, of course. He was upset by my refusal. 'This is not the wife's way,' he said. 'She must agree to all wishes of the husband.' I told him, 'You're not in Rumania any more so you got that wrong.' He never again asked me for sex, normal or otherwise.

She began to rub the sofa arm back and forth. "After I learned about him and Swaney from Lisa, I accused him directly. He tried to explain by saying there are men who like women, but they like men too. 'Not in my life,' I said."

I nodded agreeably.

"The police won't go after Rolf and Lisa, will they?" The color had drained from her over-rouged face.

"No reason to, unless you demand her return because she's underage. We can always find them and bring them back if we need to." That was overconfidence speaking, but I didn't think it would be necessary. Right then Bertalow and Swaney were the main suspects.

"I can see she's better off with Rolf," Ada Opal admitted. "If I forced her back, she'd just run again. And this gets her out from under police suspicion and any trouble that man Harris can cause. I've lost Miki, and now I've lost my daughter."

"The day they left, she and Rolf must have gotten a ride," I said. "Who could have driven them?" No reply.

Maybe they took a cab to the bus depot. I'd check as though it mattered.

The phone rang and she jumped up to take it. I followed her to the phone stand.

She lifted the receiver and listened briefly. Disappointed, she said, "Here's Wanda." She handed the phone to me.

G.P.'s leadership voice came on. "Wanda, we're meeting at the entrance of the abandoned dump. There's been a sighting of... " A brief silence before he said, "the suspect." He must have forgotten Bertalow's name. "A farmer reported a man of the suspect's description running from a barn in the direction of the dump," he went on.

"The farm right across the road from the dump?" I asked. If so, I knew that particular farm. I had parked on its access road to set the stage for the witch's appearance.

"Exactly. Took off across the road. The suspect."

"Are we talking about William Bertalow?"

"That's the one," he said confidently.

"I'll be right there," I said and slammed down the phone.

Arriving at the dump entrance, I parked alongside three patrol cars. Two were Cassvillian, dark blue with white top and doors; the other, brown, was from Watkins. The sky was cloudy. Heavy mist obscured more than a few dozen feet. The moisture in the air intensified the metallic, muddy odor of the dump itself. I stuck my keys in my pocket and zipped up the military jacket against chilly dampness.

Glancing from side to side where trash poked out, I trotted down the middle of road, feeling the switchblade strapped to my ankle. A squirrel scampered across my path. It brought to mind thoughts of William and June living on squirrel meat. Around the third bend, I glimpsed the hunting party: Bobby, Harris, Shulz, Brunanski, and, surprisingly, G.P. What was the old boy doing, joining the chase? Aiming for headlines? I hurried to catch up. The five were armed with Springfield rifles, Harris' with bayonet attached. On their hips bobbed walkie-talkies, the Cassville officers' still encased in cellophane. G.P.'s, Bobby's and Harris' were unwrapped and ready to transmit, although they wouldn't need them if they stayed packed together like sardines.

I joined the party as Bobby was instructing, "Okay, let's pair up. You sure you want to do this, G.P.?"

"What good are you if you can't join the hunt?" the old man proclaimed, wattles shaking.

"I ain't pairing up with you, Pap," Harris said.

"We need somebody to go back to base camp and coordinate," Bobby said. Presumably base camp meant the three cop cars and my Chieftain. "G.P., why don't you go back and do that?"

"I am leading the search," G.P. said in his command voice.

"Hell, I'll go back and coordinate," Harris said. "Give Pap a chance to live out his dreams." He clapped the Cassville chief on the back. It wasn't like Harris to be so generous, but before anyone could object, the sergeant had turned and was trotting back down the road.

Brunanski smirked at Shulz. "The witch bothers the Sarge."

I watched Harris retreat. Glory meant nothing if a witch got you. He'd probably sit in a squad car with the doors locked.

"With Sergeant Harris out of the picture," Bobby said, "we have a better chance of taking Bertalow alive. Wanda, you don't have a rifle or a walkie-talkie and there aren't any more to give you."

"I'm fine. I'm packing," I tapped the .25 on my hip. I wouldn't be communicating with anybody anyhow because I planned to separate from the searchers as soon as I could, locate William if possible, and recover the money. Wishful thinking there, but I had a good idea where to start, at the far end of the dump, near the glen of firs where William had last been spotted. It was where the huge tree had gone down, leaving a gouged out hole that contained the shiny ornaments Chuck found. I thought Bertalow might be able to hide in that sizable space.

While awaiting the opportunity to split, I'd join the posse to let them know I was in the dump so the dumb ones didn't shoot me.

"Wanda will stick with me," Bobby said.

"I dunno," I said. "It'd be fun to catch the bad guy all by my lonesome." Bobby smiled at Wanda's familiar macho-talk.

He turned to the two officers and tapped his walkie-talkie with significance. "Look alive, boys." Shulz drew his army knife and sliced the cellophane off his walkie-talkie. He handed the knife to Brunanski who made quick work of doing the same, even after he saw Shulz's batteries, cellophaned to the side of his unit, drop into the mud. Brunanski's batteries followed suit. It took a moment for the boys to clean them off and install them.

That accomplished, Bobby said, "Officers, you go across the road, search the old cars, every last one of them and underneath them too, and then spread out over the whole area. Call in every ten minutes. Fire a shot in the air if you come across anything and we'll be right there. Wanda, you, me and G.P. will cover the area to the right." He stepped nimbly off the road into brush and strewn trash. I followed. G.P. came along more hesitantly, watching his step and even limping slightly. Shortly, Bobby held up a hand for me to go slower. "Wait for G.P.," he directed. What was this, a babysitting party? Shulz and Brunanski, shouting at each other, fanned out across the road and disappeared in heavy mist. Bobby spoke into his squawky transmitter. "Keep the noise down, guys. Over."

The conversation stopped, and after about twenty seconds Brunanski whispered, "Established position. Over and out."

Then there were only our footfalls squishing over leaf matter and grit. I went ahead, G.P. struggling to keep up, Bobby at his side. We had just passed the glistening-wet trailer when Bobby said, "Want to rest, Chief?"

G.P. merely grunted. Admittedly it was tough going, with fallen leaves slippery from last night's rain, and the dense spread of trash and rocks. Getting a second wind, G.P. spurted past me. Taking an enormous step, he slid into standing water. For a second he remained upright, then stepped again, awkwardly, turned an ankle and went down, bracing the fall with his hands.

Bobby growled, "Damn," and brushed by me. He extended an arm to help G.P. and check his condition. That was my chance. I went around them and, with their attention on each other, I stole away.

I heard G.P. say feebly, "Damn it, I can't get up." By that time, I was in a weedy thicket. I bent low and scooted toward the trench where I'd biked. Soon all was silent except for my footsteps.

I dropped into the trench. Wet leaves made for a soft landing and squelching sounds. Kneeling and feeling soil soak through to my knees, I listened. In the distance Bobby yelled my name twice. Keeping low, I scooted along the ditch as cold raindrops began to fall. I'd convinced myself that about a third of a mile away, William Bertalow, wiry and long, was sheltering at the base of that fallen tree, near where he'd last been seen.

Before continuing the search, Bobby would have to escort G.P. back to base camp, or call Harris to come get him. Either way he chose allowed me some time. I stopped and listened. A raucous birdcall started up as wind slanted icy rain into my face. Mist obscured more than a few yards on all sides.

I trotted for a while before I stopped, placed my hands against the muddy hillside and dipped my head, taking long even breaths. The rain continued to pelt me.

Hunching low, I started forward again. Very soon I'd come upon that clump of firs, bordered by the fallen tree where William might seek refuge.

About five minutes later, I reached the narrowing and gradual rising of the trench, and then the thick intrusive branches that signaled its end. 25. in hand, I dropped to my knees and snake-crawled forward. I was becoming a muddy mess. The foliage cleared and the firs appeared, impressionistic in the steady rain. Although I couldn't see it from here, I knew that on the left, off the trail about twenty yards, lay the downed tree. I scanned the area. No movement except the slight sway of the firs. I shook rain from my face.

He came from above, large and leaping, kicking my side, blowing my breath away. He shoved my shoulder into the mud and hammered my face with a fist. My arms flailed. The mustached sweaty face glared into mine. I writhed. Harris gloated, "William Bertalow did this to you." His breath stank. A series of wrenching blows to my face slammed me to one side, then the other. He ripped off my air force jacket and tore at my shirt. I screamed. He grabbed my pants and yanked them down to my ankles, my underwear going with them. I reached my left hand toward the ankle where the switchblade was encased. Harris slugged me in the jaw. Dazedly, I felt for the .25 with my other hand, but grasped only mud. I kept screaming, but my cries were muted; he was strangling me.

Abruptly he let go, knelt on his knees, and aimed my .25 at my face. "Stop yelling or you're dead." Given the choice, I quieted. "This is your lucky fuck day," he said. "I saw that old lady burn up. I knew I seen that bike horn someplace and remembered it was on the violin kid's bike. Next time I saw that bike it was hid behind a Plinko cabin with no squeeze ball horn on it. You cleaned it up pretty good from your midnight ride." I moved my head a little. "I'm gonna fuck you, long and hard, and if you enjoy it, you might live to fuck again." No, I knew I was dead. I intended to go down hard.

He unzipped his pants and reached in. He was already hard. Then he was on top of me. I fought desperately, trying to turn my hips from him, pressing my thighs together as tightly as I could. Howling and grunting, I thrashed beneath him.

He grabbed my throat and squeezed. My sight dimmed and I felt my hands go limp. There was a thud, a sizable impact from afar. Harris' weight fell away. Above me, a face hovered, bearded, an eye dead and wandering. William's face was blackened with exposure and his breath came in wheezes.

I struggled to sit, pulling my knees to my chest to hide my nakedness. I watched stupidly as William whipped Harris' face with a tree branch. Protecting his eyes with a forearm, the sergeant rolled onto his stomach. William kicked him repeatedly, in his side and in his head, each blow bringing an anguished cry. After a while, Harris shut up and quit moving.

William stood back.

"Watch him, " I said cotton-mouthed. "He's a tough son of a bitch." William picked up Harris' rifle from the ground and tickled Harris' head with the tip of the bayonet. He kicked my pistol farther away from where Harris had let it fly. He examined the scene.

"William," I croaked.

He grabbed my hand and pulled me to my feet. "Put your pants on and get out of here," he said, voice gravelly.

I hitched up my pants. The belt sagged and the zipper was broken, but the top button worked. I struggled into my jacket. "Thank you," I whispered. "Thank you. I'm June's friend, remember?" The relief I felt was indescribable.

"Thank you so much," I said again.

In a fetal position, Harris was bleeding copiously from a cheek. He mumbled something like, "Don't, don't."

William leveled the rifle at my middle. He jerked his thumb toward the ditch. "Get outta here," he said again.

"Let's take him in together," I said. "He tried to kill me. You'll be a hero."

"No, I'm not going back. I didn't kill Plinko, but I'll never convince them."

Maybe he was wrong about his innocence but certainly right about his chances of proving it. Once riffraff, always riffraff in Cassville.

"Okay, okay," I said, "you stand guard while I go get my car. We'll handcuff him and leave him for the cops. I owe you. I'll drive you out of here. We can pick up June and the money on the way."

William's mouth fell open. "She told you? Shit, June never could keep her mouth shut."

In that instant, Harris made a move for William's leg. William smashed the rifle butt down on Harris' bloody cheek. Emitting an almost musical sigh, Harris sagged and lay still.

William fixed his eye upon me. "I was at the safe behind the desk when Plinko snuck in. He had a gun. We fought for it and it went off into his leg." The eye blinked. "I had to get money. Little Spit couldn't live like that. But I never killed the guy."

"We can beat this together," I whispered. "Trust me."

He swung the rifle back on me. "No. You get going!" The madness in his eye said last chance, better take it. I sprang for the ditch and, bouncing off the sides, I zigzagged down its narrow path.

There was no pursuing gunshot. Soon a razor-sharp pain in my side forced me to stop for air. Gulping, I swung around, making sure I wasn't followed. As I fought for breath, I heard a terrible, ungodly cry and I knew Harris had bought it. I didn't feel a thing for him. The sound just made me start running again.

Finally I broke free of the ditch and hoisted myself onto flat land. I was on familiar ground, about twenty yards from the trailer. It had stopped raining. I was shivering from fear and the cold. I zipped up the jacket over my exposed chest. I seemed to be alone; there was no sign of the searchers.

Staggering with fatigue, I headed for the pond. Fury and shame consumed me. Nearing the water, I vomited yellow liquid into a bush. After that I felt a little better, like I might survive this.

I removed the switchblade from its case and laid it next to me on the bank. My addled brain didn't want it to rust. I cupped my hands, drank from the pond, and splashed water on my face. My hair felt dirty and matted. I was shaking. The cold alone was enough to make me shiver, but part of it was the humiliation, my carelessness, that allowed the attack.

Teeth chattering, I beat my hands together. I stuck my hands under my jacket and blouse, skin blanching from my own icy touch.

I trudged along the side of the road back to my car. Rounding the final bend, I saw only one Cassville vehicle. Harris had probably driven the other to the far side of the dump. The Watkins car was also there, unlocked. I got in, phoned the Watkins station and reached a voice that transferred me to Deputy Ken Johnson.

"It's Wanda," I said, "at the dump. Sergeant Harris attacked me. Then somebody came from behind and hit him over the head and I escaped. Send for an ambulance. It should go to the far side of the dump, next to a farm and an access road where there's a grove of firs. Harris, or what's left of him, will be there." I hung up the phone.

## 54

I drove to the Plinkos, parked haphazardly, and hurried to my room. Ada Opal's car was in the driveway but she wasn't around. She was probably upstairs in the bedroom, not wanting company. That was all right with me. I hauled my old brown suitcase from the closet and opened it on the bed. I pulled change and loose items from my trouser pockets and took stuff from the pouch and crammed everything into my sparkly shoulder bag. I emptied drawers and hangers of clothes, also packed the stationery.

In the bathroom, I ran the tub water as hot as it would go, stripped off my clothes, climbed in and enjoyed the heat scorching my skin. Soaking, soaping up, I scrubbed off the felt-penned birthmark. I sank under the waves and thought how wonderful it was to be done with this. After toweling dry, I donned Wendy-clothes, combed my hair, brushed my teeth, and lipsticked up.

My face was swollen, tongue cut, and a front tooth had come loose. Purple bruises bloomed on my throat and torso. Injuries mattered little because I was alive and fleeing. I'd had enough. Money was worthless if you were physically and/or emotionally dead.

I slipped the purse over my shoulder, lifted the suitcase and trotted through the well- appointed downstairs out the front door to the Pontiac. As I prepared to close its trunk, Ada Opal emerged from the house. She yoo-hooed frantically, "Wanda! Where are you going? You're not leaving are you?" Drawing closer, she said, "What's happened to you? You look terrible."

"I'm getting out of here," I said.

"Oh, don't go. Don't leave me alone. You're my only hope for getting my money back. "

I slammed the trunk lid shut. "They'll catch Bertalow soon enough and you can make excuses to account for the extra cash they'll recover."

"But he had a partner, didn't he? Bertalow may not even have the money."

I took my hand off the trunk lever. "Who do you think the partner might be?"

She fanned her hands helplessly. "It could be anyone. Those awful Cheeley brothers. Or Carl Swaney. Or Ned, or one of the other students. They always wanted for money."

"Who else? The Culligan man?"

"That thief and his accomplice stole my money," she said. "You have to find him before the police do. Return it to me in secret. You'll be rich then. I mean for you, you'll be rich."

Even if I decided to try, I would not be the first to get to William now. Anyhow, I wanted no part of his capture. He had saved my life. But, I hesitated, I could get to June first. William was the thief. He'd stolen the money, but he'd denied killing Miki Plinko. If true, who was the accomplice?

Ada Opal had left the front door wide open, and now from inside the house we heard the phone's persistent ringing. Hurrying up the walk, she called back, "Please wait, Wendy, it might be for you." She disappeared inside.

I got into the car, but left the door open with the motor idling. Get the hell out, part of me urged, fighting with the other part that insisted I still had a chance at the bonus. The fleeing part gunned the engine while the other part kept my foot firmly on the clutch.

Ada Opal yelled out the front door, "It's Chief Cass. For you."

I shut down the motor and got out slowly. What had I been thinking? Fleeing the scene of the crime didn't look good and neither would being stopped by state cops on the highway. All thought of vamoosing gone, I trudged into the residence with Ada Opal at my heels.

G.P.'s watery voice came on the phone. "Wanda, Deputy Johnson notified us. We need your statement. Report in immediately. Sergeant Harris is in the hospital. The back of his head is beaten in and an eye has been gouged out."

I released a breath before saying, "The left eye."

"Yes. I believe so. Did you witness it?"

"No, I was out of there by then. Did you find my pistol? I lost it at the scene."

"A .25 was found on the trail. Also a walkie-talkie. You can claim the pistol when you report in. The sergeant was stripped of his coat. His weapon is also missing. Do you know who did this? Was it Bertalow?"

"I don't know; I got out of there fast. But whoever clobbered Harris saved my life. Maybe it was the witch. She seems to have borne a grudge. I was just coming to the station when you called. I'll be right there." I hung up.

At my elbow, Ada Opal said, "What happened? Tell me."

"I'll tell you later. It's almost over."

## 55

At the Beddy-Bye Motel, the black undercover car was parked five doors down from room number 8. Clever. No felon would guess that the plainclothes man who sat in the front seat all day had an ulterior motive. Bobby had told me that Number 8's bathroom window had been boarded over, so the only way out for June and the baby was through the door. William's Chevy still sat in front of Number 8 with its windshield misted over. Several other vehicles were strewn about the lot, the yellow parking lines obscured by time and the weather.

My legs were about shot as I walked to the surveillance car. Deputy Johnson was in the driver's seat.

"You minding the store?" I asked.

"Yeah. Chief Lagerquist and them are still out at the dump. I gotta be here." He blanched at my looks. "Wow. Harris did that?"

"Yes. I'll recover. Seen anybody going in and out?"

"Nope. Here's been boring. Like to have been out at the dump."

"We do what we're ordered. I'm going in to check on June and the kid. Want me to bring back coffee?"

He perked up. "Yeah. Cream and sugar."

"You bet."

I went to Number 8. Dressed in a loosely belted corduroy robe, William's wife waited with the door open. We embraced and she said, "You look awful. What happened?"

"That pig Harris tried to rape me. Your husband saved my life, but he hurt Harris pretty bad in doing it. There's a search party out at the dump now, hunting for William." I went past her into the stale-smelling room. Betty was snoozing in her buggy.

"Oh, my!" June exclaimed. "William is so brave. He'd always help out a woman. What can I do to help him?"

"I don't know. Let me think." I leaned over the buggy. "Little Spit, you need some fresh air."

"She was sick," June stated. "We had to have the doctor out. I paid cash for a house call."

"The doctor came here? How'd he get past the cop?"

"Oh, the cop came in with him. We even talked for a couple minutes. Kind of nice. Doc Klein fixed Betty right up. Other than that, it's been quiet. Real hard." June studied her broken nails.

"June, you need to leave here," I said. "William is not going to get away this time. The whole state is out looking for him. He almost killed Sergeant Harris."

"Oh," her hand came up to her mouth. She flung it aside. "No, he'll get away. He'll be back."

"No, he won't," I said gently. "It's over. You got to save yourself and your baby. Look, I'm very grateful to your husband and in return I want to help you get away from here."

"I want out so bad, but not without him."

"The cops'll catch him unless… did you and him make plans about where to meet up in case something like this happened?"

For a moment a spark lit her eyes, but then she got cagey, saying, "We never planned nothing."

"Excuse me," I said. "I want to talk to the cop outside. See if there are any plans to let you leave. It might be possible, what with them knowing they've got William trapped."

June's voice throbbed. "Will you come back and sit with me a while, no matter what the cop says? I'm real worn out with worry."

"I'll be back. Don't worry about that." I went out, closing the door quietly so as not to awaken Betty. I approached Johnson in the cop car. He was disappointed I didn't bring coffee.

"Next trip," I said. "For now, I'd like to know why, when I asked if anyone had gone into that room, you said no. Because June said a doctor made a house call to treat the baby."

"Well, sure, but I know Doc Klein. I thought you meant somebody suspicious. Anyhow, I stayed with them the whole time. Nothing was said or transferred between them, except pills for the kid and a few greenbacks for the doc."

"Okay. Concentrate. Is there anyone else who approached that room that you think is not worthy of mention?"

He got an owly look. "Man and woman and a couple kids came out of Room 5 about 7:00 this morning. Walked right past June's room to their car. Does that count? Had luggage with 'em. Got into their vehicle and drove off. Or how about the old codger that dropped off newspapers at some of the doors about an hour later? Oh, he was a big threat, that one." His voice reeked of scorn.

"An old guy? Not an old woman?"

"I can tell the difference."

"What did he look like?"

"Little guy. Bent over."

"Did you see his face?"

"Yeah. It was old. He had a ball cap on. He was looking at which doors to leave a paper at. Come on, what's with you? It's a service of the management."

"Okay." I stood back from the car. I saw newspapers still lying by three of the doors. Not Number 8. Maybe June had picked hers up. "I assume you checked that out with the manager."

He averted his face and said, "Jesus," under his breath.

"I'll get your coffee," I said. I walked around the corner to the office. The balding man behind the counter said they had no such service and did I think this was the Ritz? On my return, I gave a thumbs-up to Johnson before rejoining June. When I entered, she was rocking the baby in her arms.

"Little Spit," I said fondly.

Tears started rolling down June's cheeks. "From the day she was born, she was 'Little Spit' to him," she said, voice breaking. Betty's eyes goggled but she made no sound.

"June," I said. "The cop says the latest report is they have William surrounded, that it's just a matter of time. You gotta start thinking of saving yourself and your child."

"No. William will be back. He's smarter than they are. He'll come here. I gotta wait for him."

I sat down in the rocker. "Face facts," I said. "You owe it to his Little Spit to get out of here right now. It's what he would have wanted: his little girl gets the chance for a decent life. It's what he told me he stole that money for."

June started. "He didn't steal no money. And he didn't kill that man. William is no damn killer!"

"William told me he didn't kill Miki Plinko. I believe him. He said you have the money, that Lily dropped it off this morning in a folded newspaper."

Still on her feet, June increased her span of rocking until Betty began to whimper. June laid her in the buggy. Moving to the bed, she shook her head violently and mumbled, "No. No."

"Yes, you have the money," I insisted. "William told me so. Here's what we'll do and this is William's idea: you keep a lot of the money free and clear, enough to start a new life out west. Mrs. Plinko told the cops that the amount stolen was $10,000, to save herself some taxes. That's all the cops are looking for."

"How you know that?"

"The Plinko daughter, Lisa, told me. Remember her and me stayed with your brothers on Plum Street for a while. Anyhow, William said to return $10,000 to the widow out of fairness, so she has something to carry on with."

"Why does a rich lady need that much?" The fact June was objecting to divvying up the cash showed she might just be falling in with my plan.

"Lisa said her mom's broke now," I pressed. "Said her folks put all their savings into their music school. They scrimped and saved to set aside money for a better life just like you're doing. I'll tell the widow—"

"William did not kill Mr. Plinko!"

"I know, I know. But have a heart and be fair to those who remain. I'll tell Mrs. Plinko that I recovered the $10,000. And for my efforts as go-between, I'll take $5000 of the remainder." I had decided that, if the opportunity arose, I'd add $1500 to the $3500 promised by Ada Opal. For pain and suffering and to make it easier for June to figure out. I continued, "That will leave you with $10,000 minus what you spent already."

"Spent nothing. Been stuck in this room, ain't I?"

"True enough. Your share is enough for a very bright future for you and Little Spit. Knowing this will make William very happy, even if he has to serve a little time."

"I just got the money this morning."

"It was Lily who brought it, wasn't it?"

She nodded. Her expression changed and became sullen. She reached into her voluminous robe and brought out a palm-size automatic. My goodness, what all had that newspaper concealed? Or hadn't Bobby, ever the gentleman, frisked her fat folds properly? "We're keeping all the money," she said. "You can leave now."

I began to gentle rock the chair. "Really? You got no chance by yourself, June. Listen up, you can walk out of here with lots of cash and no one stopping you, with me backing you up every step of the way. Or, when William is caught, as he certainly will be, you'll be charged as an accomplice because this room will be searched and the money's here. What will happen to Little Spit with both her parents in jail?"

"Why would the cops believe what you say?"

"The cop let me in here without him coming along, didn't he? I don't know what more proof you want that they've come to trust me." I let that sink in before saying, "William had a partner. Was it you?"

"No!"

"Where's the Rumanian tray, June? I'll return it with no one the wiser." The tray was probably with Lily. Could Lily have been in the Plinko house with William that night? Even a witch might need to turn on a basement light once in a while.

June snorted. "There ain't no tray. We laughed when we heard about it on the radio. William never wanted nobody on that job but him. He found out about the money and the safe from Charles, and he went to rob, not kill, all by himself. A solo job. He never told me different. He would of said otherwise." Quite a lot of insistence on that one point. William never carried a gun, but was unfortunate enough to come across one that night.

I flicked lint off my trousers. "June, you're waiting in this sad lonely room for a husband who's never gonna show. And when the cops come for you, shooting it out with a tiny pistol is not the answer. What will happen to Betty? Will she get shot too? Don't you get it? Doing it my way, nobody will get hurt and nobody's gonna suspect you of nothing."

Her weapon drooped but she clung to it. I continued painting her rosy future. "Where will you go, hon, when you're free of this place?"

She sighed. "Southern California, where my sister Rita is. That's what we always planned, before this happened." She closed her eyes and tilted her head back. She looked as though she was on the beach already.

"I'm glad you'll be heading to where it's warm and there's plenty of fruit to pick and movies to see. Rita's getting into the movies out there, isn't she?"

"Rita's beautiful. Ambitious. She was always dreaming about Hollywood from the magazines in the library."

"Exactly. Okay." I eased out of the rocker slowly so as not to provoke a gun blast. "I'll transfer the $10,000 to the cops, they'll return it to the widow, and that will close that part of the case. Mrs. Plinko won't object or she'll be in even bigger trouble with the feds. It'd be smarter of me not to get involved. Puts me at risk. I should probably get out right now. It's just that your husband saved my life and I owe him big time. I told him I'd do this for him and I always keep my promises." I watched her for reaction. She had none.

"After the cops and Mrs. Plinko have the money," I pursued, "there'll be no reason for them to hold you. I'll say I found it in the dump hidden in an uprooted tree trunk. Who knows who left it there? One thing's for sure," I reiterated, "the authorities will search this room top to bottom before they let you go. So," I sighed deeply, "I'm the only way the money's getting out of here. I'm afraid I have to take it with me."

She yanked the gun up. "All of it? No!"

"They'll search everything in here," I pressed on. "I can walk out of here with that cash right now. I sure don't want the responsibility, but I don't see any other way, do you?"

She stared into space, unable to offer a Plan B. The gun continued menacing me.

She moaned, "William, where are you?"

"William will return to you," I said. "He loves you and he knows where to find you, at Rita's. Hell, he probably won't have to serve much jail time, him being a hero and saving my life and all. I'll vouch for him. Tell everyone he saved me from that evil Sergeant Harris." I outlined my plan slowly, to drive it into her slow mind. "I'll deliver $10,000 to the police for the widow. You pack up, be ready to go. I'll drive you to the bus depot. You have to leave your car here, too easy to trace. At the depot, I'll transfer your $10,000 to you, and then you and the little one will board a bus that says

'California' on the front, and be on your way to a secure, sunny life. How's that hit you?"

"We want more than $10,000. I mean we got it all now."

I sighed. "How much more?"

"One thousand," she said with uncertainty.

There went some of my personal grant. "Five hundred," I said.

"Seven fifty."

"You're a hard bargainer, June, but okay, since it's for the baby."

She laid the gun on the bed and went to the closet. Before reaching in, she faced me and said, "Lily will haunt you for your whole life if you go back on this."

"I know," I said, spreading my hands. "Three-fold revenge. Rest assured, I'm not taking any chances on that."

She rooted around in the closet and came out with a paper sack full of green bills.

I took it from her and set it on the floor. "Let's make coffee, June, and we'll drink a toast to a better life."

We went to the kitchen end of the suite where she heated coffee. After raising cups of instant to each other, we each took a couple of sips. Then I stuffed my shoulder bag with bills small and large and stuck the little automatic in my pants pocket. I hugged June goodbye. She didn't look at me. I could tell she already regretted her decision.

I strolled to the cop car, hardly hobbling at all, and motioned for Johnson to roll down the window. After he complied, I stuck a cup of sweetened, creamed coffee through. "June wants the cup back," I said firmly. I acknowledged his murmur.

## 56

I returned to the Plinko compound. The Caddy wasn't there. I removed $10,000 from the Pontiac's glove compartment and left the rest there. I dipped the $10,000 into muddy roadside water and placed it in an evidence bag. I shoved that deep into my pocket, the one without the tiny gun.

There were two loose ends in this case: a tray from the basement and Lisa's lost calfskin glove. When something has gone missing, it's always some place.

I unlocked the front door of the house and went through the kitchen and down the basement steps. The night of the murder a light had gone on in that basement.

Was the calfskin glove, blood-spotted, hidden by the killer in the basement as he or she fled? Who was William's partner? Lily? Charles? Surely not Chuck or June. Did he have a partner at all? June was sure he didn't. Was it possible that when the first bullet struck Miki's leg, William panicked and finished him off? Or had someone else, unknown to William, completed the deed?

The Cheeley boys were the only suspects besides Lily and June who were close to William. Carl Swaney certainly wasn't, although they had both been in 'The Lonesome Cowboy' at the same time. Had they talked with each other?

By that time in my ramblings, I was down the steps, past the furnace and up the steps to the greenhouse. I snapped on the light to the left of the door. I could see why Ada Opal liked this place: warm and smelling of earth. She retreated here for solace and to nurture things that didn't talk back.

And it was where gloves were commonly found. At that late afternoon hour, low light filtered through the misted windows. Right away I saw a pair of dirty white gloves on the potting bench, the flimsy kind worn by the casual gardener.

I tipped over a watering can and shook it. Dry and empty. A small bag of sphagnum moss sat on the long bench beside clay pots and a trowel. I stuck one hand in and came up with nothing but peat. Two pairs of different-sized pruning shears hung from a spike. I moved past pots bearing sod, some with wee green sprouts. I shot my penlight underneath the benches. Briefly lit corners revealed a couple of long nails and scattered dirt. There were garden tools in a wood box at the far end of a bench and I tinked through them. Two huge sacks containing potting soil and fertilizer sat on the floor by the outside door. I dug into each, fishing deep for the feel of calfskin, bringing up only sifted dirt. I couldn't force my way to the bottom of either sack, they were too big and the texture unpleasant. I brushed my gloved hands off as well as I could, not smelling them, although, like a junior high kid, I certainly wanted to.

Six flowering plants hung from chains attached to a beam running across the ceiling. I tipped each to ascertain there was no glove stuffed inside.

On high shelving against the back wall empty pots were perilously stacked, some looking ready to totter off to Humpty Dumpty's fate. I lifted down each one and looked in. Nothing but dirt. On the very top shelf I saw a large terracotta pot shoved way back in a corner where light scarcely penetrated. Several pairs of various types of gloves poked out, dainty cotton to workman's leather. Balancing after climbing onto the bench, I stretched to lift the pot down. In transport, the flimsier gloves waved, others were made of sterner stuff. I jumped down and set the container on the bench. Withdrawing each protruding glove, I laid it aside. When the space was cleared, I peered in and saw squashed at the bottom a light-colored calfskin glove. With thumb and index finger, I brought it out. There was a single spot of dried brown substance on its thumb. I placed the glove in an evidence bag for transport to the lab.

The gloves were Lisa's. Had her mention of them in her farewell letter been a ruse to protect her from suspicion? Ada Opal and Lisa. Both had access to that glove.

Footsteps tapped briskly down the basement steps. I plucked a piece of the nearest herb and skittered down the greenhouse steps into the basement proper. Ada Opal came around the corner holding a bolt rifle. "What are you doing down here?" she asked.

"What's the gun for? I'm not some hungry rabbit. How's your mother? Well, I hope." I smiled brightly.

She kept the rifle raised. "What were you doing in the greenhouse?"

"Picking herbs for dinner. I love the spice rosemary, don't you?" I waved the plant. "Can't you lower the gun, Ada Opal? You're making me nervous."

She advanced a step. "That's thyme and it won't be ready till spring. Go back into the greenhouse. I want to see what you've been up to."

"Huh? Look, if I've trespassed, I apologize." I went backwards up the first five steps. There I hesitated, realizing that the clay pot and the other gloves were still out on the bench. "What's the problem?" I asked. "Should I have stayed out of your place of retreat and reflection?"

"Shut up. Get in there." She darted up three steps and jabbed at my ribs with the muzzle, then leapt down fast, afraid of getting so close. "Go into the greenhouse, Wendy," she said, voice trembling. "Now."

Haltingly, I backed up the remaining steps into the warmish room. She followed, peered in and saw the mess. "You found the glove. Where is it? Give me your purse." Very slowly I slipped off my bag and held it out by a strap. She had to step forward to claim it. Securing the bolt rifle against her body, she rooted around in the bag and came out with the glove. With her attention diverted, I smacked her arm and the gun fired, the bullet splintering the bench before whanging into the cement floor. Ears ringing with the sound of the blast, I tried to wrest the rifle from her as she struggled to hang on. The weapon spun away and clattered against the bench. She pushed me. Off balance and stumbling, I brought my left fist up and punched her in the solar plexus. Expelling "oof," she doubled over and I shoved her out the door down the steps. As she fell she managed to grab the rail and bounced against it enough to slow her descent but she still hit the floor hard with an arm bent under her. I bounded down the steps, June's tiny automatic in hand.

"My arm, my arm," she moaned.

I retrieved my bag where it had fallen, and straddled the fallen woman, ready to handcuff her.

"No, Wendy please, I hurt," she said, rolling onto her back in agony. She held her left elbow with her right hand.

Bruised, beaten, and menaced, I was in no mood to extend mercy. But I was an ace detective, cool and measured in my responses, so I settled for pulling her to her feet by the good arm and nudging her up the kitchen steps. After I sat her down by the kitchen table, I said, "I've recovered $13,500 of your money. I'm handing over $2000 to the police; you'll get that back eventually, and I've taken out $3500 per our contract. $8000 goes to you right now." I pulled the $10,000 from my trouser pocket, counted out $2000 in big bills and restored them to my pocket. I tossed the rest toward the counter. Some of the bills fell on the floor.

She recovered enough to say, "Hide the money in the big sugar bowl in the hutch in the dining room, so the police don't find it. And keep looking till you find the rest. That's per our contract." She explored her arm with ring-heavy fingers.

The lady didn't get it. "The case is over, Ada Opal. The rest of the money is gone. $13,500 is all there is. The robber must have spent the rest."

"You crook," she howled. "You've kept it. I knew you would."

"Sue me." Gathering up the bills, I ordered her into the dining room. I followed and stuffed the money in the sugar bowl.

During my phone call to G.P., Ada Opal lay on the living room couch with her eyes closed. After confirming that the police and an ambulance were on the way, I rang off as G.P. insisted that I report in immediately.

While waiting for the mop-up crew, I sat in the easy chair opposite Ada Opal and probed. "Why'd you kill Miki? Was a tray really stolen that night?"

She sat up in agony and tackled the simpler question first. "I made up the tray. We'd had an ugly banged-up one but I got rid of it years ago. I thought I'd have to give a reason for the killer leaving by the basement." She ran her good hand over her hair. "That night when I heard the shot, I ran upstairs to see what happened. The window was open. I went straight to my husband, although I probably should have run to the window to see who it was. But I saw my duty—I went immediately to my husband to save him. He was lying on the carpet with blood on his leg. His gun lay beside him. He was pale but he still had enough strength to ridicule me. 'You stupid woman, get a doctor," he shouted at me. "'Don't just stand there, call the police. Put your finger in the dial and do it, *curule!*' That meant asshole. I'd known that for a while."

Eyes burning with grievance, she continued. "During our master classes, Miki would yank me to where he wanted me to stand. 'Over here,' or 'Over there,' he'd say as though I was never in the right place. His treatment of me undercut my authority like nothing else. I took getting pushed around as a necessary condition for our success. But, seeing him lying on that carpet, injured and still cursing me out, I saw the situation for what it was. He'd always make sure that the really talented students would love him and reject me. Like Rolf did."

She took a breath, cleared her throat, and returned to straightforward recounting. "I ran downstairs to call for help. I went to the phone but I just stood there; I didn't pick it up. Upstairs, he yelled 'hurry, you *pizda*!' That means 'cunt.' He'd called me that before, too. I swore I'd kill him the next time. Of course I didn't mean it.

"Sometimes I wake up in the night, that word echoing in my head, coming from this man who'd made me wrong about everything." Her voice became cloaked in ice. "I slipped on Lisa's glove where she'd left it on the colonnade and went back upstairs. I was on automatic. He was quiet when I walked in and even lifted his head to follow my progress. I heard his breathing, in and out, adagio, all time slowed. I picked up the gun and stood over him, just for a second in his sight so it would register. Then I pulled the trigger."

After that, until the sirens approached, she sat massaging her arm. I rested the rifle across my knees and listened to her weepy sighs.

After Shulz and Brunanski loaded her into the ambulance, I told them I'd follow along in my car. I waited until they cleared out, after which I went to the parlor and retrieved our contract from behind the painting. After tucking it in my shoulder bag, I left the house. I locked the door and left the key under the mat.

I drove to the station. In the lobby, I handed over the smudged $2000. "Discovered it in the dump, in a cavity of a fallen tree near where Harris assaulted me. Most likely, this is the Plinko loot."

Absorbing my injuries, Bobby said, "Wish you would have stayed with me. Both of us together might have captured Bertalow, brought him in together."

It was then I decided he wasn't the man for me.

I related Ada Opal's confession and produced the calfskin glove. G.P. was so pleased to have the case wrapped up that he said he would carve a Whittlin of me. "What should I call it?" he asked.

"Wanda. Wanda will be just fine," I said.

Bobby probed. "Do you think it was Harris who stole the money? Or Bertalow? I assume Bertalow was the one who rescued you."

I touched the purple knot on my neck. "I couldn't say."

"We can't rule out the witch," said G.P., adding, "You'll probably be leaving town now, so we'll notify you when or if Sergeant Harris goes to trial. He's very badly injured. Maybe he'll never recover enough… "

It felt good to give my real address in my normal voice.

Now that the state police and FBI were on Bertalow's trail, Bobby was off the case. "I'm heading out to Aurora," he informed me. "Having a homemade goose dinner with the police chief and his family today. Tomorrow I'm going hunting with him." He chuckled. "There's a possibility of the Assistant Chief position opening up there, so I'm keeping my political hand in. I'll be back in three days. Will you be here?"

That was Bobby. All business. "Sorry. I'm leaving early tomorrow," I said. "Got to get back to my own business. I guess we'll never know what we're missing out on."

## 57

In a light rain the next morning, I drove June and Little Spit to the bus station. Beforehand, in the Beddy-Bye Motel, I handed over the $10,750 in a brown paper sack. After checking it was all there, June giggled and said, "This is a new kind of social security." That didn't quite sound like June; I suspected it came from an ad in some movie magazine.

At the bus station, I bought and handed over two tickets to L.A. Wearing an ankle-length figured dress, with Betty in her arms, June climbed laboriously up the high steps of the Greyhound. From above, the driver extended a helping hand for the final tug. I watched through rain- and dirt-streaked windows as she gave him the tickets and plodded down the aisle. About halfway back, she handed the child off to an ancient lady seated by the window. One scrawny arm pressed against the glass was covered with scars. Of course, the holler fire. Lily's face in profile was deeply ridged. I reached up and tapped the window to mouth good-bye, but, occupied with Betty and June, the good witch didn't acknowledge me. It's not like I was kin.

Many hours later, when I finally pulled up to my trailer in Burton City, my brother Norris came down the steps to meet me. "You're a mess," he noted. "Typical."

"Yeah, well, I know that," I said. We hugged and I kissed him on the cheek. Thinking it over, I wasn't too surprised that, after jumping bail, he'd head here.

His wife Kathy, bouffant hair stiffly in place, was at the door. Their two kids peered from behind her.

We sat around the table in my trailer as I told a condensed version of my story. In the awed silence that followed, Sammy, the younger child, said, "Now that Wendy's back can we go outdoors?"

"What's he mean?" I asked.

Norris explained. "We've been careful. The police chief, Duane Shupe, called. Must of been about three weeks ago. He wanted to check on your whereabouts. I know an official inquiry when I hear one and it's never good, so I told him you were right here in bed with the flu. Been sick for days, highly contagious.

"But old Duane he was not convinced and said who are you to be telling me that anyhow, and I replied I'm her brother, and he thought that over but you musta said something good about me sometime." I nodded. I'd never speak otherwise of Norris to a cop.

"He insisted on talking to you right then and there, so I said 'Hang on, I'll try to rouse her even though she can hardly stand up.' When he threatened to come over, I said, 'Hold it, here she comes now. She's staggering up to the phone.' And Kathy talked to him, hacking and sniffling through her nose the whole time."

So that's where my alibi had come from.

"I'm surprised he believed you," I said.

Kathy said, "I managed, in my sad condition, to say a couple of personal things about Chief Shupe's love of WW II guns and how he got his Purple Heart. Stuff you'd told us about."

"Wow," I said, "Nice work, you saved my ass… er, behind."

The kids giggled.

A few days later Norris and family moved to the Mercury Manor mobile home next door. In the following weeks, I had a couple of lunches with Sid, but no sparks were rekindled. He's become just a very good friend.

Bobby and I exchange postcards. I sign mine "W." So far William Bertalow has not been apprehended. I believe he's the type who could survive off the land for a long time. The Cheeley brothers have not been officially heard from either. It tickles me to imagine that at this moment Lily, June holding Betty, and June's sisters with the movie star names, are sitting in the small sun-filled yard of a peach stucco home in southern California. It won't be too long before the Cheeley boys come wandering in and sometime later William will materialize to take Little Spit into his arms.

# THE END

# About Marilyn Bos

Marilyn Bos, Emeritus Professor at Minnesota State University, Mankato, is the author of three books on violin playing. She loves writing mystery novels, baseball, cats, and the violin. She maintains a private violin studio in Mankato, Minnesota.

Photo by Peter Barta

# Also by Marilyn Bos

Wendy Winkworth has just been hired to infiltrate the Burton City Hornettes and find the murderer of its star pitcher. Wendy's first problem: She's not much of a ballplayer. Second: She finds that lust, jealousy, greed, and deception are as much a part of the roster as she is. Then another body turns up.

Wendy Winkworth visits her hometown and is hired by a local teacher to find out if his ex-con mother is going to show up and ruin his chances of marrying the love of his life, who is also the richest girl in town. Meanwhile, the sheriff is trailing Wendy, either because he likes her or because he wants to stop her from looking too closely at what's really going on in town.

# Order Form

| TITLE | COPIES | PRICE | SUBTOTAL |
|---|---|---|---|
| The Stray Pitch | _____ | X $8.95 | = $_________ |
| Bubble, Roses, and Rump | _____ | X $8.95 | = $_________ |
| Switching Sides | _____ | X $8.95 | = $_________ |
| | | TOTAL | $_________ |

*(shipping and handling included)*

NAME:

ADDRESS:

CITY:                STATE:        ZIP:

EMAIL:

Enclose a check or money order payable to **Winks Books** and mail to:

Winks Books
PO Box 1827
North Mankato, MN 56002

Please allow 2 weeks for delivery.

*(also available as ebooks at amazon.com or barnesandnoble.com)*